RIVERS, WEAK MEN AND WOLVES

Hunter Letendre

Jan,

Thank you so much for everything you have done for me, and for my family. I am very happy that you are in our lives. I hope you enjoy my book, and I can't wait to read yours someday.

With Love,

(Hunter ☺)

First Paperback Edition, July 2020

Rum Ranger Press.

Paperback ISBN 978-1-7352508-0-9
Hardcover ISBN 978-1-7352508-2-3
eBook ISBN 978-1-7352508-1-6

Printed in the United States of America

www.hunterletendre.com

For Mom

AFTER AND BEFORE

We buried her beneath the ash trees, just a little ways down the road. She'd told me once how much she loved them, but no matter how hard I try, I can't remember the reason. It's silent there, cold and dead, but one day the long winter will end, and flowers will grow out of her body.

The procession was small, quiet, the attendees dressed in their very best. Among them, friends and foes came to pay their respects, as did the man who claimed he loved her.

But none of them loved her. Not like me, not how I did. Because who of them could have done what I did for her? Save her from a sickness so primal that it bore into her bones, grinding them to dust. The disease that broke her back, mottled her eyes, and burnt away her flesh until I felt as though I were staring into the face of death.

Only I loved her enough to end her suffering, give her peace, when there was nothing left of her but cinders. Because the day I came into this world she was destined to be mine, and I would always be hers.

Now it's quiet, still beneath the ash trees, and I hope a rain comes to drown me before my guilt gets its chance. But until that day, when I join her—when I answer for my sins— I take solace knowing that the dead don't mourn for us.

Knowing that what's done is done, and what's lost may one day be found.

1

1
JORAH, QUEEN OF NOTHING

For two weeks, I followed them, the black binoculars barely leaving their place around my neck. They'd become like another limb, and sometimes I found myself holding them, running my fingers over the plastic, even when there was nothing and nobody to look at.

I became pretty good at it, I think; it even started to become a sort of game. Closer, closer, creeping and edging—coming too close to being spotted, I felt the rush like a blast of wind. My insides would twist and squirm deliciously, delighted to be so nearly caught, already embroiled in new, better methods of approach.

Then I distanced myself, a few days alone, hungry, tracking—it was better that way, healthier, not watching them eat and play. My mind doing nothing but drifting while I walked;

drifting and worrying and boiling away to nothing under the heat.

I am profoundly lonely. I think sometimes that I want to die.

That's the tune my mind played to each day, the incessant skip and repeat of a broken record. Ringing in my ears, reverberating in my bones, the catchiest tune I'd heard in months. I picked at my brittle fingernails; a bit of chipped red polish still clung to them from days gone by. It would have bothered me once, but instead it seemed a sweet dash of color in a quickly graying landscape.

Each day came, just as the last. I walked, following the others at a safe distance, spying on them over rooftops and hills, bridges and cars strewn every which way. Then, come night, I liked to camp as near to them as I dared. Somewhere I could listen to the indistinguishable lull of their voices, smell the smoke of their campfires. Their mornings became my nights, and I would watch them leave, bleary-eyed and hungry—the hunt is more fun if it's a challenge, anyway. I could enter those campsites then, lay my stomach on their footprints, their coals still smoldering, and sleep until the afternoon sun burned my skin.

Those days are gone now—they've settled down, dug holes for their roots, and I've been forced to resort to other methods.

On this particular day, I was awakened by a nightmare in the early, sunrise-drenched sky. The same routine of late—the only difference the exact pattern of colors overhead, the contrast or dullness. Though I swear each morning was dimmer than the last. It was cool out, comfortable, and I tried not to think of the absurdity of how quickly it changed. It was a long, fiery summer, and it came to a fast, unnatural end. I cracked open my eyes, and all I could see was the grime I fell asleep next to. The red dirt, thick dust, dead bug—the usual.

The first step after heaving myself off the ground was checking my supplies, and when I rose each day, my bones creaked as though I'd aged forty years overnight.

Truth be told, I don't remember much after roughly four p.m. yesterday. That was right about the time I found a half-drunk bottle of scotch in the underwear drawer of M. Baldwin. At least I assumed it was his drawer, since it was his body on the couch and his nametag that stuck me in the finger while I searched him. His empty revolver that found a home in the waistband of my jeans.

I was disturbed by the house I'd woken up in. Dusty and dilapidated, a huge hole hung in the ceiling where a tree had punched through. When I went downstairs, M. Baldwin was still lying on the couch—so I guess I didn't get far after finding the scotch.

The home was eerie, forsaken, and I kept looking over my shoulder, irrationally afraid that the body that was practically nothing but bones would have moved.

There wasn't much to be found, probably why my new best friend used the last bullet on himself.

"Bye, buddy," I said to the very lifeless form of M. Baldwin, looking back briefly at his prone figure. "Cheers."

I tried to ignore the endless corpses I passed, pell-mell across the pavement, busying myself by scarfing down a few fingerfuls of meager rations. There are two types of dead you see these days: those who died first, in the initial cataclysm— now the skinless, meatless lucky ones. The bones of their necks fragmented identically, jaws either gaping or blown free.

The other type is everyone else.

I thought back to the last time I'd spoken to anyone alive. Three weeks ago, a small family traveling south; we'd exchanged only a brief, incredibly tense conversation. I'd followed them for a short while, but that night, I found myself drinking away the image of their child, her stomach distended over filthy, frayed pink shorts. I turned around before daylight.

Lighten up, I told myself, *today is the day.* I squared my shoulders, a woman on a mission—*by tonight things will be different, better. Tonight, I will feel alive.*

I paused to take a sip of water, pulling out my crumpled map in the process. I'd decided evening would be the best time to strike. Not so early as to tempt them to abandon me, not so late as to cause for alarm.

I'd found them by accident the first time, camped in a house next door one night. I'd stayed awake the entire time, terrified they would find me, preparing myself to fight if need be. Come morning, I watched them, two men and a girl—she looked just a little younger than I. They joked and laughed, organized their bags on the front lawn, shared a meal, and headed on their way.

I hadn't been able to hear them, not daring enough to crack the window from which I watched. So, I named them myself, deciding the men would be brothers (though they looked nothing alike) and named the girl after a childhood friend, to whom she bore a slight resemblance.

Watching them was comforting, knowing I was not alone,

that not everyone who still lived was suffering. Sure, their lives weren't great—but they were doing okay for themselves. They had food; I saw them eating every day, which is more than I could say for myself. A social circle, too, as twice I found them while they traded with another group. I had no interest in those others; from what I'd seen they were strange, reclusive, their women wearing only matronly gowns that fell to their ankles.

I walked for most of the day, occasionally scavenging houses, though this area was well traveled, the path worn, and there was little left to yield. No matter, we'd all be leaving soon.

I settled in a small nook, my back resting against the musty earth, occupying myself by impaling leaves on the tip of my knife. I sifted through the dirt with my boots, kicking up rocks and roots, pulling free one long, struggling pink worm.

I held the worm high, watching it squirm, wriggle up toward my fingers, a slime trail left on my skin. "I would eat you, if I was smart," I told the worm, tossing it aside, watching it glide back into the smooth earth. Burrowing its way through the long-decayed plants, through the dead animals, down to where nothing had changed.

Hours passed this way, and then the time had come. The sky was gray-blue in its evening attire, wearing clouds like a string of pearls. I debated if I should leave the food behind, but there was so little left, I didn't think it necessary. Next, my water bottles; I pulled them out, the water murky and warm, and buried them beneath the leaves. I debated drinking it all—too much on an empty stomach, the last thing I needed was for water to spurt out of my head like some horrible whale. So, I hid them, down with the worms, rehearsing my story, setting the tone, ready to perform.

The house they'd set up in sat at the end of a long, curved driveway, which seemed to melt into the trees off the main road. It was the type of home you would immediately associate with cheap beer, cheaper cigarettes, wife-beater tank tops, and men who beat their wives. Dingy, run-down, the yard littered with rusted out cars, sheets of plywood and bullet-riddled street signs—and that's just how it looked *before* the world ended.

I could see why they'd chosen to stay there, however. The trailer sat on a hill, a good vantage point, well hidden in the trees, and small tendrils of smoke poured from the metal cylinder chimney—hard to find real fireplaces these days.

I perfected my slow, sickly gait as I rounded the bend in the driveway, dragging my backpack by one strap beside me. "Hello?" I called weakly. "Hello? I need help, please."

A mere moment passed before there came a flicker of movement, the door swinging open as two men burst out, bumping shoulders, each vying to be first.

"Stop," snapped the shorter of the two. He was younger as well and less handsome, less imposing—*less everything* compared to the man behind him. "Stop, now!"

I stumbled to a halt on the gritty driveway. "Please, I just need water."

A rifle seemed to appear out of nowhere, and he took a jerky step forward. "Leave. You aren't welcome here."

"I just need a little water." I swayed dramatically, reaching into the air for support. There was an explosion as the rifle fired, and I dropped to a crouch, throwing my backpack in front of me.

7

"Geoff, stop!" the other man shouted, the handsome one whom I'd dubbed John. He grabbed the rifle, forcing it toward the sky as another shot rang out. "Let go," he snarled, finally tugging it free. "You're crazy!"

"Don't move," Geoff ordered, abandoning his "shoot first and ask questions later" method and hurrying across the gravel.

My last thought as he reached me, grabbing and twisting my arms, dropping me to my belly in the dirt, is that I am either incredibly stupid or I really do want to die.

2

JORAH–NEWCOMER, LIAR, SWEETHEART

"Good try, girl," he growled, pressing his boot harder into my shoulders. I could taste the cloud of dust that had risen in the scuffle, crunching it between my teeth.

"Geoff, get off her," ordered the other man, as he walked toward us with the speed and gait of someone who hadn't a single care and everywhere better to be.

With a grunt of displeasure, the boot was lifted and my backpack aggressively pulled from under me. I made a move to push myself up when strong hands grabbed my own and pulled them behind my back, lifting me into a kneeling position. Holding my hands with one of his own, Geoff quickly patted me down.

I let my body slump, staring bleary-eyed at the ground below me.

"Damn it, Geoff. Why'd you have to go and ring her bell so hard?"

"I hardly touched her." He grabbed my shoulders, shaking me roughly. "Hey? What's wrong with you? Where are the rest of your people?"

"I'm alone. Please, I just need some water," I grunted, my mouth still caked in dust, "I'll trade you."

Footsteps sounded nearby.

"There you are," said an exasperated Geoff. "We caught her sneaking up on camp—has some story about needing water." He scanned the trees around us suddenly, his head on a swivel.

I was hardly sneaking, I thought indignantly. In all my time following the group, I had scarcely heard them speak—here and there a single phrase, picked up by the wind. I turned toward the newcomer, the girl I had been waiting for.

"I wasn't sneaking, and I'm alone. My name is Jorah. I just need some water, I can trade you."

Her dark eyes fell on my face, almond-shaped pools of liquid night. She was short, unexpectedly so, and I doubted that if I were standing, she would even reach my shoulder. Her olive complexion was flawless, save for the dark freckles dappled on her cheeks and nose. Her thick eyebrows knitted as she looked at me, and when she spoke, it was with a light Indian accent.

"How did you find us?"

"I saw the smoke. I thought it would be worth a shot."

She glanced back at the curling tendrils rising from the chimney. "Geoff, let her go."

10

"What, but she—"

"Let her go, now," the girl interrupted. Geoff cursed and released my arms.

"Thank you," I said tentatively, climbing to my feet and nearly toppling over in the process. The other man reached out, and I eyed him warily as he grasped my arm, supporting me. I could not remember the last time I had been touched kindly, and something stirred in the pit of my stomach, a beast nipping at my organs and veins. *I am profoundly lonely, and I think sometimes that I want to die.*

"I got you, sweetheart." He smiled down at me, his grip gentle and guiding. "Geoff, go get her some water."

While a very indignant Geoff stalked off, the man introduced himself as Riley.

"And this lovely slice of something exotic is—"

"Sana," the girl said firmly, scowling at Riley, full lips upturning into a sneer. "I'm Sana." I liked that name better than the one I'd chosen for her.

Riley chuckled lightly. "Not one for the jokes," he whispered, guiding me over to sit along a short stone wall.

Geoff returned, thrusting a water bottle into my hands. Though I was not the slightest bit thirsty, I pulled it to my lips as though I had not drunk in years. The water had barely begun to trickle down my throat, however, when it was gently guided away.

"Now, about that trade you offered."

I glared at Riley, indignant, while a cool, arrogant smirk

played on his face.

"Hey, you came to our camp. You're on *our* property."

Real nice place you've got here. "I have medicine."

"You mean this?" Sana asked as she approached us. Rifling through my backpack, she procured a small, water-stained bottle of allergy pills. She walked with an evident limp; not the fake, simpering one I'd used to approach the home, but real, aching; you could see the struggle for composure on her face.

"That's my bag," I snapped. "Get out of it."

She raised her eyebrows, tossing the pack at my feet as she shook the bottle of pills beside her ear.

"This is stupid," Geoff snarled. "We don't know this girl. She could be with the group that killed Sadie."

"I've been alone since the start," I said. "That's not the only medicine I have. There's more at my camp."

"Where's your camp?"

I met Sana's eyes and gestured to the water. *Wouldn't make sense for the dehydrated girl to stop being thirsty.*

Sana sighed in defeat, signaling for Riley to return the bottle. When I finished, I wiped my mouth on the back of my sleeve, careful to catch Geoff's beady eye. "It's not far from here."

"Specific," Geoff sneered.

"Ignore him," Riley said. "What are you offering?"

I sat up straighter, stacking my spine, the rough stone wall digging into my legs. "Two tablets of Amoxicillin, five tablets of Tramadol."

I relished in the surprise that graced their faces, the intrigue. Riley's eyebrows shot into his hairline, pale-green eyes seeming to at last take a real moment to inspect me. Riley was older, maybe early forties, but still the sort of handsome that you noticed immediately. As though he threw it in your face and forced you to look at him. The rugged, good-for-nothing type that would drop your parents into an early grave. Dark-haired, straight-nosed, and blessed with light-green eyes. Tall and lean, you could just make out the tattoos at the hems of his sleeves, a deep-green mermaid tail curled around his wrist.

"What do you want for it?" Sana queried.

"Two more bottles of water, and to know where you get your supply from."

"Deal," Sana declared, glaring down the disapproving look from Geoff. "Bring us there."

I shook my head. "Give me another bottle, and I'll bring it back."

A soft sigh of relief escaped my lips as I eased my boots away from aching, blistered feet. Next, the socks, peeled away like sheets of wet papier-mâché. The cool air stung the blisters but felt incredible on my tender, pale, and shriveled feet—like some slimy creature that had been kept away from the sun too long.

I reached up into my hair next, teasing through the snarled, greasy strands, unraveling my soiled red bandana from the masses. My scalp ached in much the same way as my feet, disgruntled and weakened by its treatment. My body didn't know the world had ended. To my body, my brain had gone cold and cruel, stripping away the shampoo, clean clothes, and full meals it had known for twenty-three years. I was left with a failing, mismatched mess—a Frankenstein mass of parts that didn't really work, held together by spit and zip-ties.

My head fell back, leaning on the heavy mahogany dresser I'd forced against the bedroom door, listening to the quiet of the house and the whistle of the wind. *Alone again.* Not for long, though. Today had gone well, so well in fact that there was already a new date planned for tomorrow.

It had just been Riley when I returned, standing out on the lawn as night pulled in, a small silver flask clasped between long fingers. Though I glimpsed the crown of someone's head disappear over the edge of the roof as I rounded the bend in the driveway.

"Geoff thinks he's going to be the next great sniper," Riley muttered, glancing toward the roof. "So, if you're lying and you've got people waiting in the woods, I'd tell them to clear out."

"Just me."

Riley took the pills, holding the plastic bag up to his eyes.

"The smaller ones are the Tramadol."

"Good stuff." He held out a grocery bag, *Come Again!* painted on the front in large, cursive letters. "Your water, m'lady."

"And the source?"

He tore his eyes away from the pills. "I'll do you one better, just wait one minute."

It was eerie standing in the yard alone, the heavy blanket of night closing in, dreading the walk back to camp. The moment I'd arrived and slammed the dresser safely in front of the door had felt like the first moment I breathed again.

But Riley had returned soon, a map folded into his hands.

"Just needed to get those to Sana."

"I noticed the limp. What happened?"

He shook his head angrily, pulling the map apart. "Just some nut job, started shooting at us from the tree line a few days ago, never even saw him—clipped her in the leg."

"Damn."

"The pills will help, but anyway …" He leaned in close to me, holding out the map before us. "Like I said, we'll do you one better. With Sana hurt, we could use the extra hands. There's a grocery store just out of town; there were still supplies left last time we passed through. All goes well, we split everything four ways." There was the slightest tinge of threat in his last sentence, a warning not to cross them.

I gazed at the map. "How much?"

"Some, getting low, but we think we're the only ones who really know about it."

"Why are you showing me this," I asked, allowing a hint of teasing to enter my voice, "when I could just go there myself before you?"

"Call it a test of good faith," he quipped back, "and we have other stops beforehand."

I nodded slowly, trying not to show my eagerness. "I'll meet you there then, when?"

"It's a bit of walk from this area, so … noon, when the sun is right over your head."

I forced myself up from the floor, tiptoeing across on swollen feet, sliding into the velvety sheets of the bed. I'd been lucky, found myself a cozy little house not far from the others, clean and empty. Its owners, I assumed, had never made it back that first day. The room was pitch black, my eyes gazing upward into the expanse of nothingness, the bed so soft and unfamiliar, as though I were drifting through space.

I waited for them on the broad side of a grassy hill, one that perfectly overlooked the sea of asphalt. It was littered with abandoned cars and shopping carts, the lone island of a grocery store floating in the middle. Eerie, desolate, and deadly in its existence—a baited trap primed for the hungry. It was the *normality* of the place, I decided, which was so off-putting. The cars parked in neat rows, most of the shopping carts standing ready in their corrals.

It was as though I had arrived on a calm Sunday morning, quiet and peaceful, when only the most dedicated church goers had risen. A scene frozen and timeless, save for the three dead bodies lying face down on the pavement; bones and clothes and hair and shoes. Still, comforting, in a strange way, because that was now more normal than any Sunday trip for milk and eggs.

It felt good to have the binoculars clasped back in my hands, rigid, smooth, familiar. I alternated between scanning the road for the others and watching the grimy windows of the store with bated breath, waiting for something to move within.

I first spied the tall form of Riley, bobbing down the road, the others close behind. I skirted into the shadows of nearby brush before looping around, approaching from a road that ran parallel to the one they had taken. They needn't know I had been to this place before, watched them here, gone in after and swam in their wake, breathed the same stale air.

"Found us all right?"

"Seems that way." I hefted my bag higher on my shoulders, looking around at the store looming before us. "What's the plan?"

"Scope the outside, enter as a unit through the front doors, clear the inside," Sana replied, leaning on a finely carved walking stick. I could just make out the bulk of the bandages beneath her pant leg.

"Have you had problems here before?"

"A few loons back three weeks ago; didn't give us much trouble. They were scared half to death the moment we walked in the doors," Riley answered. "Other than that, been dead empty."

Glass crunched beneath our feet, echoing into the depths of the store. We'd done our rounds quickly, efficiently, sweeping through as a unit until we were sure it was empty. Sana crept inside now, Geoff and Riley having forced her to wait because of her leg. I, however, was much more expendable, as they'd sent me off into the depths with hardly a backward glance.

The store was more dilapidated than I'd last seen it, picked over, shelves nearly emptied. Broken glass and mounds of rotted produce littered around like a going-out-of-business sale. Flies buzzed about our heads, bumping their fat bodies off our scalps, a hailstorm of soft, winged bullets.

"Gross," Geoff spat from another aisle, "there's a body here."

I swallowed the bile rising in my throat, the stench of the store growing stronger the further I went. Down on my hands and knees, swinging my arms in wide arcs beneath the shelves. Here and there clipping something salvageable; a can of soup, a box of macaroni—and then rearing back, retching, as my fingers dipped into something squishy and far too wet.

"Here, your share." A small pile of water bottles dropped beside me, the plastic warm and soft from the months baking in the summer heat. "It's the last of what's here."

"Thanks." I lurched to my feet, brushing debris from my jeans before tucking the bottles into my still depressingly empty backpack. "Find anything good?"

Sana shook her head. "I'd say this place is about all used up."

I searched awhile longer, but soon the stench of the store had drilled a deliberate, pounding rhythm into my skull. I'd nearly made it outside when, with a sharp pang of delight, I fell back. I dropped to my knees and pulled out a perfect, if not somewhat dusty, box of red wine that had been jammed beneath a promotional display.

The three sat just outside, perched in the bed of a truck, picking through their haul at their leisure. Organizing and counting and rationing how much longer before they might starve. I envied how content they seemed together, trusting and relaxed. The familiar, gnawing hunger rose in my gut, so far insatiable.

They looked up as I approached, a hush falling over their words, guilty faces. It wouldn't have been any more obvious they'd been talking about me if they'd screamed it in my face.

"Now what?" The words tumbled out of my mouth, quieting the awkward lilt the air had taken on. *Now what?*

"We were just talking about that," Riley answered confidently, and he reached across Geoff, offering me his hand. I took it skeptically, his fingers curling around my wrist, helping to hoist me into the truck.

I settled beside Geoff, hugging my backpack to my stomach, boots curled beneath me. Geoff squirmed uncomfortably, averting his eyes.

"We wanted to know, what's your plan?" Riley continued. "What have you been doing?"

I shrugged. "Surviving," and then, as an afterthought, "barely."

"But no group? No family or friends you're searching for?" Sana asked.

"I don't have any friends or family, never had a group, just been me since the Break," I told them. *Me and the monsters and the worms.*

"You'll have to tell us how the hell you managed that sometime," Riley said with the hint of a laugh. "Lord knows we'd all be dead one hundred times over if we didn't have each other—

but look, what I'm trying to say is we like you." He splayed his hands in a gesture of defeat. "We could use some help with Sana being injured. Fair trade, work for work, protection for protection—it's really not safe for women specifically out here, not alone," he added as a side note.

Sana snorted derisively. "What Riley is trying to say is we want to know if you'll join us, at least for a little while, help get each other back on our feet." Her brown eyes were sincere, and I tried my best to hide the excitement in mine. Ignore what I knew to be true, that they only wanted me for the medicine I still had, for hadn't that been the plan all along?

I swallowed, forcing the beast back down my throat, drowning it in the emotions that bubbled up, threatening to spill out of my body and carry me away with them.

I will no longer be lonely. I do not wish to die.

3

A RELIC FOR JORAH

I hid what remained of my medicine in the battered old mailbox at the end of the trailer's driveway. Simple, easy to reach, and hidden in plain sight. I thought it would be best not to bring it all with me, just in case the others had the notion to rob me and leave in the middle of the night.

"We all sleep in the living room—it's warmer, plus the bedroom in here isn't anything nice. Up to you, though." Geoff dropped my pack haphazardly in a corner of the dimly lit room; it was obvious that he was not fond of his task of giving me a tour.

The inside of the trailer was just as you would expect. Grimy, terribly painted a dull orange, with more than a few taxidermy animals strung up on the plaster walls. They'd boarded up the windows as best they could, and the thick, if not somewhat stained carpet would make for a decent bed.

"Seen any sign of whoever used to live here?"

"Nah, you can tell the place has been picked over once or twice, though." Geoff ran a hand through his floppy, straw-colored hair, scanning the room uncomfortably. It was hard to tell just by looking at Geoff whether he was a sickly boy or a drug-addled man. Lanky and thin, he stood a head shorter than Riley, nearly the same height as me. Pale skin smattered with moles and unsightly freckles, his eyes looked hallowed, dark and sunken, his clothes hanging off his narrow frame. I was tempted to ask if he'd always looked that way or if it was a newly end-of-the-world look.

"Where's the bathroom?" I asked, somewhat awkwardly holding up a pack of wet wipes I'd found in the store. He pointed down the hall, apparently relieved to be rid of me.

The bathroom was tight and boring, the medicine cabinet empty, not even a trickle of water to be found in the faucet. The sun, now growing low in the sky, shone directly through a small window, providing the only light in the room.

I stripped down, the pile of stinking, stained clothes growing at my feet. The toothpaste-splattered mirror over the sink called to me. Filthy hair, flaking skin tinged in mismatched colors from the relentless summer, and cracked lips. I looked thinner than ever and my eyes had dark bags big enough to hold all my problems.

The wet wipes made for an adequate bath, and when I'd finished scrubbing my skin to a splotchy pink, I turned to my clothes, the only set I owned save for a few extra pairs of underwear and socks.

I was shaky, excited, and nervous. Not nervous as I had been for months, of a looming, painful death—but *old* nervous, *first date* nervous. Do they like me? Will they want to keep seeing me? How does my hair look?

Riley and Sana seemed to like me, at least enough to invite me into their group. And who cared what Geoff thought? He didn't seem to have an ounce of sway in group decisions. I liked Sana best, though she was different than I'd imagined she would be. More aloof, standoffish—but still, she was smart, reasonable, and had a handle on the two men.

When I was at last clean and had swallowed my emotions, I returned to the living room. Geoff was still there, slumped in a chair, reading a book, barely looking up as I entered. *I guess the tour is over.*

"Jorah," Sana called from the kitchen, her leg propped up on the knife-scarred table. "Give me a hand?"

I crossed to her, eyeing the bloody and sore-looking wound on her leg, the bandages littered around her.

"If you don't mind," she said, her voice strained, "Riley's off scavenging the neighboring houses, and Geoff can't wrap a wound to save his life."

"Of course, hang on." I hurried to my bag and pulled out my small box of wine, twisting the top and setting it down in front of her. She nodded gratefully, taking a long swig that I followed with one of my own.

"How did you guys end up together?" I asked her. She winced violently in my hands as I dabbed antiseptic onto the wound.

"I worked with Riley before, and we met Geoff on the road."

"Where did you work?"

"I was here for an internship. Riley was an accountant at the firm. We worked together on a few projects."

"He was an accountant?" I gaped. "He didn't strike me as the type."

She smiled slightly, a bead of sweat rolling down her forehead. "Don't bring it up to him. He hated it. But we were together when It happened, at work."

"The Break. That's what the radio stations were calling it."

She nodded. "I heard them too. Geoff's been calling it 'The Crackening.'"

Geoff scoffed. "It's funny when you think about it—you know, because of the noise."

"It's morbid," Sana snapped, glaring at him and then turning to me. "Riley and I were the only ones who made it out in our department."

I cringed, thinking of the implications of what they must have witnessed.

We sat in silence the next few minutes while I finished pinning the gauze around her swollen calf.

"Thank you," she said earnestly, admiring the clean white bandages. She paused momentarily, her brow furrowed.

"Riley and I split up right after It happened—the Break. I just holed up at home. My roommates never came back, so more food for me. After a few weeks, I went to find him. Turned out he was on his way to look for me too—it was strange, being around people again." This time when she looked at me, I could make out the sympathy in her eyes.

We relaxed for a while, stoking the fire, touching up the barricades on the windows as evening rolled in. I was just beginning to grow bored when the front door exploded inward, slamming off the wall and ricocheting back toward Riley's enraged face.

"We're screwed," Riley shouted, startling Geoff and Sana and flinging the bag he carried to the ground. He paced by the door, fuming, and I quickly edged my way around him.

"Son of a bitch," he cursed, "all our work for nothing." He spun on his heel and grabbed a shelf bolted to the wall. With a sharp heave, he ripped it down and hurled it across the room, and then stormed out.

Sana, who looked tense but not afraid, turned to me. "Don't mind him; he gets that way sometimes. He'll be back." She began gathering and sorting through the bag Riley had so haphazardly flung.

The bag held nothing but a few musty blankets and a half-chewed pack of gum, and as daytime slipped away and Sana began to light a few tea candles, Riley returned. As if on cue, Geoff rose from his seat, and the two men heaved a desk in front of the door. My stomach tightened at the realization that I was now effectively trapped with these strangers. *This is what you wanted.*

"So, want to tell us what that was about?" Geoff asked, as Riley collapsed into a chair.

He sighed and dragged a hand down his face, rubbing his dark facial hair, and then twisted to face me. "Sorry about that, sweetheart. Hope I didn't scare you."

I rolled my eyes.

"The van is trashed, absolutely useless."

Cries of outrage came from both Sana and Geoff as Riley continued,

"All of the tires are slashed, not to mention the engine is beat to shit."

"You had a working car?" I interjected.

Riley nodded. "Nearly. Been working on it for weeks, real old beater—they have better wiring than all the new shit and no computers. It wasn't fried, just old."

After a few minutes of arguing, it was determined that Riley and Geoff were dead set it had been a group they'd encountered a few weeks prior. Sana, however, didn't seem so sure.

"Why would they destroy the car?" she queried. "Why not steal it? They could obviously make good use of it."

"Hell if I know, Sana."

"You haven't even thought about that group for weeks," Sana said, her tone growing more worried by the minute. "You're sure you didn't see anyone?"

"Of course, I'm sure," Riley glowered. "A few footprints but I lost the trail almost immediately."

Still, Sana looked worried. "I think we should stick with the plan then, leave tomorrow."

"Tomorrow? You can barely walk," Geoff snapped.

Her eyes narrowed on him. "I'll be fine. I can handle myself."

Riley groaned, sinking back in the chair. "Enough. Nobody is coming for us tonight—we'll figure it out in the morning."

We settled in around the candles as Geoff cracked open two cold cans of beans and vegetables. Reluctantly, he handed me my serving, though I noticed it looked smaller than what the rest of them had.

Sana laid on her back on the ancient-looking couch, her arms folded behind her head and her eyes closed, while Geoff relaxed in his chair, hungrily slurping up the food.

Riley sat across from me, leaning against the wall with his head tilted back and legs spread. "So, sweetheart, tell me about yourself."

"What do you want to know?"

"Well, all I know is your name."

"What else do you need?" I quipped.

He sighed and seemed to think it over, then decided on asking where I was from.

"Pennsylvania—I moved this way just a few weeks before everything happened," I told him.

"Why here of all places?"

I shrugged. "Seemed less crowded here."

Riley shook his head slightly and winked. "I don't like talking about myself much either." He shot me a smile and set down his empty bowl. "Lights out, ladies and gentlemen. Back on the road tomorrow. I'll take first watch." He flicked off the lantern.

I'd made my bed a few feet away from the others, nestled in the corner of the room. My head rested on my bag as I stared up into the darkness.

You can't trust them, called the voice in my head, familiar, comforting, yet scathing. I could see her face forming—just like mine, only older, wiser; brown eyes to my blue and dark hair to my blonde. Always the more rational sister, always there to guide me. *You don't know them. They don't care about you.*

That, at least, I knew to be true. But I had asked for this, wanted it, craved it, planned it for days. Feign ill, helpless and hapless Jorah, the Jorah who needs the big, strong men to save her. Better yet, have something they need, a little bag of pills, the kind nobody's making anymore—the save-your-life and end-your-misery kind.

All I had to do was make it so they needed them.

I woke to hushed voices and a dark room; my sleepy, crusted-over eyes no longer adjusted to the dim. A tiny flicker of light from a lit match burst into existence. The three others were huddled in the corner, and after noticing my stirring, Sana held a finger to her lips and motioned me over.

Something was wrong; I could see it on their shadow-carved faces. I crouched between Geoff and Riley, the four of us forming a tight circle.

"I'm telling you, I heard footsteps," Geoff whispered, looking

28

frantic.

"Calm the hell down. You think it was just one set?"

"Yeah, but—"

Riley cut him off. "It's probably a stray dog. Nobody is going to be wandering around at night."

I had come to learn that the three of them were quite well armed. Three guns among them, the two pistols and rifle, as well as a small arsenal of knives and ammunition. I felt the weight of my knife on my hip, my only usable weapon, as the two men quietly rose to their feet.

They grabbed their weapons and, as silently as they could, lifted the desk from in front of the door.

"Once we go out there, you two stay put. We don't need the four of us running around in a panic," Riley stated to Sana and me. We nodded as he strode for the door.

I heard it more clearly then, in the silence between Riley's footfalls, in the blankness of a world gone quiet between my breaths. What I had before thought was the distant noise of crickets or cicadas had become a deeper, slower whine.

I froze, and a profound shiver glanced down my spine. It was a noise I recognized, little hisses and chirps, strange words and mangled phrases coming every few seconds. Growing louder.

"Stop," I hissed, a little too viciously, as Riley reached for the doorknob. I felt my fingers close around the hilt of my knife.

As if he had been waiting for this moment, Geoff spun around and half-raised his gun toward me. "I knew it! She's a liar, and she's working with whoever's out there," he accused triumphantly.

"No. Listen," I urged, and the three quieted, Riley's hand frozen over the doorknob.

The noises were louder now and had increased in fervor, accompanied by what sounded like the occasional shuffling footstep.

"Put the desk back," I commanded. Riley's pale-green eyes met mine, and he nodded wordlessly.

"It can't be—we haven't seen one in months," Sana whispered, her lips pressed into a tight line, her hands clamped around her rifle. Her dark skin had taken on a terrible gray sheen.

Words of reassurance failed to slip past my growing nausea, and I watched silently as Riley and Geoff swiftly hefted the desk. Hurriedly they dropped it, but as they moved to push it flush with the door, the handle twisted. I realized then why they'd barricaded the entry in the first place, as I stared in horror at the mangled bolt hanging uselessly, locking nothing, keeping no one out.

Geoff leapt backward, his gun instantly leveled, while Riley jerked to the side, pistol raised, giving Sana and me a clear view. For a moment, the handle twisted, and it looked as though Riley was about to grab for it when the door cracked open. The desk, which had been dropped near the door, only allowed it to scrape open a few inches.

I felt it in my bones before I saw it—the same visceral fear that had haunted my dreams for months, the monsters always lurking in the corner of my vision.

Red dirt, broken lock, dusty room, dead sister, dead Jorah.

A pale and sallow hand slunk from around the corner of the door. In the darkness, it almost looked normal, except for the way the stretched fingers edged around the frame like a spider's legs.

"Stop!" Riley ordered. "We are armed, we will fire. Leave, now!"

"Let me in! Now!" The cry was so sudden, so manic, that I felt as though the psychosis had leaked into my own brain.

With a sharp yell, Geoff fired at the hand. The explosion rocked the room, breaking the curtain of terror that had washed over me. The whispers and croaks shattered into a primal screech as blood splattered across the wall and the hand disappeared into the darkness beyond the doorway.

Riley sped toward the desk, ready to pursue, but I was faster. My feet carried me forward, and I threw my body against the desk, driving it the last few inches, slamming the door shut.

"Move, they'll get away!" Riley yelled, fire in his eyes as he reached for me.

"No!" Sana was shouting now. She ran to my side, throwing her weight against the desk.

"It's one of *them,* Riley!" Sana pleaded, taking the words out of my mouth. My every instinct urged me to stay braced against the barricade.

Riley scraped a hand through his hair, the other waving the gun wildly. He zeroed in on us.

"We don't know that! I need to make sure they won't be coming back."

At that moment, a force so powerful it sent me careening into

Geoff's knees rammed into the door. Geoff fell backward, his gun blindly going off, and I felt the bullet whiz past my ear.

I scrambled to my feet, Sana doing the same. Riley now worked furiously to shove the desk back against the door. The force of the collision had split a wide crack in the wood and apparently changed his mind about pursuit.

"Help!" Riley bellowed, and in an instant, the four of us had each thrown our weight into the barricade.

The screams were back and deafening, and my socks slid on the worn laminate floor. Another crash into the door jolted the four of us. Blood poured into my mouth as my teeth split my lip.

"Let us in, let us in!" came the high-pitched voices, speaking in almost unison so the words echoed.

"There's more than one." Geoff's eyes were wide with terror, searching ours for answers.

"We need to get the hell out," Riley grunted. "It's too tight to fight them in here."

"Bathroom! The window is small, but it's the only one we haven't boarded up," Sana heaved.

"Wait for a charge again, then we run. Got it?"

Barely a moment later, another collision rocked us, a larger crack splintering the wood.

"Now!" Riley shouted. In unison, we shoved ourselves away from the barrier and made for the bathroom.

We barreled inside the tiny bathroom, the window high and narrow, dim blue light filtering through.

"Sana first," Riley ordered. He took the rifle from her hands, and Geoff boosted her up. For a moment, she fumbled with the window latch, before swinging it open and scrambling through. Riley sent the rifle after her and then grasped the ledge and pulled himself out.

A resounding crash buckled the room, and Geoff's eyes met mine, his expression wild.

"Go," I whispered frantically. He looked surprised, then turned on his heel and scrambled through the window.

Why I let him go first, I'll never know, because at that moment, the realization that I had only a knife washed over me. I dove for the window, my hands latching onto the edge, sharp pain tearing through them as they sliced on the narrow frame.

"Jorah!" Sana shouted from outside.

A hand appeared in the window, reaching for me, and I leapt for it. They grabbed my wrist as I grasped theirs and began to heave me out.

Not fast enough.

I hardly heard the bathroom door slam open over the shrieking from both friend and foe, but I felt the intense jerk as my leg was yanked backward. I screamed as what felt like claws dug into my skin, pulling it apart like soft dough. I was half out of the bathroom now. Riley gripped both my wrists, but whoever was on the other side was stronger.

"Please, stay with us! Help us!"

"Give me a gun!" I pleaded. Geoff rushed forward, barely managing to pass me the pistol as I let go of Riley. I was wrenched backward, the others vanishing with a chorus of shouts.

I fell from the window and smashed face-first into the tile. Blood spurted from my nose, my lungs searing for air that they could not pull in. My vision edged with darkness, my mind shutting down, realizing I was going to die on the very day I had decided to live. I twisted and fired the gun, once, twice, three times. The screams stopped.

"Jorah? Jorah?" someone yelled from outside.

"I'm okay," I called back weakly, my vision swimming. The shouting faded, and other than a resounding ringing in my ears, I was left in silence.

They lay face down, horribly close to me. One, a large man, was fully naked, the other a frail woman dressed only in rags. Their skin was filthy, marred with scrapes, blood from two bullet holes in the bony back of the naked man pumping onto the floor. The woman trembled slightly. I couldn't see where the bullet had pierced her.

I turned and vomited onto the tiles.

When I was done retching, I lurched to my feet, my awareness reeling. The bathroom door lay on the ground, torn completely off its hinges. I could hear footsteps then, and for a moment, innate terror began to drown me. More were coming. I knew it; the others had abandoned me.

Figures rounded the corner, but instead of death, I met the wild eyes of Sana, her rifle held at the ready, Geoff and Riley hot on her heels.

4

JORAH IS MADE OF GLASS

My breath hitched as Sana worked the antiseptic into my wounds; her turn to play doctor. Jagged fingernails had been driven into my calf, leaving two lengthy gashes that, thankfully, weren't very deep.

"You don't need stitches, but you might need some antibiotics," Sana whispered as she dabbed at the cuts. I nodded, my teeth grinding together.

"I have a few more." She glanced up, and I tried to ignore the glint in her eye. *Less for her.*

"We haven't seen any freaks in months, *months*—and now we stumble on two at once?" Geoff exclaimed wildly, Sana's rifle at the ready as he paced, his eyes darting up and down the dim street. "Where are they coming from?"

"We don't know that they were freaks," Riley groaned, sitting with his head against the van. "How many times do we have to say it?"

Geoff scoffed. "What? Just because they looked a little different? No, man, I'm telling you, it's another attack. They've been up in the sky, watching us, and now they're just finishing the job!"

Geoff looked ready to tear his hair out. Riley had enough.

"Sit down, Geoff. For the last time, we haven't been attacked by aliens," he snapped, standing and taking the gun from Geoff, who almost eagerly handed it to him.

Geoff darted to sit beside me in the van.

"You saw them best. What do you think?"

I shook my head, beginning to feel nauseated again. "I don't know. It was like they looked too *fresh* to be freaks ... I think they were just crazy."

"Geoff's second theory is we're in the middle of a zombie invasion," Riley snarled, his back facing us as he guarded the van.

"Well, if they are zombies, get ready to shoot me in the head, because I'm definitely going to turn into one," I muttered, gesturing to my leg. "Actually, are you sure you still want me around? You just have more dead weight now."

"Ha!" Riley snapped. "Stop acting like you didn't just save our lives."

I couldn't help but flush and hoped they couldn't tell in the dim. "Seems to me like we found each other just in time."

None of us had taken a good look at our attackers, who still lay dead in the trailer. The corpse of the woman twitched mournfully on the tile us as we'd rushed to pack. Before we left, however, Riley had taken a powerful and well-aimed kick at the naked man, rolling him onto his back. Flushed with purple bruises, his body was speckled with slabs of dark sap, as though he had been bouncing off every tree in sight. His mouth lolled open, broken teeth and a darkness around his lips—resembling a freak, sure, but not *quite* right, at least not how I remembered them.

I felt dizzy and sick, still feeling the broken nails on each revolting finger raking my skin—wanting for my own flesh I'd left behind.

"But the way they talked, the way they moved?" Geoff continued the argument, exasperated with our lack of agreement. "They had to have been."

Sana shook her head. "Trauma can do terrible things; we've all seen how it changes people. Besides, if they were more freaks, then there would have been a second Break, and we're all still alive." She went back to binding me, leaving us in fretful silence.

When enough of the sun had risen, we began to walk, each of us eager to create distance from the trailer. Our belongings were either on our backs or piled into a rusted red wagon, which we took turns pulling along.

"So, what's our plan?" I breathed, as the driveway disappeared in the distance, the mailbox emptied of my stash of pills. I'd been forced to come clean about my hiding spot to retrieve them.

"Well, what was your plan? You were headed this way when you met us, and your life got *so* much better," Riley quipped.

"I didn't have much of one," I admitted, then after a moment of debate added, "I'd thought about going north, maybe."

"Great strategy," came the sarcastic reply.

I shook my head, slightly embarrassed at being outed by my lack of forethought. "I mean *real* north, Canada or Alaska. Or maybe Montana? Somewhere less populated, I guess." I abruptly shut my mouth, effectively killing my rambling.

Geoff rolled his eyes, and Riley smirked at me. "Caught the travel bug, huh?"

"North sounds like a decent option," said Sana thoughtfully, "but it's getting cold fast; might be risky."

"There's an air force base in Montana," Geoff piped in.

"Even with a car, it would be tough to make it before winter, and I'm willing to bet every military base is just as empty as every city. That, or it's been turned into a refugee camp, and I have no business with those," countered Sana. "How about west? Out into the plains, less people, more farmland, and if we make it through winter, the North will still be there."

We settled on that and carried on, the sun slow to creep over the horizon, keeping us on edge. I still felt strange, unsure if it was real or lingering adrenaline from my brush with death. There had been a shift in the group dynamic, a change in the air, in the way we carried ourselves around each other.

It felt good, real and visceral. The loneliness starting to ebb, knowing I was no longer alone in our extinction. All I could think was that I needed more.

We walked until the sky began to dim, and a cool breeze swept in. The temperature had continued to drop drastically, the heavens taking on a persistent hazy pattern.

"I know. I've been thinking about it, and there's a good chance it's nuclear," Sana said when I pointed out the thin layer of gray powder coating a nearby car. Soft and ashy, it clung to my skin even after wiping my fingers vigorously on my shirt.

"We've been nuked?" Geoff asked.

"Maybe," Sana answered, "but I think it's more likely that nuclear reactors are starting to fail. It's been what, five months? I don't know a lot about it but there must be some that fail with nobody to operate them—older plants that rely on cooling systems."

"Nuclear winter," I added, chilled by the confirmation of what I had suspected myself.

Sana nodded. "If that's what's happened—and it's only going to get worse. We could have frosts in a matter of weeks."

"That's what's causing the ash, then?" asked Riley, looking up into the gray-tinged sky.

Sana shrugged. "Maybe. I'm not really sure how it works. If anybody sees a library feel free to point it out."

"It could have been a volcano too," Geoff chipped in. "When the ash blocks out the sun. Err—volcanic winter?" he added sheepishly as we all turned to stare at him incredulously.

"Yes …," Sana offered, "I guess Yellowstone could have erupted."

There was a moment of awkward silence before Riley added,

"Well, damn, I always wanted to go there."

The cool air soon soothed my aching wounds and seemed to ease the cramps in my stomach. I itched terribly to eat some of the food in my pack, to drink another mouthful of water, but I restrained myself. That's all I seemed to do lately, restrain myself. Now, when the world had ended, and you'd think I would have all the freedom I could take.

That night, the four of us crammed inside a car that had rolled off the highway into the cover of sparse bushes. My leg panged terribly from the gashes, and I could tell Sana was feeling no better. We'd walked for miles on injured limbs, none of us saying how desperately we wanted distance between ourselves and our dead attackers. I was exempted from taking watch, due to my injuries, although I suspected that they still did not trust me enough to let their guard down fully.

Though nothing of interest occurred, and we woke, stiff and cranky at first light, all night my dreams tortured me. After each I awoke, head pounding, aching for a drink, drenched in cold sweat. My sister's voice still rang in my ears, the vision of her melted face and hollowed cheeks imprinted behind my eyes. *The only thing I have not lost is guilt.*

My head lolled on my neck; eyes heavy, weary of watching the wasteland roll by. I focused on turning my bandana over in my hands; the red looked nice against my tanned skin. In my opinion, my bandana was the height of post-apocalyptic fashion.

"Check it out," Riley said suddenly, and I turned groggily toward him as he gestured to a large sign just off the edge of the road. Sometime that morning we had exited the highway. It had become far too open, and we felt safer walking the enclosed backroads.

Riley bounded toward the sign, behind which a driveway led to a petite country store. I could see why he'd chosen to stop, considering we had passed many houses and stores during our walk, few of which we bothered to investigate. It was a sweet little shop, with a large handwritten welcome sign and cutesy garden gnomes peppering the lawn.

Maryanne's Convenience read another sign, written in scrawling white paint.

"I hope Maryanne's not still around," Geoff muttered. A shudder ran through me at the thought of finding some Southern-belle grandmother lying dead in her own shop.

Riley sauntered happily to the front door, grasped a porcelain garden gnome tucked into the flowerbed, and smashed it through the front windows.

"The door was unlocked."

"This way is more fun."

"He's so dramatic," Sana huffed as we followed the men inside, a fact I couldn't help but agree with. Riley seemed to have a flair for the spectacular, anything that brought him more attention.

Inside, the store was quaint and floral, labels on the shelves declaring "Indiana's Best Blueberry Jam" and "Fresh bread, baked daily."

My mouth watered.

In the end, we found no food or water, though the register was full of money, and I joked we could burn it for warmth.

"I'm picking the next stop," Sana declared, as we concurred that the store had nothing to offer. "Obviously Riley is terrible at it."

Outside, the chilled air continued to roll through, the sky a dull gray, overrun with clouds that seemed dingier the longer I looked at them. My head swam, and I grasped the nearby railing for support. *I feel strange.*

For a moment, the urge to cry consumed me. To lie down, curl up and wait for someone to take care of me, or maybe just finish me off.

Dead Jorah. Fresh wounds. The smell of blood.

"Hey, over here!"

I followed the voice around the side of the store to where Riley had found the hatch doors into the basement. A large padlock held them firmly shut—something like hope bloomed within me.

"It's locked!" Geoff exclaimed, and we all knew what that could mean—food, water, medicine. I began to feel better at just the thought.

"Stand back, I'll shoot the lock out," Geoff said haughtily, taking aim.

"Don't even think about—" Sana warned, but Geoff had already fired.

He missed, and not only did the bullet do nothing more impressive than lodge in the thick wooden doors, the proximity of the shot had us all swearing and covering our ears.

"Don't be such a moron," Riley snapped, grabbing Geoff by the scruff of the neck and throwing him away from the hatch. "That's the third time you've tried that, and it never works!"

Sana knelt by the lock, working at it with a small pin she had pulled from her thick coils of hair. I watched her, ignoring Riley as he continued to berate Geoff.

"Where'd you learn to do that?" I asked her, as Riley finished his tantrum and strode out of sight.

"Taught myself."

Geoff stood awkwardly, his face tinged red and his features skewed angrily. He took one awkward half-step away before marching off in the opposite direction of Riley.

"I swear it's been like traveling with children," Sana muttered. "All they do is bicker and fight."

"Riley seems like he gets a little violent," I commented casually.

Sana nodded. "He's just like that. He won't hurt you."

The lock gave way, and Sana tossed it to the side. "I'll open the doors; you be ready to shoot anything that might come out." To my surprise, she handed me her rifle.

With a heave, she yanked aside one half of the hatch. I peered around the outstretched gun as she pulled on the other door. I'd expected cobwebs and dust, or maybe another sallow and twisted body to come tearing out. Instead, the basement looked clean and comfortable.

I met Sana's eyes as I handed the rifle back to her, unsheathing my knife as we descended the steep steps inside.

The basement apartment consisted of two rooms, a studio and cramped bathroom. There was a cute kitchenette in the back with a doily-covered table and cozy couches corralled around an ancient television. A plush blue carpet covered the floor, and Christmas lights were strung along the ceiling. The air was stale but cool, and unlike so many other buildings, had no smell of decay.

"Pretty nice," I commented, dragging my foot over the carpet. My exhausted body ached to curl into the fibers.

Sana had crept further into the room, nosing her gun around the corner and into the bathroom. "I think it's clear."

A hooting whistle came from the doorway, and Riley sauntered down the steps. The anger on his face from before had been replaced with his usual pig-headed grin. "Well, isn't this place cozy."

We searched the apartment high and low and soon found a few dusty boxes of pasta and a kit of basic medical supplies. The drawers were filled with neatly folded clothes, though all much too large and hideously dated.

"Oh, baby," Riley cheered, holding up a dented box of cheap, beautiful, delicious, heavenly beer.

I caught a can midair as Sana let hers fall to the ground,

busting at the seams and earning her a brief yet furious tirade from Riley. We took a moment to relax, collapsing into the couches with clouds of dust rising around us, sipping the stale beer with reverence.

"I think you scared Geoff away," I said after a while.

Riley rolled his eyes.

"I'll go look for him," he muttered. Sana agreed to go too, and Riley, still carrying the case of beer, pulled one from the box and placed it on the couch beside me.

"We'll be right back, and then we can make a plan." He winked, and I smiled back appreciatively.

Alone.

For the first time since I was dragged backward onto cold tile, I was alone. I took a deep breath, the whisper of my lungs the only noise in the basement. I closed my eyes, focusing on my breathing, a dull ache having leaked into my forehead. I reached up, feeling the small lump that had formed at the edge of my hairline, yet another remnant from the encounter in the bathroom. If I focused, I could still hear the crack of my skull bouncing off the floor.

Here, though, felt safe, somewhere we could stay, at least until Sana and I had healed. Not longer, though; we needed to find somewhere better, especially if it really was going to keep getting colder. Somewhere with a fireplace and thick walls, because we would surely freeze to death in this basement.

Though I thought maybe it didn't matter; maybe we'd all be dead soon anyway.

I don't know how long I'd been asleep, but I awoke to the soft sound of footsteps descending the stairway. I stretched my aching leg, my eyes pressed tight against the overwhelming sunlight streaming from the doorway. I already felt refreshed from my nap, eager to continue the day.

"Did you guys manage to find—" My words were cut short as what felt like a baseball bat struck the left side of my head. I screamed, my eyes snapping open, my body flailing awkwardly.

"Murderer!" screeched the man standing above me, the barrel of his rifle inches from my nose. "What did you do with her?"

My head throbbed as I searched for words. The man loomed over me, his hand curled into the neckline of my shirt, his knuckles digging into my collarbone. He was very old, with tangled white hair and was naked save for a tattered bathrobe. "Who are you?" he screamed again, shaking as he moved the rifle between my eyes.

My mouth opened and closed stupidly, a fish out of water. Tears streamed down my face, leaking onto his gnarled hands. *Can't think. Can't speak.* I could hear nothing out of my left ear except for a sharp ringing.

At last, words tumbled out, sounding strange and far away. "I'm sorry … didn't know … I'll leave, s-sorry," I begged.

Sweat and spit leaked out of his face, his knuckles nearly choking me, pinning me to the couch. "I have food. I'll give it to you. Just let me leave." My voice cracked.

"Where are the rest of your people?"

"I'm alone." Panic took over. Clawing at his hands, I kicked wildly, desperate to harm any part of him. My head rang nonstop. I had never been hit before, not like this, *not like this*.

He released my shirt and took a handful of my hair as spit flew from his lips. "Liar!"

"No, I'm alone," I cried. "Let go!"

His eyes darted madly around the room, and his grip on my hair loosened. I kicked out, catching him in the thigh. He barely seemed to feel it, his hold in my hair tightening again.

"Murderer!" he roared and yanked me from the couch by my hair. My vision was spinning; it felt as though someone were drilling into my skull.

I lurched to my feet, clawing, punching feebly at his face and arm. At some point I began to scream for help. He kicked into my calf, directly over my bandages, and with a howl of pain my leg gave out from under me.

He dragged me across the room as I crumpled, incredibly strong despite appearing to be in his seventies. The reek of feces and sweat blanketed my senses.

"Get up," he snarled, yanking me to my knees and slamming my wrist down on the dainty kitchen table. "Tell me. Tell me what you did with her."

"With who?" My feet slid uselessly beneath me as I tried to push away from the table.

"Tell me! Tell me that you killed her!"

"Fuck you," I gasped, the words leaving my lips before I could register them, out and gone and no taking them back.

His mouth twitched, and he fumbled in his pocket for a moment, his rifle discarded on the floor. The knife soared through the air in a wide arc, his whole strength behind the swing. The blade stuck into the table with a dull thud.

I didn't feel the pain at first, not until I saw my fingers roll across the table, watched them bounce off the floor.

5

JORAH LETS DAN DIE AT THE END

Something like five months earlier, maybe less, maybe more, who knows these days

I sat against my bedroom wall, knees pulled up to my chest, that sick, heavy feeling unbearable in my stomach. Black, stinking tar bubbling inside. Bile painted into my mouth, eyes stinging, tinted red.

Three days. It had been three days since It happened, since the Break happened. The smell of my presumably dead neighbors had begun to waft through the vents. I pulled my shirt over my nose and mouth; I could taste the tears that soaked it.

The fourth floor of the apartment building was blisteringly hot; the central air had stopped working, but it was too loud anyway. Instead, I tiptoed from room to room or lay beneath the slowly spinning ceiling fan.

I glanced toward the bedroom door, my mattress forced up against it, the comforter thrown over the lone window. With shaking hands, I pulled my radio toward me, the buttons and knobs slick from my oily, tear-coated fingers.

It crackled to life, the lowest volume setting from which I could possibly distinguish words. "I'm telling you, John, listen to me—this is the apocalypse, this is Judgment Day—the Revelation, whatever you want to call it the end times are here. There is no coming back from this."

Hands still shaking, I dared turn up the volume, I'd hardly managed to catch a live broadcast, never more than a few words before the connection was lost or the broadcast ended. I forced a bottle of water to my lips, small sips easing the tang of salt.

"For everyone listening out there, please, stay inside. We know you want to check on loved ones, we know you're hungry, but please, you need to stay inside. We repeat, yesterday we made radio contact with a Sergeant Black out of Camp Atterbury in Edinburgh, Indiana. We have been told this is not an isolated incident. We have been told that the government remains operational. Help will come as long as you wait, again—"

There was the sound of a scuffle, a bang, and I was sure that the broadcast would cut out, when instead, a male voice crackled to life. "Reports coming in from our sister stations across the nation, everywhere reporting the same. Over half the population has been killed in the disaster of three days ago, the disaster we are now referring to as 'the Break'" Another scuffle, an angry, shouting voice ("John, they need to know!"); more silence, I couldn't breathe;

"We don't know if anyone is listening out there, but if you are, this is no accident. We have been attacked."

"You're going to cause a panic. We don't have these facts. This is all just guess-work," John's voice sounded, the two now broadcasting simultaneously. Another crackle, cutting out words as the signal wavered.

"It's no coincidence. The one-year anniversary after proof of extraterrestrial life is announced? Coincidence is an insult to everyone who is dead, everyone who will die. This was deliberate. We are being exterminated!"

"Deliberate, yes, but you have no proof this was anything but humans. Chemical warfare, new technology we don't even know about, it could—"

Then the broadcast finally did cut out, and I spent the next few minutes desperately spinning dials. Rocking to my feet to hold the radio higher, push it closer to the window. Anything, please, please, please!

The female voice returned, though it was with increasing despair I realized it didn't matter. "Again, if anyone is out there, remember you are not alone. We will get through this. Be smart, be safe. We will broadcast again soon, hopefully with more information. WVFI Radio, this is Kiera and John from the station at Notre Dame, signing off."

The radio fizzled then, a robotic voice beginning its next loop, the same information and warnings I had heard a thousand times. I switched it off and then went to the kitchen and opened the pantry. I stared at the piles of food, speculating how long I could make it last. Wondering what Kiera and John had to eat over at Notre Dame, wondering which of us would be dead first.

The power had been out for nearly twenty-four hours, and I knew that it was never coming back on. Because it wasn't just the power, the lights, the stove, the ceiling fan—it was everything. All of it as dead as my neighbors, the stench of whom was starting to drive me mad.

I first noticed it when my cellphone failed to turn on. It had been charged, at least halfway, I'd been sure of that. It was in the mere moments between setting it down to take a sip of water and picking it back up that it died. I noticed the fan next, the lull as the gears and wires were silently killed, the near instantaneous conversion of humid, stale air.

I spent hours with the radio afterward, pulling it apart, piecing it back together. Desperate for any news, any voices—but they were all gone.

I know enough about electricity and magnetics and all that garbage to know what had happened. That again, we'd been attacked, an EMP designed to cripple us further. Eliminate electronics, from phones to cars to any plane still airborne.

That evening, I lay on the floor and stared up at the ceiling fan, imagining it was on, a warm and half-drunk bottle of vodka clutched in my hand. That night, I feasted until I was nearly sick. The next morning, I poured the rest of the bottle down the drain. *There must always be consequences.*

It soon became unbearably hot without the ceiling fan, and I found myself crawling toward the window, edging my fingers beneath the curtain and prying it open, barely an inch. A trickle of cool breeze swept across my face, toying with my hair, tempting me, *urging* me.

I opened the window further, my greasy forehead resting on the sill. I closed my eyes, enjoying the breeze more than I could ever remember enjoying anything. The distant, ethereal sound of birds chirping filled my ears, teased me like the wind.

I knew then, knew in my soul that I had been wrong. That *nothing* had happened, and with almost feverish delight, I pulled back the curtains, heaving open the window with such vigor that it cracked against the stopper.

The sun shone against the bricks of my apartment building, birds fluttering by, chasing bees and blissfully unaware of the tiny spider in his web just under my nose.

Below, cars were parked up and down the street, bikes were chained to lampposts, the pastel blue sign on my favorite coffee shop reading, "Open, please come in!"

In the window, I could see a woman, her face pressed against the glass, eyes open—she could have been looking right at me. Around her head, glued to the window like a poor interpretation of stained glass, was an aura of blood.

Just beneath the window, legs still wrapped around a toppled-over bike, was another body, and another, another, another. Dried riverbeds of blood stained the roads, flowing toward the storm drains, filling them, clogging them.

I jammed my fingers in the window in my fervor to close it, though I hardly felt the pain. I choked down my vomit as I crawled back across the sweat-stained carpet, staring at the ceiling fan, imagining it was on.

On the eighth day of my entombment, while I worked to duct tape the vents closed, doing *anything* to stem the stench drifting through—I heard it.

Quiet, at first, then growing louder by the second as it beat against the roof, the windows, the walls—*rain!*

I tore into the kitchen, grabbing any receptacle I could find; pots and bowls and a packet of garbage bags. My mouth flooded with saliva, though it had been full of dust for days.

I wrenched back my curtains and heaved the window open, unafraid and uncaring of the dangers. The rain was pelting down now, a torrential storm. In the distance, lightening cracked and danced within vengeful clouds. My shaking arms held out the largest pot, drinking greedily as soon as an inch of water had formed.

It wasn't long before I was surrounded by a party of filled pots and bowls, the carpet soaked, water running down my arms, drenching my shirt. I had just begun to bask in the cool, wonderful delight of it all, when I saw her.

She stood swaying in place on the other side of the road, her jaw hanging loosely as if secured only by frail strings tied beneath her ears. On occasion, her head jerked violently, causing her jaw to snap open and closed like a broken ventriloquist's doll.

I froze in place, half out the window, heart pumping furiously, my arms already burning from the weight of the water. She hadn't seen me, her gaze fixed on the body of the biker beneath the coffee shop windows.

So slowly it was almost agonizing, I inched back inside, but the pot caught on the edge of the windowsill, and her eyes snapped toward me.

A raucous, barking screech emanated from her mouth as she lunged forward. Her skin was sallow and dry, her mouth full of dead, blackened teeth, her face painted with burst blood vessels.

"A girl!" she screeched, her jerking movements toward me speeding up. "A girl, a girl!"

I flung myself back inside as she began her sprint toward my apartment building, slamming the window shut as she disappeared from my view under the ledge.

I rushed to the door, which had long since been barricaded, and grabbed for the spear I had made from duct taping a kitchen knife to a broom handle. I sank down to the floor, opposite the window, my back braced against my barricade, digging my feet into the carpet.

I made no noise, save for my ragged breathing, clutching my spear across my chest.

She can't find the apartment. She will never find the apartment.

I had seen others like this, right after the Break. While people screamed and ran and died around me, others lost their minds. The horror of it all, a massacre of loved ones and strangers alike.

Zombies!

Had been my first thought, but after seeing more of them, it didn't suit them. These were people, living, breathing, feeling people. Trapped and tormented by the things they had witnessed, driven mad.

It wasn't long before I heard her bouncing off the walls of the narrow hallway, the garbled noises issuing from her mouth punctuated with words.

"Girl help me. Girl? Where is she? Where are we? Where is she?" Strung together like a child learning how to speak, intermittent with dreadful, agonizing shrieks. "Please, help me, please. I can't find my babies."

Her cries grew louder and louder, until, my heart in my throat, I heard her right outside the door. She was just another woman, likely not larger than me, less nourished, dying. Even from the window, I could see the black death around her mouth, both from her dying skin and from whatever she had eaten to sustain herself.

"Is she here?" came the voice, followed by a gleeful shout and a slam that jarred the walls. I'd braced myself, expecting to be rocked by the blast against my door.

But my front door did not move at all.

Another crash, and I realized she had broken into the neighbor's home—that she'd undershot my apartment by one single door.

I had suspected that I was not the only one alive in the building, holed up, waiting out the storm, but nothing could have prepared me for this.

His screams reverberated through the walls; muffled as they were, it did nothing to suppress the agony. "Help!" he shouted. There was a series of crashes, alternating with his cries of terror, and her shrieks, which seemed more and more delighted in nature.

"Jorah, help me! Jorah Sinclair!" he screamed—it was my neighbor Dan. I didn't know him well, but he had been kind to me since I'd moved here just weeks ago; returned my misplaced mail, held the elevator door open, and now *died instead of me.*

"Jorah!" he pleaded. There was another crash, and I nearly screamed as fists pounded my door, my barricade trembling and creaking. "Let me in, please! I know you're there."

"I find you, I find you."

Dan cried out, pleading with the woman to leave, that he had nothing for her. Dan was frail, short and scrawny from years of poor health decisions, and a crash told me that the woman did not care for his pleas. Their screams mingled for what felt like years, until finally, with a gurgling noise, Dan went silent.

Through the night, I endured the endless, soft squelching and humming from the woman outside my door. My body burned for days after from the exertion of bracing against my barricade the entire night through.

And in the morning, at last, I heard the shuffling footsteps as the *freak* finally tottered away, whispering, "Jorah … Jorah," as she went.

6

JORAH THE EIGHT-DIGIT WONDER

"What do you mean?" I asked, dumbfounded while the others stood around me in a fitted circle, lips in tight lines and eyes darting nervously.

"Jorah, they're gone, your fingers ... two of them," Sana repeated. I found myself starring stupidly at my clublike hand, which was wrapped thickly in layers of gauze.

"When?"

"Two days ago."

I paused, trying to think through the panic welling up inside me, a picture beginning to form in my mind. "There was a man ..."

Sana nodded. "Yes, the old man who owned the place. He came in and—"

"He hit me in the head," I interjected, cradling my wrapped hand, my eyes darting around the others. Sana and Geoff sported the concerned looks of a parent as they watched me, Geoff still holding a cup of water. Riley however, appeared stressed and grayed, continually running a hand through his hair.

"He hit you in the head, and then he cut two of your fingers off. You've been sleeping ever since," Sana continued slowly.

I looked back down at the hand in question, unable to tell if anything really was missing through the wrappings. "Which ones?"

"Your pinky finger and ring finger. There's a gash on the middle one too, but I think it's going to be okay."

"Where are they?" I asked, and Riley let out a snort of exasperation.

"She's in shock," Riley proclaimed, "or she's had her damn head bashed in too many times."

I glared at him. "I'm not in shock, although I do agree I'm going to die if I keep getting hit in the head. I just want to know what you did with my fingers."

"Here," Geoff piped in quietly, and he reached to the side of the couch and procured a small jar, in which my two bloody fingers rattled around inside.

"Oh, God dammit, Geoff. Put that shit away! You think she wants to see that?" Riley scoffed, collapsing into a chair.

He was right, and it must have shown on my face because Geoff hurriedly stowed the jar. "Sorry," he said sheepishly.

"What happened to the man?" I asked, turning back to Sana.

Her jaw clenched. "Riley happened."

"What?" I turned to look at Riley, who was staring at me, his face unreadable.

"Sorry it took us so long to help you, Jorah. It wasn't right."

"Jorah? Wow, I was beginning to think you thought my name was Sweetheart," I joked, but the others didn't laugh.

"We heard everything—well most of it," Sana began. "We were coming out of the woods just in time to see the old man head inside. We ran over, but, I'm sorry, he had a gun, and we spent too long making a plan. We were too scared to shoot, in case we hit you."

I nodded slowly, my (probably dented) brain trying to absorb information. "So, where is he?"

"Don't worry. Once he cut you, we came running in. We took him by surprise. He'd put his gun down. You'd passed out, and I pulled you away, and ..." she trailed off, looking almost sick.

"Riley beat him to death," Geoff finished bluntly, "at least, most of the way dead..." He shuddered, water sloshing out of the glass.

I looked to Riley in shock, and he grinned, though it didn't reach his eyes as he held up a pair of bruised and bandaged hands. "You're welcome, sweetheart."

I twisted around, peering over the couch toward the kitchenette, where, though there was no corpse, there was a large, wet-looking blanket spread over the floor.

I turned back just in time to see the bottom of Riley's boots disappear up the stairs and out the door.

Sana promised she had been the only one to dress me as she handed me my clean set of clothes. The shock of finding out I was two digits too short had been enough to stop me from realizing I was dressed in only an oversized pink nightgown.

"You know, this probably belonged to that man's wife," I said as I stripped off the frills and pulled on my jeans and T-shirt.

"It did, why?"

"Don't you think it's a little fucked up to dress me in the clothes of the woman whose husband cut my fingers off?"

Surprisingly, Sana shot me a grin. "I thought you'd rather have something clean to wear than be naked—or be wearing your dirty clothes which were an infection waiting to happen."

I laughed, finishing getting dressed while hurriedly eating for the first time in days. "Good point." Then I paused, momentarily overcome with gratitude. "Thank you, Sana. For everything. I'm losing count of how many times you've patched me up."

The small smile that had grown on her face faded. "You've saved us too."

"Just once, and I don't think I'd count almost getting killed by some lunatics as saving you."

She shook her head, her words laced with importance and her eyes set like obsidian. "We heard you. When the man kept asking where your people were, and you didn't tell him."

I adjusted my stance awkwardly as the memory returned. "It just seemed like I shouldn't tell him. I wasn't trying to be heroic."

"It was brave." And with that, she headed up the stairs.

Thankfully, Sana had also washed my bandana, tying it into a loop so I could pile the fabric into my hair one-handed. My fingers brushed over a rough scab knitted into my scalp. The pain in my body was no more than a dull ache, having swallowed what I was told were the last of my painkillers immediately upon waking. Sana had apologized for searching my bag, telling me she'd split the remaining pills between us, dissolving the antibiotics in water and pouring them down my throat while I'd slept.

Now I had lost my only form of power, highly doubting that the few crushed granola bars and handful of tampons in my backpack would be enough for the others to keep me around, should they finally decide they didn't want me. A small bubble of anxiety burst in my stomach at the thought of them leaving me, sneaking off in the middle of the night while I was deep in a coma of blood loss and stale beer.

They didn't leave you though, not yet, I thought, which was reasonably reassuring.

We decided to stay only one more night in the basement. My attack had set us all on edge, not to mention the damp smear of the old man plastered to the floor.

Sana told me they'd dragged his body outside and buried it, right next to a small wooden cross that had been set into the ground.

I stood over the cross now, reading and re reading the faint word that was scratched into the wood, *Maryanne*. I looked down at my bandage-wrapped left hand. Underneath the gauze, it pulsed painfully, and I felt a twinge of disgust at the thought of having to unwrap it.

You're missing two fingers! had begun to play on repeat in my brain, seeming to echo with every throb in the hand.

On the bright side, the gash on my leg no longer hurt, though it, along with where the windowsill cut my hands, would scar horribly. All I could do now was hope I didn't have any serious brain damage.

I should start wearing a helmet around, I thought to myself.

Footsteps sounded behind me, and I turned to see Geoff approaching. "Hey," he said awkwardly.

"Hey."

"Whatcha' doing?"

"Just staring at the graves," I replied, "and at my hand," I added, waving the clublike appendage around.

Geoff stood with me for a moment, as we both surveyed the earth in front of us.

"Does it hurt?" Geoff asked.

I shrugged. "A bit—those painkillers are the real deal, I'm sure it'll be much worse when they wear off."

Geoff shuddered, not taking his eyes off the dirt. "We shouldn't have buried him; he doesn't deserve it after what he did."

"I don't know ... It wasn't really his fault."

"How so?"

63

"I saw it in his eyes, heard it in his voice—not to be so poetic. The man who did this to me wasn't the same man who owned a pink convenience store with his wife—not anymore, he wasn't. He kept asking me what I'd done, calling me a murderer—I think he was talking about Maryanne."

"But you don't think he was a freak?"

"No, he didn't look like one. No broken blood vessels, no dead teeth—not that I can remember, anyway. I know your theory, Geoff." I paused, feeling sick. "I've thought about it too, but I think we just need to realize the further this goes on, the worse it's going to get for people. The freaks are dead, but that doesn't mean that everyone else is going to be sane."

Geoff nodded, fidgety, cracking his knuckles and glancing around.

"Something on your mind?"

He turned, and his dull brown eyes looked nervously into mine. "Thank you, for everything, and I'm sorry I've been such a jerk to you."

My eyebrows shot up in surprise. "I really haven't done much."

He shook his head, rubbing the back of his neck. "You saved me in the trailer, when you let me go out the window first. Why?"

"I don't know why," I answered truthfully. "I wasn't trying to save you over me necessarily, it just happened."

He nodded. "Well, still, thanks. I'm glad you're in the group."

I grinned, and Geoff flushed red. "Aww, Geoff, you're not going soft, are you?"

He rolled his eyes. "Dinner's ready soon." And he strolled off toward the house.

The night was tense, though uneventful, the watchful eyes of the others searing the back of my head. For a time, before we all fell into restless sleep, Geoff entertained us with stories from his childhood. As it turned out, when he wasn't being a neurotic, grumpy jerk—Geoff was kind of funny.

The map had been drawn out, our bags and the little red wagon packed. We had less food, less water, and less fingers than we'd arrived with.

Time to move on.

The plan was simple: keep heading west, farther and farther into the cornfields and flat land.

Riley approached as I sat beneath the shade of a tree, trying one-handed to lace my boots.

"Hey." He was holding out a handful of brass ammunition toward me. "We found the revolver in your bag while you were knocked out. I happened to have a little bit of ammo for it, so, here."

"Thanks." I'd nearly forgotten about the revolver until now, lost to the bottom of my pack with the rest of my useless belongings.

"It's a nice piece. Where'd you get it?"

"I found it on a body, a little before I met you guys."

"Smart. Not telling us you had it."

I raised an eyebrow. "Is that sarcasm?"

"No, although it would've done you some good to ask for ammo earlier, sweetheart." He half-joked, gesturing to my bandaged hand.

I glared at him. "Well, thanks." Giving up on tying my boots, I moved to stand, but a firm hand pushed me back down, fingers like snakes whisking over the leather.

"Sweetheart, I have to ask, how did you make it so long on your own?"

"What do you mean?" My tone was sharper than it needed to be, tongue like daggers and ice.

He finished the laces with a small flourish, though he stayed kneeling, eye-level. Charm and charisma radiated off him as always, and while he thought he was wooing me, I was only unnerved by the closeness. "Don't take that the wrong way; you're obviously tough as nails ..." As he glanced down at the bandaged hand, a round of pain ran up my arm as though this had offended the wound. "I just know none of us could have made it alone."

I told him what he wanted to hear, my tale of luck and woes and near misses.

He complimented my bravery, offering a shark-toothed smile.

As he left, I thought I'd begun to sort him out—it was much harder with him than the others, surprising, granted his need for constant approval and adoration. I rolled the cool bullets around in my hand, counting them, wondering who would be first to end up with one in their back.

The road is dry, and the road is endless. Those were the new thoughts intruding in my mind as we walked.

Thick dust, dry ground, endless days, gray horizon.

The conversation was bleak at best. Little to share but snippets of information we'd heard over the months.

"We've had this discussion. I want nothing to do with refugee camps. Feel free to go without me," Sana snapped at Geoff.

There had been word of hundreds of camps at the start, ranging from tent cities to repurposed apartment complexes. All erected by the last remaining vestiges of state and federal government, all just as dangerous as the road.

"Sadie, Geoff. Did you even listen to her at all?" Sana sighed as Geoff continued to pester us about the option of refugee camps. "She was at two of them, one outside of Lafayette, and I forget where the other was, but it was just as bad. Barely any food, barely any water, gangs and rapists, disease running rampant—but *sure*, big, strong Geoff Christensen, go find yourself a camp."

Riley sniggered, and I hurried to intercept before Geoff could fire off on a tangent. "Enough, guys. If we end up desperate enough, we will look for a camp, okay? Better that than nothing. As for now, we don't have the slightest idea where one would be, and I agree with Sana. They're dangerous; I saw one myself." This was true; I had seen the horrors of the refugee camps. Putrid, hellish sites—I'd lost the young couple I'd been following to one, saw it swallow them bone and all.

"What happened to being all by yourself?" Riley teased.

"I didn't go inside." For the first time since I joined the group, I felt my hand jerk involuntarily toward my chest, searching for the familiar hard plastic of my binoculars. My comfort item now squashed unlovingly in the bottom of my pack.

At midday, we wandered off the main road into a small paved area overlooking a gorgeous view of sprawling farmland. Even the gray sky and chilling winds couldn't tarnish the soft green waves stretching out toward a flat vista.

"Think we could find food down there?" Geoff asked eagerly, leaning over the barrier, as I awkwardly tried to stab open a can of tuna with one hand.

"Give me that." Riley cursed, ripping the can from my hands and giving me a look of exasperation.

"I don't think so, Geoff," Sana replied, moving to stand beside him. "It's been hot this summer, really hot, and there's barely been any rain."

"Nobody's alive to water it," I added. "Plus, that's a wheat field. What are we going to do with thousands of pounds of raw wheat?"

"Bake it into bread?" Geoff offered.

I rolled my eyes. "Sure, and we can open a bakery and name it after ourselves."

Angry now, Geoff sneered and stalked away.

"How do your fingers feel?" Sana asked as we ate.

"You mean her lack of fingers."

"Shut up, Geoff."

"Hurts," I answered, "but not too bad, more of an ache."

Sana nodded. "We need to take the bandages off soon. It should have already been done."

I shuddered. "Or I could just keep them on forever."

We finished lunch with light conversation, it was cloudy today, dull and smoggy, and we hoped the rain would come soon, as we were starting to run low on fresh water. With our break wrapping up, we were about to clamber back into the rhythm of our walk when Riley spotted something in the distance.

"Hold up," he said powerfully, peering over the lookout to the field below.

The road we were on was set slightly above the fields it overlooked, and while it gave a stunning view, it also left us slightly exposed.

"Get down," Riley said calmly, as he crouched and slowly made his way closer to the barrier before the hillside. "Its people, I think."

I dug through my pack, handing off my binoculars, which the universe had so kindly given me a reason to use, mere hours after I'd sought it.

He did nothing but curse and hand them back. Through the lens, I could clearly see the interstate on the far side of the farmland between us. It was situated lower than we were, giving us an expansive view. Abandoned cars were strewn all along it, as to be expected, but what was so shocking was the sheer number of people milling about in the road.

"There has to be at least thirty of them," I said, handing off the binoculars to Sana.

"And they're armed."

It was true, the group, appearing to be almost entirely men, even seemed to have a few working trucks at their disposal. Each one was fitted with metal and wire screens, truly giving them the ultimate apocalyptic look. I glanced back uneasily at our shabby red wagon.

"They have a fire going; looks like they just stopped for a break," Sana commented. Her face was set and taut, and I wondered if my nerves showed as hers did.

"They just stopped out in the open like that?" I asked.

"They have nothing to fear," Riley said, rising to his feet. "Let's get out of here."

We hurried down the road, and Sana told me about the group she and Riley had heard of, shortly before they found Geoff. They'd heard the tale from a married couple, the husband of whom had been badly beaten.

The couple had encountered a large and violent group, nearly fifty strong. The husband had been beaten at his initial refusal to give up their food, his wife saying nothing the whole encounter, preferring to stare resolutely at the ground. Before they left, the husband warned Riley to keep Sana close.

Her story made my stomach churn, though the group weighed less on my mind as we put distance between us—and from what we had seen, they were traveling in the opposite direction.

I stumbled suddenly over my own exhausted feet, catching myself on a nearby car. A small shriek escaped, startling the others, as I looked up into the open eyes of a young woman, her forehead leaning against the driver's side window.

If it wasn't for the gore splattered around her head like a halo, she would have been beautiful.

The end-of-summer sun had just begun to creep lower in the sky when we finally approached the sprawling suburban neighborhood. The houses, which once had perfectly manicured lawns and hosted backyard barbeques, now looked forlorn and desolate. Grass grew up to the porch, the occasional abandoned house cat slipping through the tangles. Of the houses, many had broken windows and doors ajar, and an entire street held nothing but blackened and charred remains.

There were bodies too, but that wasn't unusual, as you could hardly step these days without tripping over one. The skeletal remains of a woman dangled half out of her car, her crow-picked arm caught in the steering wheel.

"I grew up in a place like this," Geoff commented. "Less dead bodies, but still."

"Me too," Riley noted, which was surprising, as he didn't strike me as the white-picket-fence type.

As we walked down the street, a chill tickled at my spine like the ghostly hand of those who had lived here. We picked our way warily into some houses, each having little to yield.

There was one home, painted sky-blue, in which I spied the small face of a child peering from around the edge of a curtain, only to be ushered back into the darkness moments later. I said nothing.

At last, we found two homes, directly across from each other, which looked relatively untouched. "There's a good chance they only look this empty because the owners kicked it right at the start," I commented.

"Not like we haven't seen a body before. Sana, let's go," Riley countered, gesturing to her as the two of them headed for the slightly smaller home. "Meet back out here when you're done."

As Geoff and I headed toward the house, I drew my revolver from my waist. Geoff caught my eye and nodded, pulling his own gun from the holster.

"Finger off the trigger," I teased him, which was received with a hostile look.

The door swung open, filling our noses with the scent of dust and neglect, the view of a large, framed photo of a family of four greeting us as we entered. I cringed looking at their smiling faces, though I was quick to notice that the daughter looked to be roughly my size.

I headed upstairs as Geoff searched the first floor, careful to keep my gun at the ready. A search of the rooms bore very little; the family had obviously been careful to take as much as they could before they left, and I wouldn't be surprised if the house had been looted previously. I was busy picking through drawers of clothes when the creak of floorboards sounded behind me.

"It's me!" Sana shouted, and I gave her an apologetic smile, lowering my gun.

"That was fast."

She shook her head. "There wasn't much there." Her eyes darted around the room, and I noticed how she shifted her weight between her feet. I stopped gathering the clothes and stood straight.

"Are you okay?"

"I'm fine," she stated, though her voice wavered slightly. "The family was still there."

"Did they give you trouble?" I asked in surprise, crossing to the window and peeling back the curtain to look out at the quiet house.

"They were all dead. The parents … two kids. Killed themselves, by the looks of it."

"I'm so sorry you had to see that."

She nodded. "The guys are downstairs; we think we should stay here tonight and get a head start on securing the place."

"Good idea."

7

JORAH THE HUNTED

The house was secure—well, as much as we could make it, and as the light dwindled outside, the four of us sat around the kitchen table.

"There's a decent chance people could have seen us come in," Riley stated, leaning back in the chair with his boots propped up on the table, "so keep that in mind when it's your turn to take watch."

We'd boarded up the house with the careful eye an intruder may use to find weak points, and with the supply of spare wood and tools from the basement, we now felt quite safe.

"There's four bedrooms upstairs. We can all take one, and we should add an extra barricade at the top of the stairs," Sana suggested, while I busied myself preparing the night's rations.

"This is gonna be a fucking problem soon," Riley muttered as I placed down our shabby bowls. "What do we have? A week's worth, and we're already half-starved."

"We'll find something."

"Does anyone know where Jorah's fingers went? That's something."

"Hilarious," I deadpanned, glaring at Riley. "We could try hunting."

"Do you know how to hunt?"

"No, but how hard could it be?"

"Why don't we just eat the next body we find, huh?"

We continued to bicker until our bowls had been scraped clean, though my stomach still ached for food, and my hand still ached for fingers.

I was busy sorting through the clothes I'd found when someone rapped rhythmically on the door behind me. We'd all split up to separate bedrooms, and I was lucky enough to have snagged the guest room, which distinctly lacked the disturbing closeness of the personalized bedrooms of the family members.

"Come in," I called, and the door swung open to reveal a grinning Riley. A dark bottle of liquid, which sloshed merrily with each step, was gripped in his fist.

"What's that?" I asked, eyeing it suspiciously.

Riley grinned wider and winked at me, leaning casually against the doorframe. "This, my dear, is the finest hooch in this whole damn neighborhood."

"No way."

"That's right. Been distilling it myself," he said haughtily. "I can't say it tastes great, but man it does the trick." He held it out and laughed as I avidly drank from the bottle, the taste like dirt-cheap dark wine.

"God, that's good," I sighed, collapsing back onto the bed. The bed shifted as Riley sat beside me, snatching the bottle from my hands and taking a long pull.

"Nice to drink with someone who actually appreciates it. Sana never drinks, and Geoff can't stomach shit."

"You're welcome."

"I swear, the end of the world has been better rehab than actual rehab," Riley said, passing me the jug.

I looked at him in surprise. "Have you been?"

"Mm-hmm, long time ago. My ex-wife made me go."

"And you were married?"

Instead of answering, he shot me a sly grin and stuck out a hand for the bottle.

Later in the night, I sat rigidly in the uncomfortable wooden chair, staring down over the barricade protecting us from the dangers of downstairs. The alcohol warmed my belly, easing the endless knots that curdled my muscles, dampening the headache that had pulsed in my brain for days.

I felt content, knowing now the others finally trusted me

enough to let me keep watch. Knowing that they no longer feared me—or maybe they were all just too tired to care anymore if I slit their throats.

Outside a storm raged, battering the shutters and walls. We'd all felt it coming that evening, the shift of weather looming in our bones. We were like animals now, senses heightened, instincts sharpened. We'd placed every object that could hold water on the front lawn before the first drop had even begun its dive.

The morning came as a chilled godsend, the earth flooded with the rain it so desperately needed. Everything seemed greener, more alive, as the four of us stepped onto the porch. Then we ran for the pots and pans spread across the lawn, drinking our fill, water sloshing down our fronts. We bottled as much as we could, but there was far too much to carry, even with our spindly wagon, but still, we could hardly bear to let it go to waste.

"Riley, I swear if you turn around, I will shoot you."

Riley laughed, his arms going in the air in surrender, his back to us as he and Geoff kept a wary eye on the street.

"Just hurry up so I won't be so tempted," he teased, and Sana cursed at him, plunging her arm back into the freezing bucket of rainwater.

It wasn't the most pleasant bath I'd ever had. Tucked behind the corner of the house, sloshing water over myself. A mere bar of soap to work at the dirt and oils so caked into my flesh it could be my first layer of skin. I raked my nails over the soap, carving out little valleys, feeling a sense of relief that the germs and filth that clogged my fingertips could at last be washed away.

Soon we had all bathed, wrapped warmly in our freshest set of clothes, any extras washed and splayed across our wagon, and continued our journey.

I was glad to leave the neighborhood behind us, the burnt-out street of houses, the thin and frail face of the child peeking behind the curtain—the area reeked of death. And now, for the first time I could remember, my skin smelled only of soap.

"God damn, I feel good," Riley purred, sweeping the handle of the wagon from my hand with a grin. I returned his smile thankfully, stretching my aching arm, the new bottles of water doubling the wagon's weight.

The wind ruffled through my hair, drying and returning it to natural loose waves, the blonde strands fluttering in my wake like the tail of a kite. Sana reached out, pressing a small handful of crackers into my palm. Six saltines, handed to each of us in turn, our lunch for the day.

I don't think the others realized we were being followed. I'd only noticed recently myself, it was subtle, the clues, but I knew that it was real.

I knew too, that we weren't just being tailed, that what I heard weren't always the calls of real birds. I knew because I once stalked these same people, for days and days. They knew that we were being hunted no more than the worms know the world has ended.

I fell back alongside the wagon, which Geoff now pulled, the wheels squeaking and rattling over unmanaged roads. He glanced back at me, and I smiled; the group cannot stop now.

I opened my pack, which was, thankfully, quite empty. I rustled through the wagon, keeping pace, slipping bottle after bottle of water inside, stuffing a handful of still-damp clothes on top.

Geoff thanked me, thinking that I was trying to lessen the burden.

"Riley," I whispered, approaching his side, "don't look at me. We're being followed." I saw the tendons tighten in his neck, his shudder-step, the way he almost looked behind us. He hadn't noticed, but by the sly glance Sana gave me, she had.

We'd entered the outskirts of a small town, the road running parallel along shops and homes, quaint, peaceful, and becoming quickly overgrown. We'd discussed earlier to avoid it, continue our path, but I felt that it had suddenly become our only option.

"What do we do?" Riley whispered, his hand sliding toward his holster, brushing the metal of his gun.

"No." I caught his wrist, intertwining our fingers. "We don't know if we're outnumbered. They can't know we know." I looked far ahead, to where the road took a small bend, curving inward toward the shops. "There."

We said nothing as we approached the bend, Geoff still blissfully unaware, humming under his breath.

"Now," I whispered.

I darted sideways, pulling a terribly confused Geoff along toward the row of buildings beside us. Sana followed closely, while with a sharp shove, Riley sent our wagon careening off the road into a net of bushes.

We ducked low along the once-white picket fence, now speckled with mud and large swaths of paint peeling like sunburnt skin. We'd only just rounded the corner, rushing down the narrow street, when we heard them.

"Shit, they're on to us. Find them." A man's voice, gruff and commanding and cruel.

"There, the library," Sana said, pointing in the direction of a small brick building, inconspicuous and bland.

The door was unlocked as we rushed inside, darting between bookshelves toward the front windows. I collapsed on the worn carpet, back against the wall, the windows so grime-covered, it was almost like looking through wax paper.

Sana sat in a similar fashion across the large square window, strands of hair covering her face, chest heaving. Riley and Geoff beside her, crouched and grasping their weapons. I pressed my back to the wall, craning my neck around the edge of the glass to peek into the street beyond.

It was still and hushed for no more than an instant before a group of men burst from behind a home.

"Where'd they go? Spread out!"

The floorboards creaked; a shadow fell across my boots. My good hand flew to my revolver, my injured arm pressed against my chest as I looked up into the startled eyes of a woman.

She was thin, yet toned, tendons and veins unconcealed by the papery skin of her hands. She wore a floor-length cardigan, a pile of books bundled into her arms.

Slowly, I released my gun, raising one finger to my lips. *Be quiet.*

She was frozen for only a moment, then crouched, placing the books on the floor and drawing a long, serrated knife from the folds of her sweater. She crept closer, ducking against a bookshelf.

The others could see her then, shooting me panicked looks, I shook my head. *Don't move. We are all in this together now.*

"I think they got away."

"Bullshit, there's nowhere to go!"

"Nobody in any of those shops." A pause. "I think we lost them."

"Check the library."

Our eyes dart together, blue and green and brown. Movement in my peripheral vision, the woman waving me toward her, her own eyes a soft cerulean, gentle and kind.

I jerked my neck in her direction, and hesitantly the others followed. Running at a crouch, winding and twisting between bookshelves, she led us to—a dead end.

"Hurry," she whispered, clambering into the small space. The children's corner of the library, I guessed, the hard carpet floor tiled in foam mats, a stack of dusty bean bag chairs lining the wall. *Oh!*

I pulled the others forward into the corner, brick wall on one side and stacked bookcase on the other. We crammed into the space, cheek to cheek and breath to breath.

The woman and I worked silently, dragging the plush bundles

toward us, stacking them, then piling them over our heads.

Don't move, don't breathe.

The plan was so simple, so stupid, that even as we heard the creak of the library doors, I felt little doubt. Our wall was complete, stacked just low enough to be inconspicuous but high enough to hide our crouching figures, a wall of plush bean bag chairs.

I can think of nothing more pathetic than to die right now. Like a child playing hide-and-seek, Geoff's elbow stabbing me in the ribs.

His footsteps came and went, and I doubted his eyes did any more than skim over the pile. Riley's gun shook midair beside my ear, his finger twitching on the trigger. The library doors opened … and closed.

"That was the dumbest thing that I have ever let anyone drag me into, *ever*," Riley snarled almost the second the doors clicked shut, lurching to his feet and sending our wall toppling.

"Be quiet," Sana hissed, also rising. "They haven't left."

Back to the window, the woman was now keeping her distance, the serrated knife clamped in her hands.

An explosion of gunfire tore through the room, so vicious that in a matter of seconds, we had all flattened ourselves behind bookshelves.

"I saw one. They ran around the corner," a man shouted.

The woman caught my eye, her body nearly slim enough to slip beneath the shelf beside her. She didn't need to speak for me to recognize her question. I shook my head. *My group is all here.*

Her eyes widened, and in an instant, she'd heaved herself off the floor, her fingers scrabbling across the cover of a book. She hurried toward the library doors and flung the book across the street.

"Hide," Sana hissed frantically, her eyes wide in shock, practically dragging Riley away. The look on his face said he wished he could throttle the woman.

The library doors burst open, and the man fired across the room before his vision could have even adjusted to the dim. I flattened to the floor, bullets whizzing over my head. The man had hardly taken a step inside when the woman plunged her knife through his neck, his rifle dropping with him, spinning away across the ground.

"If you help me, we will help you," the woman called to me, her expression wild as she grabbed his rifle. She smashed the butt end through the window beside her, firing into the group of men who had filtered back into the street.

Sana yelled at me to follow them, that there must be a back door. I looked to her, then back to the woman. *Shit.*

I rushed across the room, dropping to my knees, my eyes closed as I fired blindly through the filthy windows. Chaos swamped the group of men, bullets raining down. Riley, Geoff, and Sana appeared by my side, Geoff bellowing a war cry as he fired his pistol.

"Gallagher's down, help me drag him!"

"There's more of them in the bank. Head for the truck!"

As quickly as the firefight had begun, it was over. My revolver clicked empty as I delivered my final shot, beads of cold sweat running down my neck.

"What the hell was that about?" Riley growled, stalking toward the front doors, rage etched into every line of his face.

I hurried after him, trying to grasp his sleeve. "Riley—" I was cut off as my nose smacked into his back. He had frozen, his body tense, flinging an arm out to push me to the side.

Framed in the doorway stood two men, each with guns raised toward us and resolute looks etched onto their faces.

"Hands up, now," the first man demanded. He was tall and broad with a thick, red beard.

"Musa," the woman gasped, leaping from her hiding spot and throwing her arms around the second man.

He wrapped his lean arms around her, dwarfing her petite frame.

"My love, are you all right?"

The bearded man had kept his sights locked on us. From the corner of my eye I could glimpse Sana and Geoff scuttling toward us.

"Lachlan, wait," the woman said, pulling herself away and placing her hand on the rifle tip. "They helped me; it's all right."

Lachlan paused, his gaze flitting between Riley and me.

"Guys, come out," I said, my hands still raised as Sana and Geoff crept toward us. "We don't want any trouble. Those men had been following us; we didn't know anyone was here."

"Who are you?"

"Doesn't matter who we are; we'll be going now," Riley

responded, gripping my arm and gesturing for Sana to come to us.

"Riley, stop," I grunted, attempting to pull away.

The bearded man stared at me then, his eyes boring into my own.

"Lachlan." The gun lowered.

The other man, Musa, had stepped forward as well, his arm still looped around the woman's waist. "It's not safe here, those men will be back with others. Come with us. Our home is nearby. It's the least we can do to thank you for helping Kara, especially since she tells me she put you in further danger attempting to help us."

The four of us paused to look at each other, a silent argument playing out between us.

"Please," the man urged, looping the strap of his rifle over his shoulders. "We owe you, but we need to hurry."

"We need to get our things."

Musa nodded. "Lachlan will go with you—Kara and I will find the rest of our group and meet you at our home."

"Okay," I agreed, after approving looks from Sana and Geoff. Even Riley didn't argue as the five of us hurried into the street.

8
JORAH'S NEW HOME

The tall, brawny frame of Lachlan stood statue-still by the corner of a home, a silent guard while the four of us worked to retrieve our wagon from the thorns it had tangled in. Despite his imposing stature, Lachlan had a kind, soft face, edged in a blazingly red and bushy beard with a matching mane of hair.

"This way," Lachlan directed, and we hurried down the road at a clip. Soon, we had left the rows of shops in the distance and turned onto a side street, the houses set back via long driveways, a smattering of trees spread around them. We reached the door, and it was immediately thrown open for us.

The room we entered was unexpectedly stylish. A charming foyer was dappled with coat hooks and family photos—all sorts of things you'd find in a perfectly well-adjusted home.

"Lachlan." The other man from the library strode forward,

grasping Lachlan's forearm as the two men greeted each other. He turned to us, dark eyes gliding over each of our faces.

"My name is Musa," he said, reaching out to shake our hands, "Musa Imani."

"Jorah Sinclair," I offered, his large, rough hand enveloping mine. I noticed his gaze drift across my bandaged arm, the gauze now dirty and tattered.

"Sana Mangal."

"Geoff Christensen."

"Riley."

Musa raised his eyebrow, but nonetheless shook Riley's hand. "Thank you for helping Kara," he said, once again looking at each of us.

"Did you find the rest of your group?" Sana asked.

"Yes, our friend Manuel managed to escape. He is a bit shaken but nonetheless all right. He is upstairs with his wife, Maria, now.

"You must know them well?" Sana queried, I presumed for lack of anything better to say.

"Yes, we were friends before. They have been living with us the last few months." He turned to me, his deep voice and firm tone unwavering. "What happened to your hand?"

A nervous laugh escaped my lips. "I was attacked … and two of my fingers were cut off."

Musa's eyebrows raised in surprise. "When did this happen?"

"About three days ago."

He shook his head. "Your dressings are filthy, Kara is a doctor. You should see her right away."

"I'll take you," Lachlan offered.

I looked to the others. Geoff gave me an approving nod while Riley stood still, his arms crossed.

"I'll come too," Sana said, and for the first time I noticed the river of blood leaking from a tear in her sleeve.

"Sana, what—"

She shook her head. "I only got grazed. I'm fine."

"If you don't mind, I would like to speak with your men," said Musa.

We agreed, and Sana and I turned to the boys. "Be nice," I instructed quietly but was met with only Riley's stoic gaze.

We followed Lachlan down the hallway into a large kitchen, dimly lit by candles as they had drawn all the shades.

"Wait here. I'll fetch Kara," Lachlan instructed.

"How many of you are there?" I inquired.

"Well, there's me and Musa, his wife is Kara, Manuel, and Maria. That just leaves Johanna; you can meet her soon." With that he headed out of the room.

I collapsed into a chair, throwing my backpack onto the kitchen island. I rubbed my good hand down my face and through my hair, pulling out my bandana.

"What do you think of them?"

Sana shrugged. "They seem all right. I don't think we're in

any immediate danger here."

"Maybe just from Riley," I muttered, picking flecks of library dust off my jeans.

"They didn't need to bring us here, offer to patch us up," Sana continued, which I agreed was a point in their favor.

Lachlan emerged back into the kitchen then, followed by Kara, the petite blonde having changed out of her cardigan, which had been splashed down the front with the blood of the man she killed.

"Hey guys, I'm Kara," she said, smiling brightly at us and shaking both of our hands. We introduced ourselves as Kara began to unpack the contents of a bag. She was bubbly and friendly, a bounce in her step while she spread out her supplies, apparently unbothered by the incident in the library.

"So, you're a doctor?" I asked.

"Yep—well okay, you got me, I was a veterinarian."

"Works for me."

She smiled again, flashing a few crooked teeth. She had a pretty face and small, thin frame, her hair tied back with a scrunchie. I noticed the deep laugh lines etched into her skin. She reached for Sana first, the blood still leaking from a long gash on her forearm.

"Thank you, guys, for helping me," Kara said as she dabbed at the wound, the tang of alcohol filling the kitchen. "I don't know what I would have done if I lost any of them."

"Thanks for not stabbing us with that knife of yours." Sana grimaced.

"The beanbag chair hiding spot was incredible, by the way," I added. "Ridiculous, but incredible."

Kara let out a long, melodic laugh, the kind of laugh only wholly likable people had. "I thought it was pretty good myself, bet that idiot didn't spare us a second glance." She finished bandaging Sana's arm; the wound, while long and painful appearing, would not need stitches. "So, tell me what happened here," she said as she gently took my hand and laid it out on the table. Sana and Lachlan sat nearby, chatting lightly.

"A few days ago, we were staying in this store; we thought it was abandoned. The others had gone outside, and I was taking a nap. There was this old man—he lived there, he was crazy, just totally gone. He bashed me in the head, we fought a little … and he chopped off a few fingers," I blubbered out, feeling my face flush.

Kara blanched. "You're fucking kidding me."

I couldn't help but laugh. "I wish I was."

"How did you bandage it?"

"Sana did it, actually. I'm not sure."

"I cleaned it up the best I could, crushed up some amoxicillin in her water," Sana answered. "The cut was pretty clean through, and there was also a bit of a laceration on the middle finger, but I didn't think it needed stitches."

"Antibiotics can be extremely dangerous if you don't know what you're doing, though I suppose the alternative is worse. How many times have you changed the bandages since?"

"Once, the day after … before Jorah woke up."

Kara shook her head, making that disapproving clicking noise. "So, you haven't even seen this without the bandages?"

"Nope."

"Well, good luck." With that she began unraveling, having to cut away the matted layers at one point. My hand ached as she worked, and she paused to dig out a few painkillers from her bag.

Soon, my hand was free, and I raised it to my face, willing myself not to burst into hysterical sobs at the sight of my missing fingers. My ring finger was entirely gone, down to just a pathetic nub extending from my palm. My pinky was in better shape, missing only until just below where the second knuckle should be. As for my middle finger, the cut was deep, Kara saying that it should have been stitched to avoid terrible scarring, but it was too late now. The stubs and my intact fingers were coated thickly in dried blood.

"Wow," I mumbled, placing my arm back down on the table and leaning into my chair, staring at the ceiling.

"It's kind of badass," Lachlan offered, and I shot him a look that made his cheeks flush to nearly the color of his beard.

"That, and it's also healing quiet well," Kara said as she inspected the tender stubs. "You did a good job with this," she added to Sana. "Do you have medical training?"

"My father was a surgeon."

Kara worked quickly on my hand, though nearly half an hour had passed before I was finally bandaged up again.

"You need to change that every day," Kara coached, "but you need to let it breathe sometimes too, so let it get air before you re wrap it."

At that moment, Riley, Geoff, and Musa entered the room.

"How are you doing?" Musa asked us as he strode toward Kara and placed a kiss on her cheek.

"Your wife is very talented," Sana offered with a smile.

Riley had crossed to me, lifting my arm and inspecting the new bandages. "How is it?" he asked, looking at me intently, as though he were trying to tell me something with only his eyes.

"It hurts, a lot," I told him, and it did, now that it had not only been jostled in a fight but prodded and picked at, "but Kara said it's healing well."

He nodded silently, surveying Kara briefly.

"So," Musa began, clapping his hands together, "you are all more than welcome to stay. We are very impressed by how you treated Kara—there's few people who would do that these days."

We glanced uneasily toward each other, Riley still seeming desperate to catch my eye.

"Would you mind if we had a minute to talk?"

"Of course." Gently, Musa guided Kara from the kitchen, Lachlan lumbering after them.

"Well?" Sana asked, as soon as the others were out of earshot.

"Well, what?" snapped Riley as he picked through the small pile of medical instruments on the counter.

"What did you talk about?"

"They just wanted to know our story, mostly," answered

Geoff, "how long we'd known each other, how things had gone. We asked about those men. They said they roll through the town every so often. They said they don't come down this way though; a few of the neighboring houses are still occupied, and they have a sort of neighborhood watch going on."

"I like them," I said. "I think they seem like good people; we should stay at least for the night."

Sana agreed, running her fingers over her fresh bandages. "It'll be evening soon. We can't go running back out with those men out there."

"Geoff?"

"Huh? Oh, yeah, I agree with you guys."

"Riley?"

There was no reply, only a scowl as he shrugged in defeat. Sana ducked into the hall, calling to the others, who reappeared, laughing and talking, breaking out of whatever conversation they had been holding.

"We'd love to stay," Sana began hesitantly, "thank you, but we would like to know about the rest of your group. Could we meet them?"

Musa smiled, his arms now wrapped around Kara. "Maria and Manuel are resting. You can meet them later at supper, but I'm sure Johanna would love to meet you now."

He left the room, pulling Kara by the hand. Lachlan jumped up and gestured toward us to lead the way as we shouldered our bags. We were led downstairs to a beautifully finished basement, clean and cozy, with a lush couch and electric fireplace. The walls were covered in family pictures, showing Kara and Musa in most of them. No children, I noticed.

The far corner of the room was covered in canvas paintings, all depicting the same meadow dotted with wildflowers. An easel stood below, where an ancient-looking woman sat on a plush chair, painting with long strokes.

"Hey, Mom," Kara called lightly, almost nervously, striding over to the old woman.

"Kara," Johanna beamed, setting down her brush and bustling over to Kara, pulling her into a hug. "When is supper ready?"

"Soon, Mom," Kara replied gently, folding the old woman's arm into her own and guiding her toward us. "There's some people here that want to meet you."

Johanna's face split into a grin as she approached us. Her hair was perfectly white, and she stood with a slight hunch. Her face was deeply lined, and she wore cheery pink lipstick.

"Are these your friends, Kara?"

"Yeah, Mom. New friends."

"Hi, ma'am, I'm Sana." Sana offered her a soft smile.

"Oh, aren't you beautiful!" Johanna exclaimed. "Such beautiful hair—and you, so handsome." She'd turned to Riley, pretending to swoon.

"You as well, darling," Riley replied smoothly, giving her his most charming smile.

"Oh, I like him," Johanna laughed, "and you! Such sad eyes, why so sad, darling?"

Geoff looked taken aback at this comment, and Johanna giggled before finally turning to me. She paused, her mouth opening and closing slowly.

"You—you look very familiar, young lady." Before I could answer, she continued, and suddenly my nerves had begun to fire off.

"Yes, I've definitely seen you before. Have you been on the television?"

Shut up! "No, I don't think I have been. I must just have one of those faces."

"No, no …" She paused, a faraway look growing in her eyes. "It'll come to me eventually."

"They're going to be staying with us for a little while," Lachlan told her.

"Who are you?" came Johanna's reply, her smile fading from her face as she gazed nervously at Lachlan.

"It's me Jo, Lachlan."

"Hmmm …" Johanna muttered. I watched Kara's face fall as the old woman pulled herself away. "My painting …" she mumbled, tottering back toward her easel.

Musa cleared his throat. "Lachlan, why don't you show them to their room, please? Then we can all have a bite to eat and good conversation."

Lachlan nodded. "Come on."

We followed him upstairs, and as soon as we were out of earshot, Sana asked,

"She has dementia, doesn't she?"

Lachlan winced slightly.

"Yeah, well—Alzheimer's."

"That's terrible," Geoff said. "My grandfather had it, just terrible."

Lachlan sighed sadly as he led us up another flight of stairs. "They had just moved her into a home before everything went down—real nice one outside Indianapolis. Her meds were keeping it under control, but obviously none of that is around anymore. God—you should have seen the place when we went to get her." He shuddered.

"What do you mean?"

"People put their elders in homes for a reason—they're too old or sick, can't take care of themselves, right? Well, when shit hit the fan, you think many people stuck around to help in the homes? It took us almost a week to go get her after the Break— God, it was horrible. Dead people in the hallways, people with all sorts of issues just wandering around. Some so sick they couldn't even get out of bed, they just laid there, dying in their own waste. We couldn't do anything."

"That's horrible," I whispered, aghast.

Lachlan stared at the ground. "It was. Johanna wasn't in great shape when we got there either. You must think too, so many of the family members don't live nearby. A lot of those old people had nobody that could come for them—dead or I'm sure some of the families chose not to come. If you can barely feed yourselves and your children, I'm sure many wouldn't even try to take on an aging and possibly sick grandparent."

"So, where's our room?" Riley asked, almost the moment Lachlan had finished speaking.

"Right, right ... this way."

Lachlan led us to a nearby room, in which two full-sized beds had been crammed. Plush blankets covered them. The pale-green walls were illuminated by a lantern in the corner.

"The bathroom is across the hall, the shower works—just no hot water. There's a bucket and sawdust for your other needs. Come down in about an hour for food."

"Thanks," I said gratefully.

Geoff flopped down on the furthest bed as the door closed, exuding a loud groan of pleasure.

"So, are you going to start being nice?" I asked Riley, who leaned against the far wall, carefully peeking around the edge of the window curtain.

"This is a joke," he scowled, flipping the curtain back in place and leaning his head against the wall.

"What's wrong with it? I like them," Sana said, her eyebrows knitted together.

"Don't you think it's a little off for them to invite us over so easily?" he snapped.

"I don't know. We did help them," Sana answered. "They seem like good people."

"What, are you scared they're gonna eat us?" I joked.

To my surprise, Riley shot away from the wall and stalked toward me. "Actually, I think you fit in here perfectly." The way he growled the word *you* sent a shiver down my spine. I took a step back, trying to put some distance between myself and his spiteful tone.

"The way you prance around like nothing is ever fucking wrong, it's like you're not even a real person," he spat.

I felt like a deer in headlights. Riley had shown his temper before, but not like this, not directed at me.

"Riley, relax," I tried, "we're all just tired—"

"Not to mention, what the *fuck* were you thinking joining her fight like that? We don't know them. They are not the group; *you're* barely in the group as it is. Next time, just shoot us all in the head and save some time." He was inches away from me now, and I could smell the alcohol on his breath. I wondered when he'd had the chance to drink.

"Riley, stop! You're being ridiculous," Sana growled, grabbing his arm and attempting to pull him away. In one quick movement, Riley wrenched himself from her grasp before shoving past us and slamming the door behind him.

"Thanks," I sighed, somewhat shakily as I turned to Sana. "Where's he even gonna go?"

"Who cares?"

"Yeah, but what crawled up his ass and died?"

"Probably Lachlan and Musa. Riley doesn't always do well with other alpha-male types. Ever wonder why it was just the three of us traveling around?"

"What about Geoff?"

"I'm a little bitch, and we all know it," Geoff huffed, his voice muffled by pillows.

We burst out laughing, and I felt like we didn't stop until we descended the stairs for dinner. Riley had returned shortly before, claiming tiredness, opting to eat something from our own rations and go to bed. None of us cared enough to argue.

Downstairs, dinner conversation was light and airy, Riley unmissed for more than the first few minutes. We dined on canned beans and fresh-baked bread, which was flat and tough, (apparently due to a lack of yeast) but nonetheless delicious. Maria and Manuel joined us, a slight Spanish couple who looked strikingly similar, with their petite features and curly hair. They were shy but kind, and at the very least, I saw no reason to be wary of them. Johanna, however, did not appear. Kara left occasionally to check on her, once returning with a splatter of blue paint slashed across her cheek.

Maria in particular was very quiet, preferring to pick absentmindedly at her food rather than speak. This, however, was explained when Kara pulled me aside, whispering that Maria had not been the same since her nephew died the week prior. A diabetic apparently, who had hung on as long as he could.

Toward the end of the dinner, Musa pulled out a dusty bottle of red wine. I forced myself to take slow sips as we cheered to new friends, close calls, and a good night's rest. Then, as we climbed the stairs to our room, I forced myself not to tear the house apart in search of the next dusty bottle.

Morning came without issue, and the house had taken on a calm, quiet presence. I awoke, feeling more refreshed than I could remember feeling in weeks. Sana was still curled in the bed beside me, snoring softly. Geoff had taken the other bed, and Riley lay on the floor, his back turned sharply to us, forehead nearly pressed to the wall. I left the room, intending to go to the bathroom but immediately running into Musa. Soon I found myself standing in the backyard with him, chilled by a cool morning breeze as I warmed my hands around a small mug of dark tea.

We stood quietly for a few moments, surveying the well-manicured garden and tall, white-picket fence that bordered the spacious yard.

"Your home is so beautiful," I commented, "peaceful."

Musa smiled. "Thank you. Kara has taken a lot of pride in it over the years."

"It's nice that you've been able to stay here."

"We've been lucky, always close with our neighbors, close with the people who lived in town. We didn't seek to harm or steal at the start; we protected each other. So far it's worked well."

At that moment, the back door burst open and Riley emerged. He had a slightly panicked appearance that turned to anger when he saw me. His eyes raked from my face to the mug cupped in my hands.

"The hell are you doing disappearing like that?" he snapped. Musa watched us with curious indifference.

"Sorry, *Dad,*" I shot back.

Without a word, he turned on his heel, slamming the door behind him.

"I'd better go after him." As I turned to leave, Musa caught my shoulder.

"Be careful of him, Jorah. He is a decent man, but he is deeply flawed."

By midday, we still hadn't left the home—much to Riley's extreme displeasure. We were fed and bathed—and at our insistence upon repaying them, had labored in the garden. I immensely enjoyed the company of the others, and as it seemed, so did Sana and Geoff. Lachlan turned out to be, despite his intimidating stature, a bit of a lovable goof—and Musa, Geoff joked, was like a spiritual guru.

Later, Sana and I sat in the kitchen, deep in discussion with Kara, who had just, to my great discomfort, re done the bandages on my hand.

"Well, I just don't see why you should have to leave," Kara stated, as she poured four small cups of tea. She handed one to Johanna, who sat quietly, drawing outside the lines in an old coloring book. "We like you guys; we ought to be sticking together."

My stomach rumbled as I sipped my tea. The meager meal of canned goods had been less than satisfactory.

"Well, we would need to talk with the guys, but I don't see why it couldn't be an option," Sana said cheerily.

"Riley's going to love the idea."

"He's being ridiculous. He just doesn't like not being in charge."

9

JAMES AND THE WELCOMING CREW

James sat bracingly on the hood of the car, the hem of his jacket pulled over his nose, head hunched down against the stench. The man next to him, on the other hand, appeared nothing but nauseated, his vision glassed over as he stared down at the pile of clothes the others were haphazardly sorting.

"Get it together, Tom," James muttered, casting a sideways glance at his companion, who now looked as though he were going to start heaving.

Tom let out a soft whimper but nonetheless straightened himself against the car.

The men around James and Tom were hard at work, their backs hunched over from the weight of the bodies they worked to dismantle. The men worked quickly, eager to be finished, stripping the fallen of anything useful, tossing the boots, jackets, and backpacks into a pile, which others loaded into the caravan.

The gated community was small and secure, with a smattering of houses down a single curved street that ended in a roundabout. Near the back sat the community clubhouse, which housed the old offices, game room, computer room, and swimming pool. The community was edged in a high, pointed metal fence, perfect for keeping out hostiles and berserkers alike.

"We've finished with the houses. Everyone here is dead, except those two." The unofficial group secretary, Jonas, scurried up to James, clutching his faithful clipboard. He was slight and young, only eighteen or so, but had proven himself adept and faithful. He gestured toward the two men on their knees, hands behind their heads. Their faces expressed pure terror, as one man could not keep his eyes off the pile of bodies beside them, the other staring frozen at the rifle aimed between his eyes.

"What's the stats on the place?"

"Same as always," said Jonas, pouring over his clipboard. "The office records show there were forty-three residents that lived here; we have thirty-two bodies. Twenty-three D.A.S., one went berserker from the looks of the house, the rest died or left on their own. So, about sixty percent as always, factoring the ones who weren't home when it all went down."

"And what's Vicars say about *them*?" James asked, pushing himself away from the car and surveying the two men.

"It's your call. He said to transfer hostage duty to you— except in special circumstances."

James nodded, and pulled a pack of cigarettes from his pocket. He grasped one between his lips and lit it, taking a long puff as he crossed to the two men, whose gaze still had not broken.

James sighed, and from his waistband he raised a gleaming silver pistol.

Now he had their attention.

"Please, we don't want any trouble. Just let us leave," spluttered the larger of the two men, his eyes trained on James' gun.

James pretended to think about it. Then with a small, forced laugh, he lowered his weapon. "All right, stand up."

The men staggered to their feet, keeping their hands tightly behind their heads, both looking around wildly, suspiciously.

"If we ever see you again, we will kill you. If we get a single whiff of your existence, we will hunt you down and kill you. Got it?" James growled, puffing on his cigarette.

The men nodded feverishly; James smiled. "Good, then in a moment you're going to turn around, and start walking. We will have our snipers trained on you, so I recommend that you don't look back, and I suggest not stopping until you're sure that they can't see you anymore."

"Thank you, thank you, sir," groveled one of the men, tears forming in his eyes.

"You're very welcome," simpered James, "now—"

He was cut off as Jonas, who had until then been in huddled conversation with one of James's men, scurried over. Standing on his toes, Jonas leaned forward and whispered in his ear.

"Oh?" said James, feeling suddenly flushed with disappointment. "Pity."

He raised his pistol and shot the taller of the men, and before the other had time to even scream, he was dead too.

10

THE CRACKS IN JORAH'S SHELL

The thick layers of gauze that had wrapped my arm had at last been shed, leaving me with only a thin covering between my mangled fingers and the outside world. It had been three days since we first arrived at Musa's home, and as I paused in our chores, something like happiness fluttered through me.

This morning we'd decided to clear out the neighboring house for ourselves—a cute midcentury home painted in soft yellow tones. Even Riley seemed to be okay with the matter, much different from the downright screaming match he'd had with Sana and me two days prior. It had ended with Geoff barging into the room, shouting that he would shoot us all if we didn't shut up, and Riley storming out, not to be seen again until the following evening. Since then, he'd become almost pleasant. *Too* pleasant.

Nonetheless, things so far had gone very smoothly at the

house. Kara said that even Johanna seemed to be a little more lucid since we arrived, a fact she relayed with tears gleaming in her blue eyes.

Food was getting scarce and would continue to do so despite Maria and Manuel having left us that morning. They had departed with tearful good-byes, furiously shaking all our hands. Maria had family only a few days' walk away; they'd wanted to leave since the start, but her nephew had been too unhealthy to make the journey. As they left, Kara had laden them with a pouch of food, and Musa slid a small pistol to Manuel.

"Give me a hand?"

I hurried over to Sana and helped her to lift the large pail of sloshing water. Even my good arm ached with the strain, but soon we'd maneuvered it into the house and poured it into a container. Musa thought it would be a good idea to keep large stores of extra water in the home, now that there were so many of us.

I still wore my red bandana woven into my hair, though these days I was cleaner. For the first time, the mirror showed something I vaguely recognized. Still so thin, with sunken eyes and yellowing teeth—but clean. Clean blonde hair, clean skin—which no longer felt as dry and irritated as it had before. My eyes seemed to shine bluer and livelier than I could remember. My clothes were clean too, and I felt as though I had regained some small part of myself in this home. I know the others felt it too. I wasn't even craving alcohol. *As much.*

Try as he might, I knew that charming, vain Riley couldn't object to the allures of a warm home and a fresh bath forever.

"Lachlan's sort of cute, don't you think?" I whispered to Sana as we headed to collect more water, prodding her shoulder and wiggling my eyebrows. I'd noticed the way he'd been eyeing her the last few days, as though she were as beautiful as the wildflowers in Johanna's paintings. "Seems to like you."

She laughed, her shiny hair woven into a fresh braid. "I think Kara's cuter," she said, somewhat sheepishly.

"Oh?" I grinned, raising my eyebrows in surprise. "Good luck fighting Musa for her."

The smile, which of late seemed sewed to Sana's face, made her virtually unrecognizable from the dark, angry, and aloof girl I had met hardly a week ago.

We passed Lachlan as we carried yet another pail inside. His red hair and beard had been combed today, giving him a much less wild and Viking esque appearance. He was busy at work building up the fence around the home, a task that was aided by the rest of the men. Kara sat in the garden nearby, pruning the vegetables, which were beginning to run low as a frosty autumn rolled in. I wondered, not for the first time, why I never saw her at any real labor.

With the cold growing steadily worse by the day, we had discussed our suspicions of nuclear winter with the others, the layers of ash like debris thicker across the landscape with each passing morning. Turns out, they'd had similar suspicions themselves, and we now agreed it was imperative that the homes be prepped for the coming cold. First, we would help fix up Musa's home, and in return, they would help us prepare the house next door for ourselves.

Sweat rolled down my face, chilling in the breeze that swept through the backyard. I took deep breaths, exhausted from the physical toil. It was always unnerving to realize how weak we all really were. Even Riley and Musa, both of whom still retained lean muscle, looked pale and tired.

We called it then and headed inside to clean ourselves before dinner. Kara had gone long ago to prepare. We crowded into the kitchen, and dinner turned out to be a bitter concoction of canned brussels sprouts and foraged mushroom soup.

"Musa, my brother, we need to throw a party," Lachlan joked as we gathered around the table, "a real party, with schnapps and the whole lot of it!"

We all laughed, adding what we in turn wished to have at this party. Geoff wished for stacks of apple pies, Lachlan for a huge roast pig, Kara and Sana both lamenting over their want for chocolate—and even Riley joined in, wishing for just one Cuban cigar, all to himself.

We ate and relaxed, and though I felt nowhere near full, the stomach pangs that had plagued me were silent.

"How's your arm?" Kara asked, peering across the table as I examined the scarred nubs of my fingers.

"A bit painful."

"Well then, I'll be right back." She swept from the room, stooping to lay a quick kiss on Musa's forehead. As she did so, he gazed back at her lovingly.

"We should get you some rings, great big metal ones," Lachlan said, reaching for my hand and inspecting the fingers. "It would look pretty badass and might protect them."

I sighed forlornly. "If only I wasn't so broke."

The table burst into laughter, which slipped into a sudden lull as Kara reappeared in the doorway, her face grave, gesturing for Musa to follow her out of the room.

"Do you think everything's okay?" Sana asked after they did not immediately return.

"Maybe it's Johanna." Lachlan offered. The older woman had been sleeping upstairs after a particularly upsetting fit instead of joining us for dinner.

Musa was leading when they returned, dark and grim, his eyes hard on all of us as he stood, powerfully and stoically in the doorway. Finally, he spoke.

"Riley, turn out your pockets."

Riley didn't move as everyone in the room swiveled to look to him, a relaxed look playing on his face. "What's that?"

"You heard what I said. Turn out your pockets."

"What's this about?" Sana asked in an offended tone, getting to her feet. Riley continued to sit; Geoff looked around at me nervously.

"I believe Riley has stolen from us," Musa said, his voice unwavering. Lachlan rose now, crossing to whisper with Kara, seeming to leave a distinct line of two sides in the kitchen.

"There's no need to get so upset," Riley intervened. "You want my pockets? You got 'em." He turned out his pockets onto the table, revealing only a few spare rounds of ammunition and a small folding knife.

"Lachlan, if you wouldn't mind, please go and get Riley's backpack."

I didn't look to Musa as he spoke, instead watching Riley's face, and for an instant I saw anger carve his features, a hint of malice behind his pale-green eyes.

"Riley, what's this about?" Sana asked, whirling on him.

He shook his head slightly. "I have no idea." He turned to me then, offering a small wink that made my stomach churn.

"Come on, man, what's this about?" Geoff pressed.

Riley ignored him, and a moment later, Lachlan had returned with Riley's backpack, which he handed to Musa. Without breaking eye contact with Riley, Musa crossed to the table and dumped the contents out.

Clothes, ammo, a small amount of food, bandages, water-purifying tablets, a nearly empty bottle of rum—and, there, at the bottom, a small folded piece of cloth. Musa grabbed it, unfolded it, and inside sat a pile of pills. "Painkillers, half of our remaining stock," Musa said, his voice grave, as his hand closed around the pills. With the other, he pulled his gun from his waistband, though he didn't raise it.

The bubble had popped—shattered, really. The illusion of safety, of friendship, of health that I had basked in for days—obliterated. I felt heavy, hungry, dirty; I could feel my heart hammering against my ribcage. Suddenly the change in Riley's mood made sense. His calm, airy presence, his anger never gone, merely morphed into retaliation.

Red blood. White pills.

"You didn't," Sana snapped, turning on Riley. "It's a mistake."

He shrugged. "Sorry, sweetheart, I did what I did." I had never heard him call Sana that before.

"Riley, what the fuck?" yelled Geoff. He turned to Musa, almost pleading. "Look, it won't happen again. He won't do it again."

"I know it will not," said Musa calmly, as I noticed that Riley had also grasped his gun, though he too did not raise it. The men stared at each other, the room incredibly tense. I barely dared to breathe. "Because he will be leaving, now."

"Gladly." Riley placed his gun on the table and began shoving the contents of his bag back inside.

"The rest of you are welcome to stay."

"Wait—wait, Musa please, he has a problem, but you can't kick him out. He's sorry, he messed up. Right, Riley?"

There was no answer, the room deadly silent, Riley slipping the backpack over his shoulders.

I looked wildly from Sana to Geoff, who both still stood, staring at Riley with rage and incredulity creasing their faces. Without a word, Sana jerked away, crossing to the door and pushing past Lachlan and Musa, who let her go.

"Why?" said Musa, after a moment of silence that seemed to flow away with Sana. Riley didn't look up, instead watching the doorway where Sana had disappeared, his face unreadable. "Why," Musa continued, his rage making his accent hard to understand, "when Johanna *needs* it, when Kara *needs* it, and you take it from Jorah as well? For what, a high?"

"Old habits die hard," was Riley's only explanation, his body rigid, hand twitching toward his gun.

"Riley—" I began, hoping that words to deescalate the situation would come to me, but I was saved as Sana returned, carrying three backpacks. She threw one across the table to Geoff, who barely caught it.

She shouldered her own, her eyes downcast, her voice wavering—though Riley now looked positively gleeful. "Thank you, Kara, Musa, Lachlan—for the hospitality."

"Sana, you don't need to leave with him. Geoff, Jorah, this is not your fault. Riley is an adult; he has made his choice," Musa appealed.

"Sana, stay, this isn't your problem," Lachlan added, stepping toward her.

She turned away, her voice hard. "Geoff, what's your move?"

He stuttered for a moment. "I'm coming with you guys, of— of course," he said, nodding to Riley and Sana.

"And you?"

I was startled by the ferocity in Sana's voice as she addressed me, the friendship we had been growing seemingly forgotten. I looked around, panicking, unsure what to do.

"Jorah, please," Musa cautioned, his eyes growing softer as they trained on me, "stay here. I know you haven't known them long. You owe them nothing."

"You aren't healed yet, Jorah," Kara furthered, finding her

voice. "Stay, it's all right."

"I can't," I gasped. The panicked feeling hadn't left. I darted forward, snatching my bag from Sana's hands. "I can't stay, I'm sorry."

I don't know why I was doing it; half of me screamed to stay—the warmth, the safety, the people—I *needed* it. I felt as though I were on the brink of some great happening, on the line between destiny and disaster.

My mind swam. "Thank you, Musa, Lachlan, Kara ... for the hospitality." The room was like ice and my words like fire in my mouth as I spat them out.

Riley offered a short, sarcastic bow, and turned, heading out of the house. I forced my feet to follow, Sana at my side, her gaze burning a hole in Riley's back.

Lachlan and Musa followed, encouraging us to stay, reminding us that Riley asked for this, that we needn't burden ourselves on him.

Musa caught my arm. "If you leave with him, it will be the death of you."

I wrenched my arm away, anger flaring up inside of me, though I knew it wasn't Musa's fault. "Good-bye," I said firmly, stumbling out onto the front steps and hurrying off after the others. Back into the evening light. Back into the abyss.

"Riley, you absolute—" Sana spat out of most vile stream of curses she could muster at Riley, at least I assumed so, because she had switched languages. Her eyes were narrow slits, and spit flew from her mouth. Geoff had resorted to quietly glowering, but I could almost feel the anger and heat burning off of him.

"Get out of my face, Sana," said Riley coolly. "Nobody forced you to come with me."

"I'm questioning why I chose to."

"Then go back!"

"Fuck you!"

"Why did you do it, Riley? Do you really need the pills that bad? I *know* you haven't had any in months. There's no withdrawal. You didn't need them!"

"Well, I guess I just wanted them."

"You mean you wanted an excuse to force us all to leave. What about Johanna, huh? Or Kara? She has cancer! *She* needed them."

"How do you know?"

"I saw her medication when I was helping her organize."

"Well, it's not my problem now." Riley shrugged it off, which launched Sana into another fit of incredulous rage.

"Guys, enough!" I interjected sharply, my head had started to pulse with pain. "We all made our choices."

"See, sweetheart gets it."

And then, I guess, I just *snapped.*

11

SANA, UNGAURDED

Her hair whipped around her head, caught in the torrents of icy wind. It fell in thick strands away from the bandana that held it together, the wild pieces framing her face and the crazed look in her eyes. Large, blue eyes, sunken into high cheekbones from hunger and malnourishment, but nonetheless beautiful—and so terrible.

"Jorah, calm down." I tried, but it was like arguing with a storm.

Geoff was slinking away, back toward the bushes on the side of the road; anything to get away from the girl with the silver revolver.

She had it trained on Riley, breathing heavily. "When we die out here, remember that it's on you, Riley," she snarled, before a bark of laughter burst from her jaws as she waved the weapon in the air, settling the tip in the center of Riley's chest.

Riley didn't dare move. *Do you feel it too?*

"Jorah, I'm—"

"Shut up!" she demanded, "I don't want to hear another *fucking* word from you. We chose to come with you. Against all our better judgment, we followed you. I know it's what you wanted; we all know it. So, make it worth our while, *sweetheart,* because I won't be dying for you. " Her words were not shouted or sarcastic, but whispered, almost in the same tone Riley used when he pretended to flirt with us. The difference, though, was her words now were dangerous, silky and predatory, and I felt that Jorah was not as helpless as she often seemed. Not as easygoing, not as real.

For the first time, I feared her.

12

THE MEMORIES OF JORAH SINCLAIR

It was still light out when we left the house, so we chose to put as much distance as possible between ourselves and the town before nightfall. Though now, as I shifted through fallen leaves for firewood, facing a night in the wilderness, I wasn't so sure that had been the best choice.

We'd gotten lucky, as far as the woods went. A short way off the main road, into the forest, sat the foundation of a long-demolished house. The concrete stood at waist height at its tallest and made a relatively complete enclosed space, save for a few crumbled walls. I offered to gather firewood while the others worked to create a shelter within the foundation. My offer went without protest; it seemed that they were quite happy to be rid of me after I'd yelled at Riley.

Just because I said what everybody was thinking, I thought angrily, kicking a stone away.

When I'd gathered enough, I returned to the camp, just as the last color of the sky was draining away to blackness.

We started a small fire, and I sat with my back against the concrete corner. It felt the safest, as behind me was sheltered, and at least I could look out to the seemingly endless forest stretching around us. We kept the fire low, so as not to attract any attention, and I shivered in the cold night air. I needed to find warmer clothes soon; a plain hoodie over layers would not suffice for much longer. Sana was curled up on the ground a few feet away, her face covered with a hat.

Riley was organizing his backpack, and Geoff was nowhere to be seen, having wandered into the surrounding woods to check the area—I guess he was too nervous to sleep without knowing what was around.

It was like a darkness had settled over the group, murkier and heavier than the true night that had set in. We were all angry—at Riley, at me, probably, at the world. I longed for the warm bed and meal at Musa's, and not for the first time did I question why I had chosen to follow Riley and the others.

I knew it was for loyalty, even though I had spent less than two weeks in their presence. They'd plucked me from a pit of loneliness and suffering, risked their lives to save mine and to save others. I felt bound to them; even the idea of being separated causing anxiety—as though we were *meant* to be a group. I had thought they felt similarly about me, judging by the way they'd expected me to leave with them, seeming not to truly question at all whether I would follow.

Did they see me as weak? As if I needed them? A lost child who was adopted into their mix, quiet, willful, but ultimately weak?

You saved their lives, I reminded myself, but as soon as the thought had processed, I wondered if it was true.

That first night, when I'd stayed behind with the lunatics in the bathroom, when I'd managed to kill them but only by the skin of my teeth, I hadn't *really* saved anyone. Without me, the others still would have gotten out of the window in time, still would have had guns to fight for themselves.

And since then? I'd had two fingers cut off and involved us in a firefight.

Now we sat here, angry with each other, cold, hungry, and back out into the void of a quickly dying world. Though at least our banishment wasn't my fault—that blame was entirely Riley's to hold.

A rustling nearby startled us all, though our fears were stilled a moment later as Geoff emerged, astonishingly, followed by two others.

"Found these two camped down by the road," Geoff said, as the slim figures of Manuel and Maria appeared behind him.

"What are you guys doing here?" I asked, bewildered, as they had left hours before we had.

"We got a bit lost, had to backtrack, and then Maria's ankle started acting up—old injury," Manuel answered. Maria forced a small, sad smile.

"Well, you're welcome to join us," Sana said, scooting over

and offering them the ground between herself and me. "Safety in numbers anyway, right?"

Manuel returned her smile and led Maria to their seats. "Geoff told us you decided to move on as well?"

"That's right, sticking with our plan of heading west," Riley answered confidently, and I shot him a dirty look. Normally, this would never have fazed him, but now he seemed for a moment to shrink under my gaze.

Serves him right.

We chatted briefly, though the arrival of two new people had done little to alleviate the tension of the group. Sana offered to take first watch, and as I busied myself preparing some semblance of a bed in my corner, there was a loud, sharp *crack* from right behind me.

I froze. The air had rushed out of my lungs, and for a horrible moment I was incapable of pulling it back in. I knew that sound; it had haunted my every waking moment for months.

I found myself suddenly back in the coffee shop across the street from my apartment. It was small and old-fashioned, with good prices and decent drinks, and the manager was kind to me. Forgivingly, understandingly kind; it was the only place I went outside my home. It was the only place I really needed to go, anyway, the walls of my pantry stacked so high with food I could open a restaurant. I had been sitting at a table near the window, sipping my coffee and watching a few dust-colored birds fight over dropped crumbs.

Then there came the noise, a loud *crack*, simultaneously overlaid by a chorus of others. Outside the window, a woman collapsed, crumpling into a heap on the pavement. A second later, before my eyes could focus on her splayed figure, a car swerved in the street and slammed into a building, the windows exploding inward.

The man who had sat in the booth near me had collapsed as well, face-first into the table, his coffee pouring out onto the tile.

I knew then that somebody had opened fire, that the women and the man had been shot. There was no other explanation.

"What—what's happening?" the barista had screamed. She was young, high-school aged, and I knew the terror and panic on her face matched mine. Five, I counted five people collapsed in the coffee shop, and it was with increasing desperation that I pushed down the creeping fact that they must be dead.

Two others had fled, and with a last look at the now-sobbing barista, I followed. Outside was chaos; more cars had collided, and people lay unmoving in the street.

Too many. I stumbled toward my apartment building, lurching out of the way as a car careened past. Everywhere people were screaming, shaking fallen companions. It felt like for every person crying and running, another lay dead in the road, their neck twisted at an unnatural angle.

I hadn't heard this many gunshots—only a few, that had all seemed to happen at once. Surely, I would have heard more?

I burst into my apartment building, more people, broken necks, blood on their faces—lying in the lobby. The elevator wouldn't come down. Two in the stairwell.

I dialed the police as I made it into my apartment, hands shaking, taking what felt like ages too long to press the right numbers. Nobody answered. But they must know! An attack of this magnitude? For I deduced that this must be some sort of terrorist attack. Chemical, maybe. I crossed to the window and wrenched open the curtains, though the scene below was one that would haunt me forever.

I relived all of this in the mere seconds between the crack and the shouting and cursing that began after.

Manuel had slumped across Maria's lap, his neck twisted backward, blood leaking from his nose and mouth.

Riley got to her first, scooping Maria under her armpits and dragging her away. Manuel rolled off her lap with a dull thud onto the ground. His eyes had rolled back into his head as convulsions wracked his body, his tongue hanging out of his mouth like a strange creature from the bottom of the sea.

"Get away from him," Riley ordered, still dragging a screaming Maria away.

I raised my revolver as I stepped toward the others, the convulsions that had rocked Manuel subsiding, his body stilling, eyes wide and unmoving.

"Wait," I said, as Sana moved toward him.

Manuel's jaw hung loosely, exposing bloodied teeth. His eyes gleamed red with burst blood vessels, and below his skin a web of destroyed veins like rivers of red and blue.

Then, from his yawning mouth issued a long, gargling laugh.

"Manuel!" Maria screamed, swiping at Riley as she dug her heels into the dirt.

I turned to Sana, fear and panic lacing her face as Manuel

began to shift, the gurgling, frothy groans still emitting from his soiled mouth. He rose, climbing to his knees as he looked out over us, his body swaying and creaking like a tree in the wind.

Red blood. Ruined veins. Broken jaws. Dead Jorah.

I aimed and took my shot—Manuel fell forward into the still-burning circle of hot coals and didn't move.

"We need to run."

"Oh God, oh God."

"It's happening again! It's really happening again."

We'd all spoken at once, the volume of fear morphing into panic as Manuel's clothes began to catch fire.

"We're all going to fucking die!" Geoff was panicking, dragging his hands through his thin, straw-colored hair. "He just turned into a freak!"

"Relax!" I snapped at him. "We don't know he was a freak." *Liar!*

Geoff was still staring at Manuel's body. "Then why did you kill him?" He looked ready to rip out his hair, which was close to how I was feeling.

"It happens simultaneously though, doesn't it?" Sana reasoned. "It all happened at once in the Break. We're safe! We're safe."

Riley was still struggling to hold Maria down. She screamed and fought him, and I wasn't sure if she wanted to run for the woods or throw herself on the fire as well. With a final cry, she swiped her long nails across his face. He released her, swearing, as she ran toward the darkness of the forest.

"Everybody, stop," Riley demanded, holding a hand over his bleeding cheek. "All we're doing is attracting attention. Shut up. There's nowhere to go; it's too dark. We stay here, and we make our stand."

We looked for Maria briefly, but tracking was impossible in the near blackness, and all of us were so shaken, we jumped violently at any noise. We returned to the fire, and the men dragged Manuel's body to the forest while Sana and I covered the bloodstains with handfuls of dirt.

It was when dawn finally broke that any of us relaxed enough to close our eyes for a few hours of sleep. It was only then that the shaking that wracked my body eased, a bone-deep trembling, that had nothing to do with the cold.

Dead Manuel. Jorah the killer. We are all going to die.

13

JAMES DURAN

The gated community, now dubbed Fort Rache, was finally purged of bodies. James had spent the last few days directing and redirecting those he oversaw. Thankless work, but still. Homes had to be assigned, defenses erected and monitored, rations distributed, and *disagreements* solved.

Vicars had been in an absolute terror for two days, when a supply run had never returned. James had led a group to investigate that morning, Vicars only relaxing when they returned with the body of a thief for him.

"Don't ever let me down, do you?" Vicars had exclaimed in his deep, haughty voice, slapping James on the back. "That's why you're my second."

"Happy to help," James told him, accepting the fat cigar that was offered and drawing a long puff. Vicars dismissed him for the rest of the afternoon.

James wasn't about to sit around, however, and found himself in the boardroom with Jonas, reviewing maps and tactics for the surrounding area.

"What's the news on the military camp to the northwest?"

Jonas dragged a finger across the map, pointing to a spot about forty miles away. "Scouts said it's pretty big, confirmed at least five vehicles. They said it looked to be about sixty military and forty to fifty civilians."

"The real United States forces?"

"Looks like it, definitely the most legitimate operation we've seen."

"Good then, far enough away they shouldn't bother us—close enough to offer a little extra protection if we need it. Is it a refugee site?"

"Not designated as one but seems like they're operating that way, much better than any we've seen, though." Jonas threw down a collection of Polaroid photos onto the table. James scooped them up, inspecting the tall barbed-wire fence they displayed. Inside was a large building, the remnants of a high school, surrounded by tents and out-of-commission school buses that looked as though they'd been converted to living spaces.

"Not a bad-looking operation," James commented, crossing the dark room to a wall covered in various documents, maps, and notes.

On one portion of the wall was a collection of photos, each with a name, date, and time written underneath.

"We lost three men last night," Jonas said, gesturing to the highest group of photos. James studied the photos; none of the men had been a great loss. "Two dead and one went berserker."

"And?"

"They're going to execute him tonight. It was Scott's brother, the redhead—Scott wanted a little time with him before he goes full berserker. I saw him earlier; he didn't even look like one yet, eyes a little red but hardly any of his blood vessels had burst, jaw was mostly intact. You could just tell though, rambling, not making any sense, really twitchy."

"How many days?"

"Fourteen."

James growled and dragged a hand down his face. He was a tall and strapping man, dark-skinned with a scruffy beard and brown almond-shaped eyes.

He cracked his knuckles, a bad habit. "Do you think it will happen again?"

"There's no reason to say it won't stop," Jonas offered optimistically, pouring over his notes on his clipboard. "But I can't tell you more than that, if it's random … if it will happen again."

"It doesn't make sense," James snapped, taking a cigarette from his pocket. "Five months later?"

"There's still hope."

But James had already stormed from the room, disgusted with himself, with his fear that in two weeks, he would be next. That it would be his body, slack-jawed, dragged off the property into the pit to be left to rot.

"Get the fuck out of the way," James snarled, men scurrying from his path like rodents.

James hoisted himself onto the front tower of Fort Rache. The first one erected, it stood just to the left of the main gates. It was a narrow tower, the top of which nestled a small, covered room, surrounded by a spacious deck that wrapped around all sides. The design had been James's idea, to create a defense tower that was both inconspicuous and highly versatile.

"I'm taking a patrol out," James stated to the man on duty. "I want ten men in twenty minutes."

He looked out to the surrounding area. The neighborhood was relatively rural, which was a large factor in choosing it. Outside the gates, the road was edged by forest on one side, farmland on the other, the nearest town a good fifteen-minute drive.

"Do you want anyone specific, sir?"

"Jonas," James said after a moment's thought, "and Bear. Otherwise I couldn't give two shits."

James was excited to hit the open road—he was craving a good fight.

James's boots crunched on the gravel as he climbed from the truck, his men following, rifles slung over their shoulders. They'd ventured out far today. James was not interested in spending another day sitting around the compound.

A few shabby houses sat on the edge of the dirt road; James directed most of the men to explore them. They carried cans of red spray paint, used to draw a large X on the door after it had been raided.

James turned to begin going over plans with Jonas, when there was a shout from near the houses. A berserker had burst out the moment the front door had been opened. Its arms looked raw and bloodied, as if it had chewed itself during its captivity. They'd known to be wary today, that the berserkers would be fresh and disoriented. Occasionally, when they were fresh, un starved and watered you could reason with them—regardless, the occupants of Fort Rache could not be bothered to try to help.

Bear had sprung forward, barking wildly and pulling on the chain that attached him to the truck. Though, after a moment, when the berserker had been eliminated, the huge black dog quieted to a soft, excited whine. Jonas hurried over to take the stats on the fresh kill.

James stood by the truck, watching the men as they swarmed over the deteriorating homes. He was about to join them when movement caught the corner of his eye. He walked toward the edge of the forest, one hand hovering over the pistol on his hip, so sure he had seen something move. He peered through the dense trees and caught a flash of movement. He crept forward. Someone was moving; he noticed the fresh trail of blood splattered on the leaves.

A woman was staggering away from him. She was very small, with lots of bushy brown hair that had become tangled in twigs and dirt. There was a huge, bloody wound on the side of her head, the gore dripping down to where it must have obscured her vision.

"Stop," James commanded. The woman looked back at him

and gave a small squeak of terror. She began to hobble faster, clutching branches for support.

It wasn't hard for James to catch her. He held her arms down, pulling her from a tangle of brambles she'd lodged herself in. The woman gave a soft whimper of terror.

"Shut up," James ordered.

"Hey, Duran caught someone." One of the men was peering through the bushes at James, who held a firm grip on the skinny arms of the woman. Not all the men were quite on a first-name basis with him.

She looked even smaller in the open, wrapping her arms around herself as she swayed on the spot, whimpering.

One of the men gave a low whistle. "Dibs on this one after Duran, eh?" He gave a booming, vicious laugh, chorused by a few of the other men who had come over to see the spectacle.

The woman had collapsed onto the ground, hugging herself and only partly conscious. Dirt, blood, and snot coagulated over her face; James felt slightly nauseated at how pathetic she was.

"What do you say, draw straws for her?" joked another one of the men. He was more of a pimply-faced boy, really, and he gave a crooked grin as his comment was met with more dark laughter.

"Enough," James commanded. Through the gathering crowd, he saw the anxious face of Jonas peering at the woman. "Look at the state of her. You're asking for some fucking diseases. She stays here."

"Who the hell says that's your decision?" growled one of the men, who appeared to be the most upset by this order. "If you won't have her, there isn't nothing to stop me." He stepped forward. He was a filthy, gnarled drunkard who had joined the group only recently. James had never bothered to learn his name.

"Do I need to remind you that you are not the one in charge here?" James snapped. "Now I say she stays here."

"Do something about it, then." He reached for the woman, a greedy smirk on his face.

Now *this* was what James had been waiting for. The man's long, yellowed fingernails had barely scraped the woman's arm when he was sent soaring backward. James stalked forward, cracking his knuckles with relish. James's men parted around him like the receding tide, leaving the filthy man crouched in the dirt. James grabbed him, delivering a series of punches to his stomach. The man screamed and flopped in the mud, as he scrabbled wildly for the knife strapped to his belt.

"Coward," James taunted, delivering a kick that sent the knife flying, breaking the man's hand in the same motion. James flipped him over and pulled him up by his shirt collar.

"Who's in charge?" James asked softly.

The man only coughed, a trickle of blood leaking from his torn lip.

"Who's. In. Charge?"

"You are."

James threw the man down, turning to the rest of the group. "Anybody else have a problem with my leadership?" There was no reply, only downcast eyes.

"Then load this piece of shit into the truck. I'd leave him behind too, but then he'd get his wish."

James stood alone as the men followed his orders. Feeling a trickle of blood run down his fists, he felt much better now.

"Mr. Duran?" It was Jonas at his shoulder.

"How many times do I have to tell you not to call me that?"

"Sorry, James, it's just that ... well I think she'll die if we leave her."

James didn't look at Jonas or the woman as he headed for the truck, wrapping his bloody knuckles in a rag from his pocket. "Does it look like that's my problem?"

14

JORAH AND THE OPEN ROAD

We never found Maria, and we never found any more food either.

Walking had long since become unbearable. Each place we stopped, each town we approached, we told ourselves, promised each other that we would find something worthwhile—but we never did. For miles, nearly every building we'd encountered had a large red X painted across the front door. After a while, we learned not to bother with those, since there was never anything left inside, and skewed our course to the north, where eventually, the X-marked houses dwindled.

This is what starving is like, I thought as I worked to keep putting one foot in front of the other. We all felt the aching in our bones and the crying of our stomachs. All I could think about was food; it was all I could dream of, obscuring almost every other thought.

Our rations were almost gone, but we had no other option than to press on. It had been eight days since we left Musa's home, and now, thanks to our pride and certainty that we would find something on the road, none of us was sure we could make it eight days back to them.

Or if they'd take us if we did.

So far, we had tried everything. When houses gave us nothing, we turned to gathering in the forest. Mushrooms, acorns, and some sort of flower that Geoff swore was edible but tasted absolutely terrible.

Currently, I struggled to walk silently through the underbrush, careful to place my feet exactly in Riley's footsteps. The two of us had decided to try our hand at hunting. Sana and Geoff felt too weak and were camped in a home not far away.

I held my revolver at the ready, prepared to turn it on any animal that wandered into our path. Riley, who had gone hunting only in his youth, grasped Sana's rifle.

Riley turned to look at me over his shoulder, gesturing to his ear, and then pointed away into the brush. I realized he was signaling the noise of a babbling river, which we could just make out over the whisper of the wind and crunching of frosted leaves under our feet.

We emerged on the bank, keeping low and quiet. A few birds flew overhead, though much too quick and small to bother wasting a shot on.

The river flowed freely, sparkling in the autumn sunshine, though aside from the birds, the banks showed no sign of life.

"Over here."

I crossed to Riley, my boots sliding in mud. He was crouched over a body, which was now scarcely more than bones and soiled clothing.

"Probably dead from the start," Riley said, "but look." He wrestled the man's vest off him, the pockets full of fishing hooks, lures, and spare line.

Riley worked to build a makeshift fishing pole while I covered the body in brush and leaves, sick from the empty eye sockets staring at me. Soon, we stood quietly, listening to the river and the wind.

"You know, I'm sorry about how things went down at Musa's," Riley said, staring out over the water.

"All in the past now."

"Well still, I'm sorry. Didn't think we'd end up like this."

"We aren't going to starve."

He didn't answer, just turned to me with his pale eyes. He stepped toward me, wrapping an arm around the back of my neck and pulling me toward him. I felt his face behind my ear, his nose buried in my hair, breathing softly, calmly. The touch was relieving, as though for a moment my fears had been swept down the river.

The days of starving had brought something unexpected along with them, forgiveness for Riley, because despite the emptiness of our stomachs, we all seemed to have little room for anger.

"What about Sana?" I mumbled.

"We aren't like that," he breathed back, "and she's not like you."

I closed my eyes, but just as I did so, there was a loud splashing in the water behind us. We broke apart, and I dove for the fishing line, the moment utterly shattered.

But we didn't care, *couldn't* care, and soon we returned with two fat fish. The four of us ate, and drank our cups of warm, boiled river water, and slept, finally, without the ache of hunger inside of us.

The next morning, we returned to the river, catching a few more fish, deciding then that our new best plan was to follow it. It took us off course, drifting and winding northward, but it didn't matter; the river gave us food, and I know we all would have followed it until it froze over.

A few days later, and we were certainly feeling better. The fish were sparse, not remotely the feast we all dreamt of, but nonetheless, it was more food than we could have hoped for. Sana had even managed to kill a rabbit that had come to drink at the water's edge.

"Hail Sana!" Geoff cheered, giving a short dance of glee. "Destroyer of rabbits!"

We camped that night under a bridge on the banks of the river. The rushing waters had led us to the outskirts of a small town. The bridge made for good shelter, and because it was on the edge of the forest, we felt safe and secure. Geoff and I worked to erect a tattered and partly collapsed tent we had found in the woods the day before.

"I miss Emily," Geoff sighed, as we worked to figure out

where each of the extremely similar pieces fit together.

"Who's that?" I had never really heard Geoff talk about his life before everything, save for a few entertaining childhood tales.

He smiled sadly. "She was my girlfriend. Well, my ex-girlfriend. She broke up with me a few weeks before everything happened. We'd been together for five years—didn't think I was going anywhere, apparently."

"What happened to her?"

He shrugged. "Don't know. I went to her house after the Break, but she wasn't there; didn't look like she'd been back either. I waited for a few days, but she never turned up. She loved camping, though. She would have been a lot of help."

"I'm sorry."

He gazed off with a soft, soapy smile, and I could tell he was lost in memories.

"You never know, Geoff. She could be alive somewhere."

"You think so?"

"Yeah, I do. Maybe off camping, and her tent is way better than ours."

"Who do you miss?"

I paused for a moment, deliberating. "My sister."

"That's all?"

"She's all I had."

"You've never mentioned her."

"I know." I willed myself to speak. "Her name was Junia. She was a good few years older than me, pretty much raised me. We never really knew our parents." The words flowed surprisingly freely, like I was talking about something that someone else had experienced, memories that were not my own. "Our godmother raised us at first, but she was old, so it was pretty much always just me and Junia."

"Where is she?" Geoff asked tenderly, pausing in his work, and from the corner of my eye, I noticed Sana and Riley still, listening.

I hesitated. "She died—just a few weeks before all of this, actually. Cancer; she was twenty-nine, it happened fast." *There was no other option.*

That evening, while the others cooked over a low fire, I wandered downstream. It had been warmer than late today, and the cold water looked inviting. I stripped off and waded in, gasping as the freezing river lapped over my skin, burning it bright red. I stood in the water, feeling the slimy rocks underneath my feet— something that once would have sent me running for the shore.

My dry and cracked skin was soothed by the icy flow, or maybe it was only the growing numbness spreading through my body. I waded deeper, the water over my chest; it felt like a band was restricting over my lungs as the waves lapped over my throat.

It was *calming.*

I didn't take a breath as I slid beneath the surface, the current pulling my hair, pushing me downstream. Fingers sliding over the rocks, algae and sediment catching beneath untrimmed nails.

I could stay here, under the water. I could stay here forever.

Let the river carry me away, somewhere clean and warm, where there was food and a soft bed, and one day I would meet the salt of the sea and finally be still. Maybe I would see my sister again.

Let me die, I thought, calmly, serenely, as my lungs began to pulse for air. *End it.*

Blue evening. Sweet water. No blood. No air. Dead Jorah.

I burst from the depths, gulping air into my lungs and forcing myself toward the shore. I crawled out, freezing, dripping, and shaking, but I felt *alive.* I flopped down on the muddy bank, the blood rushing in my veins, pounding behind my eyes. I wanted to run, fight, scream—take back what had been taken from me.

Instead I worked quickly, washing my body and clothes with my one bar of soap. I pulled on my second clean set, the ones I'd been saving since my last bath, my only others. I strode back toward camp, not caring that I was cold or that I would continue to be so, dry clothes on wet skin.

In that moment, I wished for little, cared of nothing. "I want to walk into town," I declared, lacing my boots with gusto.

Sana gaped at me. "It's nearly dark."

"And town isn't far. I won't be long, just a quick errand."

"What exactly do you need so badly right now?" Riley asked, standing with an eyebrow raised.

"Whatever I find," I chirped back. "Why don't you all come?"

"Jorah, this is ridiculous," Sana argued, "and I'm going to have food ready soon." She was currently crouched over the fire, stirring a pot of "soup". Though it was really rabbit bone broth and chunks of fish.

"Relax, I could go for a walk." Riley stretched his arms, picking up his gun and tucking it into his waistband.

"I'm in too," Geoff said.

"Come on, Sana. Might be fun," I coaxed, but she only glared back at me.

"Don't take long. You get one hour, and promise you'll come back."

"You really shouldn't stay here alone," Riley argued.

She brushed him off, looking toward the sky. "I'll be fine, just be back before it's dark, okay?"

He eyed her, but she continued, "Just go. I could use some alone time anyway. See if you can find better coats."

We clambered up the embankment on the side of the bridge, shouldering through thick brambles and brush, climbing over the guardrail onto the road. I skipped along in front of the boys toward town, the two of them exchanging confused glances.

But I couldn't care—wouldn't care! My skin still burned, and so did my blood, and my lungs had an ache for fresh air.

I hurried up the first driveway we saw toward a small house. There was no X on the door, no immediate sign of life, and I threw caution to the wind.

I heard Riley call my name as I vanished inside, but I didn't care. Didn't listen. I found my quarry moments later. It had been easy, so easy that I thought perhaps this night I was *meant* to find it.

I sat at the dining room table, my boots dripping mud on its surface as I kicked my legs up, leaning back in the chair. The amber liquid burned as I sipped, filling my chest and my ears with warmth. The boys entered as I finished my long pull, and I slid the bottle across the table toward them.

Riley caught it and for a moment looked as though he was going to reprimand me, but I made my eyes still as I stared back into his, and after a moment, he took a long drink himself. Geoff was only too happy to join the festivities.

We ransacked the house. I screamed with pleasure as I smashed a dish that Geoff tossed toward me, raining the shards across the room after a heavy swing from a baseball bat I'd found upstairs. There was no food in the home, but other than that, it seemed to have been mostly left alone. I tore through storage bins we found in the basement, procuring a few winter jackets and a stunning, floor-length fur coat that I immediately wrapped myself in.

Riley and Geoff roared with laughter as I twirled in the huge coat, the bottle clasped in one hand and my revolver in the other.

"Throw a plate, Geoff!"

"Hang on, hang on I don't know if—"

But Geoff had already thrown the plate, and I took aim. The gunshot was shockingly loud in the enclosed space, I saw Riley's lips moving as he cursed, but there was no sound save for the ringing in my ears.

"What the hell was that?" Riley swore, grabbing the gun out of my hand. "Jesus, Jorah, at least hit the plate."

He threw one himself, and with another deafening explosion,

the plate shattered in midair. We shouted in victory, and I threw my arms around Riley. He picked me up and twirled me with such vigor, the world became a blur.

We moved the party into the street, and as night drew closer, Geoff urged us to return to the bridge.

"Just a little longer, what's the hurt?" I argued, feeling slightly dizzy but so alive in the crisp air. The fur jacket was warm, though musty, and I stowed my gun in one of the deep pockets.

"Jorah, it's time to go back."

"Fuck you!"

"Riley, help me out."

"Don't be such a buzzkill."

"Sana needs us," Geoff argued, and maybe that got Riley's attention.

"All right, all right. Come on, Jorah, he's right." Riley reached for me, or maybe he was reaching for the bottle, but I danced away from him.

"Fine, Geoff can go back. C'mon, Riley, let's go have fun." I gave him my best smile.

"No, we all need to go. We can keep this up at camp," Riley said, jaw clenched, and I thought his face looked silly, very silly as he started to get annoyed with me.

"Then just leave."

"We aren't leaving you behind. You can finish your drink at camp. Let's go."

But I didn't want to go back, and they couldn't make me, because I felt like if I went back down to the river, this time I would drown myself in it.

And maybe the others too.

15

JORAH'S ROYAL COURT

I was dead or dying—I had to be. My mouth full of sand, head throbbing, spots of light dancing over my vision. My body ached, though whatever surface I lay on was surprisingly comfortable.

It turned out to be a bed, and I blanched at how filthy the covers were, how I'd had my face pressed into a stain a moment ago. I still wore my fur coat and was sweating profusely despite the frigid air of the room. The night before began to return, slowly, along with the creeping, *burning* shame. There were gaps, a lot of them. I almost didn't want to find the others and learn what events filled them in. I wanted to run and never have to face them.

I didn't get that chance, however, because as I surveyed the room, it was to find Riley standing in the doorway, leaning against the frame.

"Let's go." He stalked out, and I staggered after him, humiliation scalding my face. What else had I done? What couldn't I remember?

I stepped over a pool of vomit as we left the house. Riley walked in front, leading us in what I assumed was the direction of camp, though I could not recognize any of my surroundings.

"Riley …" I trailed off, expecting him to say something. When he didn't, "Riley, I'm sorry."

He ignored me.

"Riley, stop!" I grabbed his arm.

He whirled on me, and for a second, I braced myself, expecting to be hit. Instead he grabbed the collar of my sweater, dragging me toward him, practically lifting me off my feet. "You almost got Sana killed."

"I—what?" My eyes were glued to the large purple bruise that adorned Riley's right eye.

He released me, stalking away, dragging his hands through his hair. "While we were busy chasing you around, she got attacked."

"Oh, God."

"She's fine. We went back to camp when we heard the gunshot, but *fuck,* Jorah. What is wrong with you?"

That made me angry.

"What's wrong with me? What's wrong with *you?* The only reason we're out here is because of you and your pills." I knew that was a low blow, that I was being childish, grasping at anything I could to turn this away from me.

He got in my face. "Gonna' freak out about it again? You made your choice. I didn't force you to black out and go on a rampage."

I quieted then, angry—seething, but knowing I was just as annoyed with myself as I was with him. "What happened to your eye?"

"You punched me in the face," he deadpanned, "when I was trying to carry you back to camp."

I couldn't help but laugh, just a little. "Looks like I got you good."

"It was a cheap shot."

We started walking again. I hurried to keep pace with Riley's long strides. "I am sorry, really."

"It's fine—I probably would have been just as bad if I couldn't hold my liquor."

"How bad was I?"

He gave me a small, evil grin. "Should I start with you punching me in the face or trying to piss in the street?"

"I didn't!"

"Ask Geoff if you don't believe me."

Now I really wanted to curl up and die.

"When did you lose me?"

"It had been dark for about an hour; right after you punched me, I dropped you. You took off into the woods like a bat out of hell."

I snorted. "Great."

"But then we heard Sana's gunshot, so we left. After we checked on Sana, I came back looking, but it was no use—too dark, and Sana was so shaken, plus me and Geoff weren't very coherent. I got up early this morning and found your trail of destruction. Led me right to you."

We had passed the first house from the night before, the door wide open, and the step littered with the broken dinner plates. "It's okay, I don't blame you. Thank you for coming to get me, though."

He stopped walking just as we reached the bridge, turning to face me—handsome as always, green eyes piercing. "I had to find you. We have unfinished business, Jorah." His voice was low, showing off his smile, and the charismatic, devious smirk he often wore—it just felt different now.

We climbed down the embankment, and when we reached camp, we were greeted by a very annoyed Sana, and Geoff—who immediately gave a theatrical rendition of me, absolutely wasted.

"Piss off, Riley!" Geoff slurred, in a passable impression of my voice, "and then you punched him in the eye!"

"I've been told."

"It was awesome." Geoff finished with a grin, turning back to his work, packing up the campsite.

"That coat is ridiculous," Sana snapped at me.

"I like it; suits her," Riley countered.

I shrugged them off and kept wearing it. It was by far warmer than anything else I owned, and the deep pockets offered a reprieve from carrying everything on my back.

We were down to our last length of fishing line and final hook—so rather than chancing it breaking off again, we decided to leave the river.

More walking, and still very weak—still shamefaced and abashed from my rampage of last night. Sick with nothing but traces of alcohol in my stomach. Despite this, however, I felt more alive than I had in days. As though I had broken out of the funk I was in since we left Musa's. I was angrier now, maybe, and feeling more unstable than I could remember—but God, it was like a breath of fresh air. Like immersing myself in the icy river again, holding my breath until I thought my lungs would burst.

I wanted more.

But soon the walking got to me, and I draped my heavy coat over my backpack. Too warm for it now, but I knew I would need it come winter. The sole of one of my boots was starting to wear off, and I wore two pairs of socks to keep the blisters that plagued us all at bay.

Sana still wasn't talking to me, and she didn't seem to be much happier with Geoff or Riley. I walked behind the group, keeping to myself, wondering what we were going to do now.

Almost as though she had read my mind, Sana finally spoke.

"We need a better plan; we can't wander forever. It's going to get cold fast, and if we're out here in winter, we'll die for sure."

"So, what do we do?"

"Find a house, I think. Somewhere secluded, with a wood-burning stove or fireplace, fenced-in yard, and near the river if we can swing it."

"I'll call my Realtor," said Riley.

"I think that's a good idea." I spoke over him, directly to Sana. "We're all getting too weak to keep up this walk anyway, and if we have a place to stop maybe we can kill something big and preserve it."

"Might be able to get a car working too, if we actually had some time."

She nodded. "Geoff? Thoughts?"

"I'm with you guys, whatever you decide. It's not like I have anything better to do."

Hours of walking passed in silence, until the tempest in my stomach had finally lulled, and I realized with a jolt I hadn't asked about Sana being attacked.

"I think he was a freak," she said, hardly looking toward me. Gasps of surprise issued from both Geoff and Riley; accusations of "you didn't mention that!" flying toward her.

She waved them off, pausing in the road and finding a seat along the guard-rail. "I guess now is as good a time as any—I think there's been more Breaks, that there's a pattern; it's happening again."

We had discussed the topic at length, in the hours and days

after I'd killed Manuel. The others didn't blame me; they didn't disagree that it was the right choice. We'd all known what had happened from the moment Manuel began to shake and convulse on the ground. There was no saving him, no helping him; better to end his suffering. We were all so used to death by now anyway.

"There's something that I haven't told you," Sana began nervously, twisting her fingers in her hands. "I didn't say anything because Musa asked me not to. He didn't want to cause a panic."

We had stopped in the road, with nothing around but the cold breeze and rustle of leaves that had begun to fall far too early.

"Musa told me that eleven days before we arrived, early in the night, they found his sister dead. They'd all been outside except for her, and when they came back in, she was dead on the floor. They didn't hear the crack, but her neck was broken—he said it looked exactly like the first Break. Then, three days after we get to Musa's, Manuel breaks right in front us and turns into a freak."

"But last night, that guy didn't look like a freak. I mean, we only saw his body, but he looked normal. You said he was just another survivor," Geoff countered.

Sana shook her head. "He *did* look like one though, like a fresh one. It was darker by the time you guys got to me. He had the dead teeth, the burst blood vessels, just like Manuel—he wasn't violent, not at first, just rambling, confused—I was going to offer him help." She paused, taking a deep breath. "He jumped on me, started screaming, crying, pulling my hair…"

Guilt flared inside me, a vision of Sana fighting for her life, alone in the dark because I had to go on a bender.

"I managed to get my gun; that's when you all heard the shot. My point is, I think Manuel broke fourteen days after Musa's sister did. Now I'm not positive, but I think last night was another fourteen days, early nighttime."

"It was," Riley piped in, his expression dark.

"There's no way we just happened to be near someone that broke," Geoff protested. "We've seen nobody on the road, and then at the exact time there's *allegedly* another Break, you happen to be right next to the guy that gets hit?"

Sana shrugged. "I know it's unlikely, and this is just my theory. Maybe he had been following us, but you know how it used to be, back at the start, how it always seemed like the freaks knew where to find you. They found us when we were attacked in the trailer. That first night with Jorah—I think we were wrong; I think they were freaks too."

"But they—"

Sana was quick to cut Geoff off. "You're right, they *didn't* look quite like freaks, but just not the freaks we remember. It was dark, we were scared and in denial … and if I'm right, about fourteen days, they would have been fresh. I don't know about you guys, but when I remember the freaks from the start, all I can picture is how they all looked like corpses, right at the end. I can't explain it but … I think we need to start accepting the possibility that it could be one of us next."

She'd spoken the words that I had been too horrified to say myself. I wanted to push them back down, keep them in my stomach, where they writhed and boiled and made me sick. *Better than facing them.*

She continued, "We don't know that for sure—but the attack, the Break, it was random. I've thought about it for months and I can't find any pattern to it. Everyone we've talked to says the same, people just dropped dead, a few turned into freaks, but still— random."

"So, so, so—what? What? We're fucked? Is that what you're telling us?" Geoff snapped, pulling at his lank, straw-colored hair, his deep-set eyes wide and frantic. "Why are we even trying this shit then? We should just blow our fucking brains out now. Riley can shoot us all and then shoot himself."

"Why me?"

"I don't know. Jorah can, then."

"Geoff, stop. We don't *know* anything," I reasoned. "All we have is suspicions, and maybe it won't happen to us. Just because we don't know why it happened to some people first doesn't mean there isn't a reason."

"And if it does, at least it's a quick death," offered Riley, which I found to be reasonably comforting, before he added, "I mean, unless you're the unlucky bastard that doesn't die and becomes a freak. We'll make sure we shoot you quick then."

Geoff kept pacing. "Every fourteen days?"

"I think so," said Sana, "but we can't be sure. I guess we'll find out then."

Sana started coughing the next morning. It wasn't bad at first, but by evening, it had developed into deep, racking gasps. She insisted she was fine, up until the moment she collapsed in the road. I told Riley not to carry her, that we'd find another way—but he insisted.

We bundled into the next decent-looking house we found; it wasn't anything special, but for now, it would do. Sana burned with fever, her face white and sweaty, breath like sweet poison. It wasn't long before Riley started coughing too—I'd *told* him not to carry her.

That was two days ago.

I closed the door to my room, inhaling a slow, deep breath. It was the master bedroom, complete with an en suite. It was wholly quiet the moment the door clicked shut, closing out the sickness that had consumed every other space inside the walls. Riley and Sana barely stirred, their sleep fevered and agitated. Sana hallucinated often, and I had to wrestle to keep blankets on her as she thrashed. Riley was much quieter, and still like death. I often found myself checking his pulse, anytime I could no longer spot his shallow breathing.

Geoff was by far the best off. He was sick, but often awake and coherent. He wanted to help, but I insisted he rest. I needed him to get better as soon as he could. I knew there was a chance that Riley and Sana weren't going to make it through this. At most, I allowed Geoff to help me pin down Sana as I tried to tip water into her mouth.

I muscled my own bucket of water into the bathroom, having gone down to the river earlier, Geoff feeling well enough that I could leave the house for a while. I carried back two small pails. The walk there hadn't taken long, but it was over an hour before I made it back to the house. Sweaty and exhausted, I dragged myself inside and ate an entire can of vegetables, the first thing I'd had since Sana fell ill.

I stripped in the mirror, examining my body. For the first time in my life, I wished that I wasn't so thin. I could see all of my ribs without sucking in breath, a slight gap where my pants would stretch between hipbones. I sort of liked how my face looked, though. Not the dry, blotchy skin, the dark bags, or the chapped lips.

I looked much more angular, my cheek-bones high and severe, and the blue of my eyes deep and grim. My hair looked okay too, still blonde, still short. I tipped my chin back and I thought that I looked commanding, mysterious even—like a queen.

I could be a queen. Jorah, the Queen of the Damned. A queen for the depraved, the starving and the sick.

I could be someone to be feared.

But for now, I washed in the cold water, gathered myself, and headed back to the living room. Sana and Geoff were sleeping, but Riley was awake, his face thin and pale, and he struggled to sit up, but when he did, he gave a weak smile.

"You're going to outlive us all."

16

JAMES OF BRITTLE BONES

They'd lost two more men last night; nobody James had cared to know. They lay wasted in the pit now, slack-jawed, quiet, and waiting to be burned.

Fort Rache was quickly becoming a stronghold; James knew it had been an excellent choice of location. They'd added a few more men to the ranks recently and had taken a few prisoners as well. James couldn't understand why they kept the prisoners. For a few days, maybe, but after that, if they aren't willing to submit and join the cause, then they aren't going to. Better to kill them or let them go than keep wasting resources.

Vicars didn't see it that way, and James felt that the man enjoyed his dominion over the prisoners entirely too much. Keeping them scared, meek, starving—it was different from his power over the men, more feral and likely more entertaining.

Currently, James was busy helping to construct a set of wooden gallows on the outskirts of the fort. Toward the back, behind the main building, the fence enclosed a plain park area. Only about an acre in size, it held a manmade pond that had since long dried up, a swing set, benches, and an area just large enough to hold a garden. Though, thanks to James's suggestion, there were no tomato plots being constructed—instead, gallows and a whipping post.

James pored over the blueprints for the gallows, instructing others before running to help hoist a fallen beam. It was hard work but a much-needed break from erecting the perimeter towers—a task that after weeks had become incredibly dull.

"Vicars wants you," Jonas told James as he scurried over to him, "in his office."

Glad for the break, James threw down his tools and headed for Vicars' house. Of course, Vicars had taken the first choice of homes for himself, giving James, much to his dismay, the house directly next door. According to Vicars, if James wanted to continue being second in command, he would need to act the part—and therefore live somewhere accessible. James shared the house with Jonas and McNeal. A peaky, cruel, and balding man with a rat like face, McNeal served as an advisor to Vicars and as a weak impression of a camp doctor.

An assault-rifle-clad man stood on the front stoop of Vicars' home. He nodded as James approached and stepped aside. Vicars had decorated almost as soon as they'd moved into the community—before the perimeter fence had gone up, before they had even assigned sleeping quarters to all the men. The walls of the home were first stripped of any indication that a family had once lived there. The dining room just inside had been converted to an office, with huge bookcases behind a magnificent mahogany desk. The windows were draped in thick gold and red curtains—overall, the whole house was quite exquisite for the apocalypse. The only remnant of the former owners was the pristine, bright-red 1967 Camaro, which still ran, though you didn't dare ask Vicars for the keys.

"Ah, speak of the devil!" Vicars exclaimed jovially in his rich, booming voice.

"Hi, James," cooed the beautiful, curvy red headed woman who sat perched on Vicars' knee.

"Hello, Evangeline." James inclined his head to her as Vicars shoed her from the room. She had been found a few months prior, filthy and starving; they'd almost left her to die. Evangeline, however, never planned on that. She was as smart and cunning as she was tough. She seemed to have recognized Vicars for who he was the moment she set foot in camp, and it wasn't long before she secured herself a position at his side. She now spent her days closed inside the grand home, beautiful, quiet—tending to the potted plants and cleaning. James often spotted her watching the men from her window. She liked to offer the faintest of smiles to them. *Dare you to come take me away from here.*

"She's something, isn't she?" Vicars chortled. "They don't make too many like that anymore."

"Nobody's making much of anything anymore."

"Too right you are." Vicars tipped his glass of whiskey toward James. "Pour yourself one, sit down—we've got business."

At first glance, you wouldn't judge Vicars as a cruel or even exceptionally talented man. Short, broad, he often boasted of his Turkish heritage (on his mother's side) and his past prowess as a wrestler. Vicars wasn't particularly good-looking, with a bushy mustache and black, wiry hair, which he kept slicked back. His arms were thick like hairy tree trunks and he was always dressed his best—at least during the time he spent in his home, with his collection of beautiful women. Perhaps it was these reasons that on the occasion when Vicars revealed his true nature, it was even more disturbing.

"I heard you denied a woman to some of the men the other day," Vicars began, dark eyes meeting James's as he sipped his liquor.

"She was half-dead, sick too."

"And you beat Sean Jefferson half to death over it? Broke his hand?"

"He questioned my leadership."

"Mm-hmm, next time, kill them both. I put you in charge so that I don't have to listen to the barking of my dogs."

"Understood."

"Good," Vicars said approvingly, "I like you, James—I like your work ethic, doing good things for this place. You want to deny a man some dead slut, fine, probably keeping us all healthier." He laughed. "But if I find out you're going soft, I'm sure there's a few men who'd be happy to take your place."

"I understand. You won't hear about it again."

Vicars waved his meaty hand dismissively. "Anyway, what I

actually want to hear are your thoughts on the military group to the northwest."

"Jonas said the scouts reported around sixty fighters—"

Vicars cut him off. "Speaking of the chinaman, where the hell is he? Told him to come back after he got you and McNeal." He shook his head angrily, calling for the guard outside to go and find Jonas. "Continue."

"—and forty civilians. We outnumber them, but they certainly have more firepower and better training."

"And your counsel on it?"

"Leave it be," James said. "It's the real U.S forces. We wouldn't beat them, and they aren't likely to bother us."

"For now."

"What do you mean?"

"If it's true what they say—and it really is the old red, white, and blue, and they really are as well off, it's only a matter of time before they find out about us."

"And if they do?" James asked.

"I put you in a place of command for a reason. You tell me!"

"They aren't going to allow some of the conditions here," James conceded.

"Probably starting with your gallows." The happy Vicars was slowly slipping away. James could sense it, smell the danger in the air.

"The gallows are going to save on ammunition. They're more sanitary than just slitting throats. We already lost three men to the flu, and there's still plenty more in quarantine."

"I know that," Vicars snapped. He stood and began to pace, still clutching his glass. "I approved the plans. I know it, and I'm trusting you on this but—"

At last, the office door swung inward, and Jonas rushed inside, followed closely by McNeal, looking particularly crow like in a long, black trench coat.

"Sorry, Vicars, sir," Jonas mumbled, "it took me longer than I thought to find McNeal."

Vicars waved him off without a word, and the two men took their seats on either side of James.

"As we were discussing, the military encampment is not something we can deal with yet, but mark my words, it *will* be dealt with. I want regular scouting trips to it, only the best men, and make sure they know I'll kill them myself if they're followed back."

Jonas was furiously scribbling notes on his clipboard. James knew he always became incredibly nervous in the presence of Vicars.

"Now, what I really want to hear about is our big problem," Vicars continued.

Jonas rifled through his papers. "The pattern has been consistent, sir. Every fourteen days and twenty hours exactly."

"And you still can't tell me why, can you? *Why* certain men are breaking and others don't. Or if this is going to stop before we're all fucked."

"I—I've looked at all of the data, and I can't find any

correlation. I know it's not a disease, per se; it's no virus or bacteria."

Vicars laughed, but this time it was dark and threatening. "So, what is it, a death ray?"

James cut in before Jonas could speak. "The military group, they may know something. We could send a spy, posing as a lone survivor."

Jonas shot James a grateful look, which James ignored.

Vicars seemed to be thinking the idea over, when McNeal finally spoke. "There is another option."

"Get on with it."

McNeal cleared his throat. "An autopsy of sorts. We may be able to find the abnormality causing these reactions, should it exist inside of us."

"We've tried that. You turned the bodies into paste, and what came of it? One of our men had a fucking tumor was all you could tell me."

"Yes, but I think we may find different results using a living counterpart."

James froze. "You want to operate on living people? We don't have the supplies for that; no anesthesia, hardly any real painkillers. And McNeal, I'd say working as a lab tech or whatever the hell you did doesn't qualify you for shit."

McNeal gave James a sly, patronizing smile. "I am as qualified as anyone, and I wouldn't be completing the process alone. I only need a few subjects, perhaps one related to a previously affected victim. It would be quiet, rather clean, and informative."

"You call torture quiet and clean?" James snapped, standing and looming over McNeal, who met his gaze with calm arrogance.

"Enough," Vicars commanded, still not facing the group of men. He seemed to be perusing his bookshelf.

"What do you expect to gain out of using live subjects?"

"As we all know, when a subject was DAS—dead at the start, their entire neck, brain stem, and upper portion of the spinal column was destroyed, the process we now refer to as breaking. The progression is similar when berserkers are created, though the damage is far less severe, more varying. I believe that by investigating the area on a live host, we may be able to find clues to the causation, as the area will not be intensely damaged."

"Why not just use dead bodies that didn't break? We've got plenty of those."

To the room's general surprise, it was Jonas who spoke up. "Because there's no way of knowing if that person was ever … infected, with whatever is causing this. They may never have been in danger in the first place. We don't know if we're all at risk."

James was becoming increasingly frustrated, disgusted by what McNeal had suggested. "What's the difference between that and using a live person? None. You don't know if they—" He broke off, realization washing over him.

McNeal smiled. "*Unless* we preform our investigation on the fourteenth day, at the twentieth hour."

Jonas shuddered, and Vicars finally turned to face them.

"What will you need?"

"Three subjects should be sufficient. I would request the prisoner whose cousin broke last week, as well as the female."

"She's pregnant," Jonas chimed in.

McNeal ignored him. "Aside from them, anyone else will do. I will also need—"

James zoned out as McNeal relayed the various equipment he would require. This plan was absurd, vile, monstrous. McNeal had turned the previous bodies he had examined to pulp, and James wholly doubted that a living patient would be treated with much more decency.

"Of course, I will do my best not to kill any of the subjects, though it is likely they will die without proper equipment."

"And if none of them happens to break?"

"Then we will try again fourteen days later."

The room fell into silence, except for the heavy breathing of James as he fought the urge to strangle McNeal.

"Fine," Vicars finally said, "take what you need, except for the woman—Evangeline would never let me hear the end of it, and I really would like to avoid throwing her in the pit. Take a raiding group out and find yourself some subjects. Jonas will help you find anything else you need." Vicars collapsed into his chair, pouring himself another glass of whiskey. "Now all of you, get the hell out of my house."

The moment they stepped outside James grabbed the collar of McNeal's jacket and slammed him against the side of the building. "You're out of your goddamn mind," he snarled.

McNeal remained calm, showing only his cold, arrogant smile that James had come to despise. "Vicars doesn't think so."

"You know damn well you aren't going to find shit doing this."

"Why so soft, James? You really care about the fate of a few prisoners? You're always the one saying to kill them or let them go, and didn't I hear you savaged Jefferson the other day?"

"That was different. He deserved it. You know you're not going to find anything doing this. You just want to torture a few more people. You sadistic piece of—"

"Ah, ah, ah," tittered McNeal, "now, that is not true. I don't know what I'll find. We'll just have to see." He pushed away, and James let him go, glowering at his back as the man disappeared down the street.

"He might actually find something," Jonas interjected calmly, as James dug frantically through his pockets for a cigarette. The one perk he saw of being second in command, he wasn't going to run out of them anytime soon.

"Of course, he might," James huffed, taking off down the street, "but whether he does or he doesn't, he's going to want to try it again and again. We can't afford to lose three people every two weeks, on top of everyone who'll break too—prisoners or not." He shoved by a group of men carrying large wooden planks, Jonas jogging to keep up. "And then it's only a matter of time before it's our own people going under his knife."

"We might be able to reason with Vicars, after it's tried next week."

"Yeah, right," James shot back. "Listen, I want to know exactly when McNeal is bringing out that raiding party, and put me first on the list to go."

17

JORAH WOLFSBANE

On the seventh day of my playing doctor, Sana's sickness finally broke. She was able to sit up on her own, and she eagerly gulped down every morsel of food I put in front of her. Riley had been doing much better as well, but I still wouldn't let him do anything too strenuous.

The mood was changing considerably for the better as we huddled in the home. The crushing weight I'd endured for days had lifted, the danger passing, and I felt that if this sickness couldn't take the others from me, nothing would.

These days, Geoff was a bit of a hero as well. He'd sneaked out while I slept the previous afternoon, returning late evening, hunkered against the wind, with a backpack overflowing with food.

I swear we all could have kissed him.

That night we feasted, and for the first time in ages, none of us went to sleep hungry. First thing in the morning, Geoff and I rushed out to collect the rest of the food, as he hadn't been able to carry it all the first round.

He'd found the supplies in a small library near town. He said he had simply thought that we might enjoy some reading material. The food was in the back office behind the library's front desk. It was a donation box for the local homeless shelter, handwritten lettering asking all to please add whatever they could. I supposed anyone who knew of this had died in the Break. It was still half-full after Geoff's haul, sitting like a beacon of hope in the corner of the room. Canned vegetables, soups, granola bars, boxed pasta, bags of rice and beans, and a packet of chocolate-chip cookies. Geoff and I pored through the goods like they were the greatest treasure on earth.

"I almost cried when I saw this," Geoff said, and I gave a shaky laugh, shoving cans into my bag. It wasn't just food, either—a bottle of vitamins, soap, a pack of socks, maxi-pads, and toothpaste.

Geoff and I shared a packet of crackers as we walked, a backpack over each of our shoulders and a duffel bag suspended between us.

We did the math as best we could—enough food for about a month, if we were careful. Maybe even enough to last until November if we kept fishing along the river.

Sana and Riley were nothing but smiles when we returned, and I helped Sana shuffle over to survey the goods. We decided that we would eat a large meal that night too, both to celebrate and to regain our strength.

The next few days passed slowly, serenely, each a little less foggy than the last. The food was a godsend, and we struggled to hold steadfast to rationing. It was hard to care, however, when each time I looked in the mirror, ran my hands down my own flesh, it seemed a little more familiar.

"Jorah, I need to talk to you," Sana said as I walked into the room, carrying a pile of blankets that we were nailing over the living room windows. Ever since we had come back with the food, Sana had refused to sit around idly. She took things slowly, still very weak, but had spent the afternoon cleaning and making the house just a little more secure.

"Tonight, it's the fourteenth night, isn't it?" she whispered to me, holding up the sheets while I worked to secure them over the glass.

"Yeah, it is." I'd been planning on bringing the matter up soon, unsure if the others were aware of time due to their sickness. "What should we do?"

Sana bit her lip nervously. "Nothing we can do, is there? I think we should wait to eat; I know it's horrible, but if one of us ... well, we just shouldn't waste the food."

"Talking about which of us is going to kick it tonight?" Riley joked from across the room. Geoff's head shot up from his book, panicked.

"We've been lucky so far," I reasoned, but the room had become very tense.

"Tell that to Manuel."

Thanks to Geoff's watch, which somehow still worked, we knew that Manuel had broken around eight p.m. Sana said that Musa told her it happened to his sister early at night, so, at 7:30p.m we found ourselves waiting.

We each had our weapon loaded beside us, casting nervous glances toward each other, trying to avoid looking at the food, which sat so temptingly, ready to be eaten on the table. We'd agreed that should any of us break and be so unlucky as not to die, there could be no hesitation. The life of a freak was short and brutal, and none of us wished to live it.

"We'll wait a bit after, just to be safe," Sana said.

"I still don't see why we need to wait to eat," argued Riley. "Why not get to enjoy a last meal?"

The matter had been brought up, but nobody pushed to change the idea. I think we were all a little too nauseated to eat anyway—although if any of us broke, I doubt the others would feel up for a snack.

"Geoff, that is the most ridiculous thing I've ever seen."

Geoff had taken to wrapping layers of tinfoil around his head, crushing it down until it formed a rough helmet of shiny metal.

"You won't think so when the alien death ray gets you," Geoff snapped, finally seeming content with his protection and offering the remaining tinfoil to the rest of us. When nobody took it, he shook the box angrily. "Seriously, take it."

He looked so deadly stern, his face set beneath his tinfoil hat, that I burst out laughing.

"Screw it." I chuckled and began fashioning myself a similar helmet.

Riley gaped at me. "Not you too."

I shrugged. "What have we got to lose?" Despite endless talks on the matter, Geoff was convinced that the cause of the world's destruction was extraterrestrial related, and I had to admit, it made sense.

"If I have to wear that to survive, I'd rather die. You can all eat me after, do yourselves some good."

"We can't eat you if you become a freak," Geoff said, as if the fact that Riley might become a freak before he died was the biggest issue with eating him.

"They aren't zombies, Geoff," Sana argued, rolling her eyes at him. "Whatever happens just messes up their brains or something. They're not sick—therefore, we could eat Riley."

Geoff glared at us, mumbling something along the lines of "you don't know that".

Eight o'clock was creeping closer. We sat waiting, except for Geoff, who anxiously paced the room, occasionally adjusting his hat.

"Sit down," Sana snapped, "you're making me more nervous."

He cast her an apologetic look and plopped down on the couch between Riley and me.

We braced ourselves as the clock ticked down, not saying a word, holding our breath as eight o'clock came and went.

Then it was fifteen past, and Riley finally leapt up, demanding that we eat. We all took what felt like our first breath.

We followed him, but none of us had taken more than a few steps when a deafening *crack* split the room.

I dove backward, away from the others, the wind knocked out of my chest. Geoff screamed, stumbling over his own feet away from us. Within seconds, each of us occupied a different corner of the room, fumbling with weapons, looking around wildly for which of us had been the unlucky one.

But then, another *crack*—though this time we recognized it for what it was, and we stood still, listening to the smattering of rain on the roof. Then laughing, and finally, sitting down to eat while the thunder rolled over our heads.

I always loved to read. When I was young, needing an escape, it was always reading. Then one day it was alcohol, sometimes sex or drugs, but always alcohol. A deeper need than reading, a greater escape.

I sorted through the small pile of books I'd created, trying to remember the last book I'd read. The library was quiet and peaceful, the smell of dust and paper, dark and easy. I was drawn to the library since we'd found the food, promising myself I'd return. Geoff had offered to join me, but I told him he ought to go down to the river to try for more fish. I'd be okay on my own. I felt stronger; we all did.

A very annoyed Riley and Sana waited at the house, both itching to break their confinement, to get back in the fight.

Sana had requested something with some action, so I added a

paperback to the pile about a futuristic war between men and robots. It rested on top of the mystery novel I'd picked out for Geoff, and since Riley had snapped at me when I asked what sort of book he'd like, there was one of those middle-aged women's romance novels for him.

Despite feeling better, I was still far too weak to carry much more the mile back to the house, so after a last sweep of the library, I headed out the double doors. It was almost instantaneous that I met the two women on horseback, trotting down the center of the street, scarves pulled up over their faces to block the wind.

"Whoa, hey," the first woman said, pulling on the reins of her horse, its coat beautiful and silky black.

I hadn't even made it down the stone steps, but I hurried back up them, facing the woman as I stood on the landing, near eye level with them.

"Hey, we don't mean you any harm, so long as it goes both ways," said the other woman. She was stout and hardy, and surprisingly enough a little overweight. "Name's Kenny, this is Elise."

The taller woman, Elise, pulled down her scarf, offering me a small smile. I noticed the long rifles hoisted over their shoulders, the saddle bags seeming to burst with supplies. My hand twitched in my pocket, flexing on the cold metal of my gun.

"I'm Jorah."

"Nice to meet you, Jorah," said Kenny, in a heavy southern accent. "Any news from these parts?"

Neither of the woman seemed threatening. In fact, Elise was

looking me up and down with kind, intelligent eyes.

I shook my head. "I've been coming from the southeast. There's hardly anything to loot. Some group marked all the buildings with big red Xs; nothing in any of them."

Kenny frowned. "Pity, what about the crazies?"

"Haven't seen any for a few days."

"Did you lose any people to it last night?"

"No—" I began, catching myself at the last moment, making a hasty recovery. "It's just me."

Kenny gave a small chuckle, Elise smiling behind her. "Gotcha there. Good to know we aren't the only folks who've figured out the pattern—every fourteen days, yes, ma'am."

"Don't worry, hon, we don't want anything to do with you or your group, just looking for news," Elise added before I could speak.

"Where have you come from? What's it like there?" I asked.

Kenny sighed. "Same as everywhere else we've been, I'm afraid. Bodies everywhere, running out of places to loot. Been lucky, though, haven't met too many who aren't friendly." She smiled at me, showing her crooked teeth. "You look like you're doing all right for yourself, not as skinny as some we've seen."

I raised my eyebrows, and she gave a loud, jovial hoot, patting her healthy stomach. "We've been doing all right too. Just got to know where to look."

"Ken ..." Elise nudged her companion, the two exchanging a brief, silent conversation.

"Right, right," Kenny said, turning back to me. "We best be going. Listen though, about twenty miles from here, due north, there's a military compound. It's the real deal, United States forces. They're taking in survivors too. The place was good, safe—well, safer than any other camp we've seen."

My heart leapt. "Why aren't you there?"

"We stayed for a few days, got a little information, regrouped—it's just not our style. I say, if you're doing fine out here on your own, keep it that way—it just gets messy in those places. Worth the stop though."

"What kind of news was there?" I was excited now. News reports about anything outside your immediate circle was few and far between, if you could even say that.

"All sorts, but not too much worth listening to, I'm afraid. They're working day and night to stop us all breaking, though. Think they're making some improvement too. There was also a rumor that there's been real contact with Washington DC, say that idiot president is still alive."

"Is that it?"

"More or less—go find out for yourself." She paused, rifling through her bag and passing me a large square of folded paper. "Camp is circled in red. Avoid the highway, lot of nasty people using it. You look like a tough girl. Good luck out here, keep your wits about you."

"You too," I said, and Elise waved good-bye as the two women turned on their horses, continuing off down the street, away from the direction of our home, and soon, out of sight.

I lugged the heavy bag of books down the road, regretting taking the time to loot a few more stores. The exertion hadn't been worth the meager supplies I'd found. I couldn't stop thinking about Kenny and Elise, the kind, interesting women on their beautiful horses. All of them, thick and healthy—*you just got to know where to look.* I wish they'd mentioned just where that was supposed to be.

The longer I walked, the more tired I grew, my mind foggy, until I started to wonder if I'd made up Kenny and Elise. The two warriors on horseback, promising salvation was a mere twenty miles away, due north. Maybe they'd been just a dream, brought on by hunger or fear or guilt. At one point, I even stopped to pull the paper they'd given me out of my bag, unfolding it to reveal a map of the area, proving they must have existed.

"Hello there."

I froze in my tracks, plunging my hand into my pocket.

A man stood down the road, swaying gently, almost as if he were moving with the breeze. At first, I thought for sure he was a freak; filthy, ragged, a matted mop of hair framed his face, and when our eyes met, he broke into a wide, blackened-tooth grin.

"What's a pretty little thing like you doing all alone, hm?"

"I'm not alone. My dad is nearby hunting."

"I don't see him." He took a few steps toward me, and I could see how thin and sickly he was. He had a twitch too, and his body jerked with it every few moments.

"Stay away from me," I demanded, and I raised the gun, leveling it with his chest.

The man didn't even flinch. "Pretty little thing ..." he snarled. He still moved toward me, pulling a long knife from his waist.

I pulled the trigger and was gripped by real fear when instead of a blast, there was only a faint *click.*

My gun was empty—but I had checked it yesterday, *and I hadn't fired a shot since.* I chose to run, diving to the side as the man pounced. I rolled to my feet, dropping the bag and taking off at a dead sprint down the road. I was weighed down by my coat and exhaustion, but still, I was fast. I had always been fast.

The man let out a scream of mirth and gave chase behind me. I tore down the road. I could see the driveway of the house in the distance. Closer, closer, my stamina was dying. I had no energy anymore, and I stumbled, recovering just in time to dodge a vicious swipe from the knife.

"Help!" I shouted as I made it to the driveway, running into the front yard, I couldn't lead the man directly into the home. The yard was large, and the driveway long, but not so much that they couldn't hear my screams. "Guys, help!"

I stumbled once again, falling flat on my face in the dead and yellowed grass. I rolled over, but he dove onto me, knocking the air out of my lungs.

"Stop!" I gasped, trying to push him off. I caught his face in my left hand. I had almost no leverage from my missing fingers, but I pushed the remaining ones as hard as I could into his eye.

"Bitch!" He landed a punch on my jaw, but I fought him, still, screaming through the blood flowing from my teeth.

His rancid, hot breath made it hard to get air. I screamed and shoved at him as I felt his hands rake my stomach, scrabbling over my skin, nails biting.

"Help me!"

My vision was darkening, pure panic taking over—and then, the weight vanished.

I sat up, inexpressibly relieved, expecting to see Riley or Geoff or Sana, but instead the man was screaming now—and the freak on top of him was screaming too.

The freak had pinned the man, shrieking in her frenzy, pummeling his face with her fists, covering him in blood and spit. The freak's filthy, long fingernails, still painted pink, raked the man's face and neck, leaving deep, gory gouges. The freak was deranged, likely having turned weeks ago, her lips, teeth and skin black and cracked, every blood vessel burst, brain fried beyond any means of understanding.

I rose, ready to run, when the man managed to grip his knife and plunged it into the side of the freak's neck. She slumped off him, sputtering and gasping. He shoved the freak off himself but didn't stand. He moaned in agony, dropping his knife and clutching his face.

I moved swiftly toward him. Up close, the damage looked even more severe. His face was shredded, and one of his eyes was split in half.

"No!" he shouted, reaching for his knife, but I'd already kicked it away. Before he could stand, I brought my foot down, stamping on his throat. I kept it there, leaning into my full weight, crouching to stay grounded while he clawed at my leg. I met his remaining eye, and I think I smiled.

And when I looked up from the dead man and the dead freak,

still, nobody had come to help me.

The front door was closed but unlocked, and the house was empty. I rushed from room to room, calling for them, but they were nowhere to be found. Three backpacks and a duffel bag were missing, but still, some of our supplies lay around. There was no sign of a fight, so I deduced that they must have simply gone out. Geoff was likely still fishing, and maybe Sana and Riley had gone for a walk, to get some fresh air in their healing lungs.

But why did they take the bags? Why was my gun empty?

I pushed the bad thoughts away, choked them down, made myself a small meal and ate it. Ravenous, shaky, I noticed a fleck of the dead man's blood on my arm and scrubbed it until my skin was pink. I was sure they'd be back soon, and I couldn't wait to tell them what I'd heard from Kenny about the military camp— they would all be so ecstatic at the news.

At last, after what seemed like an eternity, I heard voices from outside. I bounded out, a grin on my face. We could leave for the military camp tomorrow, pick up the bag of books I'd dropped on the way, and we would all tease Riley over the romance novel.

I staggered to a stop on the front porch, catching myself on the railing, the fragments of my missing fingers crunched uncomfortably at the awkward angle. I surveyed the sight in front of me, allowing myself only a moment to take it in, and then I ran.

18

JAMES'S CATCH OF THE DAY

James looked up just in time to see her, the girl with the shoulder-length white-blonde hair, her face flecked with blood, a purple bruise blooming on her jaw. Looked up just in time to see her smile falter, slip away off her angular, beautiful face. Saw her run for it.

He cursed, wished she hadn't run; these men were dogs, and dogs love a good chase.

"Go get her," McNeal ordered, flicking his hand lazily in her direction. Half of the men took off after her, way more than necessary. James barked at two of them, and they slowed and returned.

"Might I remind you that this is my mission?" McNeal said, his seedy voice displaying only a hint of anger.

"And why do we need half our men running after one girl? Go check the house for supplies."

The men scurried off, and James crossed to the two bodies lying on the front lawn. Blood was still trickling from the berserker's neck. James wondered if the blonde girl had killed them.

"We got her." It took three of the men to drag the girl from around the back of the house. She kicked and screamed ferociously, while Watson, one of the few women to hold a spot in the group, trailed behind, clutching her arm as blood gushed from it.

"She bit me," Watson growled, looking at the girl with fearful, angry eyes. "What if she's a berserker?"

"Does she look like one?" snapped one of the men holding her, delivering a hard kick to her ribs. She cried out and stumbled, struggling less and less.

They forced her to her knees, holding her by her arms. "McNeal! Do you want this one?"

McNeal sauntered across the lawn, James jogging to catch up. Behind them in the home came bangs and crashes as the others ransacked it, occasionally tossing a box of supplies onto the porch.

"She's pretty, isn't she?" cackled the scrawny man on her left, "real pretty. Made a good run for it too."

McNeal held his rifle out, propping it under the girl's chin, tilting her face upward. Her chest heaved from exertion, face flushed and sweaty, her lower lip swollen and bleeding. She met McNeal's eyes, gritting her teeth, and spat a mouthful of blood onto his shoes.

Without a word, the scrawny man slapped her, so hard her head whipped sideways. James flinched involuntarily, reminded vividly of someone breaking.

"Enough," McNeal ordered, looking at the girl in disgust. "She'll do. Cuff her, load her up."

"I don't think she's alone. There was clothes hanging out back, men's clothes," said the scrawny man, James finally remembered his name was Gallagher.

"Girl, are you alone here?" McNeal asked her. She neither looked up nor spoke, still breathing heavily, staring at the ground. She wore a thick fur coat, the front of it flecked with blood.

James's chest tightened, reminded terribly of the day when he was only a child, hunting in the woods with his father. They'd stumbled upon a young wolf with its paw caught in a bear trap, howling, enraged, and terrified. James had begged his father to help it, grasping at his coat, but his father had shot the wolf nonetheless. James had never forgotten the look in the wolf's eyes—angry, terrified, defiant—neither aware nor caring that it was not James who had trapped it or that James wished it mercy.

Gallagher lifted his hand to strike her again.

"Stop," James barked. "Hitting her isn't going to make her talk." Her eyes were on him now, deep blue, meeting his, bold.

Gallagher sniggered. "Doubt that, Your Majesty. I think her pretty mouth will talk just fine."

"Over there!" Watson cried suddenly, the beefy woman pointing with her good arm toward the forest, blood spurting from the bite wound as she released the pressure.

They all turned toward the forest, and James thought he saw a flicker of movement in the trees. The girl had perked up, staring into the wild, leaning forward, her eyes fixed on a single spot.

McNeal noticed too and ordered men into the woods. James saw them then, two figures at least, darting away the moment the men took after them. Out of sight in an instant. The girl slumped, mouth slightly open, and James wondered if she realized she had just been abandoned.

They waited, but the men returned soon, having lost track of the targets before they'd even entered the woods.

"Very well, she's all we need anyway. Load her up, the supplies too. Remember, nobody touches her, not yet. We need her whole."

They dragged her away, toward the caravan. The fight had gone out of her. Her feet dragged over the leaves, passing the two bodies in the grass. She slumped as they forced her against the truck. Never speaking as they zip-tied her hands and feet. She had a red bandana woven into the blonde strands of her hair, which was forcefully yanked out and tossed onto the ground, Gallagher laughed as he did so. They stripped her of her coat too, admiring and fighting over the thick fur.

Then, just before they slipped the cloth bag over her head, James met her eyes—blue, desperately sad, and so, so angry. The wolf caught in a bear trap.

Vicars leaned back in his plush leather seat. He hadn't dismissed Evangeline today, and the curvaceous redhead sat perched on his knee, large eyes gazing around the room, lips slightly parted, as though she hadn't a care in the world or a thought in her head.

"So, it's done, got everything you need?" Vicars asked, swirling the dark liquid in his glass, offering a sip to Evangeline, who took it with a girlish giggle.

McNeal nodded. "Yes, the two we captured will be perfect, and there is plenty of time to set up the appropriate lab."

"Who are they?"

"One of them a man, mid-fifties, he said his name is Benjamin Waterly. He used to be a chemistry teacher, survived a stroke three years ago—a perfect specimen."

"And the other? The one all the men are raving about?"

"She is … difficult. She hasn't spoken a word. I estimate her to be early to mid-twenties, quite weak, though so far, she's refused to eat—although she did bite Watson. She's missing two fingers on her left hand. It's a recent wound, maybe a month old. It would be preferable if she would talk. I'd like to gather more data on each subject."

Vicars raised his eyebrows. "Feisty, eh? Maybe I'll pay her a visit." He laughed. James watched a shadow flit across Evangeline's porcelain face, gone an instant later. Vicars continued, waving a dismissive hand.

"Leave the food down there with her and let her stew for a few days. They always eat in the end."

McNeal gave a slight bow and stood, sweeping from the room in his trench coat, like some sort of bat leaving its cave.

Vicars gave a grunt of annoyance as the door closed. "Creepy bastard, isn't he? Ah well, if he saves us all, what of it?"

James forced a noise of agreement.

"Anyway, I've thought about it. I want a spy sent to the military encampment. I'd send you, but you're too valuable here. You're in charge of finding someone suitable."

"Any specifics?" James asked, relieved to be given a task he supported.

"Someone who doesn't look too threatening, but no idiots—figure it out yourself that's why I've given you the job. I want them out of here tomorrow," Vicars snapped, somewhat absentmindedly, as Evangeline had drawn his attention.

James stood abruptly, clearing his throat. "I'll start the search right away."

Vicars grunted in response, and James hurried from the room, the door swinging shut, cutting off the sound of Evangeline's laughter.

Jonas descended on him just as James stepped outside.

"What happened out there?"

"Exactly what you think happened."

"And the ones that got captured?"

"With the rest of the prisoners, I'd assume."

Jonas faltered. "I saw the girl. She's young."

James grunted.

"They're all going to die. McNeal isn't going to go easy."

"It's not my problem they got themselves caught," James

said, shoving away from Jonas and heading in the direction of their makeshift cafeteria, feeling ravenous.

Though when he sat, he found he could barely force down a few mouthfuls. He couldn't stop thinking of those eyes. Blue as the ocean, lonely as the moon.

Four days later and James had hardly thought of the girl or her coming doom. The entirety of a fresh pack of cigarettes the first night had seen to that, seeming to carry him the rest of the way.

That was all over, however, as James stood outside the entrance to the community clubhouse, its basement converted to a prison. He was here only at Jonas's insistence; Jonas having found out that the girl was still refusing to eat. He had a kind heart, that kid, and James feared it would get him killed.

But there James stood, holding a tray with a fresh sandwich and bottle of water, following Watson down to the girl's cell, Watson's arm bandaged where she was bitten.

"Good luck. She wouldn't even speak when we put her in here. Tried to feed her the next day, and she spit in my face." Watson's mulish features crumpled with obvious hatred. "Taught her a lesson for that one, but McNeal is insisting they need to be healthy, so the next step is going to be a whole lot worse if she keeps it up."

They'd erected several cells in the basement of the community's office building, which were no more than emptied-out closets and boiler rooms. The girl had been given a particularly isolated one, however, a wooden lockup built only a few feet wide in the corner of a cement side room. In her cell was nothing but a ragged blanket and a bucket in the corner.

"Good luck," Watson said again, the door swinging shut behind her.

James ignored the other prisoners as he crossed the room, edging open the far door to the pitch-black hell that the girl was kept in. He held out a small lantern before him, light flooding the space, which was musty and cold, smelling of sweat and old water.

She was there, sitting on the floor of her cell. They'd taken away the food after she refused to eat. She was filthy, still wearing the clothes they'd captured her in, arms wrapped around herself, completely ignoring the fraying blanket she'd been given.

Vicars had been serious when he said to let her stew—four days alone in the dark.

James didn't know where to start and awkwardly placed the new tray on the ground, nudging it toward the bars. "You need to eat." He noticed that she had, at least, drunk some of the water that had been left for her.

She ignored him, staring at the cement floor.

"You need your strength, trust me."

Still, nothing.

James sighed, exasperated. He'd promised Jonas he would give ten minutes of his time to this girl. He pulled up a stool, sitting down and lighting a cigarette across from her cage.

She finally looked up as the smoke drifted across the room, winding through the bars and gracing her thin face. James offered it to her, but she refused again. Her eyes traced his features for a moment, and he found himself hoping that she recognized him, knew that he had tried to help her when she'd been captured.

"You need your strength," he repeated, pulling again on his cigarette, "or you're never going to make it out of here."

That seemed to reach her, and her voice was raspy, thick. "What are you going to do with me?"

"Me? Nothing. It's them you need to worry about."

She stared at him, and after a moment's hesitation, he elaborated. "Usually they keep the prisoners for a week or so, give them a chance to choose to join the group or not. If they make it to the prison, it's because somebody in charge liked them enough to give them a chance."

She spoke again, quiet, and without question. "But that's not why I'm here."

James wondered for a moment how he had ever compared this girl to a wolf. She looked so small in her cage, curled up and skinny. Her eyes puffy from days of obvious crying, the dim light making them look more gray than blue. Hair greasy and lank, lips creased with dried blood where Watson must have hit her, her bruised jaw now a dappled yellow.

James shook his head, taking a long draw that cleared his mind. "No, McNeal took you and the other man for a different reason."

He saw the panic tighten her chest. "Why?"

James paused, deliberating. "McNeal thinks he can figure out what's killing everyone—making the Breaks happen again," he paused. "Do you know?"

She nodded, and James continued. "He's going to do his experiment the next time it's set to happen, you and two others. Cut you open and see. He thinks if he can catch it in the act, he can figure out what's causing it."

"That's it?"

James was surprised. "We don't have anesthesia or morphine. It might kill you, even if you don't happen to break that night." He said the words bluntly, surprised at himself, baiting her for a reaction.

"What will happen to me after?"

"I don't know … if you survive?" James thought it over. "Vicars appreciates strength. I think he'd offer you a spot in the group, maybe—I can't guarantee it wouldn't be as another of his wives."

"But I would get out of here?"

"I don't see why not."

To his shock, the shadow of a smile crossed her face. "I guess I will need my strength, then." She reached through the bars, snatching up the fresh sandwich and taking a bite. He noticed the two small nubs where her fingers were missing, and he itched to know what had happened.

"I'm not lying to you; this is what they're planning. There's nothing I can do to help you." He fumbled his words.

She didn't look up from her food as she spoke. "It's all right, they can't kill me."

He dropped the cigarette sharply, having forgotten about it and burning the tip of his finger. "Of course, they can kill you— knowing McNeal, he will probably try to," James said incredulously, stamping out the glowing ember.

She looked up then, her face passive. "They can't kill me, because I can't die. I can *never* die."

19

JORAH JAWBREAKER

My eyes hurt. They burn and itch, and I wish I could pluck them out.

Because why do I need them anymore? There is nothing but darkness down here, quiet, darkness, and cold. A sliver of light beams through the crack beneath the door, just enough to see my filthy hands, my missing fingers—to agonize over everything I cannot see. I may be the only person in here, but I am not alone. Guilt and anger, loss and starvation stare at me from behind the bars. Sometimes I think I can hear my sister, screaming my name from somewhere I can't reach, preaching to me everything I've ever done wrong.

I don't know how long it's been since they sat me down here. Four days, based on when I hear them feed the others, though it feels like many more.

But these days have not been useless, because they have given me time to think, to plan.

I only wish I knew *why* the others would leave me to die. What I did to them to deserve this. No, worse, why they left me to be captured. Beaten, tortured, raped—for all they knew of what might happen after.

I shivered in the darkness, curled into a tight ball, my cheek resting on the cold cement floor. Every minute I waited, waited for the door to swing open and for someone to come for me. Lay their hands on me, kill me, ruin me—then leave me here in the dark again.

I knew it must be coming, though I hadn't been touched so far.

Though, strangely enough, the dread that filled me came from knowing that I may never again leave this room. That I would stay here until my skin looked like paper and my muscles atrophied me to the floor. Maybe the darkness would blind me, give me two blue-tinged glassy orbs floating uselessly in my skull.

But by far the worst thought, was the knowledge that if I never left this room, I would never have my revenge.

They left me. Betrayed me, *lied* to me. Gave me away to this, and for what? Was I really that hard to be around? Me, Jorah, the girl who risked her life to save theirs over and over again.

I would have died for them. I knew it in my bones; they must have known too. How many times had I saved them? Nursed them back to health on food that I never got to taste?

But then I would think, *how could they have saved me?*

Outnumbered ten to one, the only logical thing to do would have been to run for it. I would believe it too, that they had no choice, and I know some part of me still hopes that they will come, smuggle me to freedom in the dead of night. But as the hours go on, I remember more clearly that my gun had been empty that day. Empty even though I had checked it the day before, taken out every single bullet and rolled it through my fingers, then put them back, the satisfying scrape of metal on metal.

So, they'd taken out my bullets, hoped that I would be finished off by something out there, taken their supplies and hidden in the woods in case I made it back. Eventually I would leave the house, and then I would be out of the way. More food for them, I supposed, the haul we had just found would last weeks longer with one less mouth.

If only I could get out of here, I knew I could find them. Work my way back to the house and the river. I'd spent days tracking them once—I could do it again.

I thought of how it would feel to carve a valley across Riley's throat. Then I cried, tears and shame burning my swollen eyes. Thought of how I'd like to see Sana drowning in the river—then I stood and screamed and punched the wall until my knuckles bled.

Geoff, well sometimes I think I'd like to see him die as a freak—and other times I miss them all so much I feel sick.

Bloody knuckles. Sightless eyes. Dead Riley. Drowned Sana.
Slack-jawed Geoff.

Jorah the Queen.

I woke with a start as the door opened, scrabbling back against the wall despite myself.

"Good luck," said a female voice. I thought it may have been the one that I bit, the one who split my lip—sometimes I tasted my own blood and imagined it was hers again.

I felt sick, though I had promised myself that I would be brave for whatever was to come.

I recognized him instantly. Tall and muscular, dark skin and golden-brown eyes. He had obviously missed very few meals these last few months. Good-looking too, not like Riley, but still, a calmer sort of handsome, the kind your parents would be happy to see walk through the front door. The heroic voice who had stopped me from being beaten, met my eyes, and felt like he'd seen into my soul—my chance at getting out of here.

So, I decided that I would speak to him, let him learn my name, see if I could find my own way to freedom.

He didn't stay for long, and when he left, he told me that he would speak to Vicars—who I assumed was in charge, to see if he could get me placed in a better room. I thought that he was kinder than he liked to admit to himself.

I felt much lighter then, knowing what was to come. Torture? Of nothing but the blood and bone—it couldn't hurt me. I would survive, and I would find my place in this group, and I would finally be what I was made to become.

I thought of his face when I told him I could not die— the incredulity, surprise, and almost amusement.

And I know what I said wasn't true, because now with the darkness back and a stomach full of food and my mind clearing,

I realize it's not that I can't die. I haven't been so lucky that death has passed me by, when billions of others dropped. No, I can't die because I'm already dead. I think I died before even the first Break, floated away with my sister a long time ago.

20

JAMES–NEGOTIATOR, KILLER, FOOL

James collapsed into the plush armchair, aching and muddy after a long day's work building up the fence. He groaned, reaching for the lamp on the small table beside him. He flicked it on, but no light flooded the room; he forgot sometimes that electricity was a thing of the past.

He felt strange, though he couldn't quite place the reason, and it only served to disturb him more. Today had been strange, that was the best word for it. After a restless night's sleep, he'd risen early, stalking out of the house he so hated to the backyard, clearing his mind with a long workout. The day had been spent working, directing men to build up the fence, deliberating on the fate of sick farm animals—hard work, *man's work,* nothing he wasn't used to.

There had been no word yet from the spy they'd sent to the

military camp; that was to be expected, but James still found himself worried over the matter. He'd chosen the man, and it would be his fault if he were a failure.

Not that James cared particularly about what Vicars or McNeal had to say, but a failure like that may be the last straw in Vicars releasing him from his position of power. He'd already been warned he was too soft, already was planning on trying to help the girl. James knew that he would never stoop to obey any other in this camp; he would have to leave if he lost his position.

James had just lit yet another cigarette when the front door swung open, and McNeal walked in. James had hardly seen the miserly old man in days, McNeal likely being too busy preparing for his experiment, sleeping in his office, reading over his torture plans. James certainly didn't mind; on the contrary, having the lurking form of a skeleton given skin absent from the house had made it much more tolerable. Now he only had to deal with Jonas following him around like a lost puppy.

"Vicars is going to meet your girl," McNeal said the moment his beady eyes landed on James.

James tensed, controlled himself, and casually ashed his cigarette. "She's not my girl, and what of it?"

McNeal raised his hands, feigning innocence. "Just passing on news. In other news, Watson says you're the only one she'll talk to. Seems like she's your girl to me. Do yourself a favor— find out her blood type, hmm? Maybe I can spare her for you to have after—can't say what state she'll be in, though."

James jerked to his feet, taking a few steps forward and leering over McNeal. "I don't care about that stupid girl, and I don't care for your news—but I am still in charge here, McNeal, a hell of a lot more than you are. You would do well to remember that."

McNeal only smiled, no doubt intending to make James even angrier, which is exactly what happened. James shoved past and out the door. Pushing his hands into his pockets, he took off for the back of Fort Rache.

James didn't even consider going to the jail. Vicars was probably there with the girl now, and why should that matter to him? He stormed past, heading for the park area at the back of the compound. There was a cluster of trees there, just beyond the newly erected gallows, the only place in the compound outside of the houses with any privacy.

James abhorred the fact that he was forced to live with McNeal, Vicars insistence was the only thing keeping him there. James stared out through the fence. This portion was yet to be completed, while the rest of the compound fence had been built up around the original wrought iron of the community. Here a large section was made only of the bars.

He gazed out into the woods. So often he contemplated leaving, taking off into the forest on his own. It had suited him just fine at the start, hunting and foraging, just him and the trees and the horrors of the world—which always seemed somehow muted in the woods. Because the woods hadn't changed, not really. Anywhere else, you could hardly take two steps without finding a corpse, broken-necked and rotting. The woods, however—pristine, quiet, where the birds still chirped, and you could pretend that the world hadn't ended.

But here now was where he needed to be. James knew that

these men needed his protection, and even more so, the innocents that these men encountered needed James too. He was good at his job, good at leading, and he would stay for as long as he could stand it.

Something moved at the edge of the trees, a shadow flitting by, but nonetheless James noticed. He peered into the woods. Squinting against the dying light, he saw the movement again.

A crazy thought appeared in James's mind that this might be the girl's friends. That they hadn't abandoned her back at that house, and any second, they would shoot him, bowl him over, and bring her to freedom.

He didn't reach for his gun.

A berserker slammed into the gate, flying out of the darkness. Its jaw dangled loosely, teeth black and broken.

"Let's go! Come on, they're going to bury us all. Burn them dead!"

The one somewhat legible sentence the poor bastard managed to emit, sandwiched between the screams and incoherent ramblings of a ruined mind. The berserker's face was covered in dried blood, bits of flesh stuck between its teeth.

James stood still, staring at the monster, studying it. They didn't *eat* people, not always; he knew that from enough time spent observing them. They preferred to dismember, shred bodies to ribbons, sometimes eat a little, but it never seemed to be the goal. James had seen them run down dogs and deer, killing indiscriminately. Once he even saw two fighting each other in a brawl so vicious, the screams brought in two more, both of whom promptly went after James himself.

The berserkers simply, didn't make sense. Something had gone wrong in their brains, turned them to mush—probably a mistake of whatever was meant to kill them.

James didn't like to think about it for long; his mind always strayed too far. Drifting out to places like China or India, where the population was so dense. He couldn't imagine anything other than streets packed full of bodies, berserkers scavenging through them like stray dogs.

Of course, he didn't know what it was like in the rest of the world. He'd heard the radio broadcasts at the start—sure, nearly everyone who had survived the Break had heard them. The problem was, they'd only lasted three days, and then the power had gone from everything, taking the last shreds of civilization with it.

"Shut up," James said finally, tearing his eyes away from the berserker and pulling his knife from his belt. Another had appeared as well, its pupils milky white against the burst blood vessels. It chewed on the bars of the fence so hard, one of its teeth shattered.

James wiped the blade of his knife in the grass, clearing it of the dark, hot blood. He passed a pair as he headed back toward the center of the fort, two of the younger boys in camp, and directed them toward the bodies. It wasn't safe or pleasant to leave carcasses lying around the fence. James himself headed to the main building, where they kept their logs and maps.

Jonas was poring over a large map stretched out over the table when James entered, scribbling in his cramped scrawl.

"Anything interesting?"

Jonas shook his head. "The usual, just marking houses we've checked and such."

"Just killed two berserkers, out by the back fence."

"Really? The raid that went out today found two bodies. Both look like they broke in the second September Break."

"Don't worry, McNeal will save us," James growled, snapping the tip of his pencil as he attempted to enter the berserker kills in the log. Keeping track of the berserkers was a recent occurrence, only done at the insistence of Jonas—probably why he received very poorly written logs from the others, often smattered with obscenities.

"You don't actually think he'll figure it out." It wasn't a question.

"No, I don't think it'll work."

"It might."

"Not with a sadist like McNeal running the experiment."

"Everyone's saying you're the only person she's talked to."

How these rumors spread, James would never understand, as he had told no one of his conversation with the girl aside from Vicars, and even then, he had omitted some details.

"Well? Are you going to try to help her?" Jonas pushed.

"It's not my goddamn business," James snapped. "Why don't you help her? Or help the other two? She's not the only one."

"Charles is a sociopath, that's why he's locked up, and the other man doesn't want my help ... I tried."

"You tried?"

"Vicars gave me permission to question him about what he'd seen out there. You know, any news he might have. I questioned him and then I told him he wasn't safe here, some of it, at least. It just didn't seem right not to warn him."

"You know we can't let them go; we'd be executed."

"I know, I just thought that maybe if he was prepared, he'd have a better chance. It didn't matter, though. He wasn't scared."

James dragged a hand down his face, craving another smoke. "Sounds familiar."

Jonas's eyes widened. "You warned the girl too?"

"Did a lot more than warn her, told her nearly everything that's coming," James admitted.

Jonas tensed, looking frightened. "Vicars won't be happy about that."

"Fuck Vicars," spat James, startling Jonas, who looked around wildly, as if their leader was about to materialize out of the walls.

"It doesn't matter anyway. She wasn't scared. Seemed like she thought it was better than what she imagined was in store."

When Jonas didn't answer, James continued, "Are you going to go see her?"

"I am. I was about to go over when you came in."

"And Vicars is there?"

Jonas shrugged. "I don't think he's gone to visit them; you know Vicars, he likes to make them wait. It's more fun that way."

Jonas's face screwed up in disgust.

So, McNeal had been trying to get under my skin, James thought victoriously. Trying to see if he would go running for her cell. McNeal seriously overestimated how much James cared, he thought smugly.

Jonas closed his notebook, slipping it into the satchel he wore across his body. "I suppose I'll head over now; I figure you don't want to come?"

"Yup."

"All right, see you later."

James returned to his work, poring over the charts and maps, reading and re-reading the same stats, though none of the material really stuck with him. James did not stay for long, his eyes growing tired, the craving for a cigarette digging into his skin.

He had just emerged into ever-growing dim, the street lit up by several small, carefully placed fires, when he heard the shouting.

Two men rushed by, still pulling on their jackets. One of them called out to James. "Someone's been attacked! They're coming through the gates."

Cursing, James jogged after the men. It was his duty to be at the front lines of all events in the fort. A small group had gathered at the gates, some working to close the heavy panels, while others carried a limp form between them.

James recognized him immediately, though he did not know his name. It was one of the younger boys James himself had only just sent out to collect the bodies of the berserkers—the nineteen-year-old son of Sean Jefferson.

"You." James roughly grabbed the shoulder of a man nearest him. "Go get McNeal and Heather, now!" He paused and swallowed. "And get Jefferson, that's his son."

James followed the small crowd as they carried the boy toward the main building, where they had equipped a medical room.

"They just came outta nowhere. Two of them, and Mike dropped the body he was draggin' on his legs—I couldn't do anything!" The second of the boys James had sent out was pale with panic, running alongside the group, soaked in blood. His face had taken on a sickly pallor, but he looked significantly better than Mike, whose head lolled as he was carried, clothes saturated with blood. James noticed several of his fingers appeared to have been chewed off.

"Where are the berserkers?" James demanded.

"Dead—they're dead. They shot them when they rescued us." The boy stumbled, craning his neck to see over the backs of the men carrying Mike. "Is he gonna die?"

James didn't answer but reached for another man and directed him to the watchtower in back. "The sound might've drawn more."

They'd reached the medical room, plopping the lifeless form of Mike down on the table. None of the limited medical personnel had arrived yet.

"Cut his shirt off," James instructed. They had one large flood light in the medical room, the only one purposed for something other than the watchtowers. James flicked it on, and the room was flooded with artificial light. The true depth of Mike's wounds was now on display, and as his cotton shirt was torn away, James doubted the boy would live.

"Move, move," came a gentle yet powerful voice. The small form of Heather shouldered her way into the room.

Only two of the men in camp had wives—that is to say, women they were married to before the Break. They weren't seen very often, their husbands preferring to keep them hidden away in the homes they had chosen (probably a wise decision). Aside from them, there were only a handful of other women in the camp. Some others, like Evangeline, had found men to protect them, and while not likely a pleasant existence, they seemed to prefer this life to the outside world.

Then there were the women like Watson, the very few who had shown themselves capable and brutal enough to stand rank with the men. James often thought they seemed far too comfortable around the likes of some within these walls.

"What happened?" Heather demanded, pulling on a set of blue latex gloves. She was a petite woman, with cropped brown hair that had begun to gray. Her features were small too—pointed nose and dull-brown eyes. She wasn't particularly pretty but was good at what she did, having been a nurse before, and had earned respect throughout the camp because of it.

"I'll send McNeal in as soon as he arrives," James told her, and she nodded without looking up.

"And don't let the boy's father in here. Jefferson, right? Don't let him in yet."

"Let's go," James said gruffly to the other boy, who'd been

206

pacing the room, his clothes sending flecks of blood throughout. James grabbed him roughly by the back of the neck, leading him out of the double doors and into the cool evening.

"Listen, go home," James instructed him. He wished he knew the boy's name. "Go home, get cleaned up, and get something to eat, then you can come back."

The boy gave a shaky nod and turned, skittering off in the direction of the rows of houses.

The chaos had begun to die down. A few men still lingered outside the building with James, two of them standing stoically as guards, large rifles barred across their chests. McNeal finally arrived, rushing inside without a word.

Jonas appeared then, bursting from the front doors of the clubhouse. James had almost forgotten Jonas had been in the building, meeting with the girl in her cell. He demanded to be filled in, but no sooner had James begun speaking when a gruff, furious voice sounded.

"Where is he? What happened to my son?" Jefferson hurried down the street, flanked by two men of equal pleasantness that he was often with. "Who was it? Who touched him, I'll kill them!" Spit flew from his lips, and his eyes were wide and maniacal, still sporting a black eye and heavily bandaged hand from the fight with James over the dying woman.

"James ..." Jonas began, but James had already stepped forward, putting his hands up. "Calm down. Heather and McNeal are taking care of him right now."

Jefferson, however, seemed to barely register James and shoved past him, throwing open the front doors.

"Stop. Nobody is supposed to go in," James ordered, grabbing Jefferson by the shoulder and pulling him back outside.

Jefferson wheeled around, his eyes locking on James. "You, you did this!" He lunged, shoving James backward.

James had known that this outcome was likely from the moment he'd laid eyes on Mike's ruined form. Jefferson was a violent man, a cruel and unpredictable rogue—one who would never listen to reason.

"What did you do to him?" Jefferson screamed, swinging wildly at James, who dodged the blow easily, sidestepping and pushing Jonas behind him in a single motion.

He could smell the reek of alcohol on Jefferson's breath, noticed the haze in his eyes—though James doubted that this would be going differently even if Jefferson was sober.

"He was attacked by some berserkers—"

"And what was he doing outside the gates? Somebody ordered him out!"

James and Jefferson circled each other in the street, the few others outside gathering around. Jefferson's cronies stood leering at James. They were large, violent men with less brains than Jefferson. If it were up to James, the trio would have been banished from Fort Rache months ago, but Vicars had an affinity for them. They ran his errands that other men quailed at, preformed the beatings when Vicars grew bored of the labor.

"Listen to me. Your boy is going to be fine. Heather told me nobody goes in right yet."

"Gallagher said *Master* James gave the order," sneered one

of Jefferson's men.

James made the mistake of looking, if only for a moment, away from Jefferson. A fist struck him in the jaw, sending him skittering backward. He twisted midair, his wrists protesting as he caught himself on the pavement.

Jefferson advanced on him, and James dodged another blow.

"Stop fuckin' running!" Jefferson roared. One of the guards advanced, raising his rifle, but James interrupted.

"Don't, leave this to me." He spat a mouthful of blood out onto the ground.

"I'll kill you for this," Jefferson hissed, flexing his hands. "Shoulda killed you the first time I laid eyes on you."

"Think this through," James reasoned, blood still trickling from his lip. "Who's going to take care of your son if you're dead?"

The two men rushed forward simultaneously, slamming into each other so ferociously they crumpled into the dirt. James caught another punch to the jaw, but with a swift, forceful kick, he sent Jefferson flying away from him.

James pinned him then, pummeling his fists into the other man.

"Enough!" thundered a voice, and James lurched to his feet, stumbling away from Jefferson and spitting out more blood.

Vicars had appeared, marching down the street with his silver revolver gleaming on his belt. The guards intervened then, heaving Jefferson to his knees, blood pouring from cuts on his face, staining his grimy black beard.

"What the *hell* is going on, Duran?" Vicars growled. "Attacking a father while his boy lays dying?"

James stared back as he wiped his bleeding lip on his sleeve. "You know damn well that's not what happened."

Vicars' eyes narrowed; black slits carved into his heavy face. "You ought to watch your tone with me, boy."

James lowered his voice but didn't apologize. "He started the fight. He didn't like hearing he couldn't see his son—on Heather's orders, not till they're finished with him."

"He sent him out there," Jefferson shouted from the ground. "If he dies it's on him!"

"That true?" asked Vicars.

James nodded, grabbing the rag that Jonas offered him and dabbing at his bleeding mouth. "Sent him and the other one out to clean up some berserkers, same as usual."

Vicars grunted, his thick fingers trailing absentmindedly over the gleaming handle of his gun. "Sounds to me like it's young Mike's own fault. Is he going to live?"

"Don't know," said James, casting a look toward Jefferson, who struggled against the men holding him, swearing profusely, "Heather seemed hopeful."

"Well, not much we can do about it fighting, is there?" Vicars said, directing the last part of his words at Jefferson. "Lock him up, let him know once we get an update. I'm not dealing with this shit anymore."

21

THE NEW JORAH

It was hard to fathom how incredible it felt to eat again, to eat *real* food again. Not canned or boxed, stale or flavorless save for flecks of campfire ashes. I never thought I would enjoy a Spam sandwich so much or feel such immense pleasure at something as simple as sipping water from a glass at my leisure.

I ate my dinner slowly, craning my neck to see glimpses of the fight raging in front of the building. My eyes had finally adjusted to the light of my new cell, a spacious and airy room on the second floor. I suppose I had James to thank for my new accommodations, though Jonas hadn't been specific.

I liked Jonas; he'd only just left a minute ago, after the shouting in the street reached us, and I could *finally* eat the food he'd brought in half an hour ago.

He was so young, and I hoped he would still be around when

I got out of here. He was smart too, the type of intelligence you could see within a few moments of meeting.

Where have you come from? How many people have you seen alive? How many have you seen break? His questions were simple, probably good data to collect, and I had done my best to answer them.

It was hard to see much of the fight from my little window, set around the corner of the building, but I could just make out the muscular form of James, circling another man like two jackals set to fight over a carcass.

I took another bite of my sandwich. I was starting to feel much stronger, now that I was eating again. Bars had been fitted over the tiny window of my new cell, as well as a few feet inside of the room, creating a barrier in front of the door. It was warmer here, cleaner and brighter. I'd even been allowed to bathe when I moved, using a small bucket full of cold water. The woman I had bit, Watson, had shoved me toward it so violently, the water sloshed over the sides.

"James wishes he could help you too, I can tell," Jonas had said. "He's a good guy, just a little tough to get to."

"He stopped me from being beat when they caught me."

Jonas nodded, smiling slightly. "That's James—he's a softy on the inside."

Now however, James didn't look so soft, pinning the man he fought to the ground and beating his face. I was curious what had happened and hoped I would find out before my purpose here came to fruition.

Nine more days to wait, nine more days to prepare.

McNeal, he was the doctor here—or some sort of scientist? I wasn't sure, I'd only seen him on the day of my capture.

"He's going to cut you open, all three of you, at the base of your neck," Jonas told me, his voice low and deadly serious. "He showed me the diagrams. He's going to do it at ten to eight, then see if any of you break."

"And if we live?"

"I don't know."

The fight seemed to have ended, those gathered dispersing. I crossed to the far corner of the room, collapsing down onto the thin mat I'd been given.

I thought of my friends, how much I missed them—though I hated to admit it. Did they miss me too? I doubted it, seeing as it seemed they'd abandoned me.

Five days since I was taken, meaning five days when I had heard not even a whisper of them. I knew they hadn't tried to come for me, because if they had, either I would have been freed or their dead bodies would have been lorded over me.

I wasn't sure who I missed the most; it varied with my moods. Sana, when I felt my best, when I felt as though I may still have chance. She'd been my best friend; I hoped she'd felt it too. I missed Geoff when I sought comfort, because of all of them, I felt he were least likely to betray me, that only he was deeply loyal.

Though it was Riley I missed most often. Callous, arrogant, sarcastic Riley—I saw him when I closed my eyes, felt his hands on me in my dreams.

Now, I find myself profoundly lonely, and sometimes I wish that I could die.

Footsteps sounded in the hallway, obliterating the comfort of memories and thrusting me back into my prison cell. Silence, momentary and familiar, and then came the jangle of keys, the door swinging inward.

The first man was stout, likely my height if not slightly shorter. Greasy, slicked-back hair, black and wiry like that of a boar. His black button-up was neatly pressed, and he wore a thick silver chain.

Vicars.

His eyes traveled the length of me before I'd even had time to take my next breath.

"Evening, miss," he said, offering a slight smile and bowing his head. James and Jonas had sidled in behind him, the gap between the door and the bars just large enough for three. "My name is Maximillian Vicars, though around here, we tend to go by last names only." He paused comically. "That is, except for my two companions here, but you've already met them."

I said nothing, crossing my arms over my chest and watching his expression.

Without skipping a beat, he continued, "But in case you've forgotten, this is James Duran, my second in command, and Jonas Chang; he handles all the record keeping and such."

"It's Yeun," Jonas piped in, but Vicars payed him no mind.

"I'm told however, that nobody has quite learned your name yet."

"It's Jorah."

"Jorah …?"

"Jorah Sinclair."

He flashed his teeth, straight yet clunky chips of bone. "Lovely name. Strange, though, I must say."

"So is Maximillian Vicars," I countered.

He laughed; this time it was a real bark of mirth. "I suppose you're right, but enough formalities. I'm here to offer you a deal."

I know my expression flickered in surprise, and Vicars noticed too, his black eyes zeroing in.

"Yes, darling, a deal. You see, James and Jonas here have told me just how special they think you are …" He trailed off momentarily, and my eyes moved to the other men. James had not looked at me once since entering, his gaze set fixedly on the wall, holding a bloody rag to his mouth. Jonas, however, seemed nervous, glancing around at each of us in rapid succession.

"What sort of deal?" I asked. *Please, anything but the next Mrs. Maximillian Vicars.*

"I was getting there—I am offering you a way out of your predicament, as I am sure my very kind-hearted men have alerted you to what you're in for." His tone had changed, morphed into a quiet, poisonous tongue.

James and Jonas had both frozen, apparently having been caught. The air had cooled in the room, a new tension forming.

A wolfish grin played on Vicars' face; he waved a hand toward them. "Doesn't matter, they're much too young and foolish to resist such a pretty face. Back to the point. They say you're special. I say there isn't much special of anything these days, so why kill it without seeing what's really going on, eh?" He paused, as if waiting for me to speak, and continued when I didn't.

"So, you come work for us, see if you fit in with the men— none of them will harm you, on my orders. Then in a week's time, if you're a good match, you get to stay. Nice and safe from the clutches of McNeal and his scalpel."

"What's the catch?" I asked, blood was beginning to pool in my palms, where my nails dug into the soft skin.

Vicars laughed again. "Too smart for your own good. The catch, I'm afraid, is I'll be needing you to spend a bit of time with my wife, for lack of a better term."

"Your wife?" I asked, taken aback. James and Jonas looked surprised as well, exchanging glances behind Vicars' back.

"Yes, my wife. I'm a traditional man, you see, and a traditional wife should stay in the home, attend to such wifely duties. My wife, however, has grown a bit weary of her time in the house, a weariness that has grown on my nerves. I only ask that you spend a bit of time with her in your off time, give her a bit of company so she stays off my back."

"But there's other women here, aren't there? Why me?"

"Yes, in Fort Rache there are other women—there are other women in my own house. But I'm afraid that they either make poor companions, or that their own men have them too busy being locked up themselves—as is their right."

"It's a deal," I said, surprising myself at the vigor in my voice.

"Excellent," Vicars said, clapping his meaty hands together, "you can stay here until we decide if you'll be joining us, then we'll find you somewhere better. Duran, you're in charge of making sure she doesn't go anywhere, and what the hell, take her on a raid tomorrow. Let's see what she's made of."

Vicars leaned into another slight bow and turned, calling for his men to follow him. Jonas scurried off, but James lingered for a moment.

"Seems like a decent deal to me," I said to him.

He met my gaze; I could see the tightness in his jaw and strain on his knuckles from across the room. "We'll see."

22

BABYSITTER JAMES

"Load 'em up. I want to be on the road in ten," James ordered, slapping the side of the truck. He was excited for today's raid, having chosen only the company he wanted. He selected a small group, those he knew to be trustworthy and level-headed. One of the men shot past him, dragged along behind Bear, the large dog barking and pulling on his leash in his strain to reach the truck.

It was frosty this morning, the crisp air burning faces indiscriminately as gear was swiftly readied. James tightened the laces of his boots once again, impatient to leave.

On the far side of the street, three forms appeared, bulky through the heavy padding of clothes. A man whom James recognized with distaste was leading, followed by Jonas, with Jorah stepping carefully in their wake. James watched the eyes of half the men around him turn toward her.

She'd been given clothes, likely from the pile they kept from raids; Fort Rache's very own secondhand store. Her ensemble was mismatched, perhaps most noticeably that she wore a large green mitten on her left hand and a glove on the other.

Though James thought perhaps he only noticed this because he knew of the stubs of her fingers that lay underneath.

"What are you doing here? I didn't authorize you joining," James said gruffly as they reached him.

"Vicars authorized it. He seems to think you aren't capable of keeping *her* from running off," the man said with a haughty and arrogant air. Conrad; hook-nosed and thin-lipped, he often served as a glorified bodyguard for Vicars, a wall of pure muscle.

"Just stay out of the way," James snapped.

The truck was beastly and rusted but had been puttering on since 1974, a computerless stick shift that refused to die. James and Jonas rode in front, leaving the others to hunker down in the bed, Jorah among them.

James peered in the rearview as they peeled out, watching her crouched down, her hair tucked into a wool hat. He'd warned the others earlier they were to leave her alone.

"I should've offered her my seat," Jonas fretted, the road bumping underneath them.

"You're higher rank."

"She's a lady."

James rolled his eyes. "And she's probably got bigger balls than either of us. She's fine."

They were headed far east today, targeting a hospital. Small and lesser known than other corporate behemoths in the area, the scouts had said it seemed abandoned. Jonas suggested the location in a briefing with Vicars and McNeal, citing that they may be able to acquire better equipment for the surgeries.

"Then maybe you'll actually be able to keep people alive." Jonas joked brazenly, a very out-of-character jibe at McNeal, which Vicars found surprisingly amusing.

"With Conrad now we've got seven. We can station one at the car with Bear, and the rest of us can go in two groups. Group one will head to the top floor and work their way down."

"And the list?"

"I'll copy it now, but we all know the basics to look for."

There was a hard rap behind them, and James looked in the mirror to see Jorah knocking on the glass in the back of the cab.

Jonas cracked the window, and her voice floated in over the rumble of the road.

"Hey, how much longer? We're all freezing back here while you two are snuggling up," she chirped, and there was a chuckle from behind her.

"We can pull over for a bit if you babies need a break," James retorted.

Jorah looked over her shoulder for a moment, speaking inaudibly to someone behind her. "Nah, but hit the gas, will you? The cops aren't gonna pull you over."

Jonas slid the window shut, a smile on his youthful face. "She's funny."

James grunted.

"She is," Jones persisted, "and it's surprising after what she's been through. She told me how she lost those fingers."

"How?" James asked before he could stop himself.

With a slight, knowing grin, Jonas explained.

"… and he cut her fingers off. He thought she had killed his dead wife or something—her group came to the rescue right after."

"Poor timing."

They pulled into the deserted parking lot and clambered out of the truck into the blisteringly cold air. James wondered for a moment how much longer it would be until freezing to death became a top concern. He relayed the plans, half-shouting over the wind, while Jonas distributed the shopping list.

"No doubt this place has already been searched, so keep your eyes open. There could be supplies where you'd least expect it."

"I found a box filled to the brim with preserved food and supplies in a library once," Jorah piped in. "It was from a food drive. There could be something like that here too."

James nodded to her, slightly taken aback by how upfront and contributing she had been thus far. He had expected her to stay meekly out of the way.

They headed toward the large brick building, the double doors of the main entrance looming before them. The parking lot was strewn with abandoned cars and skeletons. The bodies were long picked over by crows, having fallen where they stood months earlier. It was always hard not to look at the smallest ones.

The front doors had been shattered inward; the glass crunched under their boots.

"Lights on," James ordered, and flashlights were produced, illuminating the dark entryway. The flashlights were old and bulky, the same as nearly any other electronic device that was still working or reparable.

Ahead of them stood a row of receptionist nooks, three of the five with the remains of their worker slumped on the keyboard.

James peered at a map on the wall. "Perfect, let's do this, eyes open."

The group split, half heading up the staircase while Jorah, James, and Conrad remained behind. At James's direction, it had been Jonas and Bear who stayed at the truck.

The first floor was relatively straightforward, mainly offices and waiting rooms. Each person had an empty backpack, which after the first floor held only hygiene products and antacids from the gift shop. Soon, however, Jorah procured a child-sized set of crutches. She brandished one like a sword in her good hand, grasping the lower handle and bracing the rest against her forearm.

"Since nobody bothered to give me a weapon," she jibed, extending the crutch toward Conrad's face. He batted it away, scowling.

"So you can shoot us in the back? Don't think so. Speaking of, that's exactly what I'll do to you if you try anything."

"Spread out, but stay in earshot," James directed as they ascended to the second floor, moving out among the overturned desks and floor littered with papers and throat swabs.

James picked his way through the shadowed rooms, amassing a collection of packaged syringes and alcohol wipes. He soon emerged to Jorah and Conrad perched on chairs in the general waiting area.

"About time," Jorah huffed, getting to her feet and heaving her pack over her shoulder. James noticed how she struggled to hoist the bag and still maintain a grip on her crutch. Her mitten had been removed, and her fingers scrabbled over the straps.

She caught him looking and held up her hand, wiggling what was left. "Not pretty, is it? Still works though, just a little slow."

"Let's just get this over with," Conrad said, shifting the weight of his rifle on his shoulder.

They found the stairs strewn with debris and the intricate door leading to the next wing blockaded by filing cabinets.

"Weapons ready," James warned, as he and Conrad muscled their way into the hall, the cabinets screeching mercilessly across the floor.

James turned to find Jorah staring intently at a small sign on the wall.

"What's it say?"

"Oncology department," she replied almost in a whisper.

"Should be good stuff in there then, let's go," Conrad said impatiently, heading off into the dark hall, his flashlight bouncing off the walls.

It was much dimmer on this floor, with a noticeable absence of windows. Jorah's hurried footsteps clattered down the hall. "Wait up," she whispered. "I can't see a thing."

James and Jorah searched side-by-side in silence, rifling through drawers and then breaking their way into an operating room after spying a set of shiny new breathing tubes resting on a table.

"Hey, over here," came Conrad's voice from somewhere in the labyrinth.

They found him in the doorway of a patient's room, his broad frame taking up nearly all the space.

"What is it?" Jorah began, attempting to peer inside the room, but the smell had already hit them.

She staggered backward into the hallway, coughing and heaving. James held his breath as he looked inside, Conrad had already retreated, a green bandana covering his mouth and nose.

"Thanks a lot for that, asshole. Really useful," Jorah snapped, her eyes watering from the stench.

"There's a radio," James said, rifling through his bag and procuring his own bandana. "Give me a hand."

Conrad and James headed into the room while Jorah stood in the hallway, watching them sift through the mound of decaying bodies. The moment they began shifting the dead, a swarm of flies rose up around them like a black storm.

James grasped the arms of a corpse, heaving it away from the pile, maggots slopping out onto the ground at his feet. When enough bodies had been moved, he trudged through the mess of the room, finally able to reach the small radio, which sat perched on a table. James wrestled with the rigid grip a dead man had on the handset, finally forced to crack the crumbling fingers off like dried twigs.

"Why are we bothering? Barely anything electric works," Jorah said from the doorway, her voice muffled through the glove held over her nose.

"They were crowded around it for a reason, and they haven't been dead more than a month. It's worth taking."

"What do you think killed them?" James asked, as he finally left the room and closed the door on the buzzing, rancid mess.

"Who knows? Starvation or sickness, maybe. Hard to tell with the decay," answered Conrad.

A crash sounded from overhead, followed by distant, shouting voices.

They hurried upstairs, urged on by the continuous yelling, though James felt calmed that no gunshots had been fired.

"It's us," James announced as they approached the rest of the group. "Everything all right?"

"Yeah, we're all right, Dean just got a little spooked," said Tom, patting his son on the shoulder.

"Can't blame me," Dean huffed. "Look at that thing."

In the corner of the room, a berserker lay strapped to a gurney. It thrashed and screamed, albeit feebly.

"Probably been starving to death," James observed before he crossed to the beast, unsheathing his gleaming knife.

"They're in the walls! Watching!" the berserker garbled, reaching toward James, its chest heaving against the straps.

It was mere hours before nightfall when they returned to Fort Rache, having made a handful of stops on the return drive. The camp was quiet, most of the residents likely in the ramshackle cafeteria for dinner.

"Leave that for now. Let's go get something to eat," James instructed as Jorah attempted to heave bags of supplies from the truck. "Jonas, come on."

The three of them headed down the sidewalk, Jorah giving a cheery wave to Tom and Dean as they left.

"I like them; they're nice," Jorah said. "Also nice to be rid of Conrad."

"They're about as nice as it gets in here, not counting Jonas," James said, shoving through the flap of the large tent they'd erected to house the kitchens. None of the homes had been big enough to hold a kitchen for the fort, not to mention most of the appliances were nothing more than heaps of metal now.

So, instead, they'd established a large white tent in the backyard, the kind used at weddings, and set up a makeshift kitchen underneath. Mismatched picnic tables and chairs had also been dragged out to create a common eating space.

"Evening," James said to the head cook, Ramirez, as a hearty scoop of mystery stew was slopped into his bowl. The cook merely nodded, his eyes on Jorah as she approached carefully, holding out her own bowl.

"I feel like a celebrity," Jorah muttered as the two of them sat down, the eyes of everyone present turned in their direction. Jonas joined them a moment later, pulling himself away from a small group.

"James …" Jonas whispered, leaning over the table, "I was just told that Mike didn't make it."

"Shit. Any word where Jefferson is?"

Jonas hesitated. "Gone. He's gone."

"What the hell does that mean?"

"Mike died a little after we left. They say Jefferson disappeared around an hour later. He took those two guys he's always hanging around with him."

James groaned, pushing his bowl of unfinished stew away. "Better get on top of this now. Before he shows back up to kill us in our sleep."

"You should eat," Jonas argued.

James shook his head. "You two share it. Bring her back to the cell after."

He shoved his way out of the crowded backyard, pulling his pack of cigarettes from his pocket as he did so. He felt as though he had the eyes of every man in the fort on him as he left, and he wondered if word had spread that he was somewhat responsible for Mike's death. He wondered if everyone realized the vengeance that Jefferson was sure to seek.

He found Vicars in the planning office, which was unusual, as Vicars preferred information relayed to him, rather than seeing it himself. The walls were covered in the usual charts and photos, and James averted his eyes from the particularly gruesome section for berserkers.

"I've already heard about the fruits of your raid today," Vicars stated, looking up only briefly. McNeal stood at his side, beady eyes on James as he entered.

"I'm here about Jefferson."

"Fuck Jefferson. He was always a waste of resources."

"I don't disagree, but I doubt we've seen the last of him."

Vicars waved an irritated hand. "It's a problem for tomorrow. We have more pressing matters."

James turned his attention to the table in front of him, noticing a crumpled page depicting the hand drawn back of a human head and neck.

"Nothing you'd understand anyway," McNeal sneered, grabbing a folder and slipping the diagram inside.

"Duran," Vicars pressed, sifting through papers and sliding a folder to James. "This is what we need done. Afterward we can talk about going after Sean Jefferson."

James took his papers and left, letting the door slam with finality behind him. He was so annoyed with the other men, it felt like an itch below his skin. He reached for another cigarette, but his impatience only grew when he found his carton empty.

He returned to the cafeteria, intent on at least finishing his meager meal, to find Jonas already on his way out.

"Where's Jorah?"

"Fulfilling the other part of her deal."

23

JORAH THE EVANGELIST

He led me to a home in the center of the community. From the outside, it didn't appear particularly special, although it was rather grand. It was the two guards stationed in front, however, that told me otherwise.

"Stay out of the office. Stay out of the master bedroom," Conrad directed, dragging me up the front steps and finally letting go of his grip on my upper arm.

"Affirmative, Captain," I replied, mock saluting him. What sounded like a growl escaped his throat before he pushed me toward the door and stalked away.

I hesitated, wondering if I should knock, when one of the guards reached over, opened the door, and gestured for me to enter. He followed me inside, closing the door behind us and standing stoically in front of it, his rifle crossed over his chest.

The entryway was particularly grand, not what you may have expected judging from the exterior. Reddish hardwood floors and a lovely staircase, just beyond which I could see a gleaming kitchen with its dark granite countertops.

It intrigued me, so I walked toward it, calling out, "Hello?" as I ran my fingers over the polished surface. I wondered when the last time was that I had seen anything so clean.

I opened the cabinets and drawers despite myself. Here, however, the grandeur slipped, with plain cutlery and simple tableware, all distinctly neglected.

"He has our meals brought over by the kitchen staff. We never use those," came a soft, alluring voice. "But you know, it's rude to snoop."

A pretty redheaded woman stood in the corner of the room, a chain of pearls hanging around her swanlike neck. She wore a long, soft pink robe cuffed with downy feathers and no shoes. Her makeup was done as well, exquisitely so, with long false eyelashes and a heavy red lip.

"I take it you're Vicars' wife?" I said, leaning against the countertop.

She laughed, flashing her left hand. "I don't see a ring, do you? Though, I suppose I am as far as it matters."

"I'm Jorah. I've been instructed to be your new friend."

"Evangeline, and I've already heard all about you. Fancy a glass of wine?"

"Nothing would make me happier."

She poured two glasses, both as deep a red as her lips.

"So, you're the girl who's finally tamed James Duran," she said, looking me over. "You're very pretty, tall too—like a model. I'm not surprised."

I laughed, setting down my glass. "Seems a bit of an exaggeration—the James Duran part."

She smiled as well, flashing her perfect white teeth. "As far as James goes, you might as well be married. I've seen Max throw girls at him for months, and he never bites. I started to think he may want to try offering him men."

"Whatever you say." I paused, holding my glass still while she poured more wine. "How did you end up here?"

"A bit similar to you, actually." She barely drank her wine, preferring to swish the contents around the glass, watching the mauve liquid nearly slosh over the rim. "They took me prisoner, killed my boyfriend in the process."

"I'm so sorry."

She shrugged, finally taking a sip. "It's just how it is now. James actually saved me when it happened, stopped the other men from, well, doing what they would. They kept me locked up in the back seat of a car and let me rot for a few days—it was before we moved to this place. Some of the men would visit; they got through on bribes and bets. It was okay, because they would bring me things."

"Food?"

"Food, yes, and other gifts. A hairbrush or toothpaste at first, then information, secrets, things I could use to gain a little power, help myself out of my position. So, when Maximillian Vicars finally came to visit me, I was someone he may want. There was a string of executions after, my scorned lovers coming to 'rescue' me, but … here I am."

I leaned back in my chair, surveying the cunning woman before me. "And now you're here, the Queen of Fort Rache."

She laughed, dropping the dramatic air with which she had told her story. "Yes, the queen whose king sets her up on playdates to keep her off his back."

"At least you're safe."

"Ha! You and I both know there's much more than just being safe."

"Then why don't you run, do something to change your position if you're so unhappy here?"

"Oh, darling, I didn't say I was unhappy here—I just know this won't last forever. Speaking of, why don't *you* run? You could at least make it as far as the back door."

"Don't think I haven't already thought of that." I paused. "I just wouldn't say there's anywhere else for me to go."

"Cheers to that." We both took long, deep drinks. Above us, footsteps sounded, creaking through the ceiling.

"Who else is here?"

She waved her hand dismissively. "The other two. The other wives. Pitiful things, so plain, really, not good for much. Max doesn't care for them like he does for me." A hint of pride tinged her voice.

We sat in silence a moment longer, sipping our glasses, listening to the footsteps of the women upstairs.

"Fancy a walk?" Evangeline asked, "I'm just so sick of being inside these walls."

"Are we allowed?"

"Oh, I'm sure there'll be someone to argue with."

We rose in unison and headed for the front door. The guard had already opened it, gesturing for us to follow him, apparently having eavesdropped.

"Can't go anywhere without one of them breathing down our necks, can we?" Evangeline muttered, before turning to the guard. "Just a minute, honey. I only need my coat."

She opened the hall closet, and with a flourish wrapped herself in a beautiful dark fur coat. *My* coat. It took me less than a moment to be sure it was mine and to wonder if Vicars had known it was mine and known that I would see it. I briefly, stupidly wondered if my revolver could still be found in the deep pockets.

"Very beautiful," I said softly, reaching out to touch the fur, thick and coarse and familiar. *Relax.*

"Thank you, it was a gift from Max," she said absentmindedly, before entwining her arm with mine and leading me out the door. "Maybe we can get you one to match."

I'd been given a pillow (flat and yellowed), an oil lamp (rusted and greasy), and a single book (Watson's gum stuck between pages fifty and fifty-one). I was fed without schedule, seemingly

233

whenever someone remembered I existed. It was usually Jonas, once James, sometimes Watson (cram those meals through the inch-wide crack that the window opens, probably poisoned). There was a pot to piss in and a pot to wash in (don't mix them up). And aside from my few hours each afternoon spent with Evangeline, I had hardly left my cell in four days.

To be honest, it wasn't so bad. I could feel a certain softness returning to my legs, my muscles slowly untying themselves from the tangle that was created by months on the road. Now, when I ran my hands down my body, my ribs no longer played through my skin like piano keys.

There were other perks too; the air inside felt cleaner, strangely enough, as the sky outside had grown so gray that at times it was hard to tell the time of day. Jonas agreed it was nuclear fallout, the toxic snow of a winter that would be much too long.

Sometimes I caught myself holding in breath those times I was outside. A subconscious effort to keep the cancer particles out of my body.

It had worked before; maybe it would again.

It was two more days before my requests to be of some use were answered. The day of my judgment approached willfully; my reckoning, my rapture. I pushed down the laziness, the want for my plain mattress and stained pillow. *Time to be useful.*

James came to collect me early morning. Gruff, stoic James; his complexion deep and rich and flawless. He rushed me to dress, tapping his foot impatiently while I donned layers of socks and coats.

We met Jonas just outside the clubhouse, his bright pink nose and watery eyes all that was visible beneath a thickly wrapped scarf.

"Wait in the hall," James ordered as we ducked into the doorway of Vicars' home, the wind dying but the cold still wholly prevalent. A smirking Conrad and McNeal eyed me as I swept past the office entrance. Vicars leaned against his desk with a finely carved crystal glass clutched in his hand, tawny liquid swirling peacefully. The double doors closed as I took a seat on the nearby stairs. No sooner had I sat, however, than a creak sounded just behind me.

Evangeline stood at the top of the staircase, shrouded in shadows, one thin finger pressed to her lips. She descended gracefully, gesturing toward me to follow her. Around the corner into the kitchen she knelt beside a small vent. Puzzled, I joined her, though it was only a moment before Conrad's gruff voice floated through the slats.

"Twenty minutes ago, a flare went up from a scouting group that left early this morning. It went off next to that old factory building on Westend Road, about seven miles northeast."

"Duran," Vicars interrupted, "you're in charge of the recovery group."

"We also heard back from the man we placed in the military camp, Torres. Nothing big, just a note he managed to slip out, looks like they trust him enough to send him on scouting missions."

The military camp. I never learned what had become of my bag that I'd dropped in the street the day of my capture. Filled with books and supplies, the folded map given to me by Kenny and Elise perched on top. *Had they found it?*

The moment of silence ended with the surprised voice of James and distant crinkle of paper.

"They're working on a solution for the Breaks?" James breathed. "If that's true then we should leave them alone. They have a much better chance of figuring something out than we do."

Evangeline's wide eyes met my own, her false lashes fluttering in surprise. I wondered just how many of these meetings she had listened to. Her ear pressed to the wall. Her knees aching on the tile of the lonely kitchen.

"Exactly my thoughts. We keep Torres where he is, let him dig a little deeper, but we do not attack—we're outmanned and outgunned anyway."

"And my experiments?" McNeal asked indignantly.

"They continue, of course."

"We should pull back from that area," Jonas blurted out.

"And why's that?" Vicars asked, while Conrad seemed to stifle a laugh. I had the distinct impression that Jonas rarely spoke at such meetings.

"The note. They're low on food, neither of our groups have scouted some of the land near there. We should let them have it. They can't find a cure if they all starve. Plus, our presence in the area is just increasing the chance they'll find out about us."

"You want us to put our own men at risk to keep an enemy fed? We should hang you today." Conrad spat.

Vicars chuckled. There was a pause and the quiet clink of ice on empty glass. "Pull back from the area, only until we can't find anything on our side. And Duran, get going. There's men to be saved."

There was the noise of chair legs grinding over wood. "I wanted to ask you about Jorah," James began, but Vicars cut him off.

"I was wondering when you'd ask about that. Take her, she's your responsibility now. We need the room in her cell anyway. She's lucky Evangeline took such a liking to her or I'd barter her off to the highest bidder."

"Understood."

Vicars scoffed. "But that doesn't mean she can leave, so you'll watch her, or I'll have the men hunt her down with the hounds, and they can have her."

I looked for the traces of the flare against the murky swirl of the sky, though I knew I wouldn't find any. I wish I'd been able to see it, shooting up in a cascade of red sparks—I'd always loved fireworks.

The truck rattled down the road, trundling over many months' lack of maintenance. I worked on rolling the sleeves of my coat up over my hands, making a note to search for better-fitting clothes when I could.

"Need some help with that?" Tom asked, edging toward me. I offered him a grateful smile and held out my right arm, having grown increasingly frustrated with my lack of fingers.

"Can't have been fun," Tom said.

I held out the hand, inspecting it as I had a thousand times. "It wasn't."

"I trust whoever did that got what they deserved?"

"Well, how do you know it wasn't an accident?"

"Just a guess." He patted my hand as he finished rolling the sleeve, shuffling back against the wall of the truck.

"He got something, but I wouldn't say he deserved it," I confirmed, leaning my head back to watch the sky. I liked Tom and Dean; they had been kind to me since the moment I met them, before the raid at the hospital. They seemed like good people, genuine people. *They'll never survive.*

It wasn't long before we found the missing group's car. A smoking wreck, the front folded into a telephone pole. We rolled to a stop, lurching slightly as James veered into the shoulder. He hopped out of the driver's seat and crept carefully to the demolished car.

"Guess they crashed. The tracks head that way. We should walk in from here; we don't know what we're getting in to."

"Best guesses?" Dean asked as he jumped down from the truck. Dean was my age, early twenties, with a sweet face smattered with freckles. He was gangly and thin and reminded me of a healthier-looking Geoff.

"Berserkers," James said, "but it could be anything, so eyes sharp."

We began working our way toward the factory, an unsightly congruence of concrete blocks surrounded by a tall chain-link fence.

"Here," James said, holding out a rather scratched and dented handgun. "Promise not to shoot me with it."

I took the pistol, feeling the familiar weight in my hand, holding it out and peering down the sights. I grasped the metal, struggling to remove the magazine through thick gloves.

"It's loaded, I promise. Just flip the safety and you're ready to fire."

I didn't answer but gave him a small smile when the full clip of ammo fell into my palm. *Kill them all and run!*

"Over here," came a voice suddenly to my right, a voice quickened and shaky, "I found them."

Dean was pointing through the fence, to what I had at first thought was a pile of garbage.

"Christ almighty," Tom swore.

It was a pile of bodies. Fresh corpses, defiled and left behind to fester on the concrete.

"Is it …" I began, transfixed by the mass of flesh and bone that lay just a few feet away.

"It's them," James confirmed, "come on." He'd found a tear in the fence where the wire had been cut, just large enough for a grown man to squeeze through.

"The berserkers that did this might still be here," Tom warned, covering his nose with his sleeve as we stood over the destruction. "Is it all of them?"

James shook his head. "Gallagher's missing, and maybe a few

others. I don't think a berserker did this." He had crouched as near to the bodies as he dared, his gloved hand pressed over his nose and mouth. "They're full of bullet holes."

Gallagher. The man who had caught me, nearly knocked out a tooth in the process. *Shoot the others and run! Why waste your own life for any of theirs?* I took a breath, stilling my instincts, calming my panic. *You are already dead; there is nowhere else to go.*

We moved in formation toward the building, and I stepped lightly, my eyes peeled for the faintest trace of movement.

"Blood on the door," said one of our group members, a mid-thirties man with long hair and a prominent neck tattoo of a swooping sparrow.

"We'll finish the perimeter before we go inside—there's no saying that's our men's blood."

We continued to creep forward, though we had only taken a few steps when I noticed that Dean had not moved. My feet stirred of their own accord, and I walked toward him, standing by his side, following the path his eyes traveled. The door stood open, half off its hinges, a streak of blood swiped across it that faded into the fathomless dark of the factory. It was an unnerving darkness, one that seemed to swallow everything beyond the door, cavernous and impenetrable.

There was a buzzing growing in the back of my mind, and I knew what was coming in the seconds before it struck.

The freak launched toward us, screaming the unintelligible shriek of its psychosis. I raised my gun, though I was much too slow as the monster barreled into Dean's chest, knocking us to the ground and sending my pistol skittering away.

Shouting and gunshots erupted, and I rolled to my feet. Four more freaks had emerged, forming a barrier between Dean and me and the rest of the group. Freaks never lived long after they broke, and each of these seemed closer to death than the last. Their skin so blackened and bruised it could be rotten, with mouths full of teeth that could have belonged to a shark.

"Shoot them in the head or the heart!" James was shouting over the fray, and I watched in terror the moment his gun clicked empty and a freak launched itself on top of him.

I took a stumbling step toward him, but it was the desperate, panicked scream of Tom that stopped me in my tracks.

"Dean! *No!*"

Dean had also become separated from his gun and now ran in frantic circles, a freak on his heels. Tom fought desperately to reach his son, killing one freak only to have another appear in its place.

"Dean!" he screamed again.

I watched frozen, as in his desperate game of tag, Dean made a beeline for the factory, disappearing into the darkness beyond the door.

I knew in that moment that I could run for it; there was nothing to stop me. I could be back to the truck and gone long before anyone else could detangle themselves from the fray. I could find my way back to the house and the river and track down the others.

Revenge at my fingertips, I could taste freedom on my

tongue.

But there was another plan, one that was not visible to me until then. A plan where the first step was now right in front of me. *There is no God. There is no death.*

I swept my pistol from the pavement and ran toward the building. Past the door where the blood smear singed my vision like a streak of lightning, into the darkness that swallowed me whole.

The shouting and gunshots sounded strangely distant the moment I was inside, like a woolen blanket now draped over the world. Inside reeked of mildew and disarray, silent and dim—though not as dark as it had seemed before, faint light trickling in from high windows.

"Dean?" I called hesitantly, holding my gun aloft. "Where are you?"

Only silence returned my call, unwavering and murderous silence. I moved deeper into the factory, edging around tall shelves stacked with equipment and supplies.

"Dean?" called another voice. High-pitched and wavering, it sent the hairs on my neck on end. "Help me, Dean." The freak's voice echoed off the walls, pinging around the room until I could hear nothing but it and my shaking breaths.

"Where are they? Dean! Looking!"

I didn't dare call out. Instead I pressed myself against a shelf, trying to recover my bearings.

"Hungry, Dean. I hear you!"

There was a skittering of running footsteps and a raucous

scream, followed by the booming crash of a shelf collapsing onto the concrete floor. Rubble flew past my feet, and I took the opportunity, running deeper into the factory, camouflaged by the noise.

I stumbled once over a long-dead corpse, its neck bones protruding through the parchment skin. I caught myself on the side of a shelf, though the warm wetness that my hand had dipped into was more startling than any corpse.

Blood on the shelf, now blood on my hand.

I edged around the corner and finally spotted Dean through the dim light.

"Dean," I hissed, looking both ways before I rushed across the aisle toward him. The freak hunting us had gone silent, and the dark and musty factory had become wholly suffocating. "Are you okay?"

He was panting heavily, clutching his wrist where blood leaked out. "Yes. I dropped my gun."

"I have mine. Do you know where—"

Another crash broke the silence, followed by the horrific laughter that echoed off the walls. For the life of me, I couldn't tell if there were one or one hundred freaks surrounding us.

"We have to run," I urged, pulling Dean to his feet.

"They'll hear us," he whispered back, looking around frantically.

As if on cue, there was a resounding whisper that cut through me like a hot knife.

"Hear you! Bite you!"

A freak exploded out of the aisle nearest, sprinting toward us with spit flying from its slack jaw. I raised my gun, firing three times. The freak collapsed at our feet, convulsing wildly. There was a chorus of screams and muddled words from within the depths of the factory, and I could only pray that the echoes confused the freaks as much as they did us.

"Help me, now," I demanded, and together Dean and I threw our weight against the shelf to our left. It toppled over, crashing into the shelf beside it, its contents rocketing across the floor.

In the wake of the crash, Dean and I ran, vaulting over the dead freak and sprinting for the doorway. We pivoted right, another freak spying us and charging. Another pivot, stumbling through the wreckage of collapsed shelves, rushing Dean alongside me.

I was faster than Dean, much faster, lighter on my feet and more agile. He slowed us down, and my every instinct told me to leave him, but then the light of the doorway shone like a beacon.

I saw the freak from the corner of my eye. It dove for Dean, but I lunged forward, shoving him through the doorway and into the bright outdoors.

The freak slammed me into the ground only feet away from the relative safety of the outside world. I fired my gun, the shots bursting in my ears until all I could hear was ringing and my own screams. The freak's flailing limbs sent the pistol flying just moments before it sunk its teeth into my shoulder.

My hands scrabbled across the concrete around me, searching for anything I could use as a weapon. The freak's teeth dug deeper into my shoulder. The pain was excruciating, and I feared at any moment that I would pass out.

A sharp, cold something sliced into my palm, and I wrapped what remained of my fingers around it. I brought it up, stabbing it over and over into the freak's neck. Hot, sticky blood flushed out across me, cascading over my chest and filling my senses with the tang of rust.

I pushed the body, pulling myself to my feet on the rungs of the nearest shelf. The shard of glass clattered out of my hand before shattering on the floor.

Panicked voices greeted me as I limped into the sunlight. The man with the sparrow tattoo was on the ground, attempting to wrench his knife from the head of a dead freak. James stopped mid run, skidding to a halt feet from me, while Tom crouched over a collapsed Dean.

"Got him," I said weakly, "left my gun inside."

"Blake, Tom! Move them away from the building," James ordered. He turned to me, supporting me gently while Blake rushed over. "Are there any more berserkers inside?"

"Yes." I chanced a look down at my shoulder as Blake guided me into the parking lot. A flap of my torn skin hung over the neckline of my sweater like a brooch.

Tom had shattered the window of a nearby van. He unlocked the doors, and Dean and I crumpled inside.

"Dad, stop, I'm okay," Dean was saying as Tom fawned over him, wrapping his bleeding wrist tightly. "It's not deep."

"You'll go right to Heather when we get home. This is an

infection waiting to happen," Tom said, his voice garbled slightly through his ebbing panic. He turned to me, a bloody rag still clutched in his hand and tears forming in his eyes. "You saved him."

I didn't have a chance to answer, as James appeared, panting slightly, and instructed Blake to stand watch.

"What happened in there? Are you all right?"

I explained what had occurred in the factory as James pulled a clean rag from his backpack, pressing the fibers into the bite marks on my shoulder.

"Dad's right," Dean said, turning his head toward me as he slumped in his seat. "I'd be dead without you."

"We're sorry we didn't come in," Tom stuttered. "As soon as you ran in, somebody started shooting from the trees, probably whoever killed the others. We think we drove them off—it's a miracle we're all okay."

I ground my teeth as James splashed antiseptic over the bite, pressing on a layer of sticky gauze. "You should be okay, but we need to head back. You might need stiches."

"What about Gallagher?" Tom asked as he helped Dean out of the van.

James shook his head, packing his medical supplies as I worked to stem the bleeding. "No sign of him inside or out—just have to hope he makes it back on his own."

"Or doesn't," Tom muttered. "Never liked him."

We hurried back to the truck, the fog in my head dissipating slowly as I sipped from a bottle of water. My shoulder burned terribly, and I hated to think of how many germs had been in the freak's mouth. I thought, however, that as far as my recent injuries had gone, this one wasn't so bad. Not so shocking or debilitating. My lips twitched in a grin as I realized that I had finally gone some time without a concussion.

"You've got to be fucking kidding me."

We'd reached the truck—or at least, where the truck should have been. In its place was only the crushed grass and grooves in the dirt.

"Gallagher," James snarled, flinging down his bag and dragging his hands over his face.

"How do you know?" Dean asked.

"I don't," James sighed, and he dug in his pocket before procuring a pack of cigarettes. "But who else would know where we always keep the keys?"

"How much do you want to bet it was him in the woods? That he killed the others."

"Probably halfway to join Jefferson by now," Tom said as he spit on the ground in anger. "Waste of our time coming out here."

"We have the whole walk back to be angry about it," James answered. "We'll find out what happened then." He tossed the pack to Tom and shouldered his bag, starting off down the road.

We began the long walk after him, our forlorn and wounded group trudging down the unloved road. It would be hours before we reached Fort Rache.

We'd only made it about a mile when I spotted the first flake of snow drifting down between my eyes. More followed, and soon we were dusted in a flurry of the soft white spots, twirling through the breeze and catching in our hair.

"Here." Tom had caught my good shoulder and held out a very squashed granola bar. "You need to get your strength back. You lost some blood."

I shook my head. "I can't take your food—Dean should have it."

"Dean's already had some, and I wouldn't even have a son right now if it wasn't for you."

"Thanks." I accepted the offer, tearing open the packaging and throwing it in my wake.

Tom continued to walk beside me, gazing around at the snow, which fell in stronger waves with every passing minute.

"So early for the snow," Tom commented. "I can't remember the last time I saw it so soon, but to be fair, I'm from a bit farther south than here. But hey—all this snow, maybe it's here for you."

"How so?" I asked.

"Your name, it's Hebrew, right? It means early rain."

"That's right."

"Early rain, early snow—same thing isn't it?"

I forced a smile, starting to wish I could be left alone with my thoughts. "How did you know? It's not a very common name."

"I was a theology professor for twenty-five years. Must've read it somewhere. Maybe this storm jogged my memory."

We walked in silence a bit longer, my shoulder hot and tight despite the ever-growing snowfall. A groan of pain slipped through my lips.

"Let me look at that." James halted, turning and gesturing toward my wound. Carefully, I unzipped my coat and peeled back the blood-soaked shirt from my skin.

He sighed, examining the drenched gauze. "And you, Dean?"

"Hurts, but it's not bleeding so much anymore," Dean said, his voice muffled as he had zipped his jacket over his mouth and nose.

James considered him for a moment and then turned back to me, inspecting my wound one last time. "We need to stop," he concurred.

"I'm fine," I protested. "We can't have more than a few miles left."

"You're pale as a ghost, and the snow is only going to get worse. We'll find a place to rest and wait it out."

The house was terribly cold, and the floorboards creaked with every step; the echoing footsteps of the bones that lay in the kitchen. We settled in an upstairs bedroom, the snow piling against the sill of the lone window. James busied himself unpacking his medical kit, and I grew nervous that he would want to dress my wound again.

"Look what I found," Tom announced, returning from his sweep of the house with an armful of moth-eaten blankets.

We spread the blankets about, forming our own little nests and draping one of the heaviest over the window to mute the draft, and soon the room wasn't so cold anymore.

"That needs to be stitched, if you're up for it."

I flinched, my fears coming true. "Do you know how?"

"I've done it a time or two," James replied with a hint of a smile. He patted the old wooden desk chair, and I took a seat, my blanket draped over my shoulders. "This is safer than waiting to make it to camp," he said as he splashed a shiny curved needle with antiseptic.

I watched at first as he dipped the needle in and out of my skin, and once again I was strangely left with the feeling that this was not so bad. That there was always something worse.

"He doesn't talk much, does he?" I asked quietly, jerking my head toward Blake's prone figure. I could just see the wing of his tattoo draped along his neck.

"No, he doesn't. He's a decent man, though. I trust him— more than most others, at least."

"I used to be a bit like him," I said, and I found myself unable to tear my eyes from his sleeping form. "Quiet, a bit of a loner."

"I find that hard to believe." He had finished the stitching, finally, and gently applied a fresh layer of gauze.

I smiled. "Well, you don't know me very well."

"If you say so." He withdrew from my side, and I'll admit that the room seemed to grow much colder in the same motion.

"Want a smoke?" he asked, holding out a pack of dwindling cigarettes.

"I don't smoke. I'd love a drink though, if you've got any."

The small orange flame of his lighter illuminated his face for only a moment, before he once again tossed the package to Tom. "I don't drink."

I was surprised, though for politeness, I tried not to let it show. "Why not?"

He shrugged. "Back in the day, a few drinks, sure, but it's a lot more dangerous now. It keeps you unaware, dehydrates you, makes the hunger worse."

"Well, I've been drinking like a fish, and I'm still around."

He raised an eyebrow and slyly gestured toward my missing fingers and heavily bandaged shoulder.

"Oh, shut up." I chuckled, slumping back in my chair and dragging the blanket tighter around myself. "Maybe I'm down a few bits and pieces, but I'm still kicking."

"If you say so," he said again, as he took a seat beside the window, resting his back against the baby-blue drywall. "Get some rest. I'll keep watch. We'll leave when the snow dies down or in the morning, whichever comes first."

24
THE HOME THAT JAMES BUILT

The body of the deer draped over his shoulders was warm and soft, an almost welcome protection from the cold as James walked. The front gates of Fort Rache finally came into sight just down the road. Once, they had been ornate brass entries with an automated coded entrance and a 24/7 security guard. Now, they towered skyward, built up with heavy planks of wood and sheets of metal, the door secured with thick chains.

Though the security guard hadn't really changed.

James waved to the man on duty, the sentry's eyes pressed into his binoculars from the top of the front tower.

James had enjoyed his hunt, the stillness and quiet of the woods. After spending a long, cold night cooped up in that house the day before and at constant work since returning, he was glad for some alone time. He'd seen this deer the week before, passing silently by the walls of the fort. The scrawny buck wouldn't go far toward feeding the entire camp, but people would be more than grateful for even a few mouthfuls of meat that didn't come from a can.

It wasn't often that anyone succeeded in hunting, the immediate area having been stripped of most life in the first two weeks they'd arrived. Though, to be fair, for those two weeks all of camp had eaten like kings.

Today, however, was different, and as James approached, he found the head chef of camp, Ramirez, butchering a rabbit.

"Evening," James said, unloading the deer onto the table and stretching his sore shoulders.

"Nice shot," Ramirez hummed, leaning over to peer at the buck as he wiped his bloodied hands on an equally bloody rag. "Been craving venison for days."

"Try months," James huffed. "You kill that rabbit?"

"Tom's boy—Dean, that's his name, he brought it in."

"Good man."

"He's a nice kid, I'll say—heard the new girl saved his ass the other day."

"I was there; she did. He put some work in too, though."

Ramirez threw down his rag, pulling a boot up on the chair beside him, and leaned toward James, baring his teeth in a grin. "Hear she's something else, your girl. Hear you guard her day and night too."

"I wouldn't put so much stock in everything you hear." A

fleck of blood splashed James in the face as he tore at the deer hide. "But somebody's got to protect her from all of you."

Ramirez chuckled good-naturedly, turning to scrub at the blood-stained wood he had been working on. "We both know I'm not who people ought to be worrying about—unless they're scared of having their food poisoned, that is." He let out a sharp laugh. "Now that Gallagher and Jefferson are gone though, Christ, it's like a constant pissing match to see who the new meanest and dumbest bastards in camp can be."

"I think you might be able to take it, as far as dumbest goes," James quipped.

Ramirez raised an eyebrow. "Watch it. I didn't say I was joking about that poison."

"I know you take way too much pride in your cooking to poison anyone," James countered, and Ramirez once again broke into a grin. They worked in silence, Ramirez scrubbing blood stains while James carved into the deer.

"Oh, there you are."

"Hmm?" James looked up for who had entered.

Ramirez leaned over and scooped up the small pile of gristle that James had made.

"You have a cat?" James asked in surprise, now noticing the small black-and-white cat that had slunk into the tent.

Ramirez didn't answer, merely chortling contentedly as he tossed the scraps of meat to the cat.

There had been several dogs and cats living in the community when they had arrived, all desperately thin and filthy. Within a week, they had disappeared, however, slyly hunted by the group to what James had thought was extinction. This cat, however, was sleek and clean with a round, plump belly.

"I've told everyone that if they even think about harming that cat, they'll never have another meal within these walls," Ramirez huffed, wiping his hands on his apron while the cat purred ferociously.

"Noted," James replied, and before he left, his share of the venison packaged beneath his arm, he tossed a few more scraps to the ground.

Conrad stood guard on the steps of Vicars' home, his rifle pressed across his chest. He moved aside as James approached, freeing up entrance to the front doors. James was one of the only people in camp with enough authority to simply walk into Vicars' home, and James secretly found great pleasure in the knowledge that his position irked Conrad so.

"...and that's exactly what I told him," James heard as he passed through the intricate front doors, glad to be leaving the blisteringly cold evening behind him.

He dusted the shoulders of his jacket off in the hall, the fluffy snow fluttering down around him like a personal storm. He noticed the voices of the two women quiet as he walked down the hallway, soon finding them rosy-cheeked with glasses of red wine in hand.

James stopped himself from chiding Jorah for drinking so often on her medication, and instead, he gestured to her shoulder. The fresh gauze showed no traces of what the bloodied wound had been beneath. "How is it?"

She smiled back, setting down her empty glass. "Much better, thanks."

"James," Evangeline cooed, "stay awhile? We're having the best conversation."

James shifted on his feet. "Wish I could, but it's getting late, Vicars will be home soon." He gestured toward Jorah, who stood almost immediately.

"I'll see you later," she said to Evangeline, who smiled serenely back, her long eyelashes fluttering almost sleepily as she looked between them.

"It's been fun as always."

At the front door, James waited a moment while Jorah bundled into her excessively overlarge winter coat before tucking her hair into a dull woolen hat.

"They aren't going to bother you when you're with me."

"The less attention the better."

They headed out into the evening. The snow flurries had died down, and the fresh whiteness added a thin layer of beauty to the otherwise unappealing community. Jorah's bulky ensemble proved useful, as hardly a soul paid them mind as they hurried down the sidewalk. The moment they were inside the home, she bolted the door, sighing contentedly as she unwound the excessive number of garments from her body.

The early winter weather had posed several highly unexpected problems in Fort Rache, issues that many had thought they would have months longer to solve. They'd chosen this site partially because it was an older community, built when having a legitimate fireplace in your house was commonplace. Despite this, not all the homes had them, leaving many of the inhabitants of the fort crammed into the houses that did. In addition, the fireplaces only served to warm a section of the downstairs, meaning you always kept your warmest clothes on and that on the worst nights, the upstairs was practically unusable.

James thought of McNeal, who had moved out of the house and into his office in the community clubhouse. He found a sweet thrill in the idea of the old man freezing in his bedcovers.

"They're going to get used to your presence eventually," James said, following Jorah as she made her way into the kitchen. She pulled off her gloves, leaving them on the clean granite counters and inspected her hands, on which James noticed were several small red welts.

"Watson wouldn't let me wear the gloves," Jorah explained. "She had me digging latrines for five hours."

"I'll have a word with her."

Jorah shook her head. "Don't. Like you said, they'll get used to me eventually."

It was dark when Jonas arrived at the home, weighed down as usual by a small pile of clipboards and notebooks.

"Any news?" James asked, looking up from the hunk of venison he'd been working to prepare.

Jonas shook his head, dropping the pile onto the table and slumping down in the nearest seat. "Nothing worth talking about."

"Here's your jacket, Jonas," Jorah announced, holding the fabric in the air from her position on the couch, the large hole that had previously been torn in it now replaced with a small line of perfect stitching.

Jonas leapt up with a grin, taking the jacket and trying it on. "Have you thought of going forward with this?" he asked her. "You could be the community tailor. It would beat having to work with Watson all day."

Jorah shrugged, though James noticed her pleased smile. "Not really my thing, though anything would be better than digging latrines, I suppose."

"You could even branch out," Jonas continued, "start making clothes instead of just fixing them."

"I'll start the first apocalypse fashion chain," Jorah joked.

"I've heard worse ideas," Jonas responded, "but here's your payment."

"Only because you insisted on paying me."

Jonas rolled his eyes and procured a small plastic bottle, which he tossed to her. "Ramirez makes the best hooch in camp."

She twisted off the cap and took a long swig, coughing slightly afterward. "You aren't kidding." She offered it to him, and after a moment's hesitation, Jonas took the bottle as well.

"Come on, James, you too," Jorah cheered, and Jonas cracked a smile, shaking the bottle at James.

He scowled at them. "Tonight's not the night."

"Oh, come on."

"Do you want any venison or not?" James snapped, gesturing to the meat he'd been arranging in a pan.

"Fine, fine," Jorah conceded, and with a pang of annoyance, James spotted her mouthing, "someone's grumpy" toward Jonas who stifled a laugh.

Jorah and Jonas had formed a fast friendship since she'd moved into the house with them. Jonas had always been very shy, his position as a higher-up in camp coming about more from necessity for his skills than any power push he made. Their friendship didn't bother James; in fact, he thought it was good for them, though he noticed they seemed to bring out a certain childlike quality in each other that he found acutely annoying.

The house descended into near silence, save for the crackling of fire and sizzling of meat in the pan. They'd lit the kitchen and living room with a few candles, which cast shadows onto all their faces. Jonas huddled under the largest as he squinted down at his notebooks.

"What are you doing tomorrow?" Jorah asked as James divvied out their portions of venison.

"I'm not sure, why?"

Jorah shrugged. "Just if it's a raid or something, I'd like to come. Every time I see Watson's face, I want to bite her again."

James laughed, despite himself. "I'll see what I can do."

She smiled back, her cheeks slightly pink from the alcohol, her eyes soft and blue and calm in the firelight.

"You should go easy with that," James warned, eyeing the

quickly emptying bottle. "I'm definitely not taking you if you're hungover."

She waved him off. "Don't worry about me. I can handle it. Besides, Jonas has had almost as much."

As if on cue, Jonas gave a great hiccup, grinning at them from his seat and stuffing a chunk of meat in his mouth.

"Why don't you head to bed," James suggested as Jonas continued to inhale food, a sleepy grin on his face. "You promised Heather you'd be up first thing to help organize the medicine supplies."

Jonas's eyes suddenly went wide, his fork clattering onto his plate. "I forgot!" He scooped up his notebooks and bid them good night before stumbling off to the small room down the hall. It was only a few minutes later that they heard his deep snores drifting toward them.

James had collapsed into the plush chair Jonas had occupied, throwing his boots up on the coffee table as he sank into the warm fabric. A pack of cigarettes already sat on the table nearby; he fished one out and lit it, sighing deeply.

His eyes moved around the room, cozy in his bath of orange firelight. His eyes drifted to Jorah, who had pulled the edge of her collar down, inspecting the few-day-old wound on her shoulder.

"We'll have Heather take those stitches out soon," James said, and she nodded, moving from the bite to inspect the red welts on her hands. Seeming satisfied, she curled up on the couch and tucked her legs beneath her, nursing what was left of her bottle.

They sat in silence for some time, James puffing his cigarette and Jorah staring into the fire, her thin frame curled into a ball. James was just about to rise to go to bed when she finally spoke.

"Who were you, before all this?"

"Who was I?"

She nodded, not taking her eyes away from the smoldering coals of the fireplace.

"Well, I was an owner of a construction firm. I co-founded it with my brother."

"Did you like it?"

"I did. Business was good, and it was nice to work with family, surprisingly enough," James said, flicking the last bit of his cigarette into the fire and suppressing the urge to grab another.

"What happened to your brother?" Jorah continued. She'd shifted to face James, and he began to feel unnerved under her gaze, feeling for the briefest moment that she already knew all of his answers.

"I don't know. Him and his wife were visiting her family in Nevada when it all went down."

"You didn't go to look for him?"

James sighed, annoyed that she would bring up a guilt he had long suppressed. "Nevada is half a world away from here. Even with a car, it was too far. I just hoped that maybe things would sort themselves out enough that one day I could."

"Do you think he's alive?"

"What's with the third degree, huh?" James snapped. "What about you? You said you had a sister, but that's all."

Her face was expressionless, and James felt a pang of guilt for snapping at her. He was about to bring himself to apologize, to tell her that "No, I don't think my brother is alive", when she spoke.

"My parents died when I was a toddler. I don't remember them. My sister was seven, and we were raised by our godmother. She died when I was fourteen, and Junia—my sister, she took care of me after that. She even had the paperwork done to be my legal guardian and everything."

"Sorry," James grunted, looking down at the worn carpet, looking anywhere but at her.

She continued, her voice even and steady.

"My sister died of cancer two months before the Break; she was engaged to be married in June. I don't know what happened to her fiancé. I never really liked him anyway." Her tone grew steadily more strained, a shadow taking over her face.

A still silence passed before Jorah spoke again. "Can I ask you something?"

"Sure."

"Do you know what happened to my group? The day I was taken."

James paused, deliberating. "They got away—the others lost them in the woods."

"Do you think that they abandoned me? Left me here, I mean? Was there ever any hint that they looked?"

The words fell from his mouth before he could stop them. All James could do was try to make them gentle.

"I think you should forget about your old group, Jorah. I don't think that they're coming back."

She fell quiet, staring at the bottle clasped in her hands. James forced himself to speak, having found the silence even more disturbing than the conversation.

"What did you mean when you told me that you can't die? Back when they had you locked up."

She looked surprised for a moment, before her face settled back into its cool mask. "I don't know what I meant." She paused. "Sit with me?"

James rose, swiping his pack of Marlboros as he did. He settled on the couch beside her, doing his best to leave a small gap between them.

"You don't need to be afraid of me," she teased sleepily, scooting closer to him.

"I'm not."

"Well, whatever it is." She leaned against him, resting her head on his shoulder and sighing contentedly. "Night, James."

"Good night." He sat rigidly at first, but soon sleep overcame him too. Her body began to feel warm and familiar resting against his, like coming home after a long, terrible day.

25

JORAH AND THE FIRST OCTOBER BREAK

James and Jonas had both gone when I awoke, my cheek creased by the couch cushions, mouth dry, and a slight, familiar pulse behind my eyes. A bottle of water and stale chunk of bread sat on the counter, both of which took no time to devour.

I dressed, tucking my brittle locks into a hat and scurrying across the street. Conrad stood sentinel by the front door, blocking my way, pretending he would not let me in, waiting until I said *please*—the same game he made us play every single day.

Evangeline insisted on painting my nails today, picking out a sweet dusty-rose sort of color, which complemented her lipstick of the day. I relented, but only after my second glass of similar-colored wine had been poured.

"We want to look good in case we die tonight," she said, brushing mascara over my lashes, my eyes watering profusely.

We spent our day lounging beside the fireplace, reading and drinking, pretending we weren't hungry and cold. There had been no sign of James or Jonas. *So much for taking me on a raid.* I'd been told that Watson had taken ill, so there was nothing for me to do except drink and be merry.

When at last the day dwindled, the sky now merely a darker gray than it had been, we donned our coats. A crowd had gathered in the street beside the community clubhouse, men with assault rifles directing people into line. Our guard stayed with us as Evangeline and I approached, ushering us into line and then taking his place beside us.

"What the hell is this?" I asked Evangeline, our arms looped together, shuffling through the madness of bodies and cold.

"I heard Max say it's so everyone who breaks can be dealt with—less danger and mess." She frowned.

I cast my eyes onto the French doors of the building, where, just inside, McNeal would be preparing his instruments of torture. Those unwilling participants were preparing themselves in a different manner.

I spied a tear roll down Evangeline's porcelain cheek. "Don't think about them," I whispered. "There's nothing we can do."

I shuffled in place, cold and growing more bored by the minute. Men and the occasional woman still strewed into the street, before being directed to a spot in one of the many rows. I guessed that Fort Rache held around one hundred people total, maybe more. Some sat down in their spots in line, icy snow crunching underneath them; some knelt to pray.

The crowd, which had been vibrant and talkative when we

arrived, soon quieted, save for the guard's steps as they wove through, rifles at the ready. One of the guards crossed to the front of the throng, standing ahead of the closed double doors.

"As you all know, tonight Dr. McNeal is attempting the first of his experiments in order to try to discover what is causing people to break," the guard announced, his voice ringing through the crowd. A smattering of whispers and glances followed his words. "As usual, we ask for your complete cooperation during this difficult time, and please, leave the disposal of anyone who breaks to the guards. We do not want any accidents."

I swallowed, my throat tight, looking around at those who stood beside me, wondering if they would soon be dead. The minutes ticked down, the collective breath of those around us freezing in the air, rising as though smoke.

A long, piercing scream cracked through the hush. My skin prickled, hundreds of eyes turning toward the shine of artificial light streaming from the windows. Another scream, a wail of agony and anguish. It was a man's voice, and a moment later, the scream became garbled words.

"Please! Don't do this!"

More screams, another man joining in, and I began to feel a sickness rising in my stomach.

"You lied. You lied to us!"

"Oh God," Evangeline whimpered, covering her mouth with her hands, more tears glimmering in her eyes.

My chest heaved with sporadic breaths. It could have been me in there. It would be me in there now if Vicars hadn't offered a deal. *It still could be me in there.*

"Relax, everyone, everything is going according to plan," the guard shouted over the increasing murmurs through the crowd. "These people have bravely sacrificed themselves so that we may find a way to stop the breaking. Without this, we may all be doomed."

"And which of us is going to be in there next if it doesn't work tonight?" shouted an angry voice from the crowd, chorused by similar cries.

"Quiet!" the guard bellowed, hefting his rifle. "There is only five minutes until the Break, so brace yourselves."

I realized then that I couldn't see Jonas or James in the crowd. I looked around wildly, craning my neck for them. I wondered too where Vicars was—inside, probably—but why wasn't he out here, comforting his people?

The screaming had stopped, and I hoped that it was only because they had been put under anesthesia. We had found everything on the list at the hospital; there was no reason they shouldn't be able to sleep through their ordeal.

"It's okay, they'll sleep now," I said to Evangeline.

"But there was three of them. Max told me."

The cries sounded before she had finished speaking. A woman this time, begging to be set free, pleading that they didn't need to do this. Her voice was soft, cracking under the pressure of her situation. She had an accent, subtle, but there nonetheless, and with a spasm of horror, I recognized her voice.

My feet carried me forward before I could stop myself, shoving past those in line as I ran for the doors. Guards were shouting to stop. The nearest raised his rifle, leveling it with my torso. A flash of movement erupted to my right, slamming into the guard and forcing his rifle upward. James grappled with the man, the gun firing harmlessly into the sky.

"Jorah, stop!" he shouted, grunting as the guard fought back against him. I had already sidestepped them, slipped inside, basked in the warm light within.

26
SAVIOR, JAMES

"Stop! Vicars wants her alive," James lied easily, finally shoving the man away from him, who seemed to realize who he was fighting with a surge of panic.

"I—she can't go in there!"

"I know. I'll handle it. Just do your job out here."

He pushed his way into the building where the guards inside had already restrained Jorah. The typical medical room had been much too small. Instead the workstation had been erected in the building's lobby, just inside the doors.

"Get her out!" Vicars was shouting, livid, his eyes like burning black coals. Beside him stood Jonas and McNeal's assistant, holding his scalpel aloft loosely.

Jorah's eyes were trained on the woman strapped into the

third and final medical table, the other two occupied by the anesthetized men. She leaned toward the woman, straining against her captors.

Her lips moved slowly. "Maria?"

The woman turned feebly, her dark ringlets of hair falling away from her thin face, and with a pang in his gut, James recognized her too. It was the woman he had left to die on the roadside, the woman he had fought Jefferson to protect. The feeble, dying woman, whom that very night he had returned to search for, though he never found her.

"Maria," Jorah cried again, her eyes welling up with tears. "Wait, stop, let her go," she said, turning toward McNeal desperately.

"Jorah? What's happening to me? What are they doing?" Maria lay on her stomach, wearing tattered and dirty clothes. The back of her head had been roughly shaved and dotted lines drawn across her neck. You could see where her neck and shoulders had been swabbed with alcohol, as it was the only spot on her body not layered with dirt and grime.

"Let her go," Jorah pleaded again, now turning her attention to Vicars. In that moment, McNeal seemed to gain his composure, connecting the final tubes that would send Maria into a deep, painless sleep.

"Jorah, help me," she managed feebly, before the medicine took over.

Vicars shouted,

"Duran! Get her out now, or I swear I'll hang you both."

James jerked forward, hanging the rifle he carried across his back. Jorah had regained her fight, struggling in her effort to get to Maria. James stooped, grabbing her around the waist and slinging her over his shoulder.

"Stop fighting, or they'll make sure you take her place," he whispered harshly as he carried her out of the building, Vicars shouting to "Lock her up!" as they exited.

"They're going to kill her," Jorah growled, punching at his back as he swiftly carried her down the street. She was incredibly light; he could feel each of her ribs poking into his shoulders. All eyes of the crowd had turned toward her. James spotted Evangeline, hand over her mouth in shock.

"There's nothing you can do for her. You're the one in danger now."

He hurried toward their shared home, descending the stairs to the basement and finally putting her down on the unfinished concrete floor. She darted to the small window, craning her neck for a glimpse of the clubhouse.

"The Break is going to happen any minute—hey, wait!"

James had moved toward the stairs, she rushed forward, grasping the front of his coat.

"James," she demanded, "you have to help me."

"I just did."

"They'll kill me for this. They'll put me on the table next week. I'm so stupid, I know, but I just couldn't do nothing," Jorah cried out, and James was surprised to see her deep, blue eyes overflow with tears. "You have to talk to them, to Vicars."

James sighed, running his hand down his face. He wished more than anything for a cigarette right now.

"I'll talk to them; I'll do what I can."

"Thank you."

"But Vicars is going to be angry, really angry. I can't promise you'll get to keep your same deal."

"Then let me go. Just let me leave; they'll never find me."

"I can't do that." *I'm sorry*, he thought. He gripped her hands, trying to pull them from the folds of his coat. His work was not yet finished tonight.

"You can, you can if you come with me."

"I can't do that," he repeated. "Even if I could, I barely know you. I don't trust you."

"You're lying, James. You know me," she pressed, and James would never admit that the longing in her eyes was getting to him. "What is there here for you anyway?"

"Without me, those men are little better than savages. You don't know them; you haven't seen what they will do, to men or women. I can't leave."

Gunshots split the silent air so violently that both James and Jorah jerked away from each other. Jorah turned to the window, gazing out into the darkness.

"We're still alive."

"For now," James huffed, and he finally turned to leave. Despite how much he wanted to walk away, he couldn't, and he paused on the bottom step. "I'll talk to Vicars. We'll work something out. You didn't cause any real harm, hopefully."

"Thank you."

He closed and locked the door behind him, and after a moment to gather himself, he headed out of the house. People were streaming down the street, solemn faces and bowed heads, content to know they had at least another fourteen days to live.

Two bodies lay in the street, though no one stood around to mourn them. The guards were already busy cleaning up the mess, lifting the dead onto carts to bring them to the pit.

"Excellent, incredible work, McNeal," Vicars was saying as James entered the building, the smell of blood and antiseptic immediately stinging his sinuses. "Duran—McNeal's done it."

"Done what, exactly?" James asked carefully, meeting the concerned eyes of Jonas across the room.

"Well, it's going to require a few more tests. Nothing is certain, but it's a start," McNeal explained cryptically, a grin on his face that somehow made him look even more evil.

James looked around him. Blood covered the floor and the subjects, each of their necks still wide open, the skin peeled back and hanging in loose flaps.

"Charles broke, and when it happened, there was a sort of flash in the back of his neck," Jonas explained, taking his time crossing the room to avoid the puddles of blood. James averted his eyes from the splatter painting that was Charles's blood on the wall behind him.

"And the others?" James eyed the shaved skull of Maria, her form so limp.

"Alive," McNeal said, "your girl will be happy to hear. She may actually stand a chance next week."

"She won't be going on the table," James snarled, staring down McNeal. "She has a deal."

"Enough, enough—we will discuss the matter of Miss Jorah Sinclair later—McNeal I want more details. What does this mean for us?"

"The goal of tonight was to see if there would be any visible effect when the subject broke, which, as we've seen, there is. More tests will need to be run, and I will need to further train my assistants, since I'm not able to inspect all three bodies at once at the time of the Break."

"Do you think you can stop it?"

"Maybe. I have some theories now, but nothing I can do without further tests. I'll need a new third for next week, these two here should do fine for a second round. The main issue is training others, considering I can only observe one subject at a time. To only preform one trial a week would take far too long."

"Excellent, tell Conrad anything you need." He clapped his hands together, his expression happier and more manic than James could remember seeing. "Now, I'm off to find my lovely wife. Got a bit of celebrating to do."

McNeal had returned to the body of Charles, his neck splintered apart. His assistants gathered around the others, stitching them slowly back together.

James caught Jonas's eye from across the room. He jutted his chin toward the door, and with a grateful expression, Jonas rushed out after him.

"How is she?" Jonas asked.

"She's fine."

"You're going to talk to Vicars, right? Get him to keep their deal?"

James nodded. "I'll do my best."

"Was that woman part of her old group?"

James paused, kicking himself for not asking. "I didn't ask. I'd assume so. How are you?"

"So-so," Jonas admitted, casting a nervous glance over his shoulder. "It was pretty horrible; I swear McNeal looked like he was enjoying it."

"And when Charles broke?"

"After you left, McNeal finished slicing everyone open. Then him and his assistants each took a body. They had a countdown. We heard the cracks outside at the same time Charles went. It was terrible. With his neck open like that, there was blood everywhere. A bone chip hit me in the face. We all saw the flash, too, like a tiny lightning bolt went off in his head."

"What do you think it is?"

Jonas shrugged. "The most likely explanation is that we've all had tiny bombs implanted in us, rigged to go off randomly on a timer—but you can see that just doesn't make much sense either. Every time McNeal's gone into a corpse's neck, one that didn't break, he never finds anything."

"There's always the chance it's a death ray," James half-joked, looking toward a sky thick with clouds.

"I think it's more and more likely every day," Jonas said seriously. "The first Break coming on the one-year anniversary that it was announced alien life had been discovered? It's too coincidental not to be related." They'd reached the steps of the home, the dark windows looking out at them.

"Where's Jorah?"

"Locked her in the basement."

Jonas cringed. "Good luck with that. I'm going to bed. Tell her I'm sorry about her friend."

27
JORAH'S EARLY REIGN

I woke to the squealing of pigs being slaughtered, rabid, mournful cries that cut through the blistery morning air. *Food for later.* The room was cold, the fire having died sometime in the night. The base of my neck was tight and sore.

I shifted onto my back, my spine rolling with the lumps in the worn couch cushions, and I knew only that I was angry.

"Ready to go?" James asked, sipping from a flask of water, a cigarette clasped in his other hand.

The smoke burned my sinuses, waking me up. I was tempted to ask for one myself.

Outside, Fort Rache was just as it was yesterday, the day before, and the day before. The men leered at me as I passed, James too enraptured in his carton to notice. *Disgusting habit.*

He pulled me aside before we reached the gates, calluses on his hands scraped over my jacket.

"I'm sorry I can't come with you." He was sincere, searching my face. "But this is all I could work out, a few days and you're clear."

"Thank you."

He nodded, patting my shoulder somewhat awkwardly. "Oh, and here, hide it." He slipped a thin black folding knife into my hand. "You'll have your gun back soon."

I had not left the house once the day before, sitting low on the carpeted living room floor, keeping beneath the windowsills. James had been gone most of the day, Jonas occasionally returning, allowing me another chance to edge warily toward the door to answer his knocking.

In the evening, when James returned, bolting the door behind him, he had brought the news of salvation.

"You're safe, Jorah, you still have your deal."

The news had not been as relieving as I had thought it would be, a mere half-breath before my head was plunged back underwater. *Maria.*

"They have work for you, helping to fill in the pit. It will only take a few days and then you're free."

I pulled him into a hug, breathing deeply, the motion more calming and pleasant than I had expected.

"You're going to be okay. We all will be," James had whispered.

As soon as he dropped me off, he vanished, slipping inside the doors of Vicars' home.

"Hurry up, Sinclair." Conrad stood with arms folded against the backdrop of the looming front gates, his rifle looped over broad shoulders. "We haven't got all day."

The pit was not far from the fort, dug into what had once been soft farmland a quarter mile from the gates. It was unmarked, a simple mar gouged into the earth, and if it weren't for the stench, one may be at risk of falling in.

"You didn't have to do this," I said to Tom as he handed a spare bandana to me, the cloth dampened with perfume.

"I wanted to."

Tom, myself and a skinny middle-aged man with a ridiculously upturned nose were the crew to work on the pit today. Conrad stood back near the road, setting himself in a position to where the wind blew toward the pit, bringing him only fresh air.

The stranger began work immediately, driving his shovel into the crisp pile of dirt beside the pit, eager to prove himself worthy to join the ranks of Fort Rache.

"I don't trust Conrad. I wanted to make sure you were okay. Besides, I could use a bit of exercise," Tom continued, his fingers working to help tie the bandana around my head, easing the reek of death and decay.

The pit was deep and wide, an acceptable foundation to what could have been a rather nice swimming pool. It wasn't long before my hands began to blister through my gloves, every scoop of earth added seeming to do less than the last. We worked for three hours before Conrad called a break. Not that he needed one; his ass hadn't left his seat on the street barrier once. *Keeping watch.*

I stalked as far from the pit as my sore legs would carry me, plopping down on the hard, snow-dusted earth. My arms felt like rubber, hands numb and pinched despite heavy gloves. I tried to still my breathing. It wouldn't be long before Conrad ordered us back to work.

None of us saw the woman approaching, not Conrad who had busied himself with a baggie of jerky. Not Tom, who sipped his water, back to the road. Not the stranger, who lay exhausted on the ground as I did.

"Give me all of your supplies, now!" Her voice crackled and dipped, a face full of lines, pockmarks, and sparse hairs. "Now!" Her arms shook, but not her voice. As she aimed the pistol at the back of Conrad's head, his food slipped out of his fingers and into the dirt.

"I swear I'll blow your brains out," she warned as Conrad flinched toward his rifle, which leaned a mere foot away against the barrier.

Tom and the stranger had risen, one taking a half-step toward the scene, the other away.

As for me, I slunk backward, catlike, my body scraping and rolling over the ground, back into the cover of sparse shrubs. The casing of the knife James had given me nudged my hipbones.

The woman had taken Conrad's rifle, slinging it over her

shoulder. "You. Drop your holster, now, and bring me that bag."

I watched as Tom slowly undid his belt, careful not to let his fingers stray toward his weapon. He raised his hands as he stepped toward Conrad's discarded backpack. "Ma'am, you really should leave. You don't know what you're doing."

"Don't threaten me!" she screeched, her gun bouncing with her words, and I relished at the spark of disgust on Conrad's face as her spit splashed his skull.

"No threat, no threat," Tom said, now inching toward her, the backpack dangling off his fingers. "But we have a much bigger group, not far from here. It's not safe for you."

The clump of bushes I hid in was hardly large enough to cover my prone figure. Where it ended, however, dipped down low with the rolls of farmland. If I just kept creeping back, dragging myself over dirt and rocks, I could be long gone before anyone noticed. I would be fast, silent and stealthy, and they would never find me.

I looked back toward the stranger from the fort, the nostrils of his upturned nose flaring in panic, the way his feet shifted. I looked to Conrad, a pistol pinched to the back of his skull, momentarily forgetting my existence.

Run, Jorah, run!

The stranger darted, peeling to the side around the edge of the pit. The woman screamed, her pistol whipping in his direction, blowing Conrad's eardrums apart as she fired again and again over his shoulder.

In the same moment that the man fell, toppling sidelong into the half-filled pit, Conrad's elbow connected with the woman's sternum. I didn't watch her fall, only heard her screams, one last gunshot.

"Sinclair? Where's Sinclair?"

"I don't know—Jorah?"

I rose, stepping out from behind the shrubs, the woman unmoving in the street, Conrad splashed with blood, leering over her. "I'm here."

Conrad nodded, his eyes unfocused, turning back to the body.

Tom, however, his expression knowing, only looked to me with worried eyes. His gaze darted past the shrubs, down the graceful slope of the hill, out to where I could have been free. *Don't judge me for being afraid.*

Inside our home was warm and welcome, candles and lanterns glowing softly. *Our home,* it had begun to feel like that too; me and James and Jonas, in *our* home.

I slipped into the bathroom before they could realize I had arrived, stripping away my clothes, where the stench of death hung like cobwebs. Standing in the bathtub, dousing myself in chilled water from the bucket we kept inside, I rubbed the soap over my nose and mouth until it was all I could smell, all I could taste, the underlying chemical scent burning away everything else.

"There you are. I thought I heard you come in. Had me nervous," Jonas sighed as I padded into the kitchen, dressed in fresh, warm clothes, wringing my hair through a towel.

James crouched by the fire, offering me one of his deep, if not awkward smiles. The flames roared over the hearth.

"Hungry?"

"Starving."

We ate and drank and lay before the fire, James choosing to sit beside me tonight, Jonas curled like a cat in James's usual chair.

The cold had begun to overtake the house, a creeping infestation that inhabited all except the kitchen and living room. Soon we would have to drag mattresses from the rooms, string them along the fireplace, and hope someone woke each night before the fire could die and we would freeze.

I slumped across the couch, thoroughly exhausted, blistered hands balled into fists and curled over my eyes. My hair pulled with gentle tugs as James picked through it, teasing the knots and snarls. My insides felt warm and comfortable, soothed, the tang of cigarette smoke curling through the air. My last thoughts before sleep overcame me were of the rolling hills of farmland, and I knew that I had made the right choice. That I was *home*.

When I woke, the dawn crisp and blue, the house was still warm. It was a heat that seemed to linger in my bones that day, carried with me back to the pit, staying even when my blisters burst and the pus dripped down my fingers.

That night, I curled on the couch again, James coating my hands in cream, as gently as if I were a newborn.

We finished the pit on the third day, Dean replacing Tom, entertaining me as he made devil horns at Watson's back. Tom and Dean came over that evening, bringing with them a small cask of cheap gin. We sipped and laughed, James even taking one small, carefully measured swig from the bottle.

Though my hands had scabbed over and my muscles ached, I spent the next day carefully balanced between work and play. I helped Jonas organize his paperwork, barely thinking of Maria chained below our feet. I laughed as a crust of bread was stolen from James's plate by a silky black-and-white cat. In the evening, Evangeline and I organized the bookshelves in Vicars' office, a task carefully monitored by a guard but nonetheless, calming.

I could still smell the worn pages as I curled on my mattress, newly hauled into the living room, preened with fresh blankets. James lay beside me, unflinching at my touch, breathing softly, calmly, his hands curled beside my cheek, smelling of soap and spices and earth.

That night, for the first time, I thought that maybe one day I could forgive and be forgiven. That I could be washed of my guilt and pain and loss, all of it swept away in the sweet, cool waters of the river. James and Jonas and me, in our little house, on our graying street. And somewhere, out there, Riley and Sana and Geoff. Happy and healthy, in their own little house, on their own quiet street.

28

THE LOST BOYS AND JAMES DURAN

An explosion of noise jolted James awake, sending him lurching to his feet. Jorah was standing too, a crease pressed into her cheek and her hair tousled, but eyes wide and aware. Jonas had sprung awake as well, sleepy-eyed and mouth agape.

James motioned for them to be quiet. Someone was slamming on the front door. James hurried to it. Peering through the peephole, he found the irritated and stressed face of Conrad.

"Duran, open up."

James cracked the door, his pistol concealed behind the panel of wood. "What is it?"

"Vicars needs you, now."

"What's happened?" Despite his mistrust of Conrad, James let the door fall open. Conrad followed him inside as he hurried to pull on his coat and boots.

"It's the spy you sent to the military camp, Torres. Something went wrong; I don't know anything else."

"Should I come too?" Jonas piped in.

Conrad eyed him with obvious dislike. "Vicars only asked for Duran."

James had finished dressing and gestured for Conrad to lead the way. Before he stepped out, however, he turned to Jorah, his words whispered and hasty.

"I'll be back soon. Bolt the doors."

James and Conrad hurried across the snow-brushed street, the community shadowy and noiseless, save for Vicars' home, in which light blazed in every window of the downstairs.

Vicars, along with McNeal and two other men, stood in his office, each wearing a similar dark expression. Vicars gripped his glass of whiskey so tight, his knuckles were white.

"What happened?" James asked as they entered, a growing anxiety pulsing in his chest.

"We don't know. One of the scouts just came back, babbled something about Torres, and dropped dead."

"One of the scouts? Who?"

Vicars waved him off. "Some no-name we assigned to collect the messages from Torres. He had an arrow sticking out of his gut when he pulled up. Poor lad made sure we got the message, though."

"And what's the message?"

"The message is that *you*, Duran, have royally fucked things up."

"You said it yourself. He spat some gibberish about Torres, and then he died. That could mean anything," James argued back, bristling against the aggressive eyes of every man in the room now trained on him.

"The way I see it, there's only a few options as to what it means. Either Torres has gone and betrayed us, or he's fucked everything up in some way that's going to lead the goddamn United States Armed Forces right to our doorstep. Either way, *you* are the one who chose him." The whiskey glass exploded, shards of glass scattering across the room, reflecting off the candlelight.

Vicars cursed, taking a rag that one of the men rushed to give him and gripping it in his hand, blood leaking onto the rug. "Listen, it may not be too late, so you're going to do yourself a favor and go fix this. Conrad, you're going with him."

Vicars slumped down in his desk chair, breathing heavily. "I want Torres dead or extracted, and I want this mess fixed. Turn yourselves in, if that's what it takes. Just fix it."

James was enraged, his fingernails cutting into his palms as he clenched his fists. He had half a mind to tell Vicars to screw himself, to take Jonas and Jorah and leave Fort Rache for good. Though James knew he would never make it past the gate alive, that any action against Vicars was an action against Jonas and Jorah. He knew too that Fort Rache involving themselves with the military camp would likely result in more death than either side could bear.

"I'll fix it," he said, his jaw aching as he spoke from the way he'd clenched his teeth.

"Yes, you will. There's a truck being prepared for you as we speak—and for God's sake, McNeal, come stitch up my hand."

"Pull over." James swung the door to the truck wide, stepping out onto the ice-crusted road. "More blood, we're on the trail."

They found the missing truck not an hour later, the flipped-over wreck careened into a ditch off the side of the road. Conrad stood street side, his arms crossed as James crouched beside the wreckage. "I'd say he had already been shot with the arrow before this, managed to get away, crashed, and walked back."

They climbed back into the truck, the silence awkward yet demanding, angry and tense. The debris of the road had worsened with each passing day, a new detour or stop needed every few miles. A thick, blanketing snow had begun to fall, disguising the road and rubble as the gas gauge ticked lower and lower.

It took much too long to reach the meeting spot, far, far too long. The designated area was tucked away from the road, a few miles from the gates of the military camp. The snow had fallen so deep and thick that it was long before James found Torres's body, frozen and blue.

"Well, that settles that," Conrad sighed. "Pain in the ass of a trip, wasn't it?"

"He's been shot," James observed, "with bullets, not an arrow."

"Strange," Conrad simpered. "Hey, Duran, while I have you

here …"

Snow slipped from the trees with the volley of the gunshot, an earsplitting noise that rocked the clearing. Any echo died shortly after, muffled by snow.

James keeled forward across Torres's body, grasping at the fresh hole just beside his bellybutton, the blood pumping furiously over his gloved hands. They saturated in moments, now useless at stemming the flow.

Conrad leered over James, stowing his pistol, careful to trod on James's outstretched hand. He seemed to be admiring the way the blood seeped into the fresh snow. James could not speak; his side screamed in agony. He could only watch as Conrad spat on his boots. He could only listen to the gentle cascade of snowfall as it began to bury him, hear the roar of the truck's engine firing somewhere far, far away.

29

THE LAST OF JORAH SINCLAIR

Jonas sat with me for the first hour after James left. We waited in silence, nervously anticipating his return. Occasionally I rose to check that the doors were still bolted shut or to peer through the curtains at the darkened street.

It was after one of such times, when I was headed back to my seat in the living room, that I heard the unmistakable sound of someone trying to open the front door.

I stutter-stepped, turning slowly to face the door. The hallway felt as though it had stretched a thousand miles. The doorknob twisted, and the door bumped against the lock.

"Hey, Jorah or Jonas, open the door. They sent me to get you. Duran is bringing you on his mission," came a muffled shout.

Relief flooded through me. I called out to Jonas as I crossed to the entrance, peering through the peephole momentarily. I recognized the man, though I didn't know his name. He stood alone, impatiently waiting on the stoop.

"Come on, you guys need to hurry," he urged irritably.

I unlocked the door, though no sooner had I begun to pull when it was roughly pushed inward. I stumbled away, the man stepping inside as two others appeared from around the sides of the house.

"Sorry, sweetheart, only way to get you to open up." The men with him each had a gun gripped in his hand. They surveyed me with teeth bared in dark grins. "Now come with us, or we're going to go back there and blow a hole in Yeun's head."

I barely had time to think, let alone run, when the first man lunged forward and punched me hard in the stomach. I doubled over, gasping, and he immediately grabbed my hands, twisting them behind my back.

"Let's go," he said to the others, pulling me out of the house roughly, my bare feet slipping on the icy ground.

I had just begun to struggle, intending to kick out at the man nearest when Jonas appeared in the doorway, his coat half-pulled on over his skinny shoulders. "Jorah? Hey! What do you think you're doing?"

"Don't," I gasped, as he made a step toward us. The men laughed as Jonas froze.

"I'd listen to her, kid," said the burliest of the men, who then slammed the front door, Jonas's panicked face snapping out of my view.

They half-carried, half-dragged me down the street. Panic was beginning to flow through my veins, adrenaline drowning out the freezing snow and wind against my skin.

"Where's James?" I demanded. "He's going to be furious when he finds out about this."

One of the men laughed cruelly. "I expect you'll be dead long before he ever finds out this happened."

We reached the community clubhouse, empty windows seeming terribly dark and cold. Down the hallway next, we passed Watson on guard duty. She sneered at me as I was carried by.

"Ought to put a muzzle on that one," she jeered. "She bites."

The door to the basement loomed before me, chipped white paint and a smudged gold doorknob. Down the stairs, passing the other prisoners, on to the second room, my elbow caught on the rough wood as they tossed me inside. My first cell; the thin and tattered blanket still sat where I had left it. The basement was achingly cold, the air stale and reeking of mildew, worse than I remembered it.

"See you later," they teased, the slam of the door extinguishing the only sliver of light in the room.

Black room. Cold walls. No air. Dead Jorah.

I suddenly found myself wishing that I had drowned in the river all those weeks ago.

When Jonas finally came, he told me that it had been three days. He brought food with him, the first I had seen, along with a bottle of water that did not taste of dirt and mold. I ate ravenously, drinking with such vigor that the water flowed over my chin and down my neck, chilling my already frozen chest.

He unzipped his jacket too, pulling off the thick sweater he wore underneath and passing it through the bars. "It's the best I could do," he whispered. "They wouldn't let me bring you a coat."

"Where's James?" My voice was rough and scratchy, soothed only slightly by the fresh downpour of water.

Jonas shook his head. "Nobody knows. He left because there was a problem with the spy that went to the military camp. Him and Conrad went to sort it out. It only should have taken them a day or so."

My voice cracked when I spoke, and I felt tears begin to leak from my eyes. "Jonas, you have to help me, please. Go to Evangeline. We're friends, she'll want to help," I pleaded, and Jonas's face crumpled.

"I tried, Jorah, I really did—McNeal said he caught you stealing medical supplies."

"And Evangeline? She knows I wouldn't."

"I don't know, but Vicars is done. He doesn't care, and McNeal has been keeping me away from him as it is."

"But you have to have some sway. How did you get them to let you come see me?"

He looked uncomfortable, switching from one foot to the other. He spoke quietly, peering over his shoulder. "They're at the top of the stairs, two of McNeal's men, with rifles. I—I'm supposed to ask you some questions."

"Questions?"

He nodded and produced a small crumpled piece of paper from his pocket. "Just a few, how old you are, medical history—that sort of thing."

"Why?"

He bit his lip, and it was then by the dim light of the lantern he had brought that I saw the tears welling up in his eyes. "You know why."

"They're going to use me, to see if I break."

He nodded, and a tear splashed down his cheek. "Jorah, I'm sorry, I can't do anything." He lowered his tone. "I'm trying to find James; others want to help you too. Tom went out looking. He had to go on foot, but he might find him. Ramirez too, he's the chef here. He has a lot of sway, and he's sick of how things are run. Lots of men are on his side."

"It's fine," I forced, my breathing hitched, though at the sight of his expression, I tried to soften my tone. "I know you're doing everything you can."

He nodded shakily, staring down at the paper clutched in his hands. He moved to speak, but I cut him off.

"But you can tell them that they can shove that paper and their questions up their asses. I'm not making the job any easier for McNeal."

Jonas's eyes went wide with fear, and his voice shook as he spoke. "They thought you might say something like that. They told me to tell you that if you won't answer, they're going to start cutting pieces of me off until we match—starting with my fingers."

I froze, disgust and rage filling my body, all quickly extinguished by the horrible and defeated look that plagued Jonas's face. I caved, backing up and sliding down the wall, wrapping my arms around my legs. "Okay, what are the questions?"

Two more days, two more cups of acrid, cloudy water. One can of string beans flung through the bars with such force, it cracked and splattered. One night of Watson's shrieking laughter ringing in my ears.

Jonas returned once more, his eyes swollen. "Conrad came back yesterday. He—he said James is dead."

Words did not come to my lips.

"It's been snowing really heavily; the roads are practically useless. Conrad said that Torres had been long dead by the time they got to the meeting spot. He said on the way back, they had to abandon the truck. The snow was too heavy. A mob of berserkers came at them. He said they got separated, that James was overrun."

"He's a liar."

Jonas shook his head, tears dripping down his splotchy face. "I don't know. Tom hasn't come back either. Conrad's been in medical. He was real torn up."

"And me?"

It seemed that Jonas could not find words either, and neither of us spoke as one of McNeal's guards stepped from around the corner, rifle hefted, his laugh deep and cruel.

The night was long and dark, and the knowledge of what waited for me tomorrow filled my every sense. The darkness, the hunger, they called to me from the stillest corners of the room. I couldn't sleep, could hardly breathe, but I could hear them.

My sister screamed at me from behind the bars. I saw her hands come out of the darkness and reach for me, scrabbling in the air, searching for my throat.

I heard Riley's voice, calling out, telling me that I could not die—we still had unfinished business.

I thought of Musa, his kind eyes, soft voice, telling me not to follow the others out into the world. Pleading with me to stay. I was not at fault; I need not suffer.

I saw the old man's knife slash through the air, felt the sting on the ghost of my fingers.

When they came for me, I was ready, quiet, perched on my knees. My hair hung lank and greasy by the sides of my face; my eyes swollen and tight. Beneath my fingernails sat flakes of skin and dried blood, having been raked across my itching, crusted scalp.

I had been praying, something I hadn't done in years.

They carried me up the stairs, and through the large windows I could see the occupants of the fort gathered in the street, waiting to see who would break. Evangeline, sultry and poised—and Dean, standing without his father in a crowd of unknowns.

Into the lobby, Vicars and McNeal at the ready, surveying the preparations in front of them. Vicars spared me hardly a second glance. Jonas stood in the corner of the room, clutching his clipboard to his chest, his face red and swollen, the same guard that had escorted him last night standing beside him.

They forced me belly-down onto the middle table. To my right lay the man who had been captured the same day as me. He looked thin and sickly, his eyes closed and his cheek pressed to the table. To my left was Maria.

Her eyes were large and brown and scared—the same way that I had always seen them.

"Jorah," she whispered, her voice raspy, yet to my shock, the ghost of a smile traced her lips. "I'm going to see Manuel again."

I had to look away, and no sooner had I when my head was roughly forced down, my forehead pressed against the cold metal table. They affixed straps until I could hardly move, restraining my limbs, head, and shoulders.

I could see nothing aside from the table, the gray surface blurred from closeness. It would be over soon, once the anesthesia took hold, and I would sleep. I closed my eyes, imagining myself floating down the river, all the way to the ocean.

I heard the breaths still as the man beside me was put out, and then Maria, who had gone completely silent after those few words. Someone asked if they should shave my head but was quickly told there was no time—I found myself thankful for the sliver of dignity.

I felt the presence of someone beside me then, and I knew it was time. I could feel their breath on the side of the neck, expecting at any moment to feel the prick of a needle.

"You didn't really think that I'd let you sleep through this, did you?" McNeal whispered in my ear. "It's so much more fun this way. I wish Duran was alive, so he could find out."

Panic exploded through me at his words, like I'd been plunged into icy water during a deep sleep. I pulled against my restraints, wondering why I hadn't fought, why I hadn't screamed as I let them carry me. I flexed against the bonds, my struggle draining and fruitless.

"Let go of me!" Jonas's voice ripped through the tent. There was the loud smack of flesh hitting flesh and a gasp of pain. "Jorah!"

They made me listen while they sliced into the man and Maria, though they would feel nothing of it. One of McNeal's assistants counted down the minutes, closer and closer.

And then it was a blade, slicing through my skin like butter. I screamed, my own hot blood running down the sides of my neck. It filled my ears, flowed over the table, and splattered onto the floor.

Red blood. Gray table. Red blood. Gray table.

It was agony. Every muscle in my body tensed against my bindings. I thought I could hear my own tendons snapping.

Red blood. Red blood. Red blood. Red blood. Red blood.

There was another noise too, a new horror in my ear, and I realized it was McNeal, humming a tune to himself while he worked. The metal tools dug into my flesh, beyond the first flaps of skin, scraping bone, slicing veins.

Then there came the crack, deafening, earth-shattering—I heard it in every cell in my body.

I am nothing, I was nothing, and I have never been anything. I knew my head was going to explode, and I begged anybody's God to let it happen.

Somebody was screaming, and I don't know if it was me, but I just wanted it to stop so I could sleep.

Red blood. Dead Jorah.

30

SANA OF SWORD AND STONE

Sixteen Days Later

My muscles ached and burned, so tight under my skin, it felt as though any wrong movement would snap them, sending them coiling around my feet like cut rope. My skin pained me as well, dark purpled bruises on russet flesh, the occasional bloody scrape to match.

I forced myself to stand, joints cracking, feeling as though I'd aged four decades overnight. Light poured through the open flap of the tent, illuminating my sparse belongings, the bed-mat and heavy blankets taking most of the room, my backpack stealing the rest.

The sound of the horn blasted again, and it jolted me from my stupor, I rushed to lace my boots before stuffing my hair into my hat. I still was not used to my hair, even though it had been nearly three weeks since I cut it, turning the heavy strands that once reached my lower back into a short bob that barely touched my shoulders.

It was safer that way, cleaner and easier to maintain—I wondered why I hadn't done it sooner.

Outside the tent, the light was blinding. It crept up over the horizon, taunting us with rays that gave no warmth. Close to fifty tents fell into view. They weren't matching, as one might expect from a military campsite, but varied in color and size so drastically, I sometimes felt as though I was looking out over the campgrounds of a music festival.

"Mangal, present," I shouted, working to align my stiff spine. I brought my hand up in a curt salute.

Corporal Lucy Moore marched down the row that had formed before her, taking a moment to survey each in turn before she crossed to stand in front of us. Moore hadn't been a corporal for long, in fact just two weeks before she'd stood next to me in line, her tent beside my own.

That was before we lost all our previous corporals during the last two Breaks. They'd taken her directly from our group on return from a supply run, and when we saw her next, she wore her new uniform and badges, her eyes darkened by information she'd only just learned.

When I arrived, there were sixty members of the military present—mostly new recruits and trainees, though now we numbered forty-three. The civilians were dropping like flies as well. Many chose to leave, once it started to become apparent we were running out of food. Others had simply wasted away in their tents. Many had broken as well.

"Orders are simple today, so let's try to get this right. McLaughlin, you and your squadron are headed to Greenland Heights, the retirement community, I know it's a bit far, but it's large and in a secluded neighborhood, so you should have some luck. Winchester, it's your turn for cleanup duty. I've already been told there's bodies in tents thirty-four and forty-one." Moore spoke with the voice of someone who had only recently come into power, her speech strong and influential, though occasionally her commands came across more as suggestions.

She glanced down at her clipboard for only a moment, a strand of curly black hair escaping her cap. "Lastly: Mangal, Polkowski, and Muir—with me. Anyone left, go see Sergeant Black. He has jobs for you. Dismissed."

Everyone scattered; it had long been ingrained into the minds of every solider at Camp Prevail that time was of the essence. I started toward Corporal Moore, who stood waiting for us, her foot tapping impatiently. The three of us gathered around her, and she nodded briefly, gesturing for us to follow her. We headed toward the high school, one of the only buildings in camp, small and built from weathered brick. Water damage had made the top two floors uninhabitable, which led to the tent city that covered the surrounding parking lot, dotted with repurposed school buses for further shelter.

The bottom floor of the high school, which consisted of the cafeteria, administration offices, and a handful of classrooms, was strictly off-limits to all except for the higher-ups and the desperately ill. Although with the weather growing steadily worse, the possibility of disbanding the critical care unit in the cafeteria and turning it into a shelter had grown in popularity.

I felt the eyes of civilians on us as we walked, hollow-cheeked kids and, if they were lucky, a relative peeking out from the flaps of their tents. The adults were often even more decrepit than the children. It was well known in Camp Prevail that management was hanging on by a thread, the last identified eastern branch of the US Armed Forces limping along on their only leg. Medical supplies were scarce, food was a luxury—and the power and authority of the army fell more along the lines of Boy Scouts than legitimated federal forces.

"What do you think this is about?" came the whisper next to me, and I looked up into the face that still, after a month, I often found myself surprised to see again.

I shrugged in reply.

"I'd bet we're getting promoted," Lachlan continued, his large form bumping my arm. "Coolidge and Myles never came back last week, and they still haven't been replaced."

I didn't answer, though I felt a spark of excitement at that being the outcome of this walk.

We passed through the doors of the high school, Moore giving a curt nod to the two guards stationed. They returned the gesture, their eyes unblinking as their gaze traveled far and wide into the crowded parking lot beyond.

Inside was dim, with limited windows in the hallways. A smattering of unlit candles covered the edges of the floor, to be used only in the darkest of times. I had been inside the building only once before, on the first day that we arrived at Camp Prevail, starving and battered.

"This way." Corporal Moore held open a door for us, and we slid past her. The desks that had once covered the room had been pushed to the sides, leaving the center clear except for a graffitied plaster table and chairs.

Corporal Moore was by no means a stern-appearing woman. She was young and rather pretty, her face shadowed beneath her cap in the now slightly brighter classroom. Her chocolate complexion was flawless, and I thought sometimes that her eyelashes might brush her cheeks. She was sharp, though the brevity of her training meant that in the old world, she would no more be a corporal than I would be a bird.

"You've all been called here today because you are receiving a promotion of sorts," she began.

I glanced past Polkowski to Lachlan, who winked as he caught my eye, sending my gaze scurrying back to Moore. Lachlan had been forced to take a pair of scissors to his once-bushy beard and flowing red locks upon joining the military forces of Camp Prevail. He looked thinner and older without his hair, but no less intimidating. The soldiers of the camp may be starving, ill-equipped, and under-trained, but damn if they didn't look the part.

"As you all know, a month ago, we placed a spy within the compound known as Fort Rache, approximately forty miles southeast of here. Our scouts had told us Fort Rache was growing in power and numbers, leaving command to deduce that it may be wise to have someone on the inside."

The existence of Fort Rache was common knowledge throughout most of camp, with a small number of our own believed to have deserted in favor of the other compound. As far as we knew, Camp Prevail and Fort Rache were the only strongholds for three hundred miles in any direction.

"According to our spy, the fort consists of approximately one hundred occupants. The vast majority are men, and a large portion of that Neanderthals at best. The administration of the fort has left us with very few options for interaction between us. Fort Rache has a supply of food vastly superior to our own and medical supplies to rival our stock. Their weaponry and ammunition supplies are vast as well, and we believe they have two doctors." She paused, rifling through a cream-colored folder and extracting a small Polaroid photo, which she slid across the table.

The photo showed the portrait of a large man with a mop of curly black hair which had been ineffectively slicked back into a bun. He had bushy eyebrows and large, almond-shaped brown eyes.

"This is Adrian Ramirez," Moore explained. "Polkowski, I believe you were the only one who was actually here when Ramirez was. He's been stationed in Fort Rache as our spy for just over two months. In that time, he's managed to secure himself the position as the head chef of the fort. He has been an invaluable asset." She removed two more photos from the envelope and placed them beside Ramirez's.

"This is Maximilian Vicars," she said, and the photo she gestured to showed a distant, slightly blurry shot of a stout man, thick-armed and chest barrel wide. "Vicars is the leader of Fort

Rache." She rifled through the folder, fetching out a new stack of papers. "He emigrated from Turkey when he was twenty-three, after an injury put an end to his semi-professional wrestling career. Married five times with six children from four different women, all believed to have not been living with him at the time of the first Break. He narrowly avoided prison for racketeering as well as assault during his forties, clean otherwise."

The third Polaroid showed a slightly clearer picture of a younger man. He was tall, broad and handsome, with buzzed hair and dark, brooding eyes.

"I should add that much of this information is relative; it is material that we have pieced together through communication with Ramirez as well as from our limited database. This is James Duran, thirty, born and raised in upstate New York. He had a brief stint in the army, though he never saw battle and was discharged after four years." She paused, scanning the papers. "He ran a moderately successful construction company after that. Was arrested but not charged for assault when he was twenty-seven, no other crimes, never married. Duran is second in command at Fort Rache, though according to Ramirez, he is drastically more favorable to our cause as a leader than Vicars."

I picked up the picture of Vicars, holding it closely as I tried to gain a better understanding of his appearance, his face blurry in the long-distance shot. Moore waited until I had returned the photo to the table before speaking.

"It has been over two weeks since our last communication with Ramirez, normally, this would not be huge cause for concern, However, considering our last contact with him, the command of camp has decided it's time for an intervention.

During the last rendezvous, Ramirez informed us that Fort Rache had begun to use their own methods of looking for a cure to the breaking."

I felt my eyebrows raise in surprise; we had heard very little regarding Camp Prevail's attempts to find a solution. I found it hard to believe a backwater community such as Fort Rache could do any better.

Moore continued, "In addition, Ramirez hinted that the tides had begun to turn in Fort Rache, much his own doing, in persuading the population to move toward a new leader. This information, combined with the lack of further response from Ramirez and," she hesitated, "*deteriorating* conditions here mean command thinks it's time for action."

She stopped speaking then, motioning that now we could ask questions.

"Is command looking to combine forces or take them over?" Lachlan asked. He sat forward eagerly in his chair, his huge form practically spilling over the edges.

"If what we heard from Ramirez is true, and the fort really is looking for new leaders, then the cleanest course of action would be to make contact and establish a friendship—once the new command has taken control of the fort, that is."

"And if not?" I pushed. Moore had begun to look slightly uncomfortable as the conversation progressed, occasionally looking toward the door as if she expected someone higher in command to enter.

Finally, she sighed, and with a surprising air of defeat, pulled up a chair and folded into it. "Camp Prevail doesn't have the resources or the numbers to win that fight, should it come to it. We either make friends with the fort or hope they don't discover our weakness."

We sat in silence for a moment, absorbing the news, before I asked the question that had bothered me for weeks.

"And what about finding a way to stop the Breaks? Has anyone figured something out yet?"

"I don't know much about that, but listen, you're all going to be promoted to corporal," she scowled, "not that it means a damn thing anymore. Sergeant Black told me they'll have news for us on the matter soon. I don't know what it means, but you should get some answers. We just need to focus on the task at hand for now."

"And what is the task? The plan, exactly?" Lachlan asked.

"We're going to Fort Rache. If Ramirez won't bring his information to us, we'll go to him. From there, we judge the environment, extract Ramirez if necessary, leave him there if possible. No matter what, however, we won't be making communication with anyone else there just yet, not until we can report back on the situation."

The army-green truck sat concealed deep in the bushes just off the side of the interstate. We thought it best to go in on foot from there, no doubt a less conspicuous way to travel. Polkowski remained behind, a walkie-talkie clutched in his hand, Moore carrying the other. While Camp Prevail may be starving, there was no shortage of equipment. Military safeguards and resources had provided several still-working electronics that had been saved from the initial EMP. Radios, flashlights, and the heavily armored trucks to name a few. All closely guarded and distributed only when necessary.

We'd dressed in civilian clothes for the journey, layers of sweatshirts, jeans, and thick work boots as defense against the cold, much less conspicuous than our previous uniforms. I was glad for the change, more comfortable in these garments than the tight and starchy uniform.

Everything at Camp Prevail was hand-me-down unless you had gone out and scavenged it yourself, and even then, stores weren't exactly producing anymore. Every uniform given to new recruits had been taken from a soldier who had died. I recalled the last Break, in which orders had gone out for all soldiers to remove their uniforms prior to the Break. Though it was not stated, everyone knew this was so they could be re used should you die.

We traveled on the road up until a half mile from the gates of Fort Rache, our senses primed to catch anything that may approach. The snow of the previous weeks had cleared from the roads somewhat, blown by harsh winds into towering drifts. Ice crunched and crackled under our feet as we turned to sneaking through the woods.

We had taken our time before leaving camp and stopped to scavenge several houses on the way, meaning that a dim evening was just beginning to creep over the horizon as we neared the gates of the fort. Moore signaled to us to keep low, though even at a full crouch, Lachlan was at my standing height.

We'd discussed our approach to the fort at length during the journey. We had been informed of the presence of a large debris pile, located just beyond the rear walls of the compound. It was in this spot, so we had been told, that you could effectively spy on the goings-on of the camp, invisible to the guard posts on either side.

We took our time edging through the woods surrounding the fort. Silently, I commended whoever had chosen this location. The community sat at the end of the road, surrounded mostly by woods, a private sanctuary.

We reached the debris pile, a staggering mound of broken furniture and materials, haphazardly tossed just beyond the walls. It was quiet inside the camp, except for the occasional bark of indistinguishable words.

"Now, the hard part," Moore said, peering around the pile toward the walls.

The fortifications of Fort Rache were tall, though not unclimbable. They appeared to be a combination of the community's original iron-worked bars, intricate and moderately useless, and the newer addition of heavy plates. The back section differed from the rest, however, the panels varying and farther apart, as though they had run out of material just at the end.

"Remember, across the field, past the gallows, in the backyard of the first brick house," Moore said, her gaze intent on Lachlan as she repeated the directions given to her by Command. I found my gaze drawn to the sturdy, rough-paneled walls of Fort Rache, wondering what sort of community this had to be to have erected gallows.

"I know, don't be seen, don't be caught, find Ramirez," Lachlan replied in a teasing, almost bored tone. "I haven't forgotten."

Lachlan had struggled with addressing authority since the moment he'd signed up as a recruit. Normally, his sarcasm would have earned a scathing reprimand, though now Moore was much too preoccupied with the task at hand.

"I still think it should be me," I maintained, seeing my opportunity to get my last argument in. "Lachlan's too big, they'll notice him." Polkowski would have been the best option, his shorter stature significantly less obvious or threatening than Lachlan, but he had once been involved with a few men now known to be in this camp; too much risk he would be recognized.

As for Moore and me, information had long been repeated from Ramirez that Fort Rache was a less-than-hospitable place for women. Either of us walking in there would be like throwing a bone to a pack of ravenous dogs. While this made sense for Moore, who was tall and curvaceous, I felt that with my new short hair and baggy clothes, I could easily blend in long enough to retrieve Ramirez.

"Aye, but I bet half the arrogant pricks in this camp don't know what their own neighbors look like." Lachlan stepped back, puffing out his chest, his voice lowered to a deep, surprisingly aggressive tone. "Who am I? Who the hell are you? I've been here longer than half of you, now get the hell out of my way," Lachlan snarled before relaxing again. "See? Won't be hard, I've got this."

It took Lachlan a moment to find a slice of wall with enough room in the slats in which to climb, though he had only taken one step when I heard the unmistakable sound of a stick cracking behind us. I whirled around, pulling my pistol from my waist, though I was met with only the view of the darkening, shadow-cast trees.

I signaled to Moore that I was going to take a closer look. She reluctantly agreed, taking my place to watch over Lachlan as he climbed. I edged through the trees, uncertainty filling me as I distanced myself from the others. I saw the flicker of movement mere moments before I would have turned around. The pale flesh darting through the trees; surprisingly silent, bone-chillingly lithe. I crept forward, knowing what I would find, though needing to be certain.

In a clearing, just ahead, faintly illuminated by the moon that had only just appeared were two freaks. They were mangled, each more disfigured than I could remember seeing a freak before, and I wondered if they had done it to themselves. The female freak stood in place, jaw sagging and body still except for the repeated *crack* as she bounced her forehead off the trunk of a tree. The other, once a male teenager, half-crawled and half-rolled across the forest floor.

I backed up as quickly and silently as possible, scared to take my eyes off the monsters but more afraid I would stumble.

"Come on, we need to move," I whispered in Moore's ear, lightly pulling on the sleeve of her jacket. "Freaks." I jerked my head back toward the clearing.

"There's nowhere to go; we hold our ground," she said, her eyes trained on Lachlan, who was in the midst of heaving himself over the topmost point of the wall.

Laughter, high pitched and insane, erupted from the darkness behind us. Moore jerked upright, whiplashing her neck as she turned to investigate the woods, and, seeming to change her mind in an instant, whispered, "Go now, follow Lachlan."

We darted from behind our cover toward the wall, crouching in the shadows as Lachlan dropped down to the other side. He pressed himself against the slats, keeping his back toward us as he kept watch around him.

"What's wrong?" he hissed.

"Freaks," Moore said, then turning to me, "How many?"

"Two."

"Their condition?"

"Mangled but active." We could hear them moving in the trees, just beyond our vision.

She nodded, debating for only a moment. "We're going over." She crouched down, folding her hands together. I stepped in her palm and with a heave, she boosted me upward, my fingers just able to grasp the edge of the wall.

I gasped for air as I landed on the other side, still not recovered from the months starving on the road. I'd begun to suspect that my lungs had never fully healed from when I was sick. Moore, on the other hand, had been in Camp Prevail since nearly the start and was significantly more fit. She landed with hardly a sound, catlike and unflustered.

The three of us darted toward a shadowy patch of shrubs, crouching amid the thorns. I watched as firelight began to flicker into being within the fort, the wall of black, cold night steadily descending upon us.

"We couldn't risk having to fight those freaks; too much

noise," Moore whispered, "Lachlan, go, we'll wait here."

Lachlan had no sooner stood, when with a rush of fear, I caught his arm and jerked him back down.

"Look," I hissed, gesturing through our cover of leaves to the torchlight that had just appeared around the corner of the nearest house.

With increasing anxiety, the three of us pressed ourselves further into the bushes as a stream of people flowed into the field before us. For a horrible instant, I was sure we had been caught, but the group turned, moving toward the center of the field. Several men carried the torches, and they spread out in a wide circle. Light shone onto the before barely visible gallows, the knotted wood and hanging ropes casting an eerie shadow on the trees behind it. Tall torches had been stuck into the ground at intervals surrounding the gallows, which the men now lit, creating a circle of fire with only one entrance.

"With our luck, they're about to execute Ramirez," Lachlan quipped, which seemed a very morbid joke for his usual good-hearted nature.

Four figures broke away from the group, climbing a short set of stairs to the small platform of the gallows, the three rope-necklaces dancing slowly in the wind.

"That's Duran!" I exclaimed, "James Duran, in the middle." I recognized the sizable man immediately from the Polaroid. James, along with another man, each grasped the arms of a captive, leading them to climb onto small stools placed just below the swinging ropes. They draped a noose over each in turn, leaving a single hanging rope unused between them. James stepped away, to the middle of the stage, his accomplice climbing back down to the crowd.

James stood straight and stiff on the stage, his posture uncomfortable, yet powerful in appearance. The first prisoner, a man, stood with his hands bound, and I could see the shakes that wracked his body. He was small and slight and certainly did not fit the profile of Vicars or Ramirez.

The figure next to him, I realized with a hint of surprise, was a woman.

"We should go now and find Ramirez while they're distracted," Lachlan said, but Moore shook her head.

"I can see him, in the crowd."

I edged around the thistles before me, and after a moment of squinting, was able to pick out the form that most closely resembled Ramirez standing in the back of the group.

"I count fifty people," I said. "This can't be the entire town. We should wait until they leave."

Until now, all we had been able to hear was the distant muttering of the crowd, unintelligible and wandering, though now a new voice drifted across the field, strong and unwavering.

"Tonight, as the residents of Fort Rache, you all stand witness to the answering of crimes that have affected us all," James Duran announced, his deep voice bringing a hush to the gathered crowd. He spoke with power, his speech steady, angry—almost as though he had been personally offended by those behind him. *Maybe he has.*

"Looks like we may be in luck," Lachlan said with grin.

"… and Marla Watson, you stand accused of theft from Fort Rache and its people. You stand accused of murder. Do you deny these charges?"

We couldn't hear their answers, but a resounding roar of jeers and shouts rose up. Marla Watson slumped where she stood, the noose pulling on her throat, her entire body shaking with sobs. Her male companion stood still, stoic, staring into the darkness.

James Duran turned then, once the shouts had died down. He faced the first man, whose name we never heard, and with one powerful motion, kicked the stool out from under him. Marla Watson hanged next; we could hear the snap from across the field, luckier than the man, who kicked and jerked for longer than I thought possible.

I looked away, feeling sick. I released my cramped legs from their crouch, settling down on the hard dirt, my back to the gallows.

Lachlan shot me a concerned look, though it was Moore who spoke.

"They're leaving. As soon as they're clear, go find Ramirez. We'll wait here."

Lachlan nodded, his eyes trained on me, and I forced myself to ignore him. I couldn't understand why I felt so ill—I had seen bodies before, hundreds of them, no more or less broken-necked than those now swinging in the background.

We sat in silence awhile, listening to the footsteps and low chatter as the group disbanded.

"They cut them down," Lachlan said, nudging my arm.

I sighed, not wishing to be labeled as weak, and peered back over the hedge.

It felt as though my heart had exploded in my chest.

She didn't look the same, standing there next to him, watching as the bodies were rolled away, piled into a wheelbarrow. That's not to say that she wasn't recognizable—still tall and slim, still so stunning in her strange, ethereal way.

Still Jorah. With her white-blonde hair and eyes that could be their own ocean.

"Is that …" Lachlan began, his words ending as his mouth drooped open.

I nodded; all the feeling had flooded out of my limbs. I no longer felt the cold, only shock and disbelief.

That can't be her. Jorah is dead, I told myself, but the longer I looked, the more I knew that I had been wrong. We had all been wrong. That Jorah had never been dead, because she was here, as beautiful and terrible as she had always been.

Though still … different.

"What's happening? Do you know her?" Moore asked in a hiss. I ignored her; my eyes focused on the form of my friend. After a moment's hesitation, Lachlan ducked down, quickly explaining to Moore.

I couldn't hear what they were saying. Jorah and James Duran stood on the gallows stage amid the ring of torches, deep in conversation. My eyes raked over Jorah, taking in her every feature, trying to discover what made her so different from before. Trying to explain the creeping feeling of dread that pooled in my stomach like thick mud.

She looked healthier, or at the very least, like she was no longer starving. Her skin was less dry and irregular; those weeks on the road had left us all with skin like patchwork. She was dressed better too, in ripped jeans layered over leggings and a form-fitting black jacket.

She had a revolver and a long, gleaming hunting knife strapped to a belt worn loosely around her waist.

A man appeared beside them suddenly, startling me, as I had not noticed his approach. His voice carried across the now nearly empty field.

"What do you want done with the others?" the man asked, and his question, to my surprise, was directed not to James, but to Jorah.

I couldn't hear her answer, but the man nodded and hurried away. Jorah turned back to James, and as she did, I realized the difference, the dread in my gut now boiling.

It was her eyes.

I could see, even from across the field, that they had changed. Not in their size, shape, or color, but their depth. Like something dark and terrible had grown behind them. Instantly, I found myself standing on the road, weeks ago after we had been banished from Musa's home, watching Jorah as she aimed her gun at Riley in a fit of rage. Her eyes had looked similar then, dark and dead and cruel.

I felt nauseated, crouching back down behind the bush.

Lachlan's curious green eyes peered back at me. "Well? I say we should go over there right now."

"Absolutely not," Moore spat, "that's an order."

"Jorah won't hurt us; she was with Sana for months. This is probably the best thing we could have found here," Lachlan argued, looking to me, searching for my agreement, his face falling when he found none.

"I don't think James Duran is in charge," I whispered, barely believing it myself. "I think Jorah is."

"So? That should be good—not to mention she's alive. You said you found her body?"

I shook my head, not feeling like delving into the story. I turned to Moore, whose expression was of deep annoyance and questioning.

"She's my friend," I told her, though the word felt foreign. For surely, we *were* friends, but I felt in my core that it may be different now. "She's good, but I don't know if we should reveal ourselves, not like this." I trailed off, searching for the best way to explain, unable to find it.

"I just haven't seen her in a long time."

Moore gazed back, her expression wrought with stress. "If you, as her friend, don't think it's a good idea, then we *absolutely* aren't doing it." She leaned forward, peering beyond the bush. "They're leaving. As soon as they're clear, *I'm* going to find Ramirez."

Lachlan opened his mouth in protest, but Moore swiftly cut him off. "You said it yourself; she knows you. It's too risky, I'm going, and then we can get the hell out of here."

319

It was midnight when we arrived at the gates of Camp Prevail, the spotlight nearly blinding us as the guards turned on the beams. We were ushered inside, the truck squeaking to a stop, and we clambered out.

Moore, who had barely spoken a word the entire trip home, clutched the packet of papers in her hands, the only thing we had brought back from Fort Rache.

"Polkowski, you're free to go. Muir and Mangal, go get cleaned up. Meet in the same classroom as before in ten minutes," she ordered, taking off toward the schoolhouse.

Lachlan, Polkowski, and I hurried in silence back to our tents, each of us covered in a splattering of rancid blood and innards. Polkowski headed inside his tent without a word, and I wasn't sure if he was glad or annoyed to be left out of whatever came next.

Lachlan sighed, running a hand down his face. "Interesting trip, huh? See you soon." He disappeared inside his own tent.

I stripped out of my clothes outside, the icy air biting my bare skin, but it was better than filling my tent with freak guts. We'd nearly made it back to the car, Moore silent and angry, clutching the papers Ramirez had given her, when the freaks finally caught up.

I kept a small bucket of water beside my tent for cleaning, and though it was a dull gray and ice cold, it felt wonderful to scrub the dried blood from my skin. I quickly donned my uniform, thankful that it was clean, and combed my fingers through my short mop of hair.

When I had finished, I hurried out of the row of tents, not waiting for Lachlan, who I could hear rustling around in his own. Instead of going to the high school, however, I turned sharply down the next row. At the end sat a large blue tent, set in the dead grass along the pavement. The one with two brightly colored lawn chairs sitting in front and a pink plastic flamingo jammed into the dirt.

They were still awake, though I wasn't surprised, sipping from the flask of fermented apple juice that Riley was so careful to keep hidden. Alcohol was banned from Camp Prevail—not that many people had any or could even stomach it nowadays.

"Sana!" Geoff cheered, shooting me a wide grin from his position in his chair. Riley, however, merely scowled. He fished around in his pocket and procured a tiny, wrapped-up portion of a candy bar, which he dropped into Geoff's outstretched palm.

"Betting on me to die again?" I asked, not at all surprised but marginally disappointed.

"Not betting; we just take turns on each position every time you go out." Riley explained. "It's more of a gamble."

"So, sounds like you've just been swapping what's left of that candy bar for weeks then, since I'm not dead yet."

"A few other things too," Geoff said indignantly, biting off a tiny corner of the chocolate before lovingly wrapping the remaining fragments back up.

Riley held out his flask to me, but I shook my head, and with a brief eye roll, he handed the flask to Geoff instead. "What merits a visit so late this evening?"

My mouth felt dry, momentarily having forgotten why I'd

come to see them. Unable to find a good way to phrase my news, the words tumbled out. "Jorah's alive."

Riley jerked so violently in his chair that he kicked the plastic flamingo, sending it soaring across the parking lot, where it clattered away over the asphalt, just as Geoff began choking aggressively on his swig of hooch.

"You're lying," Riley snarled as he composed himself, and I was surprised by the anguish in his voice.

I shook my head. "She's alive, and there's more …" I trailed off, glancing around at the nearest patrol of guards three rows away. "I think she's the leader of Fort Rache, or at least a co-leader."

"How?" Riley asked incredulously, jumping to his feet and scraping his nails over his scalp. "They were the ones we thought killed her."

"I don't know, I didn't talk to her." I spoke quickly, my voice hushed, filling them in on the details of the day.

"Well, what are we waiting for? Let's go see her," Geoff said as soon as I was finished talking.

"We can't just go see her," I explained. "Like I said, she seems different."

"But you didn't even talk to her," Geoff objected.

"I know, but—"

"It's *Jorah*. We'd all be dead without her," he argued, looking imploringly between Riley and me.

"And she probably thinks we left her for dead," Riley said,

speaking the words that had been rattling around in my mind since I saw her. "Hell, I would, if I was her. She saw us in the woods ... and we left her."

"We didn't have a choice," I argued. It was the same conversation, the same excuses that we had told each other weeks before.

We didn't have any options.

We couldn't save her.

She was as good as dead.

"We *had* a choice," Riley said darkly, "and we made it."

We all fell silent for a moment, even Geoff, whose eyes cast downward onto the shadowy ground beneath us.

"But her body ... in the house," I whispered. My eyes stung at the thought, the memories of the scene and the horror of the days afterward. We'd seen the smoke of the cottage burning in the distance, nothing but cinders and rubble when we'd finally made it back.

The burnt-out corpse lying in the wreckage, roughly her size. Her red bandana crushed into the mud.

Riley shook his head roughly, as if trying to rid himself of the same memories. "It wasn't her; that's all there is to it."

I jerked abruptly, coming out of my stupor. "I have to go. I'll come see you guys tomorrow." I'd nearly forgotten about my ten-minute deadline, which must be swiftly approaching, if not already passed.

They bade me good night as I turned to go, each with their

own glazed eyes and faraway expressions, wondering about Jorah, just as I had been all day. All month, really.

Moore cast me an annoyed expression as I hurried into the room, slightly out of breath and rushing into my seat. It was an embarrassing entrance, seeing as Sergeant Black and Master Sergeant Carrigan were both present, dressed in their pressed uniforms and waiting patiently.

"Private Mangal, nice of you to join us," Master Sergeant Carrigan jibed, spreading his arms in welcome.

"Sorry, sir, it took longer to get clean than I expected."

"No matter, nothing has gone as we expected lately."

The master sergeant was an older man, his hair growing steadily white, it settled in thick waves atop his head. He was tall as well and sturdy—the only Master Sergeant of the entire United States Armed Forces confirmed living. Maybe the only one in the world, for all we knew.

He continued to speak, his face and the room illuminated in the shimmering light of the candles spread throughout. I could just make out the classroom posters in the gloom—overall, a less-than-professional environment for a classified meeting.

"We're here to discuss your recent findings at Fort Rache. On behalf of Sergeant Black and myself, we'd like to offer our congratulations for a job well done. Corporal Moore has already filled us in on the situation, but I would like to hear your take on it."

I swallowed, composing myself before answering. I filled

him in on what I felt about the encounter, including my doubt at my current relationship with Jorah.

"And when was the last time you saw her?" he asked as I finished, his surprisingly kind brown eyes trained on me.

"Over a month ago," I replied. He nodded, thanking me for my information.

He spoke with Lachlan next, Lachlan's description taking much less time, as he had only known Jorah for a matter of days.

"—and then I found Sana here, and Geoff and Riley, and they told me Jorah was dead," Lachlan finished.

Master Sergeant Carrigan nodded before turning to Sergeant Black. "Sergeant, if you wouldn't mind, please go and see if research is finished."

Sergeant Black nodded and exited.

Carrigan, who had until now paced the room, pulled out a seat at the small table. "I hope you understand that this could be incredible news for Camp Prevail and its people," he stated, looking between Lachlan, Moore, and me with a pleased expression. "The fact that our rival community, the one that holds our fate nearly as much as the Breaks do, now has a leader that our own most promising recruits already have a relationship with—immeasurably valuable."

I was tempted to interrupt him, to once again repeat my nerves over the entire situation, but he continued.

"Of course, however, we still have work to do to ensure a *mutually beneficial* relationship with Fort Rache, so we need to know everything you know about this Jorah. Corporal Moore has already filled us in on the few details you told her, and Sergeant Black is currently retrieving even more helpful data." He paused, once again spreading his hands in a welcoming, friendly position. "But still, everything helps."

Corporal Moore pulled out a pad of paper, clicking a pen and taking notes while Lachlan and I answered Carrigan's questions as best we could.

"How old is Jorah Sinclair?"

"Twenty-three, I believe—almost twenty-four."

"Where is she from?"

"Pennsylvania. She moved to this area shortly before the first Break," I answered after a few moments of recollection.

"Her family?"

I paused, the story of Jorah's dead, cancer-stricken sister coming to mind. "Dead. I believe they were all dead before the Break."

Master Sergeant Carrigan nodded in apparent sympathy, his questions continuing until, at last, a young and somewhat sweaty man burst into the room.

"Here, Master Sergeant, it's everything we could find."

"Thank you," Carrigan said, taking a small stack of papers that was handed to him.

I eyed the papers, confused and curious. I wondered what data they possibly could have found, what with no computers or internet access.

Carrigan placed the papers in front of us. Sergeant Black had returned as well, and the five of us sat around the table closely.

"Private Muir and Private Mangal, if not already apparent, you have both been promoted to Corporal. I am sure that you will maintain honor within this title." He shuffled the papers before him, as if anxious to read them. "Before the Break, there were many servers capable of storing information as it was uploaded to the World Wide Web. Here, we happen to be in possession of one of the very last of these data banks. The way it was stored allowed it to survive the EMPs of five months ago."

"You can access the internet?" Lachlan asked, his eyebrows raised incredulously.

Carrigan shook his head. "The internet as we knew it no longer exists. We can, however, access a *record* of the internet. These servers took a sort of picture of webpages at specific intervals, saving only the most recent data to its memory. So far, it has been incredibly helpful in many ways. Access to information that has helped us survive, to rebuild, as well as to find information on those who have wished to join us."

I was shocked, eyeing the stack of papers with innate curiosity. It felt as though a level of familiarity had been replaced in the world, like I had found a sliver of life before the Break. I wondered if I could access my social media accounts, to see photos of my family members long lost.

"Typically, there isn't much more to see than the public records or business websites of those that we research, simply average survivors looking for help," Carrigan explained, before pausing and looking down at the documents before him. "It seems, however, that with Ms. Jorah Sinclair, we are a bit luckier. If you would give me a moment."

He raised the papers, the room silent as he scanned the contents, his face unreadable.

At last he finished reading, and I wished I was better at interpreting facial expressions, though the need was short-lived, as he slid the papers toward me.

"Did you know about this?" he asked, his voice not accusing, though tense. He turned to Corporal Moore and Sergeant Black. My mind tuned him out as I dragged the papers toward me, Lachlan peering over my shoulder.

It was printed as though it had been run through a typewriter, which I guessed likely it had been. In front of me, printed on the white, somewhat crumpled papers in flawless typing lay an article from a newspaper, dated seven months past, a mere month or so before the Break.

SISTER CHARGED IN DEATH OF JUNIA SINCLAIR

It was a warm day in March when Junia Sinclair, 29, founder and CEO of the highly successful BlueSwan Cosmetics, passed away in her hospital bed. Ms. Sinclair had been diagnosed with a rare form of late-stage bone cancer four months prior. Her funeral was attended by loved ones and rivals to her company alike, as well as her faithful and caring fiancé. Those close to Ms. Sinclair described her as "wholly kind and incredibly devoted to her friends, work and God."

While at first it seemed that her death,

while tragic, was solely natural, a tip soon revealed that all may not be as it seemed. Autopsy results returned, revealing that Ms. Sinclair had in fact been smothered to death in her sleep, meaning that while her diagnosis was likely terminal, it was not her cancer that killed her.

Now, three weeks after her funeral, younger sister Jorah Sinclair, 23, has been charged with her murder. While further details are unknown, it is confirmed that Jorah Sinclair was summoned to and detained in a county jail located in Indiana, where Junia Sinclair had been living, and ultimately where she died.

A bail of fifty thousand dollars was posted by Ms. Jorah Sinclair, freeing her until her court date on May 18. A donations page has been set up for Mr. Adam Walsh, the fiancé of the late Junia Sinclair, the sisters having no other known surviving family.

31

KING JAMES

James woke with a start, lying in a puddle of his own sweat despite the frosty temperature of the room. He splayed his arms, reaching and searching for her soft figure but finding only emptiness beside him.

He felt the tide of fear give a small surge, a tug of nerves firing, enough to wake him from his stupor. Though soon he relaxed, remembering that she was no longer in danger here.

That she alone may be safe within these walls.

The dream still rattled around inside of James's mind, ever-present and vicious, living in his every moment, sleeping or awake.

"Drive it through the gates!" James shouted, bracing himself against the door of the truck, feeling the dried blood crack on his

knuckles. Only minutes since the Break should have happened—days too long that he had been away.

Tom floored the gas, and with an almighty explosion, the gates of Fort Rache were blasted off their hinges. The windshield caved inward, showering them with glass as the truck screeched to a halt. James's side screamed in protest, the bullet wound still raw and unmasked by medicine.

The moment he stepped out, the sound of screaming and gunfire magnified tenfold. In an instant, Tom had rushed toward him, pressing a pistol into his hand.

"I'm going to find Dean!" he shouted, taking off toward the smoke rising in the distance, toward the orange glow of the fireball erupting skyward. James could already feel the heat on his face from the flames, though he could hardly tell what was burning. People rushed by, warped in the chaos and confusion.

The pack of cigarettes protruded from the pocket of James's jeans, crumpled in a heap on the floor. Yet though he itched for one, he did not take any, instead crossing to the basin of water and splashing the cool contents across his still-searing skin.

It helped, but he still felt anxious, the memories still rattling around in his skull. So incredibly vivid, so lifelike, reliving it in every detail over and over again since that night.

The night Jorah proved she could not die.

James's shoulder connected with the pavement, and despite the adrenaline, he still felt the rough surface grating the skin from his arm. His side seared with pain, the twang of stitches pulling at his skin, the gunshot wound of days prior splitting open.

The berserker screamed as it clawed at James, though with a swift kick, it was launched backward. It scrambled to its feet, spastic with limbs flailing and twisting, like a rabid dog that had slipped on ice. Its jaw was more broken than usual, hanging on by mere tendons. James recognized him as one of McNeal's assistants.

Smoke billowed into the air as Ramirez appeared, connecting a crowbar with the side of the berserker's skull, finishing the monster, which collapsed in a twitching pile.

"James!" Ramirez coughed, grasping his shoulder. "We thought you were dead!"

"What happened?" James grunted as the pair ran for the cover of a nearby home, crouching in its shadow.

"Nobody knows exactly, but when the Break came, at least four people turned into berserkers, maybe more. Two of them were guards. It was chaos; somebody panicked. They took off into the kitchen-house to hide. A minute later and the whole building was going up in flames." Ramirez had to shout over the roar of the panic surrounding them, coughing as the thick smoke continued to churn in the air.

"Where are Jonas and Jorah?"

His face fell instantly, and James felt his gut twisting in anguish. "I'm sorry, my friend, I don't know about Jonas. The last I saw him he was walking in to do his job."

"And Jorah?" James pressed, now scanning the crowd of panicked people, watching as Ramirez's group moved through the mass, attempting to restore calm and eradicate the surviving berserkers.

Still, Ramirez looked pained. "They took her hours after you *left. She's been in the jail for days. I'm sorry, there was nothing that could be done." He gestured to the crowbar in his hands. "Vicars and McNeal had nearly every weapon in camp confiscated. I'm sorry."*

James dressed and made his way through the dimly lit house, the windows all blocked over to keep the heat in. He called out to Jorah, though he was not surprised when only ringing silence answered him. The office that had once belonged to Vicars caught his eye as he passed, the mahogany furniture and plush rug as pristine as ever. The room looked the same, really, save for the new piles of paperwork Jorah had spread across the desk, which had never held more than a glass of bourbon when Vicars was in charge.

The kitchen-house was a ball of fire, the flames licking the edges of the neighboring houses. You could hardly stand in its shadow, the fire blisteringly hot. The house was the last in the row, sitting on the edge of the field. It was where they had erected the fort's kitchen and cafeteria in the back yard. The house itself—smaller and lacking a fireplace, was mostly used for storage. Another pang of anguish coursed through James as he realized half of the food supply now fed nothing but the fire.

Tom, Dean, and several others were already present, desperately throwing handfuls of dirt and snow at the flames. James grabbed the arm of a man nearby as the new group ran over to help, directing him to gather the fire extinguishers in the other homes. The man nodded shakily, his eyes wide in shock, and took off toward the neighboring house, its side beginning to grow black with soot.

The chaos of the fort had begun to calm down, most residents now working as a unit to kill the storm of flames.

James checked the rounds in his gun before stepping outside, ensuring it was fully loaded as he slipped it into his holster. No guard was posted on the doorstep as he left the house. He shook his head vigorously, trying to rid himself of the memories that continually pulsed behind his vision.

Outside, Fort Rache bustled with activity. The aftermath of the Break of two weeks prior had finally been repaired, the First November Break of a few days past having been much less severe. Now the residents worked tirelessly to prepare the homes for winter. Three groups per day now left to hunt and scavenge, the clock ticking on time to recover the amount of food lost to the fire.

James quickened his pace as a chilling wind swept down the street, ducking through the doorway of the community clubhouse building. He headed into the largest of the offices inside, once the community manager's space, which had since been turned into their strategy room.

The walls were still plastered with Polaroids and notes. The section of those residents who had broken had grown so large, it now spread onto the neighboring wall. He averted his eyes from the photos, the ball of dread inside him growing heavy.

How much longer until it was he who broke? Or Jonas or Jorah? Tom or Dean?

It was only a matter of time. He could feel it in his bones.

He reached up, absentmindedly rubbing the back of his neck with one hand while he rifled through papers on the desk. He had just found his goal when a voice sounded from the doorway.

"There you are." James looked up to see Jonas, who limped into the room, a stack of books clutched in his hands.

The clubhouse sat seemingly abandoned, light still spewing from the seams. Several bodies lay in the street surrounding it, abandoned rifles splattered with mud and gore. James took off toward the building, his heart hammering in his chest.

A figure began moving as he neared, having fallen to the pavement steps away from the doors. He looked up as James approached, eyes wide with pain and fear though surging with relief.

"Jonas!" James slammed to his knees beside him. Jonas clutched his side, and despite his cries of protest, James pried back his hands. Blood spurted from a bullet hole, one almost identical in location to the one drilled into James just days before.

"You're gonna be okay. You'll be okay!" James told him. Jonas's face was pale, his shirt soaked with blood.

"Jorah ..." Jonas whispered feebly, looking toward the building. Ramirez appeared beside them, dropping to his knees and pressing his hands to Jonas's side.

James staggered to his feet. The doors loomed before him, leaking cool, artificial light. He took a step, a growing terror beating inside him at what he might find. Knowing in his heart that McNeal would not have let her live.

A cacophony of shouting erupted from behind James as she stepped into the open, moments before he would have reached the doors. She was shaky, crooked; her usually white-blonde hair had been dyed a deep red. The blood dripped down her arms, flowing across her skin like tiny rivers to where it leapt off her fingertips.

Recognition flitted through Jorah's eyes as they landed on James. Eyes that in that moment looked more beautiful and more horrible than James could ever remember.

With a heave, Jorah raised her arm, her fingers entwined in the greasy hair, displaying the severed head of Maximillian Vicars for all to see.

"How are you feeling?" James asked, gesturing to Jonas's side, where the bullet had missed his kidney by mere millimeters, passing straight through him just as the bullet that pierced James had.

Jonas grimaced, and James noticed the dark-purple bags beneath his eyes. "I'm all right, and you?"

"Better." James patted his own side. Heather had just removed the stitches a few days prior, "We're lucky, us."

James often felt he was lucky that it had been Conrad who had tried to kill him. Conrad and his goons alone, each less intelligent than the last. The designated meeting spot with Torres had not merely been a random patch of land, as Conrad seemed to have believed. Just through the trees, complete with a fireplace, medical kit, and rations, was the former groundskeeper shack of a nearby country club, without which James would have surely bled to death in the snow.

Jonas nodded in agreement. "Can't say I don't miss the few days of rest."

James, Jorah, and Jonas, along with several other Fort Rache members, had spent days in their makeshift infirmary after the disaster of the Second October Break. James recalled his shock at learning he had slept for two days straight when he woke, bleary-eyed and dehydrated on a cot in the clubhouse hallway. Jorah and Jonas had each slept another entire day before waking.

James didn't answer. Instead, he continued rifling through the papers, making a mental note to call in someone to organize them.

"You're going out looking again, aren't you?" Jonas said, his voice laced with disapproval.

Once again James didn't answer as he finally extracted the map he was looking for.

"James," Jonas snapped uncharacteristically, "you need to let it go. They're gone."

James grabbed a pen, plotting out the route he planned to take. The map was already covered with a smattering of lines and Xs. Everywhere he'd already searched for signs of McNeal and Conrad.

"For all we know, they joined up with Jefferson and Gallagher. We know they're still in the area."

"That makes it even more imperative that we find them," James argued, satisfied with his plans and stowing the map in his jacket.

"Jorah needs you here," Jonas pressed. "We all do."

"Jorah is doing just fine, and I'll be back tonight."

Jonas's face darkened, and James knew the spiel that was coming.

"I agree she's doing a good job, but you are our leader," Jonas began, but James cut him off.

"No, I'm not. We agreed on this as a community—no more leaders. There's a council now."

"The council is bullshit," Jonas spat. "It's supposed to be you, me, Ramirez, Heather, *and* Jorah."

"The people love her—Tom and Dean made sure of that; I'm better suited to advise anyway."

"But you aren't listening to me. Yes, she's doing a good job, but there's something different about her, James." Jonas's face had flushed pink as he spoke, his words blossoming with vigor. "You weren't there, and now you're so head over heels, you don't see it."

"They locked her in a cage for days, strapped her down and cut her open! Of course she's different. We've all had to get harder to survive. We're all different now," James spat, deciding then that he'd had enough of the conversation and headed for the doorway.

Jonas sidestepped, however, blocking the exit. "I thought she was dead. You didn't see how much blood she lost. The others died, and she should have too. It was chaos in the tent, after so many people outside broke *and* two of the people inside." He paused, lowering his voice and straining his words. "And then they all left, and I heard her calling out. I thought she was saying my name—" He paused, shaking his head.

James's attention had been caught; he hadn't heard that part of the story, but before he could ask, Jonas pressed on, determined to make his point heard.

"I stitched her up. The whole time I kept asking myself why

I was bothering. She was barely breathing." Tears had risen in Jonas's eyes, and James fought the urge to shove by him. "And then Vicars comes bursting back in, and I'd never seen him like that before—wild, crazed. I don't even remember him shooting me." His hand rested on his side again, touching the slightly raised area where his wound was still layered with gauze.

"Look, I know, I get it."

"But you don't listen," Jonas said, shaking his head. "The next thing I know, Jorah is standing there, completely on her own. Vicars is panicking; he's not paying attention—God, James, she killed him with a scalpel. The man must have had over one hundred pounds on her and she took him down like he was nothing—and her eyes …" He shivered. "Like nothing I've ever seen, so alive, but so distant … and she's been that way since. You know it's true."

"What, you think she's a berserker or something?"

"Of course not," Jonas snapped. "She didn't *break*, but that doesn't mean something's not wrong. She's already been through so much, and then they tortured her. They made me *watch*, James. McNeal dug into her well beyond what he did to the others, and they were asleep—post traumatic stress syndrome, you don't—"

"I'm going now." He pushed past Jonas, who finally, with a defeated sigh, let him go.

"James?" Jonas called out, peering around the doorframe moments before James made it outside. "At least go check on her first, please?"

James sighed in defeat, stepping out into the breezy daybreak.

He found her exactly where he thought he would, near the

front gates, helping to inspect and unload the new supplies and game meat being brought in.

"Hey," James greeted her, and her face split into a smile at his approach.

"Morning," she said, her cheeks rosy from the cold, her hair tousled. "Ramirez is looking for you. He needs men to help gather firewood."

James's eyebrows raised in surprise. "For the homes? There's already a group doing that."

Jorah nodded, looking away from him, her eyes narrowed as she watched a small group organize a crate of supplies. "For the pyres. I'm halting the dig of the new pit."

"We agreed burning bodies draws too much attention."

"It's better this way," Jorah answered, finally turning to look at him. "It's more sanitary; the ground is too frozen." James made a point then to look into her eyes, searching despite himself for any trace of something different, an inkling of Jonas's warning.

"What are you staring at me for?" Jorah asked him with the hint of a laugh, her blue eyes shining, the same as they had always been, stunning and kind.

James relaxed. "Nothing, just missed you."

"Cheesy," she teased. "Well, when you're done staring, go help Ramirez."

"Actually, I have plans. I'm going to look for McNeal."

Jorah's brow furrowed. "No, I think you should go help Ramirez."

"There's plenty of people who can gather wood. McNeal and Conrad are out there, along with all the men who left with them. If we don't find them, it's a matter of time before they recruit more. You know they aren't going to let this go."

While the Second October Break had been tragic, destructive, and by far the worst reoccurrence yet, it had at least given them an opportunity to drive out many of those who had long made Fort Rache such a dangerous place.

James could see the tendons twitching in Jorah's jaw. "They will come to us. You will not go to them."

Anger flared inside James. He opened his mouth to argue. *Who is she to make the rules?* But he was interrupted by the appearance of Evangeline, her red mane of hair tucked inside the hood of a thick fur coat.

"We're all settled in, Jorah," she reported. "Everyone's doing well."

Jorah nodded, tearing her gaze away from James, turning her back to him. "Good, tell Ramirez to bring over an extra ration of food for the next three days."

"Bring rations where?" James interrupted.

"Really, James," Evangeline mock-scolded, "if you weren't traipsing through the woods all day, maybe you'd know what's going on. Jorah's had me move the women to one of the better houses. Mack's wife is eight months pregnant now, and they need the fireplace," Evangeline explained before shooting James a playful smile, giving them a curtsy, and hurrying off down the road.

James turned to Jorah, intent on continuing the argument, but his words fell dead inside his mouth. He saw nothing but coldness gleaming in her stare. The ocean swept to ruins after a storm, something washed up from the depths. He could see the sinews in her jaw, wriggling and crawling like worms beneath her skin. She hardly moved as she watched Evangeline go, the huge coat bobbing up and down the muddy street.

James thought that if looks could kill, Evangeline's entire family tree would have crumbled to ashes.

32

CORPORAL SANA MANGAL

"She was always so kind, one of the most genuine people I ever met," I spoke the words assuredly, not allowing my voice to waver. "She was true, and she was brave, and she will be missed."

It had begun to sleet, small, gentle droplets pitter-pattering down around us, wetting the dirt, splattering the white cloth-wrapped body. I stepped back to stand between Riley and Geoff, hands folded, and eyes lowered to the ground.

"I'd like to say something," Geoff said, his voice taut and heavy. He limped forward, denying my offer of a supporting hand, leaning his weight on his crutch. "Kara, thank you for all that you did for us. Allowing us into your home as strangers and welcoming us back into your family now. I know I speak for the three of us, and Jorah too, when I say thank you for your kindness."

"Thank you," Musa whispered, tears glimmering in his dark eyes as he looked between us. "That was very kind."

I glanced over to Lachlan, whose face had been buried in his ragged handkerchief since the moment we stepped up to the graveyard plot, just outside the walls of Camp Prevail. He blew his nose loudly, succumbing to tears that flowed from his moss-green eyes.

Musa stepped forward. Picking up the shovel, he began to slowly lower dirt into the grave, covering the prone form that had once been his wife.

"Geoff, no, not with your leg," I said, catching Geoff's arm as he moved to help.

Instead, Riley stepped forward, grasping the second shovel and working it into the ground. Musa glanced up. The two men, who had hardly spoken since we had reunited, exchanging a brief, solemn glance.

The slush continued to sputter down until the last layer of dirt had been patted in to place.

We left Musa then, to give him time to grieve on his own, and I looked back to see him fall to his knees, bowing his head as the sleet splashed over his shoulders.

"Come on, let's get something to eat," I pressed, pulling Lachlan away by the elbow—about the highest point I could reach on the man.

"She was so good, Kara," Lachlan stuttered, tears still rolling down his face. "She didn't deserve this."

"I know, but she's at peace now. She's with Johanna," I said, awkwardly patting his arm. The news that Johanna had broken just before we arrived at the camp had been terribly sad. "She was a survivor. Even without her treatment, she lasted so much longer than doctors said she would."

Lachlan nodded, wiping a tear from his eye.

"I'm going to go lie down. Go on without me," Geoff said as we neared the row of tents in which his lay at the end.

"You all right?"

He nodded, patting his thigh. "Leg's just getting sore from all the standing. Grab me some food if you can." I watched him hobble off, ensuring he wasn't about to tip over.

The doctors in Camp Prevail didn't think Geoff's leg would ever be the same, the bones too mangled from when he'd broken it, just days before we reached the camp.

The small side building of the high school had once housed the computer lab, and as the walls were thin and the windows drafty, it had been converted to the mess hall of Camp Prevail. As well, the proximity of the lab to the cafeteria of the main building meant that portions of the kitchen could still be used.

We took our seats in a group of mismatched chairs, balancing our trays of mushy mixed vegetables on our laps. The portions were small, hardly a mouthful, and I wished it were the next day, when I could eat a better meal.

There was a rotating system at Camp Prevail, with categories split simply into men and women, with each alternating the days when they could eat sufficiently. This allowed the camp to stretch food rations further, without anyone going hungry for too long.

I eyed the much larger portions slopped onto Riley and Lachlan's plates, poking at my own small scoop sadly. A child peered up at me from the cluster of chairs nearby. I recognized her, small and frail; her only surviving family sat beside her, another girl no older than fourteen.

"Any news on Jorah? Or the fort?" Riley asked, playing with his food rather than eating it.

"No, but we're due for a meeting soon."

Riley looked out the window at the sleet still spraying over the ground. "We should go to her."

"I think that's the plan, eventually," I explained. "We need to work with the fort, they have the resources and the numbers."

Riley met my eyes, his pale green and hard. "I want to be on the team that goes."

I sighed, exasperated. "You know I have no control over that, and you know you aren't even a recruit."

"I beg to differ, *Corporal Mangal*. I think you have more control than you think," he spat, finishing his words by shoving a forkful of vegetables into his mouth.

To be honest, I'd forgotten about my recent promotion. "That doesn't change the fact that you aren't a recruit."

"It's all bullshit," Riley snapped. "The army is dead, the world is dead." He stood abruptly, glancing down at his half-eaten tray of food before he thrust it away, dropping the plate on the chair in front of the two girls. "Either I'm on the team that goes or I'll make it there on my own."

"He has a point," Lachlan said. We watched the doors swing shut as Riley stormed out, the guards shooting him disgruntled looks.

"About which part?" I grilled, with more vigor than I'd intended.

Lachlan's kind eyes landed on me, unoffended despite my tone. "He has a right to go see her, even if he's not a recruit."

"It's his own fault he hasn't signed up. I understand the system is flawed, that we aren't receiving anywhere near the training we would otherwise, but it's something. It creates order; it's kept the camp alive."

"There's pros and there's cons," Lachlan said. "Yes, overall having this system lets us be better trained, work as a cohesive unit, but it's kept our numbers down. Men like Geoff and Riley who didn't make the cut or don't want the rules, we miss out on them. Fort Rache doesn't have a recruitment system, and they've done a lot better than us."

"They're savages; you saw what I saw."

"Actually, I saw an organized system and due process."

"But the stories that have come out of the fort," I argued. "You heard what Molly's group said."

"Stories we heard weeks ago, before Jorah was in charge. I'm just saying, there's perks to both systems and flaws as well. We could learn from each other."

I didn't answer, finally scraping back the rest of my food. I gathered my belongings and turned to leave, knowing full well I was being a brat and not caring in the slightest.

"Sana, wait," Lachlan said, reaching out and catching my arm. "You know how we ended up here, how we lost the house. Musa didn't want to change either, didn't want to adapt, to get harder. He refused to do the things that could have saved us, even though they were hard. It lost us the house, and if we aren't careful, the same thing is going to happen here too."

I pressed the towel into his side, though it took mere moments for the fabric to become saturated with blood. My feet pounded beneath me, running alongside the gurney, my vision darkening as we ducked into the school building.

"Get him on the table," someone commanded, and with a brief countdown and a heave, I helped lift Polkowski onto the nearest table.

"Stop!" Polkowski cried in pain, while another solider worked to restrain him.

"Hey, hey, you're gonna be okay," I encouraged, grabbing Polkowski's blood-stained fingers and squeezing them tightly. "Look at me."

Feverish, hazel eyes flicked to mine. "Sana?"

"You're going to be okay," I repeated, working to steady my voice. "You need to try to calm down."

"Sana, what's happening?" he cried, his skin sallow as beads of sweat and tears poured down his cheeks.

I glanced at his side as a medic began to cut away his blood-soaked shirt, revealing the gaping stomach wound. "You had an accident. You're going to be okay."

He didn't answer, his hand going slack in mine as his eyes rolled back into his head.

"Everyone who isn't medical, get out," the nearest doctor commanded, and reluctantly I was swept away.

The small group gathered in the lobby as the doors to what was once the cafeteria swung closed. Most of us had been splattered with Polkowski's blood.

"The rest of his group is still out there," one of the guards who had been stationed at the gates when Polkowski had been brought in announced. "We need to organize a mission to retrieve them now."

Immediately I raised my hand, standing on tiptoe to be seen over the crowd. A voice hissed out to my right.

"Mangal!"

Corporal Moore stood in the hallway. She gestured me toward her vigorously. With a final glance to the crowd of volunteers gathering, I hurried toward her.

"Corporal, it's Polkowski. His team was attacked by freaks, and he's the only one who made it back."

"I'm aware of the unfortunate news," Moore said, signaling for me to follow her as she took off down the hallway. "However, at this current time, the plight of Polkowski is not of our concern."

"I'm sorry?"

She sighed, holding open the stairwell door. "Corporal Mangal, as I'm sure you are aware, neither of us should have anywhere near attained the rank of corporal."

"Well, yes," I stuttered, torn from my worrying at the sudden change of direction in conversation.

She continued on, the two of us climbing the stairs at a jog. "But here we are, ranked corporal, now essential members of the only known surviving contingent of the United States Army, under the command of the only known surviving master sergeant. In addition, this camp has had no contact with other leaders of *any* country or government organization since July."

We reached the top of the stairs, Moore procuring a ringlet of keys and jamming one into the lock.

I took the moment of silence as an opportunity. "Corporal Moore, have we just now heard from someone else?"

She didn't answer, instead hurrying me into the hallway and locking the door behind us. Finally, her deep brown eyes landed on me. "Sana, you are here mainly under my recommendation, and not to lessen your abilities, but we have a very limited and depleted pool of options."

I tried not to take Moore's speech to heart as we hurried down the hallway, Moore finally pausing outside a classroom door and tucking the strands of hair that had leaked from her cap back into place.

"I don't know everything we're about to learn, but it's the most important thing we have ever known. Pay attention."

The room beyond the door turned out to be the former principal's office, spacious, with a fine desk and a modicum of plush seating. The American flag hung across one wall and leaning against the other was a large whiteboard.

"Thank you, Corporal Moore. Corporal Mangal, would you

please take a seat." Master Sergeant Carrigan stood stoically behind the desk, his body pitched forward, hands spread for support over the glossy wood.

Behind him, the shades had been drawn over the window, casting us into the dim. Sergeant Black and Lachlan were already seated. A package of baby wipes was passed to me as I sat, and I began to scrub Polkowski's blood from my hands.

Once we had joined them, Carrigan straightened, his eyes briefly tracing each of our faces. When he spoke, I thought he sounded older than he ever had before, drawn and tired, and the bags beneath his eyes only exaggerated the effect.

"Three days ago was my sixty-second birthday," he began, to no other sound than the scratching of a pen as Moore recorded his every word on a pad of stained paper. "I have served as a member of the United States Army, both in combat and in administration, for over forty years. During my time in service, I received two Purple Hearts, the Medal of Honor, as well as the Distinguished Service Cross."

"All incredible achievements—" Moore praised but was swiftly cut off.

"I do not tell you this for praise," Carrigan corrected, his voice laced with strife, "but to try to find some sort of explanation for why I have been put in the situation that I have been. As I was saying, three days ago I turned sixty-two, and one week before the initial Break, I was due to retire from service."

The air in the room was fraught with tension, and I felt myself slipping to the edge of my seat, my nails clutching the armrests, sensing a great reveal on the horizon.

"I was delivered a package of information, vague, obscure, with directions to read and memorize its contents. Two days later, merely five days before the Break, the package was collected from my home and destroyed. Later, in a brief operation which I have no memory of, *this* was removed from the back of my neck."

His weathered hand flitted to the pocket of his uniform. Rummaging around, he extracted something small enough to be concealed in the palm of his hand. He passed the object to Sergeant Black, who was nearest, who after only a moment of inspection, passed it to the woman beside him.

"What you are about to see is a device all of you are already familiar with, whether you are aware of it or not. While I have shown this to some of you before, the rest I ask you please control your innate responses for the time being."

Moore, who had so far spent the longest time inspecting the device, handed it to me with wide eyes.

It was a tiny, metal disk, roughly the size of a pea, which seemed to cling to my skin as though it was covered in half-dried glue. It was flat, though with easily discernable layers and covered in minuscule, octagonal scratches like the pieces of a puzzle.

"As I am sure the rest of you have figured out, this is the device that has caused the Breaks. It is what has caused the end of the world, and each of you has one inside you this very moment."

My hand automatically flew to the back of my neck, pressing into my flesh, trying to feel anything out of place beneath the smooth skin. Lachlan reached over, plucking the disk from my hand, and inspecting it himself.

I looked around the room, my hand still searching the back of my neck. Sergeant Black and a woman whom I recognized as the head of medical both looked distinctly unsurprised by this news, their faces blank though fogged with sorrow.

"You've known this the whole time, and you've done nothing about it?" Lachlan spat suddenly, with an anger in his tone that I had never heard from him. His large hand folded around the disk; his knuckles white as though he were trying to crush it.

Carrigan sighed. "Until now, there has been nothing that could be done. Part of the package that I received held an explanation of these devices. As I stated before, vague and heavily redacted, but it stressed that they cannot be removed." He glanced toward the head doctor. "Two months ago, Doctor Lane and I voided those instructions; it was a desperate and feeble attempt to save lives, which ended miserably. The devices cannot be removed."

"Or what?" I asked, surprised by the quiver in my voice. "Do you break?"

"The package I received claimed that removing the device would be fatal. In addition, tampering with the device could cause a partial firing, damaging the host but not killing them."

"The freaks," I murmured, but Carrigan shook his head.

"What is causing the freaks is similar, but what Doctor Lane and I discovered in our test was less extreme. It seems that in some cases, instead of causing immediate death or creating a full-blown freak, tampering with the device damages the host in other ways. The man we tested—" He paused to swallow. "In what I must stress was a consensual test, he survived, though shortly after, under observation began to display increasingly erratic behavior. He became vastly more unpredictable, impulsive, and violent."

"What happened to him?"

"He killed himself after four weeks in observation," Carrigan admitted. "We have since made no attempts to remove the devices, and we don't know if that sort of brain damage would always be the result."

I didn't know what to say; thousands of questions ricocheted through my mind. I looked to Lachlan, who had slumped back in his seat, his face paling. Moore, on the other hand, looked as though she were on the verge of tears.

"These devices were planted in every human being on the planet in the months before the initial Break." Carrigan retrieved the device from Lachlan. Pinching it between two fingers he held it in the air. "If you look closely, you will see that it appears to be made out of hundreds of individual sections. This would explain why you have no memory of the disk being inserted into your body, because the disk itself never was. Instead, you unknowingly ingested these fragments over months, which then came together to form a completed disk. Dumped into the water supply, slipped into manufacturing plants, ejected out of planes— unavoidable, and the grandest feat of engineering ever seen. If nothing else, it is truly astounding technology."

"But wait," Moore interjected. "We've cut open bodies looking for the source, ones that broke and ones that died of other causes. How have we never found a disk before?"

"That I can answer," Carrigan said. "When the host dies, the disks disband into the individual tiny fragments, making them nearly impossible to see with the naked eye. I assume that whatever method was used to remove this disk from my own body also preserved it in its completed form."

"But why, why any of this? It doesn't make sense," Moore cried suddenly, seemingly forgetting her decorum, her pen and notepad falling from her lap. "Who did this? Everyone knows the alien theory. That when the drone made it out of the solar system, we finally received a signal. Then a year later, this happens?"

"Population control," Sergeant Black spoke up, the handsome man pushing himself away from the wall he leaned on. "Population control in the most effective and humane combination possible."

Carrigan nodded. "On the day of the initial Break, sixty-two percent of the disks, which at that point resided in every individual on Earth, were activated. That portion of the population perished instantaneously, leaving ample supplies and resources behind, giving the survivors a better chance."

"My sister—she was nine years old, and she was killed in the first Break! You call that humane?" Moore snapped, leaping to her feet.

"Corporal Moore, you will restrain yourself immediately, or you will be escorted to holding," Carrigan said gravely, and with a movement as though it ground her bones, Moore sat back down. Carrigan watched her for a moment before continuing. "I know how you are all feeling, and I must stress to you that I did not cause this to happen. I was merely a carrier who was chosen to hold this information. To my knowledge, I am the only one, though I find that unlikely. No, it is not fair that your sister was killed, and for the billions of people who found their loved ones dead, it was not humane either.

"I ask you this, would it have been better for those people to suffer in their deaths? A plague would have been simpler and just as effective. There are plenty of diseases of that could have achieved the same effect at reducing the population. Or it could have been bombs; nuclear warfare could have decimated the world just as quickly. Though, in each of these scenarios, people suffer. They starve, they fight, and they use up valuable resources. Would you have preferred your sister die starving, coughing up her own lungs, or instantly, painlessly?"

"I would rather she be alive!" Moore spat, her eyes brimming with tears.

"But that was never an option. From the moment this plan was put into place, people had to die. They had easy deaths, *instant*, forgiving deaths, and in their place, they left behind supplies, empty homes, and cabinets full of food. Their deaths gave the survivors a chance. We know nothing but that simple truth, that whoever did this had three intentions; to kill many, to do so quickly, and yet to leave those who survived with a better chance."

"Why sixty-two percent? How was it decided what implants would go off? Was it random?" I asked, trying to stem the thousand other questions hammering behind my teeth.

Carrigan sighed. "The packet referred to it as the Chance Probability. Apparently, the implants had another talent—to gauge a person's likelihood, their *chance,* of survival post-Break. I don't know exactly how it worked, but the implants could take readings, hundreds of different metrics—health, genetic disposition, temperament, et cetera, and calculate if a certain person met the threshold for survival. As for the sixty-two percent, I believe that was simply a computer calculation of what would be most effective."

"We buried a woman today, my friend, Kara Imani." Lachlan said, his fists clenched. "She died of cancer that was deemed terminal *before* the Break. How could she have survived this Chance Probability? Or her mother—her mother had Alzheimer's!"

"My sister was gifted! She was two grades above her age and healthy as anyone!" Moore cried. "How did she not survive?"

Carrigan looked sadly toward Moore. "Instead of going by exact age, the implants used certain puberty markers to decide when someone was mature enough to be considered for survival. Unfortunately, I believe that if you were not yet old or developed enough to hit such markers, it was simply random." He turned toward Lachlan as Moore collapsed into herself, tears streaming down her face. "As for your friend, I am less sure of the answer. It could simply have been miscalculation, or malfunction with the devices. I myself have seen many survivors who seemed very unlikely to have been in that top thirty-two percent—perhaps they simply slipped through. It could also be, however, that there was something about these people that offset the other readings. Intelligence, certain aptitudes, bravery, or strength—something that overruled the conditions of their bodies. I'm not sure which, if either, is the answer."

"But who caused this? Someone had to make the devices, and I'm assuming set off the EMPs too."

"Yet another aspect I do not know. The common conclusion that most of you had reached was that this extermination came from somewhere beyond our planet. While you knew nothing of the disks, you know that it is unlikely that humans held that sort of technology to kill with such precision, and to come on the day exactly a year after the public learned of extraterrestrial life? It seems far too clear to point to the most obvious answer. Though now, with what I have told you, I hope that you may have come to the same conclusion as I. That this is indeed *alien* technology, but humans had a hand in this as well."

The room held a ringing silence. Carrigan seemed to be giving all the opportunity to speak, but when no one did, he carried on.

"I do not have all the answers. I fear in fact that I know scarcely a fragment of why this has happened to our world. However, the reason I gathered you all here today is because the time has come that we are able to stop these repeating Breaks. As you know, three days after the initial Break, nearly all electronics were destroyed by an EMP. Cars, phones, planes—nearly anything that ran on electricity, and especially if it required fragile computer chips to run, was destroyed. The package I received informed me that in addition to causing such destruction, these EMPs had a second purpose—to destroy the chips inside each survivor."

"But it failed," I filled in, glancing around the room. "Instead of destroying them, it damaged them, and that's what's causing the new Breaks."

"Precisely my conclusion, Corporal Mangal," Carrigan confirmed, "though it cannot be said if this effect had been on all of the devices. Some of them may have been destroyed, or all simply damaged. What matters is that, at last, we believe we have found the one place where we may be able to turn them all off." He gestured to the whiteboard that leaned against the wall. A large map had been taped to it, an X marking the location of Camp Prevail, and much farther away, another.

"This is where we need to go to stop this. It is the nearest location capable of broadcasting the signal needed to shut down the devices. The problem, which I present you with today, is that we have no hope of reaching this location on our own. Not without creating a drastic risk of losing the entire party along the way. As well, we would be leaving all who stayed here in an incredibly vulnerable position."

"Fort Rache," I whispered to the silent room, and all eyes flicked to me.

"Precisely," Master Sergeant Carrigan said, "Fort Rache, our only hope of reaching the station before the next Break."

33

JAMES THE JESTER

"This is wrong."

"No, this is justice." She didn't meet his eyes when she spoke. Instead, she stepped away, taking her place on the stage.

The walls of the fort had been mended, built higher, stronger than ever. The gates had been repaired also, sturdy, heavy metal sheets lining them, kept watch over by a flawless around-the-clock guard system. The rubble of the burned-down house had been cleared away, the blood-stained floors from McNeal's trials soaked in bleach.

All in a few short weeks.

The supplies lost in the fire had nearly been restored, the lot now kept in multiple locations throughout camp to prevent a recurrence. The new pit had been abandoned, piles of firewood kept beneath tarps in its place—unless of course anyone felt strongly enough about the fallen to dig them a grave in the frozen ground. It was rare that someone did, but should the inclination grip them, a small graveyard had also been plotted out.

Order had been restored. The people were happy, healthy—as much as possible given the circumstances. Women had emerged from the woodwork, now safe to travel throughout the fort without needing constant protection. Those who disagreed with the new order and had not left in the aftermath of the Second October Break had been driven out.

Or hanged.

Or in the case laid bare before James that very moment, *burned.*

"Taylor Gallagher, you stand accused of the murder of Blake Henley, theft of a truck and supplies belonging to the occupants of Fort Rache, as well as mutiny and desertion against the fort." Jorah's voice rang out over the crowd that had gathered in the field. Beside her, two large men grasped the thin shoulders of Gallagher, holding him steady while he cursed and spat at Jorah.

The air swirled with frosty gales, the frozen grass crunching beneath the feet of the citizens as they shifted in place, trying to stay warm. All were wrapped heavily and tightly in their winter gear, a mismatched kaleidoscope of salvaged clothes. Except for Jorah, whose thin jacket remained open, her chest heaving with presence and vigor as she spoke.

"Many of you knew Blake Henley," Jorah continued. "I had only the pleasure of spending a short time with him, on the very mission that set out to find and rescue a group of missing people, a group that Taylor Gallagher was a part of." A vicious roar of jeers and shouts rose up from the crowd. James watched as a rock came sailing from the back, striking Gallagher in the chest. "It was during that mission that my group and I were attacked by not only freaks, but an anonymous gunman from the woods. After our narrow escape, we returned to find that the sole survivor of that group had stolen our truck, never to be seen again. Until now, when in the dead of night, he returned, intent on taking from us again! Determined to find more of you, to try to convince you to betray this fort, just as he did!" Jorah's voice had exploded with passion, her words laced with revulsion, the crowd cheering wildly with her, hurling insults toward Gallagher, who had begun to cower.

"Kill him!" someone screamed. "Blake was my friend! Kill him for what he did!"

"Blake was a hero! He alone noticed the intruder, he *alone* confronted him, and in return for his valor, he was stabbed and left to die." She threw her arm out, pointing to the dark patch of grass where Blake's body had been found the day before, the bird tattoo on his neck splattered with blood. "We are a new people, here and now. We have survived while billions have perished. We have built this place for ourselves and for our children to thrive, and we will no longer bow to the cowards and monsters who wish to take it from us!"

A chill was spreading through James. A sheer power was radiating off Jorah, mixing with the crowd and spreading through the air like wildfire.

"You can stop this," a voice said beside him. "You can stop this right now."

James shook his head. "I can't, besides, he deserves to die."

"Aye," Tom agreed, "I'm not saying he shouldn't die, but not like this. Burned at the stake, the mob mentality of it all—it's too much. It's asking for trouble. Gallagher has friends out there, Jefferson, McNeal, Conrad—everyone who deserted is still out there."

James's eyes flicked to Tom, the older man's gaze reproachful. "I can't stop this now. It's too late. She has a power over this place that I never thought possible. I can't question her now, not in front of everyone."

"What do you have to say for yourself?" Jorah asked, turning to Gallagher.

The thin, balding man looked up toward her, his small and watery eyes narrowing. Bruises and cuts canvased his face, his dry and cracked skin making him look even more of a ruin. There was a pause while he seemed to study her. Then, with a wild cackle, he turned to the crowd, screaming out over the jeers.

"I say I should've killed that bitch when I had the chance!" He spat toward the crowd, the brown glob of saliva landing in the murky snow.

Jorah nodded to the men holding Gallagher as the crowd screamed. The whole of the fort had gathered for the execution, save for those currently on duty. James spied Evangeline in the back of the crowd, her expression still and stoic.

"This can't be allowed to be a common thing," Tom pressed, nudging James's arm. "You need to take the power back. Jorah is a good leader, the people love her, and this place has changed for the better with her, but she *needs* to be checked!"

James did his best to ignore Tom, watching as the guards dragged Gallagher to the pyre that had been constructed just that morning, the handiwork of those who had been closest with Blake. Gallagher's face had taken on a wan, sallow pallor. James could see the beads of sweat that began to roll down his face despite the cold, the gravity of his situation seeming to dawn on him.

"Wait!" Gallagher called out, yelping in pain as his arms where bound roughly behind him, binding him to the main beam of the pyre. "Please, wait. I'll talk. I'll tell you about the others!"

James jerked forward, ready to call off the execution at the prospect of information. Jorah, however, seemed to have predicted this and caught his eye, silently nodding to him as she stepped toward Gallagher.

The crowd had quieted, listening intently for what would come next.

"Talk, then," Jorah said, almost distractedly, as she procured a golden Zippo lighter, running her fingers over the metal.

"I—I, cut me down first!"

Jorah shook her head. "Talk."

"They're camped out by the river. Maybe twenty miles east, just off Mast Street. There's a big bend and this old gray mansion they've taken up in."

"How many are there?"

"I don't know."

"Liar," Jorah sang, flipping the lighter to life. Gallagher gave a shout of fear, and the crowd screamed with mirth.

"There's forty of them, and they're finding more all the time!"

"Is that it?"

"What else do you want to know?" Gallagher cried.

Jorah held up the lighter, the small flame flickering. She appeared to think for a moment, then to James's shock, the ghost of a smile graced her face. "Nothing."

She tossed the lighter toward the pyre, the blaze instantly catching on a pool of gasoline, sending tongues of flame shooting toward Gallagher.

"No! You said if I talked, please!" he screamed, straining against the bonds.

"We will pay for this," Tom said gravely, though James hardly heard him, his eyes trained on Jorah as she stepped away from the flames, the crowd parting for her as she left the pyre.

"Have mercy," Gallagher gasped, "mercy!"

She paused, turning back to Gallagher while he tried to dance away from the flames. "Mercy? Just like you had for Blake? I don't think so," she said, her voice cool, eyes emotionless. "There is no mercy in this land, not for men like you."

"What the hell was that?"

The numbness that had enveloped James had depleted with the crowd as they flowed out of the field, the remnants of the pyre crumbling to ashes. Anger had spread through him then, filling the void while he hurried after Jorah, following the mop of blonde hair that bobbed down the street.

"Can't let you in right now. Sorry James," the guard at the door had told him, a younger man whom James had once taught how to shoot.

"Step aside."

"I'm sorry. She said she doesn't want to be disturbed."

"I would think I would be the exception to that rule," James growled, his fists clenched as he willed himself not to throw the boy aside.

The guard stuttered, his eyes flicking between James and the door. "You—you're right, I'm sorry." He stepped aside, and James hurried passed him, slamming the door to the sound of "Please tell her I tried to—"

Now James leaned over the grand desk, supporting himself with fingers splayed out over the wood.

"He was going to give us information, details that we *need*," James pressed, as Jorah at last turned her gaze from the window.

"I figured he would let you in," she commented, crossing the room and sifting through a cabinet.

James paused, surprised. "Of course he would, I have just as much power here as you do."

To his further shock, a sort of simpering smile spread across her face. The effect was not a pleasant one; her features seemed shadowed in the dim light, and combined with her smirk gave her a sort of dark quality. "A leader who has to state that they have power is no leader."

She locked her gaze with his for a moment. Then, as though she had taken a knife to the cords of tension binding the room, she laughed.

"I'm just saying, James, that it wouldn't hurt to be a little more forward. The people love you, they love *us*, and we should show them that we're a team." Her expression had softened, glass clinking in her hands as she poured herself a tall serving of brandy. She shook the dark liquid toward James, though she did not seem surprised when he declined the offer, merely rolling her eyes good-naturedly and stowing the decanter back in the cabinet.

She took a dainty sip. Crossing the room and placing the glass on the desk, she wrapped her arms around James.

James sighed, folding into the hug, burying his face in the soft, sweet-smelling hair. He fell back after a moment, though he kept his hands on her waist.

"But I'm serious, Jorah, you need to consult me before you do something like that, and the rest of the council. It's in place for a reason."

"The rest of the council doesn't want their jobs," she pressed. "You and I are the decision makers, and they know that; the council should be consulted only on big decisions."

"Executing a man in cold blood, just moments after he promised us valuable information? How is that not a big decision?"

"He deserved what he got. He told us what we needed to know. That group is not a threat to us."

James looked at her incredulously, though his gaze was met with only annoyance as she pulled herself away, her back to him while she sipped her drink.

"I'm just trying to do what's best for the fort. The people need us," James said, following her across the room as she moved to pour herself another glass. As she raised the decanter, he caught her arm. "And I'm trying to do what's best for us."

Her gaze narrowed on his grip on her wrist for a moment, before flicking to his face, her features soft. "I know. I love you, James."

"I love you too," he sighed, cradling her cheek in his hand and pressing his forehead to hers. "We will figure this out."

He released her, and she smiled, taking a sip from her fresh glass. "That reminds me, Jonas needs you."

James laughed. "How did that remind you that Jonas needs me?"

She grinned. "Because Jonas loves you too," she quipped. "Go see what he wants, and I'll meet the two of you to eat in an hour."

"Sounds good." He kissed her on the cheek, debating with himself whether he would grab his pack of cigarettes before leaving.

Feeling a new sense of cheeriness, he decided against it and exited.

"Ms. Sinclair asked if you would be so kind as to relinquish your guard post," James said to the boy as he emerged. "Don't worry, she isn't upset with you," he added, feeling pity at the terrified look on the young man's face.

James stepped away, intent on finding Jonas, though with a

sudden, strange urge, he peered back at the home.

Jorah stood in the window once again, surveying her kingdom before her, eyes unblinking, expressionless, her nose mere inches from the window. James swiveled around, searching the street for what she was looking at. When he found nothing unusual, he turned back to the house.

But she was gone, disappeared back into the quiet home, its empty windows staring out at nothing, just as it seemed she had.

A jerky laugh escaped James's lips, much to his own surprise, and he started off down the road once more, bundling into his jacket. He resolved to tell Jorah later that her antics were starting to creep him out, sure that they would share a laugh over it.

"What do you think of the new people?" Ramirez asked, before emitting a loud groan of exertion as he heaved another plank up to James.

It had been three days since Jorah had failed to show up for dinner with James and Jonas, though that had hardly been surprising, as shortly after James had left her, a group of eleven survivors had arrived at the gates, begging to be let in.

James grasped the rough wood, still seething over the events days before. "I haven't talked with them much since we first let them in."

"So, you're still angry about it."

"How do you know I was angry in the first place?"

"Half the town heard your row over it with Jorah!" Ramirez exclaimed with a hint of mischief. "And let me say, she is *much* scarier than you when she's angry."

"Fuck off."

"Now, now, there's a whole lot of people mad at you right now for questioning their queen. Don't need me off your side too."

"We just restored our supplies; now we're feeding them indefinitely while they heal. Eleven more people. I don't know what she was thinking." James fumed as he worked to secure the board in place, narrowly missing his thumb with a swing of his hammer. "What's your opinion?"

"Finally consulting another council member, eh?" Ramirez teased. "Just kidding. I think it was good of her. We could use more numbers. It's more mouths to feed, but so long as they turn out to be all right and pull their weight."

"That seems to be how everyone else is thinking too," James huffed. "I swear if we had tried this crap under Vicars, there would have been a rebellion."

Ramirez shrugged. "Vicars and Jorah are two very different leaders, and now Fort Rache is a very different place."

The day was much warmer than the weeks of late, and James had taken the opportunity to gather a group to help construct a rudimentary stable. Recently, a supply run had returned with four live pigs, the only survivors of a petting zoo a few towns over. Until now, the animals had been kept in one of the fenced-in back yards; it was now time for a better solution.

"How do you want the entrance, Duran?" one of the workers

called.

"Low and tight to keep the heat in," he called back from his perch atop his ladder.

The building of the stable had to be done quickly, as it was only a matter of time before relentless and heavy snows would come. They could always build a better barn once spring arrived. A larger space would be needed, as with any luck, they would have a new litter of piglets by then.

They continued to work, soon sweating under the sun, though it was a greatly welcome change to the usual brittle cold. Just as James had climbed down from the ladder, dismissing the men for a brief break, a voice called out to him.

"James?"

He turned, at first unsure who had spoken, before he spied the form of Evangeline standing in the shadows of a home nearby. Her face was devoid of its usual makeup, her lips cracked and dry, wisps of her typically voluminous red hair fell lank and dead from her hood.

"Evangeline, what can I do for you?" James asked, trying not to be obvious that he noticed her abnormally disheveled appearance. "I haven't seen you around much."

"I've been staying in the house we set up, you know, for some of the women. Mack's wife, Kendra, she just had the baby, so I've been helping." She paused, glancing around at the slew of men resting in the grass. "Could we go somewhere private to talk?"

"Of course," James said concernedly, leading her to a more secluded spot among the rows of homes. "Is something wrong?"

James had always admired Evangeline, her courage and fortitude. She was a clever woman, one who had not yet let this world beat her down, who instead had managed to climb the ladder until she had settled alongside Vicars comfortably. Now, James sometimes wondered how she had been coping with a lesser lifestyle. Judging by her appearance, not very well.

Evangeline looked around once more, nervously twisting the hem of her sleeve, "I think something's wrong with Jorah." The words tumbled out of her mouth as though she couldn't stop them, her pale eyes filled with anxiety.

"Not you too," James snapped, with more annoyance and vigor than he had intended.

"I—I'm sorry, it's just—"

"No, no I'm sorry, tell me why," James said, softening his voice, unnerved by the panic that had sprung onto her features.

"I think that you both are doing a great job here. Things have never been more peaceful and safer, but …" She trailed off, biting her already damaged lips. "Maybe the pressure, maybe it's just been a little bit much for Jorah."

"Evangeline," James said sternly, "tell me what's happened, I promise you aren't going to be in any trouble."

It seemed he had guessed her fear correctly, as with a sigh of relief, the words began to tumble out of her. "There were two things, really. The first was a few nights ago. I woke up to Kendra's baby crying, and Kendra hasn't been feeling well, so I thought I would let her sleep and handle it. I was rocking him, had just got him to stop fussing when…" She shivered, twisting the coat so hard, her knuckles cracked. "It was Jorah, she was just outside the window. It was the middle of the night, and it was freezing out. But she was just standing there, staring inside, staring at me and the baby with this *expression* on her face. It was like there wasn't a single thought in her head, but at the same time it was so angry, so unnerving."

James felt his teeth grinding in his mouth, the burning, molten dread dripping back in his stomach. When he didn't speak, Evangeline continued.

"I didn't know what to do, so I just ignored her. I put the baby back down, and when I looked again, she was gone." She looked up into James's eyes. "Does Jorah sleepwalk?" she asked, almost hopefully.

"Not that I know of. What was the second thing?"

"Now, please don't be mad, but I went into your house yesterday," she began. "I wasn't snooping or stealing, I promise. There was no guard. I knocked, but nobody answered. I was only coming to look for one of my hats that I thought I may have left behind in my room when I moved out."

"Go on."

"Well, like I said, nobody answered, and I needed to get back to help Kendra, so I just went in. My room was upstairs, the big one at the end of the hall, so that's where I went, but—" She seemed to blanch at the memory, once again looking around in terror. "Just go look for yourself, okay? Please."

"We don't use the upstairs. The fireplace heat doesn't reach. It's too cold."

"Just promise me, go look in my old room."

James sighed. "Okay, I will, and I'll talk to Jorah. You're right that she has probably just been a little stressed out, but you know her. She loves this place, and she wants nothing more than to protect it. She would never hurt you."

Evangeline nodded. "Yeah, thank you, James." And with that she scurried off.

James watched her go, pondering briefly what could possibly be hiding upstairs to have spooked her so badly. However, there was work to be done, and he decided that finding out could wait.

"Think she'd go out with me?" Ramirez asked as James walked back to the group. "She's looking a little skinny lately, but damn, I don't mind so much."

James didn't reply, prompting Ramirez to backtrack.

"I'm just kidding, mostly. Is she all right?"

James turned to Ramirez, once again craving a cigarette and damn near on the verge of retrieving one. "Does Jorah seem off to you? Different?"

"Well, I can't say I knew what she was like before all this, never even spoke with her until she walked out holding Vicars' head." He stretched out his hand, mimicking the blank look that Jorah had worn as she'd displayed her trophy. "You worried?"

"No," James lied, "but some are, Jonas and now Evangeline."

"From what I've seen, Jorah's tough. She's a strong leader and a good person—even if she's scary as shit sometimes. That being said, you've known Jonas and Evangeline a lot longer. And I know, I know that you and her are on some crazy romance spree, but that doesn't mean you aren't missing anything."

James sighed, annoyed with the turn in his day. "Thanks for the shitty advice."

Ramirez laughed good-naturedly. "I'm known here for my cooking, not my advice. Get used to it."

Smoke rose in billowing black spirals over the treetops, the signal that fresh bodies were being burned. Mostly berserkers that had been caught lurking nearby, only one man from camp, a loner who'd been unlucky enough to catch a stray bullet that should have added another berserker to the pile.

James turned his back on the angry cloud, ducking inside the dimly lit home before him.

"Check under the sink," he ordered, pointing in the direction of the trashed kitchen. "And make sure it hasn't expired."

That morning Jonas had come to James with the idea of searching surrounding homes for fire extinguishers, a runoff idea stemming from the disastrous fire weeks prior. In addition, James had been instructed to retrieve more building materials.

James waded through the house, and upon finding nothing of consequence, shouldered open the jammed back door to the yard. Old tires and sheets of aluminum and plywood littered the yard. There were several old cars as well, which James made note of, as some of them might learn to run again with a little love.

"Back here." James summoned the rest of the crew, and together the men worked to load materials into the truck waiting out front. It was tiring work, cold sweat forming pools beneath their heavy layers of clothing.

"Heads up!" Tom shouted as his form appeared in the doorway of the house, two bright-red fire extinguishers cradled in his arms.

James turned to see the child wander out of the woods, his jaw broken, and clothes tattered over stretched and sallow skin. He moved toward them slowly, nothing but a sad croaking noise emitting from his gaping mouth.

"I've got it," James sighed, retrieving the pistol from his belt. The other men turned away from the sight, back to their work, desensitized. James felt very little as he fired, reminding himself that this was not the first berserker child he had seen and likely would not be the last.

"You all right, man?" James asked, noticing the tears that had welled in Tom's eyes as he approached the older man.

"Just looked a little like Dean is all, when he was that young."

"Dean's doing good things these days," James answered, unsure of what else to say. "You should be proud."

Tom nodded, offering a slightly teary smile. "Been hard letting him go out without me, but I know I won't be around forever. The boy needs to be able to take care of himself."

"People at the fort like Dean; he's in good hands," James said gruffly. "Jorah likes him too, so he's extra safe."

James turned, though instead of seeing comfort on Tom's face, he was met with an appraising gaze.

"There's something I need to talk to you about, it's about Jorah."

James's first reaction was annoyance, though he held his

tongue, turning away from Tom as he stooped to gather more wood. "What's that?"

"I should have said something a long time ago," Tom began, "but I didn't want to put her in danger, and then she was safe and became our leader—a good leader too, and I didn't think I needed to. But now I fear I've made a mistake."

A low, distant rumbling cut through the air, interrupting the retort that had been on the tip of James's tongue.

"What the—?" James murmured, looking up at the truck speeding toward them. "It's one of ours!" he called out, settling the anxious converging as men hurried to investigate the noise.

"Looks like Jonas," Tom said, his brow furrowed.

A moment later, the truck had screeched to a stop, snow and ice spinning out behind it as Jonas jumped out, his eyes wide as he rushed to James. "Someone came from the military camp. They came to speak to Jorah," he burst out.

"You mean to speak with the leader of the fort?"

"No, they came for *Jorah*. They knew she was there. She wouldn't let anyone else into the meeting. I came as soon as I could."

"Go, now," Tom said immediately. "I'll finish things here."

James nodded to him gratefully, jumping into the passenger seat as Jonas floored the vehicle in reverse.

"What do you mean she wouldn't let anyone in?" James demanded as soon as they were speeding back down the road, glad they had chosen a nearby house to gather supplies. "She's in there alone with them? Did she know them?"

"I was at the gates when he showed up. He said he came from the military camp—Camp Prevail, it's called, and that he knew Jorah and wanted to speak with her."

"And the guards just let him in—and then left her alone with him?" James's body had gone so incredibly rigid, he could almost feel his bones scraping together.

"We told her what had happened. I ran off to get Ramirez. When I came back, they were both in the office. She told the guards not to disturb her."

James opened his mouth in rage, but Jonas swiftly cut him off, his eyes still wide and anxious.

"Before you ask, we did order them aside, but it's her new men, from that group she let in last week—it seems that her authority is the only one they recognized. When we realized they weren't going to let us in, I came for you as fast as I could. It's the only thing I could think to do, rather than starting a shootout in the street."

James took deep breaths, trying to stem the anxiety and fury frothing within him. "It's okay, you did what you should."

"There's something else," Jonas said, glancing toward James. "Evangeline is missing."

"What do you mean, missing?"

"Kendra says she never came back to the house last night— says they didn't think too much of it. I guess Ramirez asked her out the other day, so they thought she was with him. Nobody has seen her since noon yesterday."

"Fuck!" James cursed, resisting the urge to slam his hands on the dashboard. He shook his head violently instead, grinding his molars to dust. "One crisis at a time."

They pulled up to the gates, the heavy doors immediately opening for them. James had his feet on the ground the moment the bed of the truck cleared the gates, taking off at a brisk jog toward the center home of the complex.

"Oh, you're all in for it now," he heard Ramirez say to the guards stationed outside the front door.

James approached the steps, where two men stood with rifles slung across their chests, staring down at him smugly.

"Step aside," James ordered, doing his best to remain calm.

"We have orders not to let anyone inside. There is a diplomatic meeting in process," answered the taller of the two men, the arrogant smile on his face growing more infuriating by the second.

"Whose orders?"

"Jorah Sinclair."

"Well, I am James Duran, and I am *ordering* you to step aside," James growled, his fingers twitching toward his pistol.

When neither of the men spoke, James drew the pistol, leveling it with the taller man's chest. "I understand that you are under the impression that Jorah is the sole leader of this fort. Due to your status as new citizens here, I will forgive this misjudgment." James radiated nothing but pure authority as he spoke, his voice booming, eyes narrowed warningly. People had begun to gather in the street behind him, curiously watching the scene unfold before them.

"Step aside now, and I will consider not exiling you from the fort." James finished.

The two men exchanged a brief glance, the smug grins having been wiped from their faces. Without a word, they lowered their rifles, stepping aside and leaving the path to the door clear.

James rushed inside, Jonas on his heels, while Ramirez ordered a group of nearby men to relieve Jorah's guards of their post.

"Jorah?" James called as he burst into the house, whirling around, looking for things out of place. The office doors had been closed, the blinds drawn; James threw the door open.

Jorah stood beside the magnificent mahogany desk. A half-finished glass of whiskey was all that sat on its surface, discarded.

She hardly looked up as they entered, her dead eyes trained on a man who knelt on the floor across the room, his hands raised in surrender.

"What the hell is going on?" James spat, looking between the tip of Jorah's revolver and the kneeling man, her finger resting steadily on the trigger. "Who is this?"

"My name is Riley," the man answered, glancing over at James and Jonas. "I've come from Camp Prevail; I came to talk to Jorah."

"Why?"

Jorah had still not spoken, her stormy gaze trained on Riley, the gun steady in her grasp. Riley glanced toward her nervously before looking back to James. "There's another group coming to talk soon, the leaders of the camp. They need your help. I wasn't going to be allowed to come. I only wanted to speak with Jorah."

"How did you know she was here? What do the others want from us?" James questioned, his own pistol still gripped in his hand.

"They've spied on your camp before," Riley said. "I don't know exactly how." His gaze fell back on Jorah. "Sana came once. She was so glad to see that you were okay, and then she told me and Geoff, and I had to come see you. Jorah, we thought you were dead."

It was then, finally, that Jorah spoke, and her voice grated like a knife dragged across steel. "Liar."

A panicked expression spread across Riley's face. "I'm not lying, we thought you were dead—if we had known there was any chance, we would have searched for you." Nervously, he attempted to stand, but again sank to his knees as Jorah cocked the revolver.

"You left me to die. You took the bullets out of my gun."

"No! We never would have."

"Enough!" Jorah screamed.

Without a second thought, James's feet carried him forward, his body jerking in between the outstretched revolver and Riley's shocked face. "Stop."

At last, she looked at him, her features distorted. "Move!"

"No, you can't kill him." James paused, trying to level his voice. "Not until we meet with the rest of his group."

Jorah's eyes fluttered wildly, her manic expression sending

tendrils of dread tunneling throughout James's body, but he pushed them away. "We'll put him in the jail, we will meet with his group, then we can decide what to do with him." James raised his hands calmly, his heart pumping. "Think of the fort, Jorah. Killing him could start a war."

She didn't answer, her chest heaving, and the gun lowered a few inches. Without moving, James glanced to Jonas and Ramirez, both frozen in the doorway. "Take him to the jail. Make sure there's a guard stationed at all times."

The two men moved, grabbing Riley by the elbows as he stood, albeit shakily, and pulling him out of the room.

"Jorah, you can put the gun down," James said evenly, reaching out and resting his hands on the cool metal, pushing it toward the floor.

As the gun lowered, it was like the strings holding Jorah upright were cut, and her body sagged toward the floor. The gun tumbled out of her hands, landing on the plush carpet with a muffled thud. She met his eyes, and in that moment, her gaze looked just as deep and as sad as the first day he had seen her.

Bluer than the ocean, lonelier than the moon.

34

SANA, LEADER OF MEN

My nerves hadn't ceased to writhe and burn since the moment I stepped out of the classroom, and now, two days later, I was on the verge of taking Riley up on his offer of a drink.

I'd sworn the two to secrecy before divulging what I'd learned. I dragged them outside of camp on the premise of a fresh-air walk, so as to avoid anyone hearing the shouts of rage I knew would come.

Now, I stared around at the inside of my tent, my half-packed duffel bag lying at my feet.

What do you pack for a mission that you may not make it back from?

So far, warm clothes and even warmer clothes and the few rations of food I had lying around. I glanced down at the one photo I still had, weathered and torn, depicting my parents and me on vacation when I was only a baby.

Gingerly I lifted it, running my fingers over the frayed image before tucking it safely into my breast pocket. I decided to leave behind my extra pair of boots; they would only weigh me down.

"Sana, you ready?" Lachlan called from outside.

I hefted my bag, zipping the near entirety of my belongings inside and stepped out into the cool daylight.

Lachlan's uniform looked clean and orderly, his own pack slung over his broad shoulders and his now-short red hair slicked down beneath his cap.

"Looking dapper," I commented, and he responded with a warm smile.

"Wanted to look good in case this is the last time anyone here sees me."

"Fair enough."

Together we headed to the main entrance of the camp; Corporal Moore and Master Sergeant Carrigan were already present, loading the truck we would take with our meager supplies. Sergeant Black had elected to stay behind, the only high-ranking member of the army left in Camp Prevail, should we fail to return.

"Are you sure you're up for this?" I asked Geoff, who stood to the sidelines beside Musa, leaning his weight into his cane.

"Absolutely," he said, his expression set and determined.

I nodded, stowing my bag on the truck. It had taken mine and

Lachlan's combined efforts, but we had finally convinced Carrigan to bring Riley and Geoff to the meeting with Jorah. Should all go to plan, they would then remain behind in Fort Rache, instead of continuing with us to the radio tower.

"Where's Riley?" I asked, glancing around.

"I haven't seen him since last night; he was gone when I woke up."

"Well, he better show up soon, or he'll miss his ride."

"He doesn't know he's invited to come; I never got the chance to tell him," Geoff said.

A clump of disappointment formed inside my gut, weighing down the promise that I had felt for the coming meeting. I had been excited at the prospect of the four of us being back together once again.

"He's probably just off moping in the woods," Geoff continued sourly. "He'll just have to see Jorah when you all get back from saving the world."

I forced a smile, turning to Musa, who clasped my hands in his own. His dark eyes were sad today, drawn and distant, and I thought he looked much older than I had ever seen him.

"Good luck, Sana," he said almost in a whisper. "Tell Jorah I say hello. Tell her I'm sorry."

"Sorry for what?" I asked. "And you can tell her yourself when you see her."

A small, sad smile graced his face. "Be brave, Sana. This is what you were always meant to do."

I accepted his words with a slight nod, holding back the urge to question his cryptic declarations. I climbed into the truck bed, helping to pull Geoff aboard while Lachlan passed up his cane. A small crowd had gathered to see us off, rumors having spread throughout camp like wildfire as to the reason for our mission.

"Good luck, Sana," a young woman yelled from the crowd, I gave her a slight wave, feeling my cheeks turning pink.

"Isn't that the one you've got a crush on?" Geoff teased, prodding me in the side.

"Shut up," I hissed, taking my seat in the truck bed, eyeing the crowd of thin, hungry faces watch us go.

Wondering if I would ever come back to this place.

The road to Fort Rache was shrouded in trees. Bare and lifeless, they stuck into the sky like a skeletal ribcage, driving into the belly of the beast.

We stayed low in the truck bed, as per instruction, as the gates of Fort Rache came into view—the only sort of protection we would have should the occupants choose to open fire. I glanced up through the slats of the reinforced truck bed, its walls having been built up higher with strips of wood and fencing.

"Stop. Turn off your vehicle and exit with your hands raised," called the gruff voice of a man. I could just see his torso standing atop his guard post, the perfect place in which to keep watch over the only road into the compound.

Or to shoot us all dead in a matter of seconds, I thought bitterly, scrunching down further, my legs bent awkwardly against Lachlan's.

"It's them," another voice called, "they're here."

My head jerked toward Lachlan, his face displaying what I suspected was an equal amount of shock to my own.

How did they know? he mouthed, and I shook my head in response, feeling the pit of anxiety in my gut give an unpleasant shudder.

We heard the doors of the truck opening next, the footsteps of Moore and Carrigan as they climbed out.

"I am Master Sergeant Thomas Carrigan. I come from Camp Prevail. We have come to ask for your help, as well as in the hopes of brokering a peace deal between our two communities." Carrigan's voice did not waver for a moment, and I wished desperately I could see more than a mere sliver of the gates.

"How many are with you?"

"Five, there are three more in the bed."

"All of you, out now," a new voice sounded, familiar, and slightly panting as though they had just run to the gates.

With a look of finality toward Lachlan and Geoff, we pushed ourselves to our feet. We were careful to keep our hands in the air as best we could while we climbed from the truck, Geoff hobbling forward with one arm raised above his head while the other clutched his cane.

"How did you know we were coming?" Moore asked as soon as the five of us had formed a line. My heart hammered in my chest at how completely exposed we were.

"One of your people, Riley Daniels, he arrived at our gates this morning," James Duran said, and while his voice did not sound angry, his dark tone still caused pangs of anxiety to ricochet through me.

"We did not authorize Riley's coming here," Carrigan responded quickly. "He has acted of his own accord in doing so."

"We figured," James replied with a hint of sarcasm. His dark eyes scanned us, holding still only briefly on Geoff and his walking stick. "Leave your weapons in your truck. If you bring any inside, it will be a regrettable choice."

The gates swung forward as five Fort Rache men marched out, their eyes trained carefully on us as we unclipped and unburdened ourselves from our guns and knives.

"If Riley's already blown this, I'll kill him with my own fucking hands," Geoff growled, leaning against the truck for support as he undid the fastenings on his holster. "Couldn't wait to see Jorah, could he?"

Though I said nothing, I agreed wholeheartedly, doubting if I had been this upset with Riley since he'd stolen the painkillers from Musa's home.

"What is this about?" James asked Carrigan as the gates of the fort swung closed behind us. James and several of his men stood in a firm line between us and the rest of the community, making it clear that for the time being we would not enter any further.

"It would be best if we could talk in private with whomever your leaders are. This is not news for the general public," Carrigan said carefully, and I noticed for the first time how deceptively powerful-seeming Carrigan was. While James Duran had thirty fewer years on Carrigan, the two men still stood shoulder to shoulder, dark, authoritative, and imposing.

James glanced back to the rest of us. "Which of you is here because you know Jorah?"

Carrigan and Moore both glanced back to me, and taking my cue, I stepped forward. "My name is Sana; this is Geoff and Lachlan." I gestured behind me. "Geoff and I were in a group with Jorah for months—Riley too, she's our friend."

"Mm-hmm," James muttered, eyes narrowed, "and I don't think I need to ask how you knew about her. I hear you've been spying on us for weeks."

If the tension has been palpable before his words, it was downright booming now. Though only for a moment, as with an exasperated sigh, James Duran continued.

"But I guess I can't get too upset about that; we've done the same to you."

Now *that* was surprising news, as we had not been sure if Fort Rache was even privy to our existence, let alone keeping tabs on the camp.

"Please, Mr. …"

"James Duran."

"Mr. Duran, the news we carry is of the utmost importance, and I am afraid we are on a very tight schedule to deliver it," Carrigan pressed. "If you would just give us some of your time."

James nodded, and relief dripped into my body. "We can talk; the rest of the council is already waiting."

He began to lead us down the street, armed guards still accompanying our every step. The elegant houses of the fort were mostly brick and rather large. Many of the windows had been boarded over, likely to retain heat, I suspected. Glancing down the street, I could see where it ended in the main office building, the type that usually held the community manager's office or a clubhouse sort of lounge. To its left I knew to be the field, the one with the gallows, where the fence was just underbuilt.

"Mr. Duran, where is Riley?" I asked, earning a sharp look of disapproval as I quickened my pace to near James.

"Riley Daniels is in holding." He paused, glancing back at me. "It was the only thing I could do to keep him alive."

"What do you mean?" I asked, but the procession had come to a halt before the largest home in the complex, as well as the grandest.

"Come on," James ushered, leading us into the foyer of the home. To our left stood a set of intricate glass French doors, and just beyond them, standing at the edge of a large desk, was Jorah.

She didn't speak as we entered, nor did she seem to blink, her gaze unwavering as it passed over each of our faces in turn. We continued to the back of the long room, lined with tall bookshelves and cabinets of a deep, glossy wood. We turned to face her then, and it was only at that point that I noticed the others present in the room.

The first was Ramirez, stout with his mop of black hair and scraggly beard. We'd been given strict instructions before leaving not to expose Ramirez's identity. This had been accepted easily, as we all knew that revealing that a man on the council of leaders was our spy would no doubt anger the rest of the fort.

A member of their guard closed the doors once we were all inside. Turning to face away from the office, you could just see his figure through the patterned glass.

"As I said, my name is James Duran. This is Adrian Ramirez, Jonas Yeun, Heather McCallister, and Jorah Sinclair."

Carrigan nodded to each in turn. As he took a step forward, I began to feel as though we were standing in a grand throne room, waiting to be judged by the king and queen of the land.

"I am Master Sergeant Thomas Carrigan, this is Corporal Lucy Moore, Corporals Sana Mangal and Lachlan Muir, and civilian Geoff Christensen. We are here to ask for your help."

"Ask away," James said. He folded his arms over his chest, his jacket riding up and revealing the pistol holstered to his belt.

I glanced to Jorah. Her eyes were locked on Carrigan, and I could tell she was doing her utmost not to meet my stare. *Does she really think we left her to die?* I wanted so badly to call out to her, go to her, hug my friend who I had thought I would never see again.

But I didn't move, and neither did her gaze, her eyes cold and jaw taut. She looked different, and I knew that I had not been imagining it that day we had witnessed the hanging—something had changed inside her, and it scared me.

"We believe that we have found a way to stop the Breaks," Carrigan began, and there was an audible intake of breath from across the room. "There is a sort of radio tower that we can only hope to reach with your help. It is there we may be able to send a signal that will stop the Breaks."

"You're going to need to tell us more than that," James said, at the same time Jonas gasped.

"How do you know?"

Carrigan began to explain, even going so far as to remove the tiny disk from his pocket. Jonas jerked forward at the sight of the device, the first and longest to inspect it, and even the indifferent yet cold look on Jorah's face twitched as it passed through her fingers. The only area of explanation where Carrigan seemed to hold back was on the dire situation of Camp Prevail. He only asked that, in addition to an entourage from Fort Rache accompanying us to the tower, a handful of provisions and men be sent to Camp Prevail in our absence.

There were only a few moments of silence when he had finished before Jonas spoke, the young man once again holding the disk. "Even if you reach the tower, and if it's right for sending your signal, how do you know how to shut them off? If the devices are partially damaged, like you said, how can you know they can even receive any signal?"

"I told you that I was given a package of information, informing me of the devices, of what was about to occur. I was ordered to memorize its contents, and then it was destroyed. Well, there was one part that wasn't."

I turned to Carrigan, confused as I had yet to hear of this, and watched as he pulled a small, slim silver tablet from within his pocket. It was completely metal and no thicker than a pencil. Flawless, unmarked steel, except for a tiny screen that blazed a row of numbers and letters.

"That has been nothing but a blank screen until three days ago when it turned on of its own accord. I believe it to be the kill code, per se, for the devices."

"Incredible," Jonas whispered, staring at the device, "this is incredible. I thought it must be something like this, an implant, but wow—it's ingenious."

"And they can't just be removed?" James asked. "You say that removing them kills the host?"

"Removing them will not work, nor should it be attempted. I believe our only option is to get that code to the tower, preferably in less than two days, as I'm sure you know that is when the next Break is set to occur."

James nodded, and in a determined voice, he said, "How many men do you need?"

"A smaller crew to come to the tower; for that we mostly lack the gas to reach it in time. As for protection at Camp Prevail— five to ten should suffice."

James opened his mouth to speak, but to the general surprise of the room, it was Jorah who stepped forward.

She leaned over, taking the small disk from Jonas, and pinching it between the few remaining fingers on her damaged hand, holding it in the air as she seemed to inspect it. "How many fighters did you say you have in Camp Prevail?" she asked. "How many civilians?"

For the first time, Carrigan hesitated, though only for an instant, his eyes trained on Jorah. "Twenty-six fighters, including the four of us, and approximately thirty-two civilians, mostly women and children."

"So, less than we have, but not by much—and still you ask us to send you not only men, but provisions as well, why?"

"Camp Prevail is not nearly as well protected as Fort Rache. We have less food, our people are generally weaker, and we cannot leave them on their own considering we don't know how long we will be gone."

A small, deadly smile had grown on Jorah's face, spreading over her pale skin like mold. "Liar."

"Jorah—" James moved to interrupt, surprise and sudden anger radiating off him, but she held up a hand, pressing on.

"Why would Riley come of his own accord when you chose to bring Geoff and Lachlan? Why do we need to send you men and provisions for a trip that will take less than four days total, when we are only marginally better off?" The vigor in her voice was growing steadily with each word, an unsuppressed hatred beginning to billow out of her. "I can think of no pure reason."

"Jorah, please—" I began, trying to calm the storm I could feel approaching just as intensely as if a true hurricane were at our doorstep, but she cut me off.

"Sana!" she mocked. "Sana and Geoff and Riley, why do you expect us to believe your story when we all know you left me for dead? James was there that day; he saw you run! So, you send Riley ahead of you, send Riley to woo me and cry to me and promise it was all a misunderstanding?"

"We *did* think you were dead," Geoff implored, taking a few shaky steps toward her. "Jorah, we never would have left you."

"Liar!" she yelled, and her voice rang, bouncing off the corners of the room. "You saw them take me—you *saw* it. I know you did. You left me. You took the bullets out of my gun."

"We were outnumbered ten to one," I pleaded. "We came back for you, but then we found the house had burned down, and there was a body in it. Jorah, we thought it was you, it was so burnt—wait, what do you mean, 'took the bullets from your gun'?"

James made a sudden, jerking motion that failed to go unnoticed. "Enough. If you would excuse us while we discuss." He crossed to the doors and opened them, murmuring to the guards before stepping back and gesturing for us to leave. "We'll have an answer for you soon," he said with an air of finality.

I led the group as we sidled past Jorah, whose breath was coming in ragged bursts. It was then, as I neared her, that she finally met my gaze.

And I could see that Jorah was gone.

35
TRAITOR JAMES DURAN

"They are *lying* to us," Jorah pushed as soon as the doors had swung closed. "If we go with them, send men to their camp—we'll all be dead come morning."

"I disagree," Ramirez said. "It makes sense, the devices, the station, even the fact that Carrigan has that information. There aren't many master sergeants; it makes sense that he could have been told all this."

"Then you're a fool," Jorah growled, her head snapping toward him.

Emotions bubbled inside of James. He gazed at Jorah, her face flushed with rage.

"Can you give us a moment?" James said, turning to Ramirez, Heather, and Jonas. "Please."

They exchanged glances before nodding and slipping past James into the entryway, the door clicking closed behind him.

"Jorah," James whispered calmly, reaching out to set his hands on her waist. His fingers had hardly brushed her when she jerked away.

"Don't touch me," she seethed. "As far as I'm concerned, you're a traitor now too."

James bristled at her reply. "Why? Because I think they might be telling the truth?"

"You know what they did to me. You told me yourself that you thought they left me—do you remember? Now they show up here with a story, and you're ready to give everything up for it? Everything we've worked for." She turned away, hunched over the desk, her nails burrowing into the wood.

"I have never said that we should go with them or give them men."

"I want them dead," she whispered suddenly, and then she turned, a manic, gleeful smile on her face. "I want them dead; I want them hung for what they've done. Lying, treachery, attempting to take from the fort—they deserve it."

It was then, when she turned, that James finally saw it. That *thing* that for weeks he had caught naught but glimpses of, the glimmer of something terrible lurking within her.

"You're right," he said automatically, working to keep his voice level.

She perked up at his words, her frenzied smile spreading. She danced toward him, grasping his fingertips. "You mean it?"

James forced himself not to recoil. He nodded, and again she swayed forward, graceful and grinning as she placed a gentle kiss on hip lips. "I'm so glad."

James placed his hands on her waist and pushed her back a step. "But not all of them, just your group, the ones who betrayed you."

Jorah hesitated, and then nodded. "When should we do it?"

"Soon, but we have work to do first. We need the fort to know they deserved it."

She nodded vigorously. "What should I do?"

"For now, you should go rest." James said, brushing a hand down her cheek.

"Why?"

"Because you need your strength, and the others know that you'll never believe their lies. You go and rest, let me handle this. I'll tell them we need more time to think. They can wait outside the gates for now."

She thought it over for a moment, and then her eyes narrowed, focusing on James. "You would never lie to me, right, James?"

"Never," he replied firmly. "Get some rest. I have everything handled."

He followed her to the living room, tucking her in and placing a glass of whiskey beside her. She laughed at the gesture, waving to him as he slipped the door closed.

Immense relief flooded James the moment he had a solid panel between him and Jorah. Nothing but chaos rocketed through his brain as his legs, seemingly of their own accord, carried him toward the stairs.

It grew steadily colder as he climbed, like summiting a mountain. At the top of the stairs, the hallway seemed to bend away from him, darkness seeping in as though the very walls repelled light and warmth.

The door of the room stood ajar, and with each step toward it, he heard Evangeline's voice growing louder in his ears—*just promise me, go look in my old room.*

Light filtered in through the thin curtains, which had been swept closed over the window. The room looked normal, tidy, the bed made, and drawers pushed in.

It was a moment later that the smell hit him.

Fighting back waves of nausea, James tiptoed across the room, praying that Jorah would not hear him. James had a sinking suspicion of what he might find in the moments before he opened the closet door.

The closet, at first, seemed wholly normal. It was empty except for an overturned bucket, which sat in the center. As James reached for it, something caught his eye. He craned his neck around the side of the wooden sliding door. The white paint had been scratched off in a single large patch, the paint replaced with writing. Words had been carved into the side of the door, hundreds of them. Some appeared as though they had been carved with a knife; others held the distinct, shallow appearance of fingernails scratched bare.

It didn't matter, though, how the words had been carved, because they all said the same thing, over and over again:

Red Blood. Red Blood. Red Blood. Red Blood.

He tipped back the bucket then, seeing only the edge of what lay underneath, something he thought had long been destroyed. It was sickening, to say the least, seeing the rotting eyes of Maximilian Vicars peering back at him.

James found Jonas and Ramirez in the planning room, the two hunched over a map, hundreds of gruesome Polaroids as their backdrop. The group from Camp Prevail sat just outside, waiting patiently in the chairs once reserved for visitors to the community, waiting to speak with the manager.

"James, I know what you're going to say, but I think they're telling the truth—" Jonas began as soon as James burst into the room, quickly closing the door behind him.

"I know," James cut him off, "I think they are too."

"About time!" Ramirez exclaimed. "Where's Jorah?"

"Resting, but we don't have much time. She thinks that we'll be executing her old group soon."

"Christ."

"We need to plan, and we need to move fast. I'll call them in."

"Wait, James," Jonas said, "there's one thing that doesn't make sense. Jorah said you told her you thought her group abandoned her. Did they?"

James froze, hands cramping from being so tightly bound into fists. "After we found her—McNeal's men, they were just bored, and they torched the house. Jorah was already on her way back here as a prisoner when it happened."

"But they said there was a body inside?"

"When we found her, there was a body of a man in the yard and a berserker woman that Jorah had just killed; it must have been one of them. Jorah asked me weeks ago, and I didn't tell her—I didn't tell her because I didn't want her to leave. She would have gone to find them if she knew."

"And her gun being empty?"

"That, I don't know."

The others quieted, taking in the newfound knowledge.

"You can't tell Jorah, not yet," Jonas said, his expression solemn.

"I know."

"But one day you'll have to."

"Jorah has been the one with the real power since the moment she killed Vicars," James explained. They'd just used the better part of the last half hour describing the events that had occurred within the walls of Fort Rache over the last few months. From Jorah's capture, to McNeal's experiments, to Jorah's miraculous escape and rise to power.

"The people love her, and not to mention she has her own slew of guards," Jonas continued. "She let them in a few days ago, a power move on her part, now that I think about it. She's too unstable to reason with. After you've stopped the Breaks, when you come back as heroes, then we can get our power back." Jonas turned to James, his voice lowering sympathetically. "And maybe then we'll be able to help Jorah too."

James nodded, looking around at the group before him. He paused on the shorter woman—Sana, he remembered. She had the distinct appearance of an old soul, with dark hair and skin, her eyes like black slits as she appeared to scrutinize his every word. She caught his gaze and seemed to take it as an invitation to speak.

"We can't leave Riley behind; she wants him dead."

"We can't break him out. There's no time, and her men are stationed there. It's too suspicious if we try."

"She'll kill him."

"No, she won't," Jonas interrupted. "I'm changing the plan. I'm staying."

"Absolutely not," James snapped, swooping down upon his friend. "It's too dangerous, and you'll be useful at the station."

"I have a duty to the people here. Jorah won't hurt me," he said confidently, "and I'll make sure Riley isn't harmed either. I have a plan, and I'll have Tom to help me. I can work on the missing Evangeline situation too."

"We can't leave Riley," Sana repeated, turning to Geoff and forcing him into the conversation. "It's no better than what Jorah thinks we did to her."

"It is better," Jonas pushed. "I promise I'll keep him safe."

"There's something else you should know," Carrigan interrupted; his voice weighed ominously.

James wasn't sure how to feel as Carrigan explained. It was as though a balloon of relief had sprung up inside him, only to be weighed down by dread.

"You're saying that she might be brain damaged now? That when McNeal messed with the chip, it caused her to be like this?"

"If she was never like this before, then I'm almost certain."

Now that he knew this, it was like pieces of a long-lost puzzle were appearing in his brain. Bit by bit the picture formed.

It wasn't Jorah that was like this, it was the chip in her head.

"Do you think that when we shut down the devices, she might get better?" James asked hopefully.

It was Sana who spoke now, her face pained, but James saw too the glimmer of hope in her dark eyes. "I hope so, but I don't know. We don't know if it's just the chip or if there's been permanent damage."

James leaned away from the desk, now aware that he had been practically doubled over. "It's a chance, there's hope," he said firmly.

"Let's get to it, then. We don't have time to waste," Ramirez announced, clapping his hands together.

James nodded, turning and forcing himself to leave the room. He pushed down the fear all too easily now, nearly immune to it, barely feeling how sick it was making him.

James crept into the home, careful to step only in the places he knew the boards would not protest. The others had gone, slipped away on the guise that the meeting had ended; Jorah's men none the wiser. Jonas had already begun his work, winding and sneaking through the fort on silent feet, speaking only to those he knew could be trusted.

She was sleeping when James entered the room, silent, peaceful breaths past soft, full lips. James reached for his backpack, though he froze, unable to stop himself from edging to her side. Her whiskey glass was empty, tipped over on the floor. He crouched beside the mattress, level with her sleeping figure, powerless as he reached out to brush the strands of white-blonde hair from her face.

She looked so peaceful when she slept, like the Jorah he remembered, the Jorah he loved.

"I'm going to fix you," he breathed, tracing the sharp curve of her cheekbones. "I promise."

He placed a soft kiss on her forehead, gathered his bag, and left the room. He could think of nothing else but her as he crept through the fort, making his way past the field, to the little spot where the wall just wasn't quite right.

Her laugh, her voice. The way she was so kind, so sincere— loyal, and candid and brave. The girl who gave everything she could for others. The girl who was as gentle as a bird and as vicious as a caged wolf.

But she was gone now, replaced with something terrible, beautiful but manic.

He took the bag of hurriedly gathered supplies from Jonas, then, turning back at the last moment, he pulled his friend into a hug.

Then James climbed the fence and was gone.

36

THE QUEEN OF THE DAMNED

Jorah

My fingernails are sore, burning. When I open my eyes, I see that I've scraped them ragged on the wood of the floor.

Blood drips down my hands, marking the white sheets, staining them.

I leave, pulling the wolf-fur coat from its place in the closet, donning it, wrapping myself in the thick fur, though I can't remember the last time I was cold.

Cold. Even the memory of the sensation feels distant, dreamlike. Like a recollection from your childhood that you aren't sure if you imagined.

When they tell me that the others are gone, I force myself not to draw my pistol and shoot them all dead.

"Where's James?"

They tell me he's gone too.

Then I learn that I've slept through the night; today is a new day. But still I am so tired.

They tell me Evangeline is still missing, and I'm confused, because they should have found her body by now.

I touch the wolf's fur, dense and coarse. *Traitorous, lying bitch.*

"Jorah."

Jonas approaches me, a smile on his face. It's fake, but he thinks that I don't know.

"Hey, Jonas."

"I have good news. The supply run that just came back killed a deer, a big one too. It was Dean that shot it, Tom's son."

Tom's son, Dean.

"That's great. I'll have to congratulate him when I see him." I smile. Somewhere inside, I do feel happy. I want my people to be fed, to thrive. I know that's what I want. I've only ever wanted to keep them safe. Bring books back for them, treats and prizes.

I remember a pile of books, ones that I lost somewhere along the road. There was one that was special; it was going to be funny, a joke. I remember it was for Riley. I remember Riley is here, waiting for me.

I think about going to him, killing him, ending it all, but then I think it can wait. Let him sit where I sat, cold and scared as I was, just for a little while. I'm headed to the front gates when I see Dean, and I hurry across the street to him.

"Congratulations on the deer, Dean, you should be proud."

He smiles back, ear to ear. "Thank you, Jorah. You should join me and Dad for dinner later. I know he would like it."

"I'd love to."

And then I'm happy again, knowing my people are going to be fed, that while many others will go to sleep hungry, my people will not know that pain tonight. It's what I want for them. I know that it is.

Maybe when James gets back, I'll feed him to them.

James

The journey had gone smoothly so far, nothing more delaying than the occasional stop to move debris from the road. They'd seen two berserkers, the decrepit forms lurching after them as the trucks flew by.

"If we keep up this pace, we should make it in in time, but it's going to be close," Sana said. She was constantly reading and rereading the crumpled map. "We got lucky with the weather, if only it can keep holding off a few more days."

They'd managed to secure the second truck on the pretense that Ramirez was taking it on a supply run and collected James on the side of the road just a few miles outside the walls of the fort.

"Would you stop talking? I'm trying to sleep," Ramirez grumbled from the back, rolling over in the cramped back seat.

This was the first time Sana had ridden with them, declaring at the last stop that if she had to sit in the truck bed for one more moment her legs would fall off.

They pushed onward silently for some time, Ramirez's snores the only station the car radio would turn to.

"I can't believe Riley did that," she muttered to herself. "He must have stolen a car. There's a couple that we keep outside the gates. Nobody would have noticed."

James grunted in response, wondering if Jonas really could keep Riley Daniels safe.

"I need to tell you something," Sana said, running her fingers over the map, "but first, I need to know why you trusted us."

James glanced at her out of the corner of his eye, hands tightening reflexively on the steering wheel. "Not about to betray me, right?"

She let out a shaky laugh. "No. But why? Jorah said you both thought we left her, betrayed her, so why trust us? I wouldn't, if I was in your shoes."

He turned to look at her, not caring that the road was flying by them. He was unsure of how to answer, but the look on her face suddenly made it all too easy. "You know why."

She sighed, looking back out at the road and the taillights of the other car. "Because you know that the house burned down, and you didn't tell Jorah."

"I didn't want her to leave," James admitted. "She would have left."

"I don't blame you, but there's something you should know."

She dug around in her pocket, removing a folded sheet of paper, which she held tightly in her hand.

"What is it?"

"Don't crash the truck," she warned, and then she began to read.

Jorah

I find myself sitting behind the desk; the room is full of candles. In my hand sits a small ornate glass, a dark amber liquid sloshing inside. I take a sip, and it burns my teeth and gums. I feel better.

"Jorah, did you hear me?"

"What? Sorry, just thinking," I say, looking up into the face of Jonas as he peers over the desk. There are others behind him too, Heather, two of my guards, a few of the members of the fort who like to be involved.

"I think we need to evacuate the fort. We can send everyone to Camp Prevail," Jonas says, and there are murmurs of agreement and argument behind him.

The past hour comes flooding back into my mind, clearer now than when it had occurred. I straighten in my seat. McNeal and Jefferson's group had finally reemerged, taken two of our men hostage while they were out on a supply run. They cut one of them to ribbons, then sent his head back with the other.

I recall meeting the man at the gates. He trembled while he held the blood-soaked sack.

"They said to hand over Duran and surrender the fort, and nobody else has to die."

"How many men, how well armed?"

"We know for certain about McNeal and Conrad, the eight men who left with him during the Break, the four that left later, and Jefferson and his two cronies." Jonas takes a deep breath. "But Shamus—the man who returned—he said they've got numbers closer to forty now. Turns out Gallagher told the truth, and that's only what he saw, all men … save for some prisoners." Jonas swallows, and I notice the sickly sheen of fear coating his face. "And we know what they're like. They won't make peace, they won't show mercy—they're coming to take the fort."

"Surely, we're in better shape than them," a man says, stepping forward. "Eat better, trained better; they'll never make it past the walls."

"We'll gun down plenty of them, sure, but they could get in. A truck could drive straight through the gates. Duran and Tom did it once," says another.

Duran.

"Where is James?" I blurt out, looking around, feeling strange at the confused faces looking back at me. *Shit.* I remember. "I mean, have you heard from him?"

Jonas shakes his head, holding up the handheld radio, which he said James had left for him. "The signal isn't going through, but I don't think they'll be back in time."

"The Break is tomorrow," I say, thinking out loud, as that seems to be the best way to make my brain work. "Right afterward is when they'll attack; that's what I would do, when we're scrambling."

Jonas nods. "Jefferson and Conrad may be morons, but McNeal is not. They'll have a plan."

"But what if they know that's what we'll guess? They could come tonight to trick us."

"No, it doesn't make sense for them to come tonight; it will be tomorrow. It will be much easier for them to dispose of their men who break on the road than it will be for us inside the walls," I say. "Either way, preparations begin as soon as this meeting is over."

"Preparations?"

I stand, taking another long swig from the glass, feeling stronger.

"I want everyone who can fight pulled for training. I want extra fortifications fit on every guard tower, as well as the houses with windows overlooking the wall. Anyone with military experience will be brought to me."

"Jorah, it's a lost cause. Even if we beat them back, we're going to lose half our people in the process."

I feel the hot torrent of anger building inside of me, like jets of boiling water firing off in my body. "We will *not* lose this place."

"The people should have the choice to leave, the sick and those who can't fight."

"Camp Prevail is a dump. If we lose this place we may as well shoot each other."

"We will build a new home," Jonas argues, and I can tell he's feeling brave. "The people have a right to choose if they live or die."

"Let me speak to them."

James

"I don't believe it."

"Neither do I."

"You—you don't?" James stumbled over his words, searching for the answer.

"Maybe the Jorah of today, how she is now, but before?" She swallowed, a terrible sadness creeping into her features. "She risked her life to save us within a day of meeting us. A day later, she risked it again to keep us safe—and she lost her fingers for it. *Days* after that she joined a shootout to help a stranger." Sana turned away from him, and James noticed the heaviness in her voice when she spoke again, the tremble in her words. "The Jorah I knew wouldn't have murdered her own sister. There's no way."

James was silent for a long time, lost in thought, not caring that his eyes burned. Miles had gone by before he spoke again.

"Tell me more about her, before."

"What do you want to know?"

"Anything, everything."

When Sana looked back at him then, she was smiling. "Should I start with how we met, or the time her and Geoff tried keeping out the Break by wearing tinfoil hats?"

413

Jorah

"Scouts just returned. McNeal's group is on the move. They've got cars; they'll be here by tonight."

"And the plan?"

"Going accordingly so far," Jonas says, scanning through his notebooks. "The truck is about to leave for Camp Prevail."

"How many are going?"

"Eleven—most of the women, the baby, the sick and wounded."

"Tell them they won't be welcome back."

"Jorah …"

"We don't need cowards among us. They won't be welcome back."

I am at the gates when I feel the prod on my shoulder.

"Miss Sinclair, I've just overheard, they're planning on sending the prisoner out with the women and the baby, going to sneak him out in half an hour."

I restrain myself from jerking away from the touch, shrugging off the filthy hand. He's one of my new guards, one of those I let inside in exchange for loyalty. His freckled face looks down at me, evidently pleased with himself over his discovery.

"Thank you." I begin to walk away, but something tells me to turn back. "Go and find Jonas. Tell him they need his help at guard tower three, immediately."

The door swings shut behind me, cutting out the light, filling my senses with only the musty smell of the basement. The scent of neglect and cold.

I prop open the door, the darkness of the cellar shooed away as light floods inward. I carry my lantern before me, placing it on the small wooden stool that still sits mere feet from the corner cell. The same stool where James had sat when he first came to visit me.

Riley looks up as I approach, and I see fear flashing in his eyes. I feel satisfied seeing it, as though I've just had a full meal.

"Riley."

He stands, somewhat shakily at first, but then strong. "Jorah, please, listen to me."

I stand just far enough from the bars of the cell that he cannot touch me, and when I do not speak, he does.

"I'm so sorry, Jorah. I'm so sorry." He leans against the bars, and I can smell his sweat and his suffering. "I'm sorry for everything."

I can see him now—despite the dirt and the bags beneath his eyes, the addition of temporary years from starving in a cell, I can see that he is still Riley. Tall, lean, and handsome Riley. His dark hair has grown, so has his beard, and just beneath the edges of his sleeves, I can see his tattoos.

There was one that I had always liked, and I can just see the faded edge of green ink, a mermaid's tail wrapped around his wrist.

"I'm sorry for everything," he repeats, "for getting us kicked out of Musa's, for being cruel to you, taking you for granted, and Sana and Geoff." The words pour out of his mouth, precarious, but growing in intensity. He reaches out to me, and I can't remember stepping forward, but now his hands are cupping my cheeks. "I'm sorry that we left you." His nails press into the sides of my skin. "We should have looked harder, looked longer—but Jorah, I swear to you, we thought you were gone.

"It was me that emptied your gun. I did it the night when we were waiting for a Break. I know it was stupid, but I swear, I just didn't want you to have to be the one to shoot any of us, if we turned into freaks. I wanted to save you from that—we wouldn't have been your responsibility to end." His fingers press into my cheeks, gripping my jaw. "You left before we woke up that morning. I didn't have to time to slip the bullets back in. Jorah, I was so scared. I'm so sorry."

"You're lying," I breathe.

He shakes his head, hands trembling. "I'm not, Jorah. Please, trust me. Trust me like you did at the start, before you even knew us."

My face feels wet, my eyes sting—burning like my nails and the roots of my hair. Burning like every nerve in my body has burned for weeks.

Riley pulls me forward, kisses me, and I feel nothing but the recognition that it is tears flowing down my face. I meet his eyes, so green.

"I never trusted you, Riley. I knew you, from the start. I'd followed you all for days. I knew your every mannerism before you knew I even existed." My whole body shakes, unceasing and agonizing. "I shot Sana, I destroyed the van—I just wanted to be part of the group." My eyes squeeze shut, forcing back the tears that burn like fire. "I was so lonely, and you left me to die."

Then he gasps, jolting away from me, and when I look down, I see that I've plunged my knife into his side.

James

They stood on the edge of the field, overlooking the sea of dead grass, its shore an abandoned parking lot.

"That's it?" James asked, coming to stand in line beside the others, the tiny army ready to wade through the waters.

"That's it," Carrigan said, glancing down at his still-ticking watch. "We have fifty minutes."

Geoff was left behind, the consensus that his injured leg would only slow everyone else down. The glass doors of the building had been shattered, leaves and other debris blown inward. Carrigan crossed to a map on the wall, scanning it for a moment.

"Third floor."

The climb went smoothly at first, until they found the stairwell to the third floor had been haphazardly barricaded with furniture. Office chairs, desks, and tables thrown pell-mell down the staircase.

"Hurry, form a line," Ramirez ordered, taking second behind James. Everyone grunted and heaved as they tore at the barricade, feeling the seconds ticking down.

Soon, it was clear enough for someone small to wriggle through, and Sana did so, disappearing for a moment as she checked the hallway for danger.

"Hurry," she urged, her mop of jaw-length dark hair reappearing, all that was visible over the pile. "I can pull someone up from here."

James was the last to reach the third floor, insistent on clearing nearly all the debris. It helped to ease the dread inside him, knowing at least that they would not be trapped.

"You still haven't told us how we're going to do this. The building obviously doesn't have power," Moore said as they took off down the hallway, following right on Carrigan's heels as he led them through the deserted and musty corridors.

"The system has backup power, it was all included in the—" A yellowed body exploded from a doorway, careening into Carrigan and slamming him to the ground.

James skidded to a stop, throwing out his arms to stop the others from flying onward.

"Get back!"

Carrigan screamed as the berserker tore into him, the body a pale blur, except for flying streaks of blood.

James fumbled with his gun, the iron sights catching on his holster. Another berserker came hurtling out of the room then, its skin an ashy-gray, its jaw hanging on by fibers. Gunshots exploded in the hallway, and James dove forward, tackling the berserker off of Carrigan and dragging it across the hallway.

"Move!" somebody screamed, and there was an almighty crash; dust and water splattered James as he finally freed his weapon, shooting the berserker point-blank.

The ceiling had caved in. Wiring, piping, and tiles barred the middle of the hallway, trapping Carrigan and James on one side. Water spurted from a broken pipe, mixing with the pools of blood on the floor.

James rushed forward, grabbing Carrigan beneath his armpits and dragging him away from the rubble.

"Are you okay?" Sana called, peering through the debris.

"I am—Carrigan's bleeding bad." James stripped off the top layer of his clothing, pressing it to the large wounds on Carrigan's side.

"We're all okay. Moore's rifle went off when the second freak jumped her. It took the ceiling down."

"Start clearing it!" James called before turning back to Carrigan. The older man's eyes were wide, his face splattered with blood.

"There's no time," he said.

"You're going to be okay," James promised, the blood rushing over his hands. "You'll be okay."

"Stop," Carrigan ordered, his eyes locking on James's face. "Listen to me!" He reached up a bloodied hand, clasping it around the back of James's neck and pulling him down, his voice coming out in a rushed, frantic whisper.

Jorah

I feel as though I have just woken up as the door to the house slams behind me, jerking me from my sleep. I look down at my hands, bloody—whose blood?

Riley's blood.

I burst into the office. It's dark; only a few candles remain lit. My hands shake violently as I try to pour a drink, amber liquid sloshing over my skin, running red and falling into my cup. I drink it anyway.

"Jorah?'

I swivel around, whiskey splashing over my skin. "Tom, what brings you here?"

A strange look is etched into his face. "Are you all right?"

"Yes." I force myself to breathe evenly, steadying the shaking in my hands. "Just nervous."

He nods. "So are we. I tried to send Dean away, but he wouldn't go, he believes in you."

I say nothing, watching him, my hand shuddering out to support myself on the edge of the desk.

Tom doesn't break his gaze, his dull, small eyes, face coated in laugh lines watching me. "My son is staying here for you, Jorah. My son is prepared to die for this place, for you."

"I'm sorry."

"I've made my peace with it, and I've believed in you too. We worked hard to convince people you were right for this place, would make it better."

"I'm trying."

"I know you are, but there's something I need to know— before we fight, something I should have come forward with a long time ago. You asked how I knew what your name meant, 'early rain.' I've known for months, recognized you the moment I laid eyes on you. I remember the news stories."

I can feel the alcohol settling in my system, the shakes in my hands easing, I stand straighter.

"Jorah, did you kill your sister?"

"Yes."

He doesn't seem surprised so much as saddened, and as he steps forward, I half expect him to draw his gun, to finish this. "Because she was dying?"

The words fall out of my mouth. "You don't know what it was like, seeing her suffer like that, seeing her *change*." I can see her, her face, her beautiful features caved in, sunken eyes and jagged cheekbones. "I had to do something. I couldn't let her hurt anymore." I feel as though I am pleading with Tom, begging for forgiveness like a child gone crying to her father. "I didn't have a choice."

"I understand," Tom says. "Jorah, I do. Your sister understands too."

"You don't understand!" The words come in a violent, screeching torrent. "Not unless you saw it, smelled it, *witnessed it* with your own eyes. She was dead long before I touched her. I didn't have a choice!"

Gunshots explode beyond the walls of the house. We both

turn, our eyes searing as the light of a huge fireball erupts through the windows.

"Dean," Tom breathes, giving me one last look before turning on his heel and running for the door.

The whiskey glass flies across the room, shattering on the wall, the dark liquor splashing to the floor. The Break hasn't happened yet; it's too early for them to be here.

I find myself in the bathroom, heaving over the sink, my bloodied fingers clutching the stained marble. Only eight fingers, cramped and slipping in my own mess.

When I look in the mirror, I see her. Clear as day, looking back at me. Junia and I. No worse than the day she died, no less tormented than me now.

My mind clears.

Outside a battle rages, gunshots fly by, blasting through the boards as the fence begins to splinter apart. A truck has been used as a battering ram to try to force open the gates. It now sits in a smoking wreck, foiled by the two vans Fort Rache had parked just inside the doors.

I search desperately through the smoke billowing into the air, at last spying the familiar figure, crouched by the corner of a home.

"You were right!" I cry over the chaos, clasping Jonas on his shoulder. "You were right."

A body plummets from the guard tower as fire begins to spread to the walls.

"We have to get everyone out now. They'll kill every single one of us."

"There's no way," Jonas shouts, his eyes wide with terror. "They're coming over the walls!" I turn to see the figures that had begun to appear at the edges of the walls. Many are shot down and beaten back, but steadily more torsos appear, heaving themselves to our side.

"Get everyone you can, bring them to the field. They can climb over the wall and take to the woods."

"We don't have time!"

"It's the only chance," I urge, grabbing Jonas's arm and heaving him upward. "Go!" I shove him forward, and he stumbles at first, before righting himself and taking off toward a group of nearby men.

I run in the other direction, my eyes locking on the small groundskeeper shed hidden behind a grouping of shrubs.

"Help me," I order the two men who had taken cover in its shadow, and together we heave the doors open.

The inside holds little useful, gardening tools and old fertilizer, but there, in the middle, sit three large canisters. I heft two, pushing one into the arms of each man, the smell of gasoline clashing with the burning smoke.

"Pour this all along the walls, soak them, get the wood, get everything, then go to the back of the field and climb the fence with the others," I shout to them. They stare back for only a moment before each takes off in another direction.

I grip the last canister, running for the nearest house, sloshing the gas over the front steps. I force open the door, dumping the gas onto the floor and screaming for anyone inside to leave, to run for the field. I repeat this at the next house, and the next, until the canister is emptied.

Malicious voices echo through the camp now, the hunters coming for their prey. A figure runs by, and I burst from my hiding place, latching onto his arm.

"Dean!" I run with him, the two of us rushing for the field, others running with us. As we near the final home, I stop on my heel, dragging Dean to cover.

"Dean, listen to me," I say, shaking him, his face lit with adrenaline. "Dean, I need you to do something for me, okay? Go to the jail, here." I fumble in my pocket, extracting a ring of keys. "Run there, don't stop for anything. There's a man in the basement cell, he's hurt. Help him, get him over the wall with the others."

"What are you going to do?" he asks frantically, taking the keys, his head on a constant swivel.

"It doesn't matter. Just do this, please, and then get yourself out of here." He nods, lurching to his feet in a half-crouch as he turns to run.

"Dean, wait!" I burst out, lunging forward and catching his arm again. "Tell them I'm sorry. Tell them all that I'm sorry for the things I've done. Tell them I love them."

James

Without a word, James let the rag fall from Carrigan's side. He stood and broke into a run down the hallway, cries of "Where's he going?" echoing behind him.

He found the room easily, nothing extraordinary, a simple plaque on the wall, having just learned that hundreds of these exact rooms existed across the world. He held the small metal tablet to the handle. There was a soft click as the door unlocked, just as Carrigan had said it would.

Inside, just as Carrigan had described, was a simple computer monitor, dusty yet undamaged. James moved in a deep fog, closing the door behind him, sitting down in the plain office chair. He barely registered the awe of the screen flicking to life, the small tablet vibrating in his hand, the jumbled letters and numbers still burnt onto its screen.

He typed in the code and as soon as he had finished, a box appeared on the screen, alongside a countdown—fifty seconds remaining.

Press 'Enter' to reset system.

Note: Resetting system is suggested in circumstances of implant malfunction.

Note: All damaged implants will be automatically activated and destroyed in event of reset.

The hope that had once bloomed inside of James crumbled to dust, suffocating him. There was no saving her. He glanced at the countdown—thirty seconds until the Break. Thirty seconds until countless more survivors would die … twenty seconds until maybe he would die too, and that didn't seem so bad, because then he wouldn't have to choose.

I'm so sorry.

Jorah

"Where is James Duran?" comes the booming, gleeful shout, the revelations of a man who knows he has won. "We know he's still alive."

"Climb!" I urge, using all my strength to boost someone over the fence, most of the others already waiting on the other side.

"Jorah, it's too late," Jonas cries beside me, as we turn to see the army advancing upon us, Jefferson at its head, with Conrad only steps behind him.

"Give us James Duran!" Jefferson screams again, swiping his assault rifle between each of our forms as we work to load people over the fence. "Or everyone is going to die."

"Get them out, and then yourself," I say to Jonas, grabbing his hands and clutching them. "Promise me, no matter what."

He nods wordlessly, and I turn from him, drawing my pistol as I march out into the field, the army of thugs halting as well.

"James Duran is gone," I call. "He's miles away."

"It's that white-haired bitch!" Jefferson cackles, slapping a disgruntled McNeal on the back. "Thought you said you killed her?"

"I thought I did," he growls back, staring at me with furious eyes.

I can feel the blood running down my hands as my nails cut into them, and I will myself to stay present, just a little longer. My brain pulses, trying to drag me back down to the abyss.

"Well, if it can be avoided, let's not kill that one. Hard to find them pretty these days," Jefferson jeers, earning a boisterous cackle from the men behind him.

"I've had dibs for weeks," Conrad says with an evil grin.

"Leave now, and I will allow you all to live." I force myself to stand straight as I speak. "Stay and you will die."

Horrible, evil laughter springs from the crowd, Jefferson the worst of all. "Actually, I think I'll just kill you now." He pauses, grinning maliciously. "Unless you want to tell me where Duran's gone?"

It takes only a second to glance behind me, and it is Riley's eyes I meet, only for a moment, as he is eased over the wall. Jonas plants a foothold after him. I turn back.

"Enough of this!" Conrad barks, a dark gleam in his eye, smoke from the gates still billowing behind him. He raises his rifle.

But I am quicker, just as I had always been. I plunge my hand into my pocket, scooping out the singed gold lighter, the same one I had used to burn Gallagher alive. I aim to my left, pinning a sheet of metal lining the wall in my sight. The lighter is already soaring through the air before Conrad's shot catches my shoulder, pain bursting through my every nerve.

The wall explodes into flames, the gasoline firing off until within only seconds we are in a ring of fire and smoke. The men scream, scattering as the fire catches the trail of gas, igniting the houses beside them. Jefferson is knocked to the ground; a boot catches him in the temple.

I rush backward, the sight of the small gap in the wall keeping me going, the opening growing smaller and smaller as the flames close in.

I go crashing down the moment that the bullet tears through my calf, my face bouncing off the ground. I whirl onto my back, Conrad advancing toward me, rage caked on every inch of his face, blood and soot splattered like freckles.

He raises his weapon, aiming for my nose, and I close my eyes. I feel peace in this moment, painless despite the flames creeping toward me, burning my flesh pink. I feel nothing but peace.

There is a deafening roar. My eyes burst open as a torrent of bullets from behind me slash through Conrad, splintering his bones and shredding his flesh.

Then there is a crack, deafening, ringing in my ears.

And then my sister is standing before me, and everything is okay.

James

Three days later

The day was warm, well, not warm, but at least the cold didn't singe your skin.

The supplies that could be salvaged from Fort Rache came trundling into Camp Prevail in a long line, its residents cheering and whooping as they watched. James stood just outside, observing the procession, his new home looking cheerier than he could have imagined it.

Fort Rache stood abandoned, a smoldering wreck, unsalvageable, the dead of three nights prior now buried within the walls. James himself had buried Evangeline, her skin as white as the snow she had been found under, the word *traitor* carved across her flawless forehead. *She wanted me to tell you that she's sorry for everything.*

"Want to take a walk?" a soft voice said, gently placing a hand on his arm. He nodded, turning and following her away from the hustle and bustle of camp, into the woods, to where all they could hear was the soft bubbling of a creek.

"I want to kill McNeal. I want it to be me," she said, staring out over the water, "but I understand if you want the honor."

James shook his head. "You can do it, I got to catch him." There had been little more satisfying in James's life than the feeling of McNeal's bones cracking under his fists.

She nodded, and the two of them stood in silence a moment longer, feeling the breeze, watching the temporarily unfrozen water bubble and boil. An impermanent relief; winter would still come for them all.

"I just don't understand," Sana said suddenly, turning to him, "about Carrigan."

James shook his head. He had told them before, everything he knew, everything Carrigan had told him while he lay dying. "There was never a package of information, never an operation to remove his device—he never had one—Carrigan knew it all, the whole time."

"But he told you it *was* aliens? I don't understand."

James sighed, feeling numb to it all. "Alien technology, something they discovered two years ago; it's the whole reason why all this happened. Somebody out there told somebody here to do this. Carrigan was part of it from the start." A cynical laugh burst out of James. "Alien technology but with a human hand is what he said. That's why it malfunctioned, why they needed people with a kill switch just in case. The technology was far too advanced to be damaged by EMPs—those were only meant to hinder the surviving population. He wasn't the only one, just the first to bother turning it off. It was supposed to shut off on its own, and when it didn't, Carrigan was alerted.

"They released the partial knowledge about discovering extraterrestrial life on purpose exactly a year before the Break. There needed to be a scapegoat, a common enemy for the world to band together against." James dug around in his pocket, pulling out the crumpled piece of paper that had printed from the computer the moment he reset the system.

"It's all in here, and more."

Sana took the paper softly, stowing it in her coat. "One day people will have to know what happened, but for now, we have something else to do."

James nodded, looking around where they stood. "Here will work just fine, I think."

"Why here?"

He gestured around them, toward the trees, which would hold no leaves for many months. "These are ash trees; they're Jorah's favorite. She told me once, but I can't remember why."

Sana smiled, looking to the trees. "I know why, because they were her sister's favorite, too."

EPILOGUE

The day was hot, so hot that you were forced to find the nearest shade, to lie in the soft grass, listen to the breeze and the chirp of birds.

"One more story, please Auntie?"

"One more. Which one?"

"The one about the beginning, with the white-haired queen," the little boy begged, his mop of straw-colored hair flopping as he leapt up and down with excitement.

"Okay, okay, relax." The woman chuckled, settling back down in the grass. The little boy smiled brightly, crawling up beside her and resting his head against her leg, his fingers toying with the grass.

"Long ago, the world was a very different place. It was crowded and busy, with buildings as tall as the sky, lights as bright as you can imagine, and more people than you could ever meet."

"And children?"

"So many children." She smiled, tousling his hair. "The people were incredibly smart, and they spent years and years growing their cities, growing their knowledge, until one day they reached the moon, and years later, they reached the very edges of the stars. Now, until then, the people had never heard of any others in the universe, not on any of the stars or the planets or the moons that they could see. It wasn't until they reached beyond those stars that they found them, but things were far from good. The others told them that they were in grave danger. That now that they had reached beyond their limits, others would come, others who didn't want anyone else to be able to reach beyond their own stars."

"And they killed everyone!" the boy shouted.

"Excuse me," the woman reprimanded, earning a squeaky "Sorry".

She continued, "In order to protect themselves, the people were told they needed to hide. So, they did, in the only way they could figure out how. They set against their own people. Many of them died. Society and their cities and technology were destroyed, but it was the only way that they could hide from the others in time."

"And then you met the queen—you and Daddy and Riley."

Sana nodded, pinching his cheeks lightly. "Yes, but she wasn't a queen then. She was just a young woman, the bravest and the kindest that I ever met."

"What did she look like?"

"Well, if I had to guess, I would think you had a little crush on this queen," Sana teased, and the boy blushed.

"You can't *like* someone from a story, Auntie Sana."

Sana laughed, the sound beautiful and ethereal as wind chimes. "Well she was tall, with blonde hair that was nearly white, and eyes so blue the ocean would be jealous."

"I want to see the ocean."

"And one day you will," she promised, looking up at the figure now crossing the field toward them. "Look who I see," she whispered teasingly, and the boy jerked upward.

"Dad!" he cried, jumping to his feet and running into the arms of the man. The boy flew into the air, spinning around with screams of laughter.

"Geoff, come and help me up, would you?" Sana called as Geoff continued toward her.

"Please, I'm older than you. You act like you're eighty."

"I've got some apocalypse years on me," Sana quipped as Geoff grasped her hand, leaning on his crutch as he pulled her to her feet. "Where's Emily?"

"Making lunch, and it should be ready. James and Lucy are coming too."

"And Riley?"

Geoff shook his head. "Haven't seen him in a few days—but you know he always turns up eventually." He twisted around; the little boy had disappeared from his side. "Jorah? Where'd you go?"

"I'm here," the young boy called, peeking out from around the tree, blue eyes that neither of his parents had playful and shining. "I haven't gone far."

THE END

Acknowledgments

Thank you so, so much to everyone who supported me while I wrote, edited, re-wrote and obsessed over this book. From the first days of writing, to the final weeks of agonizing over a title. Thank you for helping me keep my sanity. I will do my best to remember you all when I'm famous.

A special *thank you* for the time and effort that was given to this book goes out to—

My Partner— Alex Autenrieth

My #1 Fan— Dad

My First Readers & Helping Hands—
Raquel Pratte, Trish Autenrieth, Taylor Roy, Sean Kohlbrenner, Jaxon Letendre & Hannah Stumbaugh

My Artist— Olivia Cargnel

My Editor— Joel Pierson

My Muse— Ranger

Made in the USA
Middletown, DE
08 July 2020

12158477R00262